SWORD AND SCION

THE ALLEGIANCE OF AVARICE
Book 2

JACKSON E. GRAHAM

YOUNG**OAK**PUBLISHING

Young Oak Publishing LLC
Hayden, Idaho

Young Oak Publishing LLC
P.O. Box 682
Hayden, ID 83835

Cover design by Bobooks
Logo design by KJ Designs
Author photograph by Rachel Stewart Photography

http://jacksonegraham.wixsite.com/jackson-e-graham

Library of Congress Control Number: 2018907816

ISBN: 978-1-950917-90-7 (sc)

PRINTED IN THE UNITED STATES OF AMERICA

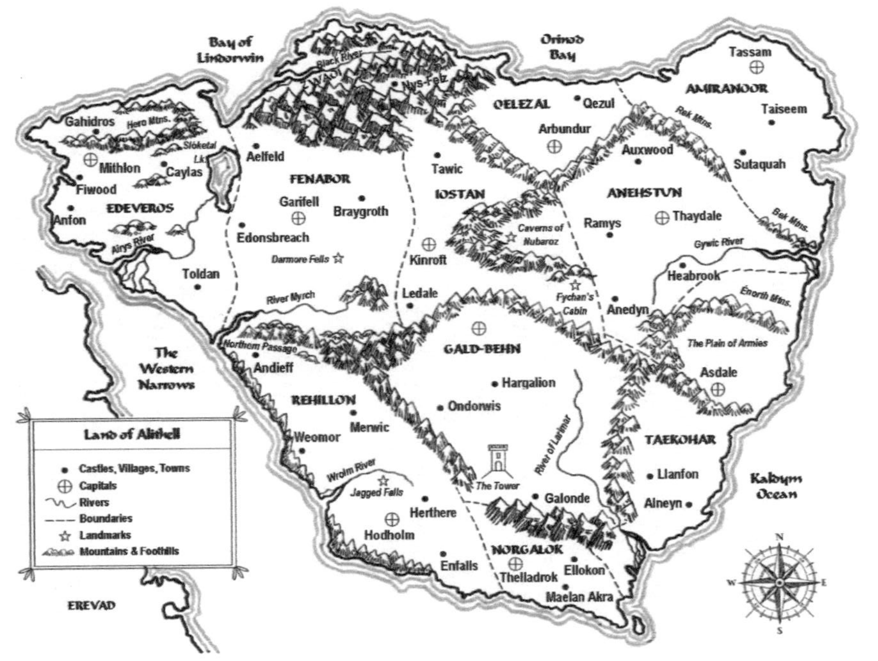

Bay of Lindorwin
Orinod Bay
Black River
Nys-Felz
Tassam
QELEZAL
Qezul
AMIRANOOR
Taiseem
Gahidros
Hero Mtns.
Arbundur
Rek Mtns.
Slóketal Lk.
Aelfeld
Tawic
Auxwood
Sutaquah
Mithlon
Caylas
FENABOR
IOSTAN
ANEHSTVN
Fiwood
Garifell
Braygroth
Ramys
Thaydale
Bek Mtns.
EDEVEROS
Anfon
Edonsbreach
Caverns of Nubaroz
Gywic River
Airys River
Darmore Fells
Kinroft
Heabrook
Toldan
River Myrch
Ledale
Fychan's Cabin
Anedyn
Énorth Mtns.
Northern Passage
GALD-BEHN
The Plain of Armies
Asdale
The Western Narrows
Andieff
Hargalion
REHILLON
Ondorwis
River of Larimar
Weomor
Merwic
TAEKOHAR
Land of Alithell
Wrolm River
The Tower
Llanfon
Castles, Villages, Towns
Capitals
Jagged Falls
Galonde
Alneyn
Kaloym Ocean
Rivers
Boundaries
Herthere
Landmarks
Hodholm
Mountains & Foothills
NORGALOK
Enfalls
Ellokon
Thelladrok
EREVAD
Maelan Akra
N
E
W
S

PRONOUNCIATION GUIDE

<u>Places</u>

Andieff (pronounced: **On**-dye-ff)
Anehstun (pronounced: **Ah**-ne-stoon)
Enfalls (pronounced: **En**-falls)
Gald-Behn (pronounced: **Gahld-Ben**)
Herthere (pronounced: **Her**-theer)
Hodholm (pronounced: **Hod**-holm)
Iostan (pronounced: **Eye**-oh-stann)
Merwic (pronounced: **Mer**-wik)
Nys-Felz (pronounced: Niss-**fellz**)
Qelezal (pronounced: **Kell**-eh-zall)
Rehillon (pronounced: **Rey**-hill-on)
Taekohar (pronounced: **Tay**-ko-harr)
Weomor (pronounced: **Way**-oh-more)
Zwaoi (pronounced: **Z-why**)

<u>Characters</u>

Amnedd (pronounced: **Om**-nedd)
Ayleril (pronounced: **A**-luh-ril)
Beydan (pronounced: **Bay**-dun)
Caywen (pronounced: **Kay**-when)
Eyoés (pronounced: **Aay**-oh-ess)
Gwair (pronounced: **Gwhere**)
Gwyndel (pronounced: **Gwin**-dell)
Hranfist (pronounced: **Ron**-fist)
King Fohidras (pronounced: Fo-**high**-dras)
Kiffyn (pronounced: **Kiff**-in)
Rodmer (pronounced: **Rod**-mer)
Vikar (pronounced: **Vyker**)

<u>Months for the World of Alithell</u>

Iaudyn
Nósor
Dichán
Biarron
Iaulan
Merchen
Yílor
Thurdál
Aevoran
Rotanos
Rynéth
Bivyn

**Don't miss these other titles by
Jackson E. Graham:**

Sword and Scion 01: Into the Dark Mountains

Sword and Scion 03: The Reign of Delusion

To God and my awesome editor,
who helped bring this book to life.

A man in his castle, sitting on a hill,
The Richest Lord be his name.
His halls of gold, a radiant glory,
Bespoke of thralldom, a tragic story.
Eyes blinded, he no longer saw
The serf's toil, his hopeless misery.
Stricken by sickness cruel, the villein fell,
Yet the Richest Lord cared not.
When foes came, spears bristling for war,
With limbs torn, the Richest Lord fell
Alone, with none to care.
No more do they shine, in luminous fame,
The halls of the Richest Lord.

The Lay of Treasures, Unknown Author
Circa 1361 SE

"So give your servant a discerning heart
to govern your people and to distinguish
between right and wrong."
(1 Kings 3:9, NIV)

"Stop judging by mere appearances,
but instead judge correctly."
(John 7:24, NIV)

PROLOGUE

15th of Nósor, 2202 SE

A Forester never runs, Kiffyn.

Emerging from the safety of a secluded alleyway, a lone figure in soaked Forester garb stumbled into the road, his gaze darting to far reaches of the darkness. Matted brown hair stuck to his forehead, and droplets of water traced down his scarred chin. He patted his chest pocket to assure himself the message was there.

I can't let my brother down—or Gwyndel.

Furrowing his brow, the Forester stepped further into the open, scanning the surroundings for sign of his pursuers.

The light of the full moon shone upon the town of Merwic. Glistening in its light, puddles of rainwater collected in the hollows of the uneven cobblestone streets. The crack of thunder's whip resounded overhead, spurring on the night rain. Steadily beating on the wooden roofs of the commoners' homes, the storm lulled the townsfolk into a deep sleep with its soothing words. Again, thunder tore through the sky, a streak of bright blue partly hidden by the clouds. None stirred. The steady drone of rain upon the cobblestone filled his ears. A surge of fear raced through him as he considered the possibility of ambush. Silently, the Forester drew his knife and clenched his jaw.

No Phantom Leaguer will take this message from me.

A spinning blade raced past his head and embedded into the nearest wall with a hollow thud. The Forester leapt behind a stack of firewood, searching for the hidden enemy with wild eyes. Startled, a pair of rats scurried into the darkness.

"Kiffyn," crowed a voice from across the street. Laced with a sly, silky civility, the man's speech eerily reminded Kiffyn of a thin dagger, hidden under the folds of a man's cloak. Always there, but never seen—until it is too late. It was a voice impossible to forget.

Amnedd? Couldn't be—not after the ambush at Braygroth...

Gripping his knife, the Forester peeked around the stack of wood, suppressing the urge to shiver in the cold. Although concealed in the shadows of a nearby shed, Kiffyn recognized the vague outline of a man.

"I know you have the message," Amnedd continued. "Come now, how much is this parchment worth to you? I will pay handsomely, should you accept my offer." The very suggestion made Kiffyn's blood boil. Drawing in a slow breath, the Forester glanced to the side. A movement from an open doorway made his eyes narrow.

He's trying to draw me out.

Glimpsing a forgotten barrel to his left, Kiffyn quietly grasped the lid by its handle and pried it loose from the barrel. He glanced down the street, recognizing the steepled roof of the local Farmer's Guild. Although his original plan demanded he be the one to deliver the message he carried, it was clear that carrying this out would be impossible.

Bryoc will be able to do what I cannot.

"Do you wish to spend your blood on this *sopping parchment*?" Amnedd inquired. Immediately, a man burst from the open doorway, hurling a javelin towards the Forester's exposed position.

Deflecting the attack with his makeshift buckler, Kiffyn hurdled the stack of firewood, knocking several logs to the ground. Fixing his gaze on his goal, he raced towards the Farmer's Guild. With a silent anger, the Phantom Leaguers followed, their pursuit hidden from the moonlight. Kiffyn's heart leapt into his throat as he slipped on the wet cobblestone. Shakily recovering his balance, he burst into the Farmer's Guild, the door bouncing back on its hinges. Seizing the door handle, Kiffyn slammed the door shut and barred it.

Woken from sleep, a man cast aside his blankets and leapt from his bed across the room. With a cry, the man searched about the room and fumbled for the pair of shears hanging on a nearby wall.

Kiffyn extended his hands to dissuade the confused man. "It's me, Bryoc!" he exclaimed, casting aside his shield and pulling the folded parchment from his chest pocket. Bryoc recognized his friend's voice and ceased his frantic scramble.

His eyes widened at the Forester's grim and harried appearance. Rushing to his friend's side, Bryoc laid his hands on the man's shoulders. "By the blight! What's wrong?" he gasped.

Kiffyn shoved the message into the man's chest along with a sack of coins. "Take it, Bryoc!" he ordered, his voice stressing the urgency of his command. "Ride for the Northern Passage and deliver this to the Baron of Taekohar! You will be safe once you pass through the towers."

Bryoc hastily stuffed the message in his shirt pocket, then shoved a loaf of bread, the sack of money, and a sheathed dagger into his satchel. He put on his boots and wrapped his cloak about him. "What about you?" he inquired. Running footsteps sounded outside the door.

Trembling, Kiffyn pointed to the back door. "*Now!*" he shouted. Bryoc paused, took one last glance towards his old friend, and fled out the back door into the night.

Kiffyn gripped his knife and turned back towards the main door. There was nothing more he could do.

"Set it on fire," Amnedd hissed from outside. "I want him alive."

1

Racing over the long, flat plains, a crisp morning breeze rippled through the grass. Trees of a deep spring green crowded together as one forest. The calls of birds echoed from the skies above, hearkening the arrival of a new day. Proudly standing over the horizon, the sun cast its light upon Asdale's new keep.

Strong, finely hewn stones set fast against the next to form the keep's solid walls. A thick mortar held the stones together as brothers. Arrow slits and small windows dotted the tower's walls, providing not only light into a spiral stairway within, but a protected view of the castle grounds without. At its base, a large wooden door guarded the entryway. Fastened to the front of the door, interwoven branches of iron formed a closely-knit forest design, its craftsmanship indicating the position of the one residing inside.

Around the base of the completed keep, wooden structures were stationed in the wide, cobblestone courtyard. The braying of work mules and bellowing of oxen issued from several temporary buildings. Bales of hay were stacked beside each structure to provide food for the animals within.

Although the surrounding land had remained tranquil throughout Castle Asdale's construction, a thick wall surrounded the keep and its completed courtyard, acting as both a boundary and a secondary defense should the need arise.

Only a few people walked inside this inner plaza surrounding the keep, ferrying tools and other supplies to the workers in the outer courtyard through an open gateway.

Hemming in the castle grounds, the thick outer wall rose from the ground with each newly placed stone. Laborers carefully trod upon the wooden scaffolding fastened to the wall's surface, smoothing out layers of mortar and placing new stones. Below, one man's continual steps powered a large wheel, which in turn lifted stones up to the workers on the wall by a pulley. The grating sound of stone on wood melded with the din of the worksite as three men moved heavy blocks of stone towards the lift upon a rolling cluster of logs.

Carts passed through the ruins of Asdale's main gate, bringing in loads of stone from a nearby quarry. As the carts dropped off their loads, masons gathered around the stones with their chisels and hammers, slowly forming useable bricks from the rough, uneven chunks. Beneath the roof of a simple shed, master builders gathered together, measuring both wood and stone for the construction. Craftsmen worked alongside both masons and woodcarvers, producing beautiful embellishments. Each man desired to do his best to restore the cornerstone of their territory.

A tall figure in a green cape strolled among the mass of laborers, observing their duties. Eyoés' emerald robe shone brightly in the morning light, its bottom hem coated with the morning dew. Underneath his robe, a tunic of a thick cloth protected him from the crisp breeze. The hard lines of struggle and anger had faded from his appearance, replaced by a confidence hinting at inner change.

Seeing a group of stonemasons, Eyoés entered their midst and turned to the leader of the group. "Good morning, Llew! How does your family fare?" he inquired with a smile of genuine interest.

Standing from his seat by a crate of tools, Llew extended a hand of welcome towards the Baron. "They are faring well, my friend," he replied, his tanned face upturned in a wide smile. "I received word that my son was apprenticed to the Bowyer's Guild in Alneyn. My wife Lilien and I are very proud."

Eyoés raised an eyebrow. "You should be! When I was young, I was apprenticed in the Leatherworker's Guild. It stretched my free time too thin, and I neglected my work. I found it was *my* hide that got tanned by the master!" he joked. The surrounding stonemasons burst into laughter. Although Eyoés remembered the story behind his jest with regret, he cast aside his remorse and joined their merrymaking. Giving a final wave, Eyoés patted Llew on the shoulder and continued on his walk.

As the laughter of his companions faded behind him, Eyoés' smile dwindled into a thoughtful look. The journey to Zwaoi had waned to distant memories four years after his installment as Baron. With a sigh, Eyoés shook his head and looked at his boots.

My past mistakes still pain me. And they are not the only thing.

At the thought, he frowned. Glancing up from his musings, he watched as the laborers about him sweated and spent their strength to fulfill the dream of Asdale's future glory. Eyoés adjusted his robe.

Much of the construction is funded by my wealth. Without resources, these walls would never be finished.

Although he knew what would come next, Eyoés found it upon him before he could stop it.

Why should I use my resources solely for paying off expenses? Even my father never saw this much wealth. Surely enjoying a good portion will do no harm.

Eyoés stopped in his tracks. His eye caught sight of a nearby worker. Wiping the sweat from his brow, the man struck up a conversation with a companion, eyes glowing as he withdrew a note from his pocket and boasted of its contents. Eyoés forcefully looked away, rejecting the thought of misusing his wealth.

Indulgence often leads to sacrifice. These men have families, and homes to return to. If I spend increasing amounts of my wealth, I could find myself pressuring them to work faster so I might keep more. As it says in the Proverbs—fixing on the cares of life choke out the truth. Refrain from considering wealth as something to be desired.

"Eyoés!" called a voice from behind, waking the young Baron from his troubled musings. Turning, Eyoés quelled the unease within him and forced himself to appear normal.

Striding down the grassy thoroughfare, a man clothed in a fine, deep blue tunic hastened towards him. Embroidered upon his leather vest, ornate designs accented his neat appearance.

Eyoés could not help but appreciate the man's fine apparel, recalling its ample price. "What duties need to be taken care of today, Ayleril?" he asked.

Slowing to a walk, the man smiled. "We will concern ourselves with the duties of the Baronship later," he replied. "For now, I simply wish to walk with you back to the keep." Nodding, Eyoés gestured for him to continue alongside. During the years following his return from Gald-Behn, Ayleril's wisdom and knowledge had proven to be invaluable. What might have transpired had the King not sent the man to assist him, Eyoés would never know. Eyoés strolled beside his advisor, running a hand through his hair as he tried to ward off disconcerting thoughts. Ayleril set his hand upon the Baron's shoulder, seeing the signs of his inner struggle. "What troubles you?" he questioned, the concern in his eyes prodding at the young Baron's reluctance.

Sighing, Eyoés regarded the keep with a pensive gaze. "I'm still not accustomed to my position, even after four years," he revealed. "The power, the wealth —it all continues to be strangely foreign. I find myself enticed by these very things, despite my attempts to remain impartial. I fear what it means to be Baron. If the authority of this title leads me into wrong, I want no part in it."

Glancing towards Ayleril, Eyoés found himself surprised at the man's nod of understanding. "You feel you've stepped into the dragon's mouth, do you not?" the elder asked, looking Eyoés in the eye. The young man's silence answered in the affirmative. "Eyoés, the Baronship is not a quest for control and fortune, but a position of leadership over your fellow man and stewardship over the wealth given to you," Ayleril continued, sweeping his arm across the span of Asdale's ruins. "When a man finds himself in authority, he is tempted to rule others with tyranny, and believe he is superior to them. In truth, he is under the King's rule as much as the next man—he has just been given the responsibility of caring for those who can't always care for themselves."

Eyoés regarded the workers toiling around him, his forehead wrinkled in thought.

Such things might be true. Yet, this responsibility tempts me.

Refraining from more troubling talk, the two continued towards Asdale's keep, discussing the duties and responsibilities of the day.

Striding through the corridors of the keep's lower levels, Gwyndel brought a shaky hand to her forehead as the voices of several aides and servants joined together in a single clamor for her attention. She adjusted the collar of her mulberry dress and fixed her gaze on the door to the castle kitchens.

"Lady Gwyndel, the menu for the workers' noon meal is yet to be arranged," one of the servants said, lifting her voice above the others in order to be heard.

Gwyndel forced herself to nod. "I am heading toward the *kitchen*, Erynn," she sighed, her ears ringing.

As one voice fell, another took its place as one of Gwyndel's aides struggled to move closer to her. "You must remind Baron Eyoés to draft his letter—"

Gwyndel raised a hand to ward off the woman's remark. "Yes, Margred, I remember! Eyoés must write a letter to Lord Brol of Nubaroz to finalize the arrangements for the Gesadith trade—you needn't remind me," she interrupted. Gwyndel shook her head and tried to hurry her pace to escape the constant demands.

How could anyone stand such chaos? I am barely able to sustain my duties as Steward, let alone find time to enjoy myself.

Closing her eyes, she tried to shut off the voices of her nagging companions. A longing within prodded the regret over her incapability.

I wish I was fit to deal with the demands of this high position. So many opportunities to steward what King Fohidras has given, and yet I constantly fall short. Perhaps I am not doing enough.

With their questions answered, the women fell back, their footsteps scurrying across the stone floor as they hurried to accomplish their next task. Following

Gwyndel silently as he waited for his opportunity to speak, an older man in Forester garb laid a hand on her shoulder. The roughness of his fingers hearkened to the life of an archer.

Gwyndel turned, taking a deep breath as she realized the aides and servants had left. Looking into the familiar man's eyes, she sighed. "Dugal, you've held your tongue for quite some time—for which I am thankful," she admitted, indicating he should speak.

Looking away as he gathered his thoughts, the man released Gwyndel's shoulder. "I regret to be the one to tell you this," he spoke, his expression pained. "But the leadership of the Forester Assembly has brought forward a new recruit to replace you, should you deem them skilled enough."

Gwyndel stiffened, her mouth agape as the realization of her fellow Forester's words sank in. "A replacement?" she stammered, unsure if she had correctly understood.

Turning away, Dugal held his hand to his forehead. "All of us at the Assembly wish you were still among us," he insisted. "If we were to have our way, your position would be left open until your eventual return." He paused, considering his own words. Then, he turned to where the young elf stood, silent as she hung her head in shock and thought. "You *will* return, won't you?" Dugal inquired, his face downturned.

Not venturing to speak, Gwyndel pictured the determined, yet downcast faces of the Assembly. Many among the Forester ranks had forged a camaraderie with her. A multitude of friendships had sustained her when her family had been assumed dead. Gwyndel swallowed. The familiarity and passion for her former life among the Foresters stirred up a longing within.

Should I approve the Assembly's replacement, it would suggest that I would rather stay in this castle than return to the way of life I've always called home. It would be betrayal.

Lifting her head, Gwyndel met Dugal's gaze and nodded. "In time, I will return. Tell the Assembly I wish to have more time before making a decision," she declared.

Dugal pursed his lips and rested his chin in his hand. "I cannot assure you how long they will give you," he said. "Perhaps I can convince them to give you until Fall. That is all I can promise—and I promise loosely."

Stepping forward and extending her hand, Gwyndel nodded. "Until then," she said, the unsteady satisfaction in her voice less than assuring. Dugal clasped her hand briefly and turned away, striding in the direction of the keep's entrance.

As he turned around a bend in the corridor, Gwyndel hastened to the kitchen, her mind swimming in a sea of thoughts.

2

The repeated hammering upon the chamber door startled Eyoés from sleep. Sucking in a quick breath, the Baron swiftly sat up and tossed the blankets aside. Beams of moonlight coursed in through the chamber window to light the room, keeping the shadows cornered in the recesses. Hung upon the farthest wall by a single iron rod, an ornate tapestry silently rippled in the night air. The dark green background morphed into a hazy emerald in the calm moonlight, and the golden emblem of fire emblazoned upon it seemed to come alive to pierce through the darkness. Eyoés forcefully looked away from the beautiful piece of art, growing increasingly uncomfortable at the blatant reminder of his authority. Stationed beneath the crowning emblem stood a desk, upon which an inkwell and pen awaited their next use. Crowding a solitary bookshelf, numerous volumes held knowledge within their covers. Other than this, a solitary chair, and the comfortable bed opposite, the room possessed no further furnishings.

The clang of a metal gauntlet bashed against the door to his chamber again. For a moment, the images of Skreon's pallid face flashed through his mind. The return of the nightmare shocked him with a momentary fear.

Tense, Eyoés swung his legs off the side of the bed and silently pushed himself to his feet. Wrapping his fingers around the handle of his sword and grasping the scabbard in the other, he stepped towards the door. Contrary to his fearful emotions, Eyoés knew the nightmare had no grounds for belief. Still, the stark memory of his dark quest preyed at his nerves.

Eyoés began to draw his sword. "Baron, sir—this is an urgent matter. You are sorely needed!" whispered a voice from behind the door. Closing his eyes, Eyoés let out a steady breath as the vision of Skreon dissipated. He seized the door handle and opened it.

A soldier stood in the doorway, caught lifting his gauntleted hand for another knock. Shuffling in place, the guard stroked his greying beard, as he paused to consider his words. "What is it, Kaven?" Eyoés questioned, leaning closer towards the man.

Briefly glancing down the spiral staircase, the soldier turned to Eyoés. He gestured down the steps. "A messenger has just arrived—from Rehillon. He claims he has a message of utmost importance, and nearly knocked down three of my men in order to get it to you," he answered. An unintelligible shout rang from the bottom of the stairs, tinged with a determined desperation that arrested Eyoés' attention. With a brief nod, Eyoés pushed past the guard and raced down the stairs, nearly tripping over his night robe. Moonlight flashed across his face as he passed the keep windows. He ignored the chill night air biting at exposed skin. Another shout rang from below as Eyoés and the soldier arrived at the bottom of the stairs.

Eyoés halted. Underneath the tall ceiling of the main hall, a skirmish had broken out. Holding out their hands in peaceful gestures, three guards attempted to hem in a disheveled, harried man. Wearing a muddy, soaked cloak, the messenger clutched a small buckler he'd wrenched from one of the sentries. Dark patches underneath his eyes hinted at near exhaustion. His wild gaze bespoke a stony determination all too familiar to the Baron.

He is consumed with an unflinching resolve—as I once was.

With a cry, the messenger lashed out at the nearest guard, knocking him soundly on the side of the head with the buckler. The guard stumbled back, grimacing in pain, then returned to the fight, trying to tackle the man as he swung at a second soldier.

Eyoés interceded before more violence could take place. "Hold your attack! You wish to speak with me?" he shouted, hoping he could break through the focus of combat. At his voice, the messenger turned, baring his teeth in anticipation of another foe. His anger faded into relief as his eyes glimpsed the symbol embroidered upon Eyoés' robe.

Casting aside his buckler, the messenger shoved past the guards and stumbled towards the Baron, shoving his hand into his chest pocket. "Baron Eyoés?" he inquired, his voice weak. Eyoés quickly nodded and moved to keep the messenger on his feet. Withdrawing a wrinkled, wet parchment from his pocket, the man extended it towards the approaching Baron. Eyes rolling into the back of his head, the man collapsed onto the cobblestone floor with a thud. The wet parchment fell from his hand and landed at Eyoés' feet.

Cradling the folded parchment in his open palm, Eyoés sat impatiently waiting for Gwyndel to arrive. Although the messenger now lay in the hands of the local healers, the sight of the man nearly sacrificing his life to bring this message to him instilled a sense of dread he could not ignore.

Eyoés examined the tapestry hanging above his desk. The candle's light spread wide over the lower half of the tapestry, leaving the upper half shrouded, as if to speak of things underneath the surface, hidden by deception. Eyoés frowned.

The creak of his chamber door swinging open caused him to turn. Closing the door quietly behind her, Gwyndel stepped closer and tightened her scarlet robe. Her curly red hair hung in a tangled braid, hinting at her sudden wakening. The dark patches underneath her eyes and small stress lines on her features gave Eyoés a pang of regret. Work and strain had remained her constant companion for the past few years.

She rubbed the sleep from her eyes. "You sent for me?" she said, her furrowed eyebrows revealing her confusion.

Eyoés held the message close to the candlelight. "A messenger from Rehillon delivered this before he fell unconscious," he explained with a thoughtful expression. "I wanted to make sure we read it *together.*" Gwyndel nodded, stepping closer. She appreciated his consideration, a confirmation of the change he had undergone.

Laying the wet message on his desk, Eyoés gently unfolded it, careful to keep it from tearing. As Eyoés finished the last fold, he smoothed it out upon the wood surface. Squinting to read the washed out text, Eyoés began to read aloud.

Eyoés and Gwyndel -

If all has gone well, Kiffyn will have arrived at your halls. Dark things have come to my knowledge, and I fear who to trust but you. Fly to Rehillon as soon as you can, and enter quietly. I believe the Phantom League has plans against the territory. Tell no one about this, save Ayleril. I shall await you at the bridge to Merwic.

Gwair

Eyoés fell backward against his chair, staring blankly at the candle upon his desk.

Pacing about the room, Gwyndel clenched her hands into fists and turned towards her brother. Memories returned at the mention of her Forester companion. "Kiffyn was to deliver this message?" she mused aloud, visibly agitated. "Where is he? I wish to speak with him."

Eyoés abruptly stood from his chair. "Kiffyn is not here," he answered. "The man who delivered this missive—I've never seen him before."

Gwyndel's gaze darted towards the chamber door. "How do you know? You've met Kiffyn before?" she said. Eyoés nodded. One year, during the annual assembly of the Five Heroes, he had seen a younger man accompany Gwair. Gwair had introduced the man as Kiffyn, his younger brother. Eyoés appreciated the young Forester's wit, personable attitude, and determination. Although Eyoés had seen little of Kiffyn since, the memory continued to make him smile. Oftentimes he had wondered whether Gwyndel and Kiffyn had met.

"Yes, I've talked with him before. I remember his face," he explained, snatching up the message from the desk. "The messenger that delivered this to me is *not* Kiffyn." Gwyndel looked away, her gaze flitting around the room. She paused, recalling fond memories of Kiffyn shielding her from the taunts of local ruffians. At the thought, her eyes filled with an inner glow of gratitude.

Even when we did not know each other, he stood up for me.

Her chest tightened at the thought of him in danger. Clenching her fists, she started towards the door. "The messenger—he'll know what happened," she said.

Eyoés grabbed her shoulder to restrain her. "He's unconscious, and will most likely remain so until a few days have passed. We don't have much time," he insisted, pulling her away from the door. "We must follow Gwair's instructions." Gwyndel hesitated. The nagging thought of unfinished work about the castle put a knot in her stomach.

Is it right for me to leave one duty in order to fulfill another?

She glanced towards the door, her lips pressing in a slight grimace. "What about my responsibilities?" she inquired, conflicted.

Eyoés waved his hand dismissively. "Ayleril will make a fine Steward," he answered, releasing Gwyndel's shoulder. "I am sure of his capabilities."

Glancing once again towards the door, Gwyndel nodded in agreement.

I could use a break, and Kiffyn needs our aid.

She stepped towards the door and pulled it open. "I will prepare my things," she asserted, pausing to make sure her brother had spoken all his thoughts.

Eyoés pondered in silence, staring out the window into the night sky. "I must leave the temptations of my position, and this new unrest in the Kingdom sickens me," he mused aloud. "We leave for Rehillon at dawn. And this time, we come in strength."

3

Gwyndel's boots rustled through the layers of pine needles, leaves, and branches as she strolled along the hidden forest path. The gleaming light of dawn shone through the evergreens, glinting dully off the deep green boughs. Her gaze wandered, taking in the familiar sights and smells of her old home. Wisps of moss hung from the branches about her, and overgrowth obscured the path before her feet. Although she was alone, Gwyndel flashed a quick smile of embarrassment as she struggled to maintain a steady course. Over the course of her time in Asdale, the Forester skills she had nurtured in her training had become slightly rusty due to lack of practice.

The scratch of claws against bark startled her as a squirrel raced to the safety of the boughs above. Laughing at her own alarm, Gwyndel took in a deep breath, her nostrils tingling at the pungent scent of pine. It was good to be home.

However short my visit may be.

The lightness in Gwyndel's eyes faded as the forest opened ahead of her into a small clearing. A heaviness weighed down her shoulders as the familiar sight of her treehouse came into view. Despite the occasional cluster of moss clinging to the walls and roof, its appearance had changed little.

Walking towards the remnants of the rotting tree trunk nearby, she retrieved the wooden crook hidden within. She sighed heavily. While co-ruling Castle Asdale, her former cabin had been a reliable source of relief during the hardest times. With a distant stare, Gwyndel recalled her frequent retreats to her home—times of thought and repose amid the stress of her life.

One day, I shall become a Forester again, and leave the chaos of civilization behind me.

She unhooked the small pin from the bottom of the balcony with her crook and watched the ladder tumble down. Returning the crook to its hiding place, Gwyndel scrambled up the ladder and stood upon the balcony. She glanced back into the forest from which she came. Gwyndel wet her lips as she thought of Eyoés awaiting her return, assuring himself that Gibusil's saddle—and their supplies—were securely fastened. Despite her brother's objections, she had insisted they stop at her former home to assure it was securely locked up. She would not entertain the thought of her place of solace being vulnerable for a long period of time.

Grasping the wooden door handle, Gwyndel gave it a firm pull. The door held fast, assuring her the lock was in place. Satisfied, she turned and began to climb the conifer that anchored the cabin in place. A thick branch hung slightly above the roof, offering her safe access. Gwyndel felt the bark scrape against her hands and legs as she slowly made her way across the branch. Once above the treehouse, she leapt onto the roof with a thud. Cut into the shingles in front of her was the vague outline of a secret hatch. Before fully delving into her duties as Eyoés' steward, Gwyndel had found enough time to construct the unusual safeguard.

There should be little danger of intrusion with this new design.

Grasping the discreet handle, she pried the hatch open and descended down the wooden ladder to the interior of her home. She let the hatch fall behind her as she descended the last half of the ladder and set foot on the wooden floor. At the sight of the familiar furnishings, Gwyndel frowned, her emotions mixed. A nostalgia permeated the space as memories of her brother's first appearance returned to her.

He's changed much since then.

The thought of Eyoés reminded Gwyndel of her present duties. Crouching by the side of the bed, she retrieved several wooden boards stored underneath, along with a box of nails. Boarding up the windows and door would discourage any would-be intruders from their intentions. Gwyndel cleared her throat as she gathered up the supplies in her arms, forcing herself to remain focused on the task at hand. She started towards the door.

Her eyes alighted upon the old, crinkled map upon her desk, causing her to pause. She had purposely left it undisturbed after their return from Zwaoi as a reminder of their journey. Although thrilled by the idea of another adventure at her brother's side, Gwyndel pressed her lips together in reluctance.

Maybe—just maybe—Eyoés will soon be ready to shoulder the complete responsibilities of Baron himself. And when he does, I will not be torn from my home again.

Three sunrises had crossed the horizon before Gibusil sailed through the fair skies of Gald-Behn, below the veil of gilded clouds. Keeping their westward course, Eyoés gently handled the griffin's reins as the quiet breeze brushed against his face. He closed his eyes, taking in the scent of honey upon the wind. A wave of excitement coursed through him at the reality of their new journey.

And this time, I am not burdened by my own foolishness.

Within the boundary of the King's land, the temptation of his status seemed trivial, and the beautiful willow copses and unending plains below calmed him. A strong desire to linger took its place. With a tinge of regret, Eyoés knew it could not be so.

All things happen in the King's timing. Gwair needs me.

Turning in his seat, Eyoés looked to Gwyndel. Silent, she gazed off into the distance, her features soft and peaceful in the King's realm. Eyoés smiled and faced forward. "I haven't had time to tell you this," he began. "But I want to thank you for helping me navigate the Baronship these past few years. Without your help—"

Gwyndel set a hand on his shoulder with a smile. "I am merely assisting you with your responsibilities. In time, you will have the wisdom needed to fulfill your position," she replied, looking off into the horizon with a sigh. "I eagerly await that day,"

Not detecting her longing, Eyoés laughed. "I still can't decide if I'm eager or anxious about that day!" he exclaimed. He slightly corrected their flight path. Eyoés opened his mouth to speak again.

Eyoés.

Recognizing the voice, he set aside his conversation for another time. Eyoés closed his eyes to block off any distraction to the Guide's voice.

Yes?

He smiled, as if conversing with an old friend. The voice returned.

Do not relax your guard. The mission to which you travel will endanger not only your life, but your purpose as well. Beware the charm of gold and the company of evil.

The voice fell silent. Eyoés' smile faded as his mind raced away, absorbed with the thought of riches and power over his people. He abruptly shook away the thoughts entangling him, repeating the warning under his breath. Worry and despair began to well up within, upsetting his stomach.

Am I doomed to be haunted by these thoughts of greed?

Forcing himself to quell his rising anxiety, Eyoés spurred Gibusil onward.

I must get to Gwair—I will not let my own fear account for the fall of Rehillon.

Seated behind her brother, Gwyndel closed her eyes, letting the warm caress of the wind sweep across her face. Memories of Kiffyn returned in a perplexing combination of fondness and dread…

4

17th of Dichán, 2185 SE

Gwyndel cried out as another clod of tightly packed dirt slammed into the side of her head, knocking her to her knees. Through the throbbing headache pounding in her skull, she heard the taunts and laughs of the three young Forester Initiates. Their Master left them unsupervised, preoccupied with tending a wounded man who had stumbled into their camp that morning.

Nausea welled up in Gwyndel's stomach with each blow. Sickened by the pain and hurt, she gagged. At the sight of their prey in such misery, the ruffians increased their taunting. More clumps of mud flew through the air and pummeled her.

Clenching her fists, she sobbed in anger, her tears tracing paths through the dirt speckling her youthful face. Gwyndel pounded the ground with her fist and fell onto her side.

Where are you Fychan?

A large pinecone struck her cheek. As a trickle of blood rolled down her face, she confronted the reality of her situation. In Fychan's absence the delinquent Initiates were emboldened to act on their malicious impulses.

"Go back to the desolate wilderness, elf!" they shouted. "Your kind has no place here!" Gwyndel choked down a sob and curled into a ball.

They're right. I have no home—I'm an outcast. Why did the King let this happen? Why did he not let father live?

Grinding her teeth, she wept. She pulled the brown peasant's hood down over her face. Anger flared against her tormentors. Sheltering her face with her hand, Gwyndel cast a dark glance at the sky above.

If the King really cares for me, he would bring a miracle!

More flying debris cut her legs and bruised her body, causing her to wince. Pounding with the strength of anger and childish frustration, her heart sped faster. She waited in spite with a hidden hope for a miracle.

The pinecones and small stones continued to fly. Crying out, Gwyndel felt the added insult of fallen pine needles pricking through her clothing. With each passing second of torment, Gwyndel slumped further into the depths of despair. Closing her eyes, she wrapped her arms around her body, unable to fight any longer.

A sudden shout startled her. Bewildered, she let out a yelp and opened her eyes. Crashing through the brush, a young boy about her age brandished a long branch above his head. The standard brown hood identified him as a Forester Initiate. He bared his teeth in indignant rage. "Leave her be!" he yelled, charging into the midst of Gwyndel's tormentors.

The taunts of the other Initiates turned into a frantic yelping of pain as the strong oak branch pounded them repeatedly, driving them back. Releasing the projectiles in their hands, the ruffians fled the scene, now bleeding and bruised themselves. Gwyndel watched them disappear into the brush. Shaking, she sobbed, her thoughts confused.

Throwing aside his improvised club, the young boy turned to where she lay. His blonde hair bounced about his ears as he raced to her side, his face ashen. As he knelt at her side, Gwyndel rolled onto her back. Sobs racked her frame as she wiped away her tears of joy. As Gwyndel sat up, her arms encircled her savior in an embrace. Tears welled up in the boy's eyes as he saw the fresh terror in hers.

He held her head steady with both hands. "It's alright! I swear by my honor they will never hurt you again," he vowed, tears coursing down his cheeks. "Master Kerron will dismiss these shameful troublemakers from the Forester service."

Chin trembling, Gwyndel embraced him, weeping openly on his shoulder. "Thank the King you came, Kiffyn," she muttered between sobs. "Is it true what they say? Do I deserve to be cast out for being an elf?"

Squeezing her tightly, the boy collected himself. "That is nonsense—and don't you *ever* believe it," he replied.

5

Clouds gathered. Casting dark oaths at the lone griffin, the overcast sky threatened to unleash its stormy wrath upon the two travelers. After three more days of traveling, the shining plains of Gald-Behn had faded behind them, obscured by the misty crags of mountains. Bent on his mission, Eyoés ignored the dreary weather, pulling the hood of his cloak lower over his face. Gwyndel followed his example, bowing her head to shield herself from the wind. A powerful gust surged against Gibusil's wings, nearly unseating the two riders. The griffin quickly compensated, giving a warble of inquiry as to the riders' well-being. Eyoés patted Gibusil's feathery hide and guided the griffin to a lower flight path above the treetops to avoid the angry gales.

Below them, dark green conifers clustered together, lush with ferns and other growth. The musty odor of the moist earth rose from below, the rich brown tones of the forest floor nearly masking the silent watch of several deer. Tightening her cloak to ward off the crisp air, Gwyndel leaned forward. "How far until we reach Merwic?" she inquired, scanning the path ahead for sign of a settlement. Releasing the reins, Eyoés retrieved a compass from his belt and flipped the cover open.

He glanced back and forth between their course and the instrument in his hand. "Based off our first estimate, we should be arriving sometime today, as we've been making good time," he responded, returning the compass to its place. "Keep a vigilant watch—we'll fly low to mask our approach." Grasping the reins again, Eyoés brought the griffin even lower, nearly on top of the forest canopy.

Several minutes passed before Gwyndel pointed off to the southeast. "There," she said. Eyoés followed her arm to where several pillars of smoke rose on the horizon. He nodded and corrected their course, urging Gibusil to a quicker pace while glancing to the sky above. Frowning, he searched for any sign of the sun, hoping to determine the time of day. As if to deny him his goal, the clouds thickened above him.

We must hurry. If we don't catch Gwair before evening, he might have returned to a temporary encampment.

He didn't have long to wait. Not far ahead, the forest abruptly halted outside the town limits. Cobblestone streets weaved through rows of houses and storefronts. On the farthest side of the village, large plots of farmland sustained the local people. Eyoés watched as several farmers labored diligently at the plow, guiding a team of oxen down the length of their plots. The smells of civilization and fresh food carried on the wind towards the riders.

Fly to Rehillon as soon as you can, and enter quietly. I shall await you at the bridge to Merwic.

As Gwair's warning returned to his memory, Eyoés searched for a place to land unseen. His eye caught sight of a small break in the treetops. Gibusil, sensing his master's wishes, pulled his wings inward and ducked through the break in the trees. As soon as they were within cover, the griffin quickly popped its wings open to slow their descent, coming to a gentle landing upon the forest floor.

Removing his cowl, Eyoés dismounted, extending a hand to aid Gwyndel's descent. With a grateful nod, she took his gloved hand and hopped to the ground. Eyoés patted Gibusil's neck in gratitude, marveling at how much the griffin had grown since their first adventure. Around them, the forest opened into a narrow channel of sparsely treed ground. Large clusters of ferns dotted the forest floor, growing through the thick layer of damp pine needles. Moisture hung in the air about them, reminding Eyoés of the forests of his home following a spring rain.

Peering through the trees, Eyoés glimpsed the edge of Merwic directly ahead. Squinting, he caught sight of a large stone bridge.

If all has gone well, Gwair will be waiting there.

He clenched his fist as he considered the possibility of Gwair's position being compromised. Turning on his heels, he briskly removed his sword from Gibusil's back and buckled it around his waist.

Should things go awry, I will be ready.

Gwyndel began to unfasten their supplies from the griffin's back. Shaking his head, Eyoés set a hand on her shoulder. "Stay here with Gibusil. A lone traveler is often ignored, but two earn a look of interest. We can't take any chances," he insisted.

Casting a wary glance towards her brother, Gwyndel released their supplies. "You think there will be trouble?" she asked, briefly glancing at the town between the trees. Despite his attempts to remain positive, Eyoés knew it would be foolish to not account for the worst.

He swallowed. "First, I will contact Gwair. If I am not back by nightfall, fly to Gald-Behn and get help. Until we get a more detailed explanation from Gwair, I don't know who we can trust," he answered, turning away. Without another word, he strode in the direction of Merwic. As he disappeared into the thick brush, Gwyndel stroked Gibusil's feathery wings.

If he disappears as Kiffyn did…

Wiping debris from his worn cloak, Eyoés emerged from the forest and examined his surroundings. Because of the urgency in Gwair's message, he had left his Baron's clothing in Asdale. The common clothing he now wore offered a better chance of remaining unnoticed. Directly ahead, the land dipped into a steep divide, spanning a relatively short distance before sloping up again to a flat grassland, where the town of Merwic sat. Spanning the width of the divide, a stone bridge provided easy passage for those wishing to enter the town. Moss grew between the cracks of stone, giving the structure the appearance of age. Walls about waist height lined either side of the bridge to ensure safe passage. Directly in front of Eyoés, a road passed in front of the bridge, leading to the next town. The rough appearance of the structure spoke of a clever, coarse people.

Trying to avoid the looks of several people heading for the road beyond the bridge, Eyoés pressed his lips into a firm line and feigned the study of his fingernail, searching for any sign of Gwair as he started toward the bridge.

His heart beat faster as he searched the faces of the crossing people, not recognizing any. Stepping onto the stone pavers, he increased his pace. As he reached the apex of the bridge, he stopped.

Leaning against one of the side walls, a man in ragged clothes admired the surrounding wilderness. Eyoés narrowed his eyes and stepped closer, trying to get a look at the man's face. A two-toned hood of faded red and yellow sat loosely over his head, but his tall, burly frame hinted at his identity. Glimpsing the approaching man, the lone peasant turned slightly. Eyoés let out a quiet exhale as he recognized Gwair. Assured they were not being watched, Eyoés nonchalantly rested against the wall beside.

With a nod, Gwair leaned close to Eyoés. "You received my message, then," he whispered, not looking directly at Eyoés to avoid any chance of suspicion. Eyeing several nearby locals, Gwair repeatedly clenched and unclenched his fists, as if in preparation for a fight. Eyoés felt a rising unease inside at his companion's nervousness.

I've never seen Gwair so agitated. There must be a reason.

The conclusion sent an involuntary shiver through him. Recovering from his momentary lapse of awareness, Eyoés glanced toward Gwair. "Yes, but Gwyndel and I know little," he replied in a low tone. "What can you tell us?"

Gwair shook his head ever so slightly. "Not here," he insisted, his hand slipping into a small bag on his shoulder. He briskly removed a large chunk of bread, a potato, and some jerky from within. "Give this to Gwyndel, then come straight back to the bridge. We'll head to the Crooked Heel together and talk there." Clapping his hand on Gwair's back, Eyoés waited for the passerby to disappear from view before quickly returning to the forest with Gwair's gift in hand.

The two heroes strode down the cobblestone street, Eyoés following several paces behind Gwair in an effort to remain unnoticed. Seeing no need for such measures, Eyoés had quietly objected, reasoning the people of Merwic would not be aroused to suspicion at the sight of two men walking beside each other. Still, Gwair had insisted.

"If I am being watched, it would be foolish to pair up." Despite this reasonable explanation, Eyoés still found such lengthy measures strange at best. Watching Gwair turn a corner in the path ahead of him, he pursed his lip. His friend's excessive attempts at total secrecy seemed unnecessary.

Perhaps a deeper understanding of the situation at hand will help me make sense of his concern.

As he rounded the bend, Eyoés saw Gwair standing below a large wooden sign. Coming to a stop at the door to the establishment, Eyoés wrinkled his nose at the grotesque representation of a broken heel painted on the sign.

"Welcome to the Crooked Heel," Gwair chuckled under his breath and waving his hand towards the door. "Let me do the talking, and we should be free to speak —some." Raising an eyebrow, Eyoés stepped towards the door and opened it. A waft of warm air shot out from within, carrying with it the smells of sweat and beef. Taking in one last deep breath of fresh air, Eyoés entered, followed by Gwair.

The din of conversation nearly drowned out every other sound. Huddled around their tables, patrons laughed, argued, and discussed with their fellows, drinking and eating as much as they could afford. Several homemade chandeliers hung from the ceiling, providing enough light to see comfortably by. Far to the back of the room, a long bar provided extra seating and a place to order.

Walking around Eyoés, Gwair led the way and strode towards the bar. Eyoés edged around several seats as he followed.

The bartender watched Gwair set an arm on the bar. "What do you want?" he inquired, his voice less than welcoming. An air of tension lay about the place, strengthened by the dark looks of the customers.

Taking stock of the situation, Gwair adjusted his manner. "Something to eat," he replied curtly. Expecting the new customer's temperament to match the mood of the townsfolk, the bartender nodded in turn and ducked through a doorway leading to the kitchen. Eyoés set a hand upon his companion's shoulder and gestured towards an open table. Gwair nodded in confirmation as the bartender returned with a plate of beef, bread, and potatoes. As the man set the plate upon the bar, Gwair slid several coins towards the bartender, retrieved his food, and started towards the table they had chosen.

As he sat down, Gwair set the plate upon the table and took a quick look around to make sure they would not be overheard. Briefly closing his eyes, he paused for a moment. Then, taking the utensils in hand, he began to carve up the meat. Rubbing the back of his neck, Eyoés cleared his throat.

Gwair saw his friend's hungry look. "We're sharing," he explained, retrieving a second set of utensils from his bag.

Leaning forward, Eyoés took the utensils. "You've never been so anxious. Is this situation truly so dark?" he said, keeping his voice low.

Glancing around once more, Gwair nodded, seeing his friend's interest. "I fear it is worse. Over eight months ago, a terrible rainstorm swept through South

Rehillon, spoiling the grain crops in Hodholm, Herthere, and Enfalls. Many were struggling to feed themselves," he answered. Eyoés looked firmly at his companion. Several times, he had heard of such things being common among the rural workers of the land. Sometimes, the workers at Asdale even mentioned the struggle, worried they would return home to find their families starving. A pang of compassion accompanied the recollection.

"I have heard of such things occurring across Alithell," Eyoés mused, taking a bite of bread. "I assume there is more." Gwair sighed, anxious to unload the burden of his unease and find a way to solve his predicament.

"Baron Vikar saw the need to intervene—and secured an agreement with a trader to import a new, more sustainable grain. 'Everwheat' if you can believe it," he continued, chuckling bitterly to himself. "It worked—for a while. The tax was so high, even the Baron struggled to pay!"

Intent on Gwair's words, Eyoés frowned and crossed his arms. "Why would Baron Vikar accept an agreement even he could not pay?" he asked, his suspicion growing.

Gwair shook his head. "The trader enacted the tax *after* the agreement. Out of desperation, the Baron didn't protest the extra expense, hard pressed to keep the people's food supply stable," he answered through his teeth. "We were all fooled because of our fear and desperation. When one of our payments failed to

arrive, the trader cut us off and ceased trade altogether
—"

A sudden shout of anger rang through the tavern. Gwair jumped, hand reaching to the dagger at his belt. Two men threw their seats backward into the laps of several other patrons. The older of the two, whose wizened appearance hinted at years of hard labor, shook his fist at the other.

"Your 'savior' is nothing but a fraud! Baron Vikar has led Rehillon in many years of prosperity!" he shouted, his voice hoarse. A spiteful laugh burst from the younger patron. Seeing the dark, fevered hatred in his eyes, Eyoés stood and pressed himself against the wall, gesturing for Gwair to follow after.

The angry youth seized the elder's shirt. "Do you not remember the terror of the Addiction? Vikar—that swine of a man—nearly caused our ruin. Long live Throst Ravenstrong!" he yelled in return. The elder man's eyes darkened in disgust at the very name. With a roar, he threw a wild punch. Seeing the blow, the youth swiftly stepped back to avoid it, drawing a small tool knife as he did so.

Gwair needed no instruction as chaos erupted and the two men fell at each other's throats. Amid the confused customers, Eyoés and Gwair fled—but not unnoticed.

Unflinching at the erupting chaos, a man in commoners clothing stood near the door, observing their escape with a dark eye.

6

Bursting through the trees, Eyoés and Gwair stumbled into the small clearing, tripping over several unseen tree roots. Gwyndel gave a small cry and leapt up. Instinctively, Gibusil leapt to her side with a growl, then relaxed as he recognized Eyoés.

Gwyndel hurried towards them. "What happened?" she asked, glancing over their shoulders for sign of any pursuers. Gwair shook his head, his arm around the young Baron's shoulder. Recovering his breath, Gwair gestured they should sit, ruffling Gibusil's feathers with his hand as he walked past. Turning around, Gwyndel opened her mouth to speak, then hesitated as she considered her words.

Should I ask about Kiffyn?

Guessing at her intentions, Eyoés set a hand on her shoulder and shook his head. Gwyndel flashed a false smile and drew back, despite her worry.

What if Gwair does not know of Kiffyn's disappearance? I do not want to be the bearer of ill news.

"I apologize for the sudden exit, Eyoés," Gwair sighed, seating himself beside the beginnings of a campfire. "I should have suggested we discuss matters in the safety of the forest. It would have been a wiser decision, but my inability to identify the enemy has clouded my judgement." Waving the matter aside, Eyoés sat beside his fellow hero, warming himself by the fire.

"That is the least of our concerns, it seems," Eyoés said, regarding Gwair with a questioning eye. "Tell us more about the strange circumstances you were speaking to me about—before we were interrupted."

Gwair nodded, turning to Gwyndel. "I shall," he began, noticing the food he had sent her laying half-consumed by the fire, "once I have explained the matters we have discussed to Gwyndel." Without the fear of being overheard, he recounted the startling details of the past events to her. Although familiar with Gwair's words, Eyoés found himself again unsettled.

Does Gwair's story correlate to the tavern brawl? Who is Throst Ravenstrong?

He tried to make sense of the strange affair as Gwair recounted the circumstances that had beckoned them there. Gwyndel's eyes narrowed as she pondered the meaning of the strange incident. "So if I understand you correctly, your people were in the midst of a crop failure, as a result of a severe rainstorm. The Baron of the territory contracted an agreement with a trader to import a certain Everwheat grain into Rehillon. When no payment was received, the trader cut off all access to the grain," she affirmed, raising an eyebrow as she regarded Gwair. The hero nodded.

Eyoés interjected before Gwair could continue. "One of the ruffians in the tavern spoke of a Throst Ravenstrong—what does he have to do with this trading dilemma?" he said.

Gwair looked to the ground, his gaze troubled. "He took action when nobody could—I will speak of that soon. Baron Vikar and the Council of Lords were helpless to stop the people's suffering. After several days, I noticed I did not feel like myself after consuming Everwheat bread. Suspicious, I ceased eating any of my personal supply. I found myself struggling against delirium. Through sheer force of will, I suffered through several weeks of pain, but recovered," he continued. "When the supply of Everwheat grain began to run out, the people of Rehillon began exhibiting strange symptoms—ranging from mood changes and insomnia to delirium, tremors, and in some cases, near madness. Left with little food after the rainstorm, the people were instructed to eat oats—*horse feed*—in order to survive. Their suffering furthered my suspicions." He tried to hold in his just indignation.

Eyoés glanced toward Gwyndel. Although he had yet to know the results of this revelation, a nagging tension began to build. Gwair continued. "I knew something sinister was rising in our land, and traced the path of the Everwheat trade to the Darmore Fells in Fenabor. My companion and I located one of the farms growing the grain. By questioning the planter heavily, I uncovered the truth—prior to shipment, the Everwheat flour was purposely mixed with Ossinder powder," Gwair explained.

At the mention of the plant, Gwyndel gasped. "Ossinder?" she asked, her posture stiff. "That herb is unlawful in Alithell!" She recalled the several times she and Fychan had foiled traders dealing in the addictive plant. Gwyndel leaned closer towards Gwair. "The Phantom League controls much of the Ossinder trade, and makes a considerable profit," she said in a low voice.

For a while, Gwair said nothing, instead clenching his hands into fists. He took a deep breath to steady himself. "Yes—the grower himself filled his pockets with the League's gold, in return for poisoning the flour. The revelation both angered and disquieted me. Upon my return to Rehillon, I shared my discoveries with the Baron. I also received word that Lord Ravenstrong had discovered an antidote to remedy the Addiction's symptoms. Because of Throst, the Everwheat addiction was broken," he said. "I knew if the Phantom League was to carry out their treasonous acts, there must be a trustworthy force prepared to combat them. I secretly tasked my closest aides to raise up a band of Loyalists to thwart whatever might be in store. I instructed Kiffyn to carry a message to Asdale. He was to arrive at the Farmer's Guild here in Merwic, to meet with a friend and refresh his horse before moving on," he sighed, meeting their gaze. "But I hesitate to face this evil alone. That is why I sent for you. I fear the Phantom League has their eyes set on bigger things—things I have yet to discover."

Locking eyes with Gwyndel, Eyoés paused, pressing his lips together in thought. A desire to help his fellow hero in his time of need pressed him to accept the mission.

The mission to which you travel will endanger not only your life, but your purpose as well. Beware the charm of gold and the company of evil...

His chest tightened as the Guide's warning returned. It was apparent the company of evil would be ever present.

Could this mission result in my downfall?

Fiddling with the hem of his cloak, Eyoés considered the possibility. He eyed Gwair. The man's gaze was haunted with the uncertainty of his predicament. Through their several years of friendship, Eyoés had come to know of Gwair's determination and unwillingness to compromise.

Should I do nothing, Gwair will fight whatever enemy he is faced with—and he could die as a consequence.

Eyoés looked to Gwyndel. Although she did not have as strong a friendship with the man, it was clear what she thought. She gave a light nod. Despite the conflict between his own aversion and Gwair's need, Eyoés was resolved.

Leaning forward, he set a hand on Gwair's shoulder. "A Hero stands beside his brother despite the risk. We will stand with you," he declared.

Gwair smiled as he clasped Eyoés' forearm in gratitude. "I give you my thanks," he said, the unease in his manner replaced with a strong confidence. "Kiffyn would have swanted to join us—I am glad he is safe in your halls." At the mention of the Forester, the light in Eyoés' eyes faded. Noticing the worry in his friend's eye, Gwair glanced to Gwyndel. She turned away, biting her lip to hide her anxiety. As Gwair's forehead wrinkled in confusion, Eyoés pulled his arm from his friend's grasp and laid a comforting hand on his shoulder.

"The man who delivered your message was not Kiffyn," he explained, looking downward.

Gwair's eyes widened in horror. "What?" he muttered, leaping to his feet.

Standing, Eyoés met Gwair's gaze. "The messenger who came in his place fell unconscious from exhaustion. When I spoke with the local healer, he told me the man wouldn't awaken for several days. We decided to hurry to your aid rather than wait for an answer," he said. Gwyndel hurried to comfort the stricken man.

Gwair returned the expression of sympathy, then left Gwyndel's embrace, his face darkening. "Our mission is all the more urgent, with Kiffyn gone," he said, struggling to compose himself. "A platoon of my Loyalists followed me here from the capital and are stationed around the town, should I need them. Tomorrow, I will return with them before the sun rises." Briskly, he turned away. Before Eyoés and Gwyndel could give another word of encouragement, Gwair disappeared into the forest, seeking a place to mourn the disappearance of his brother.

7

As the moon faded from the sky, the forest was overtaken by a total darkness—the inky black mire that plagues the land before the approach of dawn. Everything under night's banner morphed into an ebony horde, as if to fight off the coming light. The haunting calls of owls echoed from the conifer boughs, startling Eyoés from sleep. He sat up, momentarily confused by the darkness. A tingling grew in his chest as memories of his first black night in Zwaoi overwhelmed him. Casting aside his blanket, he shuddered and reached for his sword. As he grasped the handle of his blade, Eyoés remembered where he was, and Gwair's promise.

A platoon of my Loyalists followed me here from the capital and are stationed around the town, should I need them. Tomorrow, I will return with them before the sun rises.

Eyoés bowed his head in relief as the howling cries of Zwaoi faded from his thoughts. "Gwyndel," he called in a low voice. Eyoés heard the rustling of blankets as his sister woke.

For a moment, Gwyndel said nothing, gaining her bearings. Then, with a burst of bright flame, their campfire sprung into life, causing the both of them to squint. With a growl of irritation, Gibusil woke, tucking his head closer to his body to block the light. Replacing her flint and steel in her nearby pack, Gwyndel rubbed the sleep from her eyes. "Gwair must be on his way here," she observed, stifling a yawn.

Taking both of their blankets, Eyoés stood, neatly folding each and shoving them into the supply pack. "I expect we will form a plan when he arrives with his Loyalists," he reasoned, buckling his sword belt. "It will be a challenge to discover the Phantom League's intentions *and* find Kiffyn."

Their discussion ceased as a glow appeared through the maze of trees, illuminating the bark of several conifers with a faded orange light. Through the gaps in the trees, Eyoés glimpsed a number of silent, mounted figures carrying torches. Hearing the approach of an armed company, Gibusil came to his feet, at the ready. Eyoés moved to the griffin's side, hand placed soothingly on its shoulder. As the squad emerged from the forest, the tamed light of their torches melded with the wild flame of the campfire. Riding at the head of the group, Gwair raised his clenched fist. Immediately, the Loyalists reined in their horses and sat upright at attention.

Gwyndel cocked her head, impressed. Their training combined with the loyalty burning in their eyes gave the appearance of a well-experienced outfit.

Eyoés nodded to Gwair and gestured to the Loyalists. "How long have you been in command of these men?" he inquired, his tone approving.

Gwair smiled. "Several months. Many of them were once members of the Northern Guard, as I once was, many years ago. It takes strength and courage to withstand the grueling training demanded of them," he explained, voice full of pride for his men and his home territory. "Once discharged after ten years of service, many return to their homes. I am grateful to the King these men have come under my command."

Regarding the Loyalist troops with a newfound respect, Eyoés stepped forward and bowed. "As are we," he agreed. When his men saluted in response, Gwair gave the command to stand at ease and dismounted, tying his horse's reins to a tree. The large group of men dismounted and moved into the clearing with their steeds, quietly chatting among themselves. Gwair sat beside the campfire, leaning closer to Eyoés and Gwyndel to speak privately.

Gwyndel spoke first. "What is our plan?" she asked, removing a map from her pack. She untied the leather strap wrapped around the parchment, spread the map open on the ground and used several stones to keep it open.

Gwair nodded in appreciation. "With Kiffyn gone —" he began, giving a false smile to hide his anxiety. "Our goal is divided. If Kiffyn is to be found, we can no longer stay a single force." He indicated Merwic on the map. "Some of us must search for my brother, while the rest return to Hodholm to investigate a potential plot," he maintained. "I suspect the Phantom League has their hand in my brother's disappearance, and their reasons for doing so could very well tie in with their work in the capital." As Gwair spoke, the image of his brother surfaced, bringing a pang of guilt and loss with it. He cringed.

I sent Kiffyn into danger. I should have done more to ensure his safety.

Briefly raising a hand, Eyoés interjected before Gwair could continue. "If too many of us return to Hodholm, we could gain unwanted attention," he pondered, chin resting on his hand.

Gwair tapped the map. "A large force is easier to conceal in the wilderness. The Loyalists would follow Kiffyn's trail, while a smaller party would travel to Hodholm," he agreed.

At the mention of Kiffyn's trail, a jolt of hope ran through Gwyndel, followed abruptly by confusion. "Where do we pick up Kiffyn's trail?" she questioned.

Gwair stabbed his index finger at another town on the map. "Only a fool would enter foreign territory and not assure a quick escape, should the circumstances demand it. The only path to exit Rehillon is through the Northern Passage. The Phantom League will most likely be stationed in Andieff in order to keep a steady watch on their escape route," he speculated with conviction. "Because Kiffyn got the message past their guard, the League doesn't know *who* the letter beckoned. The small contingent will first assemble in a place near Andieff to discuss the next move before retreating to a place of safety. Even if they are no longer there, enough information could possibly be gathered to point to their current location."

"What are we waiting for?" Gwyndel questioned. Eyoés looked to the sky, grabbing his cloak and fastening it around his shoulders.

"We don't have time to discuss any longer. Dawn is nearly upon us," he agreed. Eyoés spread the dying coals of the campfire with his boot and smothered it with dirt. Striding toward the nearby pack of supplies, he removed his water skin and unplugged the opening. The fire hissed in anger as a large splash of water finished it off.

Gwyndel stepped towards Gwair, glancing longingly towards the Loyalist ranks idly talking among themselves. "Send *me* with them—to look for Kiffyn," she said, shouldering her bow. Gwair paused, regarding the Forester as he stroked his trimmed beard. His eyebrows furrowed as a fear within prodded him to object.

I sent Kiffyn into danger to face an unknown foe. Is it right to ask others to brave the same danger?

The responsibility for the demise of his own brother and possibly two of his close companions troubled him. Sighing, Gwair forcibly ignored his misgivings.

Just because I ask does not mean they have to accept. It is their choice to put themselves in danger, not mine.

"Kiffyn was a friend of yours, wasn't he?" he asked. As Gwyndel looked downward, she affirmed what Gwair already knew. Kiffyn had often spoken of Gwyndel as a dear friend and fellow Forester. Before Gwyndel could repeat her wishes, Gwair turned toward the Loyalists gathered together. "Captain Beydan!" he called.

Standing at attention, one of the Loyalists strode towards his commander. In the light of the nearby torches, his worn leather jerkin and gloves were a dark tan, and the sleeves of the shirt underneath were emblazoned with military insignia. Sheathed at his side in a plain leather scabbard, a strange weapon caught Gwyndel's eye. Even when sheathed, the sword's shallow curve and claw-like tip was apparent. Although she had never seen one firsthand, Gwyndel recognized the weapon from her Forester training.

A falchion.

As the man approached, the sheathed weapon knocked against his thighs. Beneath a prominent brow, his two steely hazel eyes cast stern looks to those present. Long hair swept behind his shoulders, and a thick beard masked much of his features.

Shoulders back, Beydan saluted his superior. At the man's arrogant bearing, Gwyndel clenched her jaw. "Yes, High Marshal?" Beydan said, casting a fleeting glance at Gwyndel while standing at attention.

Gwair saluted in return. "You are to travel to Andieff in search for Kiffyn, as I instructed you last night," he commanded, gesturing to Gwyndel. "Gwyndel, daughter of Élorn and sister of Eyoés Kingson, will accompany you."

Stiffening at the command, Beydan examined the Forester before him with a scowl. With a growl of spite, Beydan looked away from her in disgust. "She'll never keep up the pace, Forester she may be," he objected.

Frowning, Gwyndel tensed, firmly crossing her arms in a show of defiance.

I'm not sure I have the patience.

Gwair's expression darkened. Taking a step forward, he locked a stern glare on his subordinate. "Captain Beydan, you are a member of the Northern Guard and under my command. I may not be in active duty, but I still carry the honor of my rank. If she slows the pace, you *match* it," he ordered. "For the entirety of your journey, Gwyndel is to be alongside you. Give her the use of my horse. Understood?"

Clenching his jaw fiercely, Beydan took a step back. "Yes, High Marshal. We will find Kiffyn," he answered, his voice stale as he struggled to control himself.

With a decisive nod, Gwair gestured at his troops. "Get the men ready to ride," he declared. Saluting his superior, Beydan spun on his heels and started towards the troops, growling orders.

As the Loyalists prepared to set out, Gwair shook his head and turned to Gwyndel. "Forgive him for his behavior," he apologized, his gaze flicking upward. "He struggles to control his resentment."

Gwyndel glanced toward the Captain with a sigh. "What happened to him?" she inquired. Watching his men get into neat formation, Gwair paused.

"He tells us nothing, yet there are rumors he suffered a tragedy concerning his own brother," he speculated. "Unless he willingly speaks about the past, it will remain a mystery. I hope he does not cause you much trouble.”

“Gwair and I must then be headed for the capital of Hodholm,” Eyoés reasoned aloud, joining his two companions. “I overheard, and packed your supplies in the spare sack, Gwyndel.” Shaken from her musings, the elf murmured her thanks, embracing her brother. After several years of being ever at his side, she struggled to leave him behind. Reluctantly releasing Eyoés, Gwyndel blinked away tears. Eyoés leaned over and plucked Fóbehn, the blessed bow, from where it lay by his boot alongside its quiver and extended them both to his sister.

Gwyndel regarded the weapon quietly, then cleared her throat. “Are you sure you don’t want to take it?” she asked. Fóbehn brought back many memories.

Eyoés nodded. “It will serve better in the wilderness than in the courts of Hodholm. We were meant to use it, not be afraid of it,” he insisted. Shrugging the quiver onto her shoulder, Gwyndel took Fóbehn into her hand. The beauty and familiarity brought a smile to her lips. And comfort.

Eyoés laid a hand on Gwair’s shoulder. “We must make for Hodholm—Gibusil will bear us there in haste,” he announced, making his way to where Gibusil waited, playing with a solitary fern.

❖

15th of Biarron, 2202 SE

Two days of rain and battering wind came to pass as Eyoés and Gwair forged their path to Hodholm. Gibusil continued on against the cold, his golden feathers stained dark by the rain. Wrapping their soaked cloaks about them, Eyoés and Gwair said nothing, watching the horizon for sign of Hodholm. Eyoés fingered the griffin's reins with one hand, and clutched his compass in the other. Even as he searched for their destination, his thoughts journeyed on another course.

I cannot help but worry for Gwyndel's safety—yet I know the importance of this mission to both Gwair and the people of Rehillon. I must focus on the task at hand, and leave Gwyndel in the Guide's hands.

His eyes narrowed as he struggled to focus. After years of being at Gwyndel's side, leaving her—no matter for how long—made him anxious. Forcefully setting aside such thoughts, Eyoés glanced over his shoulder. Wrapped tight in his cloak, Gwair looked off into the distance, his brows unconsciously furrowed. Eyoés hesitated to break his companion's deep concentration.

His thoughts are elsewhere, as are mine. We both fear for our family.

Patting Gibusil's wet feathers with his gloved hand, Eyoés released the reins for a moment. "You are close to your brother," he said.

Gwair blinked as the voice interrupted his thoughts, then paused as he considered Eyoés' statement. "We've shared much of our lives together. Whenever one of us struggled, the other would be there to come to his aid," he said, with a slight smile. "Once, we journeyed with our family from our hometown of Merwic to Andieff to visit old friends. While our elders discussed matters, Kiffyn and I found ourselves alone and free to explore. We fashioned swords and bows from branches and trekked further into the forest than we were allowed. I nearly fell to my death in a hidden ravine. I do not know what would have happened to me had Kiffyn not been there. More than once we have saved each other."

Eyoés chuckled and turned away, taking hold of Gibusil's reins. His smile faded as he envisioned Gwair's brief tale.

Until I met Gwyndel, I had no sibling to share such memories with.

A resentment rose within, a remnant of his old self. Shaking his head, Eyoés refused to be embittered.

The past cannot be changed. I am grateful for what the King has given me now.

Eyoés emerged from his thoughts as Gwair pointed to their right. Below, the forest broke away into a wide expanse of fields. From the view above, walls of round stones appeared as interlocking pieces of stained glass, sectioning off each farmer's land. Several small cabins were built on each plot to house the families toiling to make a living.

In the center of the expanse, a sprawling castle watched over a town built outside its thick walls. Upon the battlements, soldiers milled about, keeping a watchful eye on the land. Within the castle walls, a wide square keep nearly spanned the diameter of the inner courtyard. Parapets and towers bristled from the keep's walls, like an army of spears. Each grey stone was tainted dark by rain. A faded red flag flew above the keep, emblazoned with a blue shield encompassing three drops of amber surrounding a single conifer.

Taken aback at the sheer size of Hodholm, Eyoés shook his head in disbelief.

One day, Asdale might grow to this magnificence.

The thought caught him off guard as he remembered the size of his home castle before the destruction. He mentally compared the two capitals.

Perhaps such things will come to pass in time.

Gwair set a hand on Eyoés' shoulder and pointed to a small hill below, crowned by a large section of isolated trees. "Quickly! Land in cover before we are seen," he urged. Brought back into the reality of their mission, Eyoés abruptly steered Gibusil towards the trees below.

Hidden inside the cover of thick brush and trees, Eyoés and Gwair dismounted from the griffin's back, rainwater dripping from their clothing. Underneath their feet, the rocky, uneven ground defied their presence. Above their heads, the boughs of the evergreens shielded them from the weather.

Gwair removed his sword from their supplies and fastened it around his waist, his wet hands squeaking as they slipped across his polished leather belt. "I will acquire a horse in the town and enter the castle first. The garrison will have been expecting my return," he explained, beckoning Eyoés toward the edge of the copse. Gwair pointed toward one of the towers on the battlements. "Don't fly to the gate until you see me hang a red blanket over the topmost window. I will assure the guard does not apprehend you when you arrive. We will continue on from there." Eyoés squinted, making out the topmost window Gwair indicated. He noted its placement and nodded in agreement. Assured Eyoés understood, Gwair emerged from cover, hurrying across an open field in search of a horse from the nearest cabin he could find.

Crouching behind an old stump, Eyoés fingered the pommel of his sword, watching the tower window like a hawk. The damp, musty scent of rotting wood mixed with the sweet smell of cedar and pine. Beside him, Gibusil lay uncomfortably in the confined space of the copse, attempting to rest. Eyoés wiped his sweaty palms on his clothing.

Has Gwair been discovered by the Phantom League? Is he distracted by some pressing matter? Why this delay?

For a moment, he considered making his move without Gwair's signal. Then, with a growl of annoyance, he discarded the thought. "The Phantom League could not have discovered his intentions so soon," he assured himself. Gibusil lifted his head as his master spoke, ears cocked in anticipation of a command. Catching the movement from the corner of his eye, Eyoés ruffled the griffin's feathers. He glanced back towards the tower.

The window was now marked by a red blanket. Eyoés stood and whistled a command to Gibusil. As the griffin rose, the young Baron leapt onto its back. Gibusil tensed, then sprang upward, the power of his legs propelling him through the canopy of boughs. Once its wings were clear, the griffin gently issued from cover. Eyoés guided his steed on a low flight path toward the castle gate.

Landing before the gates instead of landing within the courtyard will make us seem a lesser threat.

He hesitated, flexing his fingers as he loosely grasped the reins. Because of the strict measures Gwair had taken to make it appear as though he had arrived separately, it was unclear how his own arrival would be received.

Gwair will assure I am allowed in when I land at the gate.

Eyoés jumped as cries of surprise and fear rose from the town below. He glanced downward, stomach clenching as he watched the townsfolk rush for cover under Gibusil's shadow.

Things do not look welcoming...

His head shot up at the sound of orders barked from the castle battlements directly ahead. Swarming to their posts, the soldiers prepared to protect their capital. As Eyoés came closer, he recognized the hulking shape of ballistas upon the battlements. The guards cranked back the drawstring.

Gibusil plunged downward, out of sight from the soldiers above. Pulling up before they hit the ground, the griffin landed in front of the castle gate. Shouts erupted from the battlements, and the gate swung open, revealing the iron teeth of the portcullis. As the metal barrier began to lift, Eyoés saw a group of troops race toward them, weapons drawn and ready for combat. As the jingling of their armor mixed with the orders of the officers, Eyoés dismounted and unbuckled his sword belt. The portcullis lifted.

"Hold your fire!" Gwair bellowed as he rushed down from the gatehouse. At the sight of Gwair, the troops fell back from the gate and saluted, casting suspicious glances towards the newcomer. Eyoés slumped against Gibusil and took a deep breath to calm himself.

Gwair will act as though he hasn't seen me for awhile. I have to make this look convincing.

As Gwair stepped into the entryway, his expression visibly brightened. He extended his arms in welcome. "Eyoés! Welcome!" he exclaimed, approaching his disheveled friend. With a shaky laugh, Eyoés returned the gesture and embraced him. Gwair's new, fine clothing contrasted starkly with Eyoés' plain sodden rags.

"It's good to see you, my friend. I am glad I was finally able to visit," Eyoés replied with his best excuse.

Releasing him, Gwair stepped back and wrapped his arm around his companion's shoulder. "I am thankful as well," he chuckled, leading him towards the gate. "Come now, I will find you a room and a place for Gibusil to rest and dry his wings."

9

Several long, wide stairs spread out before the two heroes, twinkling with the glint of rainwater upon their surface. Falling in line behind them, several guards kept up a steady march, their chainmail clinking against their steel vambraces. The steady beat of rain had momentarily abated, ceasing its attack on the unyielding stone structure.

Gwair ascended the steps to the central keep, with Eyoés following close behind. The towers sprouting from the keep observed their approach like silent giants. As they drew nearer, the sentry posted at the entry saluted and tapped the large door with the tip of his pike. At the signal, the door swung in on its hinges to allow admittance. The guards fell back to allow the two to speak in private as they entered.

A wide vestibule stretched out to either side of them. Crafted stonework pillars supported the structure at every corner. Tapestries hung in several places along the walls, paying homage to previous rulers and events. Creamy white tiles covered the floor under their feet, reflecting the overcast light streaming in from several nearby windows. Before them, a second set of stairs led through an arched opening to the main level. A scarlet carpet graced the middle of the stairway, guiding them through the maze of passages and halls.

Eyoés lingered, continuing to appraise the castle's grand architecture. Everything around him seemed aged with history.

"Astonishing, isn't it?" Gwair marveled. Eyoés set one foot upon the first stair and turned to examine the space from another angle.

"It whispers of the past," he thought aloud, his gaze finally coming to rest on his companion. "I have seen few places like it, except the royal city of Gald-Behn."

Clasping his hands behind his back, Gwair ascended the stairs alongside Eyoés, his footsteps silenced by the carpet. "Hodholm has stood for centuries as our capital. It was constructed during the War of Adrógar as a refuge and fortress for the armies of men, as was Asdale," he commented. "Many tales have had both their beginning and their end in these halls—some are still being written."

Leaving the vestibule behind, they reached the top of the stairway. The scarlet pathway beneath their feet divided, leading down long hallways to either side of them. Large windows at the end of each passage provided light along the breadth of the hall.

Casting several furtive glances in either direction, Gwair pulled Eyoés into a nearby corner out of sight. His countenance darkened with a seriousness Eyoés had never seen in him before. "Be *careful* what you say and do," he whispered in warning, his gaze darting to possible hiding places. "Our enemies are rife in this place. Be on your guard, and trust *no one*, even if they seem to be a friend. Until this is over, our thoughts are our own." With a final study of the surroundings, Gwair stepped into the middle of the hallway. The light from the windows fell on him, and his dark expression lifted, as though the light had washed it away.

Hesitant, Eyoés stepped out from the corner. The uncertainty of a secret mission confounded him as it clashed against his desire for open talk and direct measures.

There must be a way to make a direct move against our enemy. Why don't we simply...

His thought trailed away as he realized there were no options. The Phantom League's goal lay wrapped in secrecy, and the identities of those directly involved were hidden with excruciating care. Until the conspirators made a move, any step against them would could cost them the element of surprise. The Phantom League would have little mercy for newfound enemies.

Am I fit to handle the situation?

Unwilling to consider the possibility for the time being, he waved it aside. Eyoés hurried behind as Gwair moved down the hallway to their right.

I will follow Gwair's lead. In time, I will know what to do.

Further down the hall, Gwair stopped in front of a plain door and removed a set of keys from his robe. As Eyoés caught up, Gwair inserted a single key into a small keyhole above the door handle and twisted. With a click, the locking mechanism gave way, and Gwair pushed the door inward. Eyoés stepped past his friend and entered.

Against the far wall, a single window allowed light into the room. Three pillars supported the vaulted ceiling, the upper half of each blossoming with intricate stonework. Wood planking, worn from years of use, covered the stone floor. A bed was placed against each of the side walls, layered with thick blankets. A wardrobe stood in the far corner, accompanied by a bookshelf and desk.

Standing in the doorway, Gwair pointed to the wardrobe. "The servants will place our bags here when they are finished with Gibusil. In the meantime, you can get yourself a fresh set of clothes," he said. "I spoke privately with Baron Vikar while you were waiting for my signal. He'll be expecting us."

Rounding a corner in the hall, the two came to a halt before a crafted oaken door. An iron owl knocker hung on the middle of the door, regarding the heroes with wide eyes. Clutched in its talons was a heavy metal ring. As Gwair tapped the ring against the wood with a hollow thud, Eyoés glanced behind to assure they were not being observed. They heard the shuffle of feet not far from the other side of the door.

"Enter," commanded a voice within. Leaning against the door, Gwair pushed inward and quickly entered with a bow. Eyoés scanned their surroundings a final time. Satisfied their entry would be unseen, he turned and stepped inside.

The cold point of a dagger pressed against his throat from the side as he entered. Eyoés froze and looked sideways into the narrowed eyes of a man his age. Stubble covered his square jaw, and unruly red hair crowned his head, combed in an attempt to tame it. Eyoés clenched his jaw as the man's hard gaze pinned him to the spot.

"Who's this?" the man inquired briskly as his blade drew blood.

Eyoés started to speak, then saw another figure move out of the corner of his eye. "Stand down, Rodmer," a strong voice ordered.

The man pressed the blade harder against Eyoés' neck. Then, with one final stare, he withdrew his blade and sheathed it. "Yes, Uncle," he muttered. Regarding the man with irritation, Eyoés wiped away the blood from his neck and shut the door behind him.

Moving from behind his desk, a tall, dominating man extended his hand in greeting. The blue coat he wore clung tightly to his broad frame. Atop his high forehead, finely trimmed grey hair set him apart from his unruly associate. His presence exuded the same sense of power and control as did Gwair's. "My apologies for my nephew's behavior. The stresses of the current unrest have worn at his nerves," he declared. "Allow me to introduce myself. I am Vikar. Baron of this territory." Eyoés took the man's hand and met his gaze. A fearful tension permeated the Baron's gaze, out of place with his strong demeanor. It spoke of hidden fears he desired to keep to himself.

Eyoés gave a quick smile. "Eyoés Kingson, Baron of Taekohar and member of the Five Heroes of Alithell," he spoke in return, looking about the room. Covered in loose documents and stationery, a desk was stationed to the right of the far wall. Two large chandeliers hung from the ceiling by chains. A large bed stood in the leftmost corner of the room, and a large, lush rug in the Eastern style of Amiranoor decorated the floor.

Baron Vikar nodded and indicated a cluster of chairs in the middle of the room. Eyoés and Gwair gave a nod of thanks and sat, glancing briefly at each other as the Baron seated himself across from them. "Welcome to Hodholm, Eyoés. Have you come to gain inspiration for the design of Asdale?" Vikar remarked.

Eyoés sat up in his chair. When Vikar waited expectantly, Eyoés searched for an appropriate reply.

A short answer will provide just enough information to satisfy.

"I've come to visit Gwair. We haven't seen each other since the last gathering," he quickly added. The Baron of Rehillon nodded, stroking his greying beard.

Vikar turned to Gwair. "You've brought him to aid us?" The older hero nodded sharply in the affirmative. Confused, Eyoés shifted in his seat, eyes darting to Gwair for confirmation. He did not meet Eyoés' gaze.

"You seem a trustworthy man. Gwair has told me such quite often," Vikar noted. With Gwair's insistence on complete secrecy still fresh in his memory, Eyoés simply nodded, rather than endanger himself with words.

Noting his friend's watchfulness with approval, Gwair leaned back in his chair. "I have complete confidence in Eyoés," he said. "He is a welcome ally in this time of crisis."

They sat in silence, and Eyoés privately willed Gwair to end the meeting. Vikar cleared his throat. "Forgive me, I haven't introduced you to the rest of those present," he said, standing from his seat. "You've already met my nephew Rodmer."

Pushing away from the wall, the young man approached, his red hair defiantly falling over one eyebrow. "I apologize for rushing to arms," he reassured. A warm smile eclipsed his hard gaze. Eyoés gave a quick smile in return.

Vikar turned and pointed to one of the corners of the room. "And this is my daughter, Caywen," he concluded. Previously standing in the leftmost corner of the Baron's quarters, a young woman approached. Tucked behind her ears, her straight, raven hair descended past her shoulders. Beneath thick eyebrows, two piercing eyes were set wide on her round face. Her appearance was lofty, yet her bearing told of a spiritedness more fit for an adventurer than a Baron's daughter. She could be no more than Gwyndel's age.

Eyoés bowed in return. "My Lady," he said.

Caywen smiled and inclined her head. "It is a pleasure to meet you, Baron Eyoés," she laughed. "You needn't bow to me." Clearing his throat, Eyoés stood.

Before he could speak, Gwair set a hand on his shoulder and cast a furtive glance to the door. "We'd best depart," he interrupted with a smile. "Eyoés and I have much to discuss."

Catching sight of the piles of documents upon his desk, Vikar sighed. "And I must return to my duties. We shall meet again, Baron Eyoés," he said. With a final bow, the two turned to leave. Eyoés opened the door and passed through. As Gwair passed by, Vikar grasped his shoulder and briefly whispered in his ear. Then, with a nod, Gwair took his leave.

Eyoés forcefully shut the door to their quarters and turned to face Gwair. "You trust them?" he asked, incredulous.

Standing in the middle of the room, Gwair turned, confused. "What?" he remarked.

As Eyoés took a step forward, he set a hand against the center pillar of the room. "Vikar asks questions. What if he uncovers our plan?" he protested. "What about his nephew? Rodmer's hesitance to withdraw his blade speaks to me of questionable motives."

Gwair violently shook his head and stood facing his fellow hero. "I have spent years in service at Vikar's side—I trust him," he insisted. "Vikar honors the King and *truth*. That is why the current state of affairs has worn on his nerves."

Eyoés met his gaze. "How are you sure he has not deceived you?" he accused.

Gwair stepped forward, leaning close to his friend's face. "He wished to determine your honesty, and my witness to your story," he answered, keeping his voice low. "And even if he was the villain, what would Vikar gain by undermining his own rule?"

As Eyoés considered Gwair's words, he came to a new realization.

Of course! My anxiety over the situation has command of me.

Bowing his head, Eyoés sighed. "Forgive my rashness. I am still growing in my skills of discernment," he apologized.

Gwair set a hand on the youth's shoulder. "You don't have to shoulder the weight of Rehillon's burden alone. With the Guide's wisdom, we will find the *truth*," he answered. "Is there something in you that is stirring up unease, aside from our present circumstances?"

Eyoés paused, momentarily taken aback.

Could there be something else at the root of this?

The more he considered it, the more the Guide's warning returned. Looking up, Eyoés stepped past Gwair and wandered to the bookshelf. The volumes beckoned to him with their intriguing titles. Several chip marks on the shelves indicated use.

Running his hand along the wooden frame, Eyoés glanced over his shoulder. "When Gwyndel and I were traveling over Gald-Behn, the Guide spoke to me," he explained. "For now, I'm still contemplating his meaning." As soon as he spoke, Eyoés knew he had revealed only part of the truth.

I understand temptation is ahead—but will I succumb to it?

10

20th of Biarron, 2202 SE

A thick fog descended over the rolling moors of Northern Rehillon, accompanied by a harsh, chill wind. As the gale's strong voice roared across the landscape, the mottled grass and scrub bushes trembled in fear. Mice fled into their burrows to escape. The pungent stench of peat and wet earth mixed with the fresh scent of rain as the clouds wept.

Standing firm against the storm of rain and wind was a single tree, nearly the height of a man. Crooked, its trunk and branches were stained dark with rain and covered in lichen. A cluster of red leaves clung to the branches in defiance of nature itself, seeming to encourage any small beast to fight against the wind's tyranny. A family of voles huddled under its sheltering branches, their heads emerging from within a small hole in the tree trunk. Amid the onslaught, the defiant tree stood—an image of courage despite the odds.

Above the chaos rose the dull pounding of hooves. Steadily, it grew louder. Then, like a flash of lightning, a dark brown horse charged past with its rider. The voles fled into their shelter. Knocked off their limbs by the sudden brush of wind, a pile of red leaves fell to the earth, trodden into the mud.

Spurring his horse onward, the rider adjusted his hood. A brown cloak rested over his plain clothes, soaked by the rain. From his appearance alone, he seemed to be no more than a commoner—a trader perhaps. His eyes would cause one to hesitate. Dark with untold knowledge, they gave him the sinister look of one whose mind was full of secrets. Such a conclusion was not far from the truth.

To his right, the rider spotted the black speck of Andieff in the distance, partially shrouded by fog. Although slower, it was necessary to take the indirect path if one's arrival was to go unobserved. He urged his horse to greater speed.

The foothills before the mountains loomed directly ahead, sloping higher and higher until vanishing into the low-hanging clouds. As the rider neared them, the ground sloped steeply downward to a ravine, hidden from view by the deceptive rolling moorland. Pulling the reins to slow his steed, the cloaked rider descended into the ravine, his horse's hooves churning the grass and wet ground underneath. He threw back his hood and dismounted.

Beneath the rise he had just crested was a gaping cavern in the ravine wall. Its placement was so situated that it was undetectable without knowing where to look. Clumps of brush and grass clung to the top edge of the cave roof. A thick layer of rock supported the wet ground from beneath. At either side of the cavern entrance was a cloaked figure, hidden in the shadows of the overhanging rock. Peasant hoods masked their features, and wool gambeson armor covered their upper bodies. Daggers and other tools of their dark trade hung on their belts. Lingering in the shadows, a black mist darted further into the secrecy of darkness, briefly catching the rider's eye.

As the rider tied his horse to a nearby rock, the guards nodded in welcome. The scout returned the greeting and hurried into the depths of the cave, leaving the dim light of the moor for the enduring darkness of the underground. The chalky odor of subterranean water permeated the bowels of the cave. Torches were strategically placed along the rock walls to provide enough light to see by, but to keep the deeper recesses and crevices in shadow for cover. While passing by, the scout noticed the dark figures of several of his fellows hidden throughout the cavern. For treacherous men, caution and secrecy were valued above all else.

As the man journeyed further into the cavern, his steps became more hesitant. A growing nervousness churned his stomach. No matter how many years he had been in his leader's service, the very presence of him exuded a cold hate. The man swallowed to keep his cool. The illusion of inky mist residing in the depths of the cavern did nothing to aid his efforts.

The long tunnel came to an abrupt end, blocked by a solid piece of stone. Acquired through trade, a single Gesadith lamp lit the space with a pure white light—an unadulterated glow out of place with where it now resided. Noticing the messenger's arrival, a bulky man stood up.

A layer of chainmail covered his gambeson. Upon his broad shoulders, a wolfskin fought off the cold drafts of air. His face struck fear into those under his command. His grey beard and hair accentuated piercing green eyes, which were as deep and brilliant as the trees after a fresh rainfall. His appearance was akin to an old wolf, cunning and savage in his ways—a wolf ready to pounce at any given moment.

Lowering his eyes, the messenger kneeled, clenching a fistful of his cloak. "Amnedd, I come with grave news," he said, forcing his voice to remain steady in pitch.

Amnedd regarded his fellow Phantom Leaguer. "Speak quickly, for your companion already delivered the news that the people are suspicious of the fire in the Guildhouse and Bryoc's disappearance," he warned.

The messenger looked up, noticed the dark gleam in Amnedd's eye, and lowered his head once again. "I saw Gwair at the Broken Heel Tavern in Merwic—and he was speaking to another I did not recognize," he divulged.

Amnedd's eyes darkened, and he bared his teeth. "He seeks his brother," he growled. The Phantom League scout noticed a dark shape in the back of the cave and peered around his leader to examine it further.

Curled in a ball in the shadows, was Kiffyn, bruised and nearly unconscious from beatings and torture. He muttered incoherently under his breath. The Phantom League scout consulted his superior. "Should we flee the territory—and kill the hostage?" he inquired, laying a hand on the handle of his dagger in anticipation of his master's command.

Eyes narrowing, Amnedd paused to consider the ramifications of the news.

If there truly is someone on our trail, they will bring a large force. We cannot stand against such numbers, and they will surely search the moors surrounding Andieff. The chance of discovery is too great so close to town.

At the obvious conclusion, Amnedd curled his lip and kicked the stone wall with his boot. He recoiled at the thought of being forced to relinquish his prize without standing his ground. Amnedd spat at the ground.

I would rather die than flee. Such an escape would rob me of my reward and my pride.

Seizing the shirt collar of the scout at his feet, Amnedd hoisted him off the ground, his gaze wild. "We will *never* run!" he hissed through his teeth. He released the man's shirt and pushed him away. "Leave the hostage alive—should Gwair learn we slew his brother, he would pursue us across Alithell to achieve recompense. We cannot risk such a compromising situation," he ordered with a wicked smile. "We will relocate to the ruins of Weomor in a day. From within the remains, we will pick them off one by one." The Phantom League scout hastily nodded and departed to relay the order to the others, his footsteps echoing off the stone walls.

Turning on his heels, Amnedd regarded the silent form of Kiffyn. "You heard," he said.

Silence answered him, then the grinding of rock as Kiffyn pushed himself up from the gravelly cave floor. Trembling with exhaustion, he lifted his head to look at his captor. A large bruise surrounded his left eye, and various clotted wounds and scabs covered his exposed skin. "You are taking a risk, Amnedd," he wheezed, grimacing as his broken ribs restricted his breath. "You'll face failure again, just as you did at Braygroth."

Kneeling beside his suffering hostage, Amnedd inclined his head close to Kiffyn's ear. "When your brother comes to save you, you will watch him die alongside those who were fools to follow," he mocked with a grin.

Kiffyn's eyes watered as he shook his head and retreated with his back against the cave wall. "One who commits evil deeds in darkness cannot stand against the strength of the light. You will be robbed of your triumph," he coughed.

The scornful satisfaction faded from Amnedd's face. Wrapping his hand around the handle of his dagger, he pulled it from its sheath. At the harsh sound of scraping steel, Kiffyn winced and pushed himself against the stone, eying the blade warily. The long, Rondel dagger seemed a dark thorn in the light of the Gesadith lamp.

Amnedd strengthened his grip on the dagger. "I believe its time for you to bleed again," he hissed. "This time, you *will* be silenced—and reduced to a muttering beast!"

Down the length of the cavern passage, Kiffyn's screams startled those on watch.

11

22nd of Biarron, 2202 SE

Struggling with the overcast clouds, the afternoon sun lit the forest below with a bright light as it fought for dominion in the sky. An army of trees reached up to cheer for the sun's victory, their rich brown trunks covered in bright moss. Crowding close together over the forest floor, the trees spread their roots in the multitude of undergrowth. The ground rose and fell like the hills, buckled by years of growth and change. Stumps of dead trees wore thick mourning robes of moss and fern, weeping for their broken halves. Old Man's Beard hung from the branches and boughs above like thin, tattered cloth. Although pungent, the scent of moist growth and crisp air attracted no attention from the Loyalists weaving through the forest like a long thread.

Atop their horses, they silently guided their steeds through the thick trees. Packs of supplies were split between each man to ease the load of the group, which stretched like a serpent to what seemed the horizon. In truth, although their combined number was small, the illusion worked in their favor to increase their numbers. Each member was clothed in the style he favored, and appeared as a strange gathering of commoners. Despite the impression of disorganization, a common cause united them into a single force.

At the lead, Beydan scanned the path ahead for danger, while assuring correct navigation. If trouble did come, he would not be caught off guard.

Immediately behind him on Gwair's tawny horse, Gwyndel followed, Fóbehn strapped to her shoulder along with its quiver. Nine days of travel had brought them to the far reaches of Andieff—and none of it had been pleasant. Trying to remain compliant and kind despite Beydan's arrogant behavior had been a losing battle. Gwyndel shifted in her seat and avoided looking at the Loyalist Captain.

Every comment I've made has been met with a challenge, and my efforts at reconciliation have been in vain.

Looking through the branches above her, Gwyndel forced herself to patience and remembered her goal.

I am here for Kiffyn.

Surveying the forest before him, Beydan raised an open hand to signal a halt and brought his horse to a stop. The men waited obediently in line, their horses pawing at the ground.

Turning his steed around, Beydan brought his hand down. "We camp here. Dismount!" he ordered. Although difficult terrain, he knew the thick forest would provide better shelter than any open clearing. At the command, the troops dismounted and spread out across the immediate vicinity, while relaying the order to those in the rear. Upon finding an adequate place to camp, the men unloaded their simple tents from their saddles. Each man hung a long canvas sheet over rope between two opposing trees, staking one end of the canvas to the ground while folding the longer side underneath to create both a second wall and a dry floor to sleep on.

Observing the camp's construction, Beydan and Gwyndel dismounted and tied their horses to the nearest tree. Gwyndel furtively watched him from the corner of her eye. From her brief experience, it was clear that starting conversation would produce unseemly results. That, however, did not stop Beydan.

Watching the Forester he despised from the corner of his eye, Beydan noted the camp taking shape. "We made good time in our travels," he began. "I believe we will rescue your Forester companion within the next few days. I expect there will be little trouble from the radicals who hold him—such people have sharp tongues but dull blades when the time comes."

Gwyndel stiffened, hand grasping the rope tight. "They are the *Phantom League*," she replied through her teeth. Beydan turned toward her and paused, a knowing grin building on his features. Her irritation was obvious.

Watching her reaction, he turned back to the growing camp. "Ah, yes. The dreaded Men of the Dagger. As the saying goes, a trained sword will often put the rogue's dagger to shame. Surely, the talents of the Northern Guard are more than enough to deal with such scoundrels."

Gwyndel turned to bark a retort—then stopped herself. Over their travels, she had fallen for his deliberate jabs. Gathering herself, she realized a non-combative reply would keep a lengthy argument at bay.

She took a deep breath. "Your training puts you in a good position, then."

Her hopes were dashed as Beydan turned to her, eyes lit with a prideful triumph. "At last! You see my view," he exclaimed with a satisfied smile.

Gwyndel's eyes narrowed and she forcefully stepped forward. "I believe you misunderstand me—" she began. The Captain ignored her comment with a dismissive wave and turned away, beckoning two of his troops.

"Wilfrith and Sighere! I am in need of your stealth," he shouted. At the sound of his voice, the men abruptly ceased their conversation and shed whatever light armor they wore as they hurried to their Captain. Their years of arduous service in the Northern Guard had hardened their emotions to the gruff commands of their leader. Standing straight, they saluted Beydan and awaited further orders. Beydan nodded in curt approval. "Enter Andieff and search for any possible evidence to where the Forester is located. As soon as you discover a strong lead, return and report to me," he concluded. With a final salute, the two men raced off into the forest.

Night fell upon the silent tents of the Loyalist camp. Torches fought against the curtain of blackness.

Above, the moon sought solace and hid its face behind the clouds, giving permission to the stars to light the land. Gentle starlight glittered upon the fern leaves, contrasting with the wild, untamed flame of the torch. Hidden by the night shadows, several of the Loyalists stalked the borders of the camp, peering into the darkness for sign of a threat. In the middle of the encampment, a campfire burned and crackled in a small cleared section of ground.

Sitting in front of the flames to fight off the night cold, Gwyndel awaited the return of the scouts. She wet her lips, scanning the mass of brush and trees around her. Occasionally, a glimmer of light pierced the black expanse as one of the guards passed by, torch in hand. Gwyndel stifled a yawn. She looked at the stars above, and her thoughts began to wander.

Does Kiffyn see these same stars? Or is he shut up in darkness, tortured by the Phantom League?

Gwyndel shivered at the image of her old friend screaming in pain while she lingered in idle thoughts. Shaking her head to free herself of the nightmare, she stood from her seat by the fire. For a moment, her anger and frustration at Beydan lost its strength.

I will not stay in safety and silence while Kiffyn suffers. With the King's help, I will push through.

Gwyndel jumped at the sudden rustling of brush nearby. Emerging from cover, a dark figure set foot within the camp's borders. A glimmer of torchlight issued from behind a tree, accompanied by a challenge from one of the sentries. The figure gave a short reply and saluted. As the man neared one of the standing torches, his face was illuminated.

One of the spies.

The sentry gave a brief welcome and continued his rounds. Watching the figure stride toward a large tent stationed roughly in the center of the encampment, Gwyndel hurried to intercept him. Her fists clenched as she thought of Kiffyn's suffering.

I must know what to do next. If he receives word first, Beydan could very well keep the information to himself.

Gwyndel raised her hand. "Wait," she commanded firmly.

Recognizing her voice as that of a superior, the man halted and turned at attention. "Yes—my Lady?" the man replied, unsure of how exactly to address her.

She ignored the man's awkwardness. "What have you found concerning Forester Kiffyn's whereabouts?" she inquired. The man swallowed and pulled back slightly. Years of service under Beydan's leadership insisted he refuse and report directly to his Captain. He began to object.

"Please," Gwyndel insisted. The Loyalist paused at the unease in her tone and the persistence in her eyes.

Shaking his head he stood at ease. "I guess it won't hurt no one," he sighed with a countryside accent. "There is a trader—smuggler more like—who could very well be allied with the Phantom League. It's quite amazing what you can learn in a day of casual talk." He smiled at the last words. As she turned the information over in her mind, Gwyndel bit down a smile.

If this smuggler knows where the League took Kiffyn, we can catch them by surprise.

Gwyndel's eyes sparkled. "You are dismissed—"

Beydan's laughter cut like a sword's edge. "Well, well—the Forester fancies herself the Captain, now?" he sneered, issuing from the night shadows and standing beside one of the pole torches. The excitement from Gwyndel's expression faded. Stiffening, the spy avoided his Captain's gaze. In the flickering light of the torch, Beydan's mocking grin seemed of molten bronze, lined with shadowy fangs. His expression darkened into a snarl as he stepped forward and thrust his face into Gwyndel's. "I'm warning you. Usurp my position like this again, and I'll leave *you* behind," he snapped, baring his teeth. "I respect Gwair—and that is the only reason why you're still here."

Glaring at the Loyalist Captain, Gwyndel drew in steady breaths to suppress her urge to retaliate. For several moments, neither budged for fear of giving the illusion of backing down. Then, abruptly signaling for the spy to follow, Beydan turned away and strode to his tent.

12

The following morning, Gwyndel brushed aside the canvas door to Beydan's tent and stepped inside. She squinted as the morning sunlight was amplified by the white walls. Although compact, the structure was tall enough for her to stand upright. Scattered across the canvas floor were Beydan's few possessions—namely several items of clothing, stationery, a few wrinkled parchments for the occasional missive, his bedroll, and his sword.

Looking up from the journal in his hand, Beydan glowered from the far corner, sitting cross-legged. "I'd prefer you not trod on my few humble belongings," he muttered. Gwyndel glanced at her feet and noticed an odd piece of parchment under her boot. Mumbling her apology, she stepped off of it and moved toward Beydan. Guessing at the reason for her intrusion, Beydan abruptly closed his journal and set it aside, along with his quill pen and inkwell. "Sit," he ordered. He quickly suppressed a smirk of quiet triumph as she obeyed. Catching a glimpse of the strange scar on her cheekbone, Beydan raised an eyebrow. "Unusual mark," he noted, gesturing toward it.

Gwyndel let a lock of her hair down to obscure it from view. "None of your concern," she said, not meeting his gaze. The Captain pursed his lips. Though curious, he decided to set the matter aside.

A woman's scars are of little importance to me.

Gwyndel took a deep breath. "You've been told about the smuggler," she began, annoyed at what she perceived as a delay.

Beydan nodded briskly. "And more. Since you cheated me out of hearing the news first, I might as well tell you the rest of it," he asserted with a bitter smile. "This smuggler—Brecc is his name—dealt in Everwheat before trade was cut off from Southern Rehillon."

Raising an eyebrow, Gwyndel leaned slightly forward. "And?" she asked expectantly.

With a bark of resentful laughter, Beydan frowned. "You know the rest—there is a reasonable connection between him and the Phantom League," he growled. "If he knows where his kindred spirits took the Forester, we can deceive him into telling us—or force him to."

Gwyndel drew back and folded her arms across her chest. "And how do you plan to accomplish this?" she questioned. As Beydan smirked in triumph, her stomach clenched into a knot. His smug excitement warned of questionable behavior.

"Our smuggler's a drunkard," he said. "Give him what he wants, and he'll be loose with his tongue."

Gwyndel's eyes widened and she stood, shaking her head. "Knowingly tempting a man with his weakness is cruel! Surely there must be some other way," she insisted. "What about bribing?"

Standing, Beydan scowled at her and set his stance wide. "Money is a weakness for any ordinary man," he retorted, "but I am the Captain of this division. We will get Brecc to talk *my* way."

Stepping forward to refute Beydan's order, Gwyndel opened her mouth to speak—but Beydan shoved her back. The elf recovered her balance quickly. Beydan cocked his head and narrowed his gaze. "Go ahead. Insist on your way, on your leadership," he challenged. "And pray my accusations of insurrection do not stir the men to action."

Instinctively, Gwyndel stepped back, her blank, harried gaze refusing to look Beydan in the eye. Beydan sat and reached for his book. "We will try to locate Brecc this evening and learn what we can," he concluded. Beydan raised his hand to wave her away, only to find himself alone within the walls of his tent.

As the sun began its descent into dusk, they reached the town of Andieff. Rays of golden sun tore through the veil of clouds, and the cool air fought to establish its place with the coming night. The dirt path crunched under Gwyndel's boots as she kept up with Beydan's steady pace.

Wet moorland rose and fell about them, barren of trees. On either side, the faded, distant forms of mountains could be seen. The peaks seemed to rush ahead of them, coming closer with each step until they loomed upon the horizon ahead. Standing tall, the grey mountains encroached on either side, forming a single causeway ahead that allowed narrow passage to the land beyond. Scattered throughout the Northern Passage, watchtowers stood like stone trees, their shingled roofs sharp and pointed. From the numerous vantage points, the steely eyes of the Northern Guard scrutinized all who entered and departed Rehillon's borders.

Compared to the towers' might, the town of Andieff seemed but an unimpressive bush, lazily sitting upon the open moorland. A small, simply constructed archway allowed entrance into the town. Guarding the entrance, a single commoner leaned against the arch, loosely holding his spear as he gazed off into the distance. Gwyndel glimpsed Beydan scowl at the man's lax duty.

The people have come to rely on the Northern Guard to protect them from danger.

They passed through the arch and into the town, unseen by the idle watchman. Clenching his jaw, Beydan stooped and picked up a stone. While walking, he turned back to the guard and threw it. He quickly turned away, suppressing a laugh as the man yelped in pain and woke from his stupor. Gwyndel pressed her lips into a tight line and glanced at the Captain. Clothed in the fine robes of a well-to-do merchant, Beydan carried himself highly, and with a disarming smile.

The wealthy, haughty role suits him all too well.

Gwyndel casually adjusted her linen headdress. Although she appeared calm and collected to the townsfolk, she seethed inwardly at posing as the merchant's wife. She frowned.

When this is over—

She stopped herself as she glimpsed a movement out of the corner of her eye. Prior to setting out, Beydan had given strict orders that several of the men trail them in case of trouble. Setting aside thoughts of irritation, she examined the town with a watchful eye.

Constructed of rough stone bricks and roofed with shingles of slate, the stumpy houses seemed like stone hills, rolling back and forth across the span of the town. The bustle of the townsfolk waned as workers returned to their families for a night of peace. Others started toward their favorite tavern or the homes of their companions.

As they passed an alleyway, Beydan suddenly stopped and grasped Gwyndel's shoulder to stay her. Making sure those who remained in the street were paying little attention, Beydan stepped into the shadow of the alley, closely followed by Gwyndel. Although partially hidden by the shadow, Gwyndel recognized the second scout Beydan had sent into town the previous day.

After glancing to the street to assure secrecy, the man locked eyes with his Captain. "Brecc is at the Tower-Tree Inn," he whispered. "Turn left at the second street and you'll find it. He'll be wearing a worn, blue merchant's robe—can't afford a new one with his drinking habit." Beydan gave a nod of understanding and the scout turned and dove into darkness.

Quietly emerging from the alley, they followed the spy's instructions, hurrying at a fast walk until they stood before the inn's entrance. A small lantern hung from the awning above the door, illuminating the entry. Painted on the door was a grey tower, sprouting pine boughs from its walls. Beydan quickly pushed the door inward and stepped in, holding the door slightly ajar for Gwyndel.

She hesitated mid-step, her conscience prodding her.

I am about to partake in Beydan's plan—and purposely tempt a man with his vice.

Feeling Beydan's sharp eyes upon her, Gwyndel avoided his gaze. She began to move back from the entrance, but imaginings of Kiffyn, bruised, starving, and broken, haunted her and compelled her to follow. Taking a deep breath, she entered. As she brushed past, Beydan shot her a glare of warning and shut the door behind them.

Unlike many of the taverns and inns they had seen, a single large window allowed the fading light into the dining hall and entryway. The establishment was small, with only a few tables neatly set about the room. Sitting at a small desk by the left wall, a small, wizened man sketched odd drawings in a journal, muttering strangely to no one in particular. From the back of the room, the reedy drone of a bard's bowed lyre filled the room with its dreary tale of rain and wind. Patrons gathered around the tables, ignoring the arrival of the newcomers.

It didn't take long to find their target. Sitting alone at one of the smaller tables, a man in old, soiled robes gazed longingly at the bar on the opposite side of the room. A dark beard covered his mouth and chin, and his oily hair was pasted back from his forehead. Even from a distance, his appearance breathed mischief. At the sight of Brecc, Gwyndel leaned back slightly, her stomach heavy with guilt at what was to come. Beydan had no such hesitation. Feigning having just seen the lone man, he made a straight course to the man's table. Gwyndel followed, cringing as she regarded the other patrons.

Beydan's fortunate nobody pays attention.

Watching the two of them casually taking a seat opposite, the disheveled merchant nodded in welcome and curiosity. Beydan leaned against the tabletop and smiled disarmingly. "Evening," he said, casting an indifferent glance to the muttering innkeeper. "Food any good?"

Brecc gave a stifled laugh and raised an eyebrow. "Not worth your while. Old Albern's fare is such filth it makes us sick. Been that way since he journeyed out into the nearby moors to hunt for some extra food. The desolate land drove him mad," he stated, thumbing at the muttering sketcher.

Beydan nodded in understanding and gestured toward Gwyndel. "My wife was afflicted with the Addiction as soon as the trade ceased. She's been mute with madness ever since. We had dealt in the flour in the southern towns and lost much of our wealth when no one wanted to buy the remaining stock," he sighed. To maintain the ruse, Gwyndel stared blankly at the table and said nothing.

Brecc's eyes glinted with a common sympathy. Eyeing the other patrons warily, he leaned closer to Beydan. "So did I," he whispered. "Thought the new source of income would stay longer than it did—nay, it was no more than a passing interest. Now I wear these rags and trade in those cheap mountain spices just to make ends meet." The smuggler extended a hand of greeting. "I'm Brecc," he introduced.

Grasping the man's outstretched hand, Beydan smiled. "Sawel of Garifell," he replied.

Cocking his head, Brecc pursed his lips. "Fenaboran, eh?" he noted. "What brought you down into Rehillon?"

Beydan nodded and leaned back upon his chair while regarding the silent form of Gwyndel. "Peasant revolts, taxes, and the hope of valuable southern goods to trade," he lied. Behind the mask of casual conversation, he cringed.

I haven't set foot in Fenabor since I was a boy.

Hoping the man wouldn't detect his deception, Beydan swallowed.

Brecc didn't seem to notice. "I always thought the profits were better up north by Garifell," he mused, "but I wouldn't know—never gone much farther than the Darmore Fells."

Quietly letting out a pent up breath, Beydan nodded towards the bar across the room. "Can I get you something to drink?" he inquired.

At the words, Gwyndel averted her gaze and bit her lip to force herself to remain passive. Underneath the table, she clenched her fists against the pain in her chest.

This is wrong!

Furtively looking to Beydan, she stilled.

There is nothing I can do.

Glancing toward the bar with a longing eye, Brecc shook his head. "The wife's demanded I quit," he sighed. A wave of relief quelled the rising guilt within Gwyndel.

Beydan casually shrugged and raised his eyebrows. "What could one drink do?" he maintained, the words sending Gwyndel into more misery.

As he paused to consider it, Brecc said nothing. He looked sideways to where Beydan sat. "Well," he replied with a knowing smile, "if you insist." Rising from his chair, Beydan strode to the bar. The innkeeper, setting aside his journal of strange imaginings, moved to serve the customer. Beydan returned with a pitcher, two mugs, and a plate of cheese and crusty bread. He set them on the table.

Eyes widening at the amount of drink, Brecc looked to Beydan. "I am my own man, after all," he remarked.

Flashing a smile, the Loyalist Captain took his seat. "So you say," he muttered under his breath. Gwyndel watched in dismay as one drink led to another, each draught taking more light from the man's eyes than the last. Before long, Brecc sat hunched over the table, clutching the last remnant of drink in his hand.

Growing smug with the triumph of his plan, Beydan gave a hard smile and rested his chin in his hand. "You said you used to trade in Everwheat," he began, keeping his voice low to avoid being detected by the other patrons. "Who did *you* work for? My employer worked on the shores of the River Myrch."

The smuggler took a deep draught of ale and gave a contented sigh. "Some group outfit," he stuttered, bleary eyed. "Called themselves the Specter Guild, or somethin' of the sort." His speech slurred with the strong influence of the drink. Closing her eyes, Gwyndel shook her head and did not look upon the man's moment of weakness.

Feigning interest, Beydan leaned forward. "Do they still trade? I might want to seek out an assignment with them," he continued, suppressing a smile.

Brecc clumsily pointed toward the door of the establishment. "You have a desire to join, you got to become a Peddler for 'em—and be willin' to withhold the goods if they tells you so," he ranted, waving the mug in his hand. "I overheard 'em talk about how they were going down to Weomor to deal with some character—" His words trailed off as he sank onto the table, unconscious.

Beydan smiled and nodded. "I'll look into it," he spoke under his breath. Standing from his chair, he pulled Gwyndel to her feet. As they passed the innkeeper's desk, Beydan set several coins upon the man's table to pay their dues. Before any questions could be asked of them, the two disappeared into the growing dark.

13

Face pensive, Eyoés sat on the edge of his bed, resting his chin on his fists. Weaving around the central pillars of their quarters, Gwair paced about with hands clasped behind his back.

Gaze fixed on the wood floor, Eyoés let his hands drop. "You told Vikar to tell no one about this meeting?" he asked without looking up.

Gwair nodded to himself and leaned against the nearest pillar. "I did," he answered, looking to the door. "If we can have our meeting before most of the castle staff is roaming about the halls, there will be a good chance we will not be overheard."

A knock on the door made them jump. Keeping his weight on the balls of his feet, Gwair ventured toward the door and leaned against it. He gently tapped a series of knocks on the wood and waited for a reply. A single knock and two scratches quickly followed—the signal Gwair and Vikar had previously agreed upon.

Looking to Eyoés, Gwair nodded and quickly opened the door. Vikar hastily stepped inside and Gwair shut the door. He twisted the key in the locking mechanism and tested its strength.

Satisfied, he returned the key to his pocket and motioned for Vikar to sit in a nearby chair. "Are you sure you were not followed?" he inquired, leaning against the door to listen for footsteps.

Vikar nodded and sat across from Eyoés. "I left my quarters before Caywen and Rodmer were awake. I told no one, as you requested," he answered. Gwair retreated from the door and leaned against one of the pillars.

Eyoés paused. Since his last meeting with the Baron of Rehillon, he remained undecided as to which trail to pursue first to start unraveling the plots of their hidden enemies.

It would be best to further understand the situation before acting.

Looking to Baron Vikar, Eyoés leaned on his elbows and folded his hands above his knees. "Gwair has already told me about the Everwheat crisis," he began, keeping his voice low as a precaution. "I want to hear your side of the story."

Shaking his head over the memory of the root of his troubles, Vikar began. "News came of people suffering—struggling to feed their hungry children and wives as their crops were destroyed by the rain," he explained, gaze downcast. "The news distressed me, and I sought a way to ease the people's struggles. My advisor, Hranfist, seeking to relieve my anguish, proposed a solution. Everwheat, he called it—the crop that mocks the cold."

He looked into Eyoés' eyes. "Hranfist negotiated a trading arrangement for me. Even when faced with the supplier's heavy prices and taxes, I agreed, ever thinking of my starving people," Vikar continued, his voice cracking. "For two months, I paid the tax, the price for trade—everything! But when the supplier sent me word that my latest payment had not been delivered, I objected. I had entrusted five of my most loyal troops with the payment, and they had confirmed the delivery upon their return. Regardless, the trade was cut off, leaving my people in the throes of addiction."

Eyoés stroked his chin. "Surely you suffered from the ill effects?" he questioned.

Vikar shook his head violently, his expression hurt. "I thank the King I did not. I had not exhausted my extensive food stores, so I never had to purchase Everwheat flour for my own use," he said.

Pausing, Eyoés regarded the Baron. Dark bags hung beneath his eyes from lack of sleep, and lines creased his forehead.

He speaks the truth. He truly cares for his people.

A pang of conviction hit him as he recalled his own struggles.

What do I value more—my own position or my people?

Shaking his head to dispel his rising guilt, Eyoés focused on the task at hand. "When I first arrived in Rehillon, I heard of a Throst Ravenstrong. From Gwair's story, he seemed to have some connection to the Addiction," he recalled. "What do you know of him?"

Although barely noticeable, Vikar's expression lost its tearful passion, replaced instead by uncertainty. "Nearly two months ago, he brought forth a remedy he insisted would cure the symptoms of the Addiction," he explained. "Although skeptical, the Council of Lords and I decided to give his solution a chance. I'm grateful the remedy worked." Standing from his seat, Baron Vikar looked from Eyoés to Gwair. "However, the people have been in turmoil over their allegiances ever since. Those who are loyal to me have been put at odds with those siding with Throst. There is even dissension in the Council of Lords," he declared. "I fear the people will be torn apart by war."

Gwair abruptly stepped forward, his incredulous stare fixed on his leader. "Surely it will not come to that!" he exclaimed, glancing to Eyoés. "I have seen strife among our people before, and we have triumphed, with the Guide's help."

Setting a hand on the warrior's shoulder, Vikar clenched his jaw. "It is as the Proverbs say—when the people are divided, strife will follow," he sighed.

Eyoés stood and raised a hand. "Your advisor, Hranfist. He recommended the Everwheat trade, did he not?" he cautiously suggested. Vikar nodded.

"I have told you this before. You suspect he has an unspoken allegiance with the Phantom League?" Gwair ventured further.

Pacing about the room, Vikar stroked his beard in thought. "I have had that suspicion myself, since Gwair explained his discoveries in the Darmore Fells upon his return," he admitted. "If Hranfist is truly a Phantom Leaguer, how will you expose him? To openly act would invite the enemy to retaliate, and his quarters are at the top of the eastern tower. He maintains the wooden stairs leading to his quarters so they would announce an approaching intruder—Hranfist has always had a fear of ambush."

Eyoés halted, brows furrowed in thought.

Ambush?

Vikar turned to face Eyoés and Gwair. "The Council of Lords is meeting today. Perhaps you can uncover more there," he proposed. "I can convince the Council to let you partake in matters."

A smile grew on Eyoés' face as he arrived at a conclusion. "So we shall—and I believe I can get Hranfist to expose *himself.*"

14

Gwair pushed open the door to the Council chamber and entered with Eyoés following behind. Eyoés glanced at Gwair—although the Baron had ensured their welcome, he was unsure if it would be a glad one.

I have little right to meddle in the affairs of Rehillon—and my role as one of the Five Heroes has not much legend as of yet to back my cause.

Gwair discreetly raised a hand and nodded to dispel his hesitancy. "We will be fine," he whispered. "Vikar will secure our place."

Satisfied, Eyoés stepped further into the room. Faded slate tiles ran the length of the floor, meeting up against walls of mottled grey stone. Shields emblazoned with various standards hung upon the walls. A meeting table was surrounded by crafted maple chairs carved with the coat of arms for each Lord. On the farthest wall, a large window was placed well above their heads. Conversing with each other in low tones, three noblemen wore surcoats bearing their individual coat of arms over ceremonial armor. Eyoés glimpsed Vikar standing in the back of the room. Beside the Baron, a short man clothed in a red and brown robe whispered in Vikar's ear. His pompous expression and his square jaw gave him a shifty appearance. Eyoés clenched his jaw.

That must be Hranfist.

The hushed sound of conversation was cut short. Feeling the tense, irritated looks of the council, Eyoés froze, taking a sudden interest in the shields hanging from the walls rather than meeting their gaze.

One of the Lords stepped forward, throwing a hand toward the two heroes. "Why have they come? Show them out," he cried. Standing beside the wall, two guards hurried toward them and gestured for them to leave.

"That will not be necessary, Haral Rhys," Vikar shouted, pushing his way through the crowd of Lords.

Turning at the sound, the nobleman who had spoken bowed, his face tight with irritation. "But they have entered without invitation," he objected.

The Baron waved the matter aside. "Baron Eyoés Kingson has already witnessed the strife of our people when he set foot in our land. And Gwair is our brother," he reasoned, "What have we to conceal that is not already known to them? They are Heroes of Alithell, and we owe them our respect. Let us begin our session." With a sigh of agreement, the Lords relented and took their seats. Saluting their superior, the two sentries guarded the entryway.

As the Council seated themselves, Vikar set a hand on Eyoés' shoulder and nodded toward the nearest wall. "You both may watch, but do not venture to speak. The present circumstances of our lands have worn at their patience," he whispered. Exchanging a glance of understanding, Eyoés and Gwair strode to the side of the room and turned to face the Council table.

Vikar took his place at the head of the table and cleared his throat. "When last we gathered in this room, we agreed Throst Ravenstrong's remedy for the Addiction would better the people," he began, his gaze wandering to each of the three Lords. "Yet now our decision is being questioned?"

One of the Lords leaned forward to distinguish himself from the others. "Look around you, man," he remarked, stabbing the table with his index finger. "Our people are divided because of it! If we do nothing, our people, the Rehils, could be plunged into civil war. Do you not remember the Dwarf Draed from your books? I could not bear to see Merwic descend into such chaos!" At the mention of the infamous Dwarf Civil War, Eyoés cringed as memories of his angry, insolent behavior in Lord Ardul's halls resurfaced. He forced himself to focus.

Such behavior is behind me. I will not dwell on the past.

For a moment, the Baron's brow wrinkled in painful recollection, then was quickly hidden. "I know of the Dreyd, Agnar Crawbrand, and I too wish to avoid the Dwarves' fate," he agreed, placing a clenched fist onto the table. "But should we have withheld our aid in our people's time of need? Surely there must be a way to restore order."

Giving a cry of exhausted irritation, another nobleman pounded on the table with both fists. Eyoés recognized him as the one who had opposed their entry. "Force Gerall Bardmond to use the Northern Guard to subdue the people—at least then we shall have peace," Lord Rhys shouted.

Immediately, Lord Gerall leapt from his seat. "Lord Rhys, I will never allow the Guard—my fellows —to do what what you propose! For years I have lived with them, breathed with them, and have seen them die. The Northern Guard is a strong protector, not an enforcer of such folly as yours!" he exclaimed.

His face red with anger, Vikar Amberster drew his dagger and slammed the pommel onto the table. The noblemen involuntarily jumped in their seats at the powerful blow. The Baron turned to the cause of the dispute. "Lord Rhys, consider your words before you expose your imprudent thinking before the Council!" the Baron roared, staring darkly at the hasty Haral Rhys. Silenced by Vikar's anger, the man backed down and swallowed.

With a nod of satisfaction, Vikar sheathed his dagger and turned to Gerall. "Lord Bardmond, I will never force the Northern Guard to coerce our citizens," he reassured, his voice calm. Briefly closing his eyes, Gerall bowed and seated himself.

Watching the proceedings with increasing discomfort, Lord Crawbrand raised a hand of inquiry. Noticing the nobleman's gesture of respect, Vikar motioned for him to continue. Lord Crawbrand gently stood from his chair. "Perhaps—"

The chamber door opened. Standing at attention, the two sentries saluted as a single man entered the Council room. As he approached, the noblemen whispered to themselves. Eyes narrowing, Gwair assumed a solid stance and crossed his arms. Intrigued by the behavior of those present, Eyoés examined the newcomer closely.

A white surcoat bore his coat of arms, two ravens above an open book. Much of his long, dark hair hung over his shoulders, while a section was loosely bound behind his head in the fashion of young nobles. A finely trimmed beard and mustache gave him the appearance of stateliness, and his expression bore an air of respect and confidence. From the reactions of the Councilmen, Eyoés reasoned as to his identity.

Throst Ravenstrong?

At the recollection of the tavern brawl, and the strife and disquiet of both the Baron and Gwair, Eyoés stepped back, pressing himself against the cold stone wall to appraise the newcomer unobserved.

Striding to his seat at the table, Throst flashed a smile, the warmth in his demeanor visibly stirring those present. He bowed to Vikar. "Please forgive my tardiness," he apologized. "I pray I have not interrupted the discussion."

As the youngest Lord sat, Vikar nodded in welcome. "You missed little," he admitted, adjusting his seat. "You were saying, Lord Crawbrand?"

Clearing his throat, Agnar continued. "Perhaps Lord Ravenstrong should be the one to restore the people's unity," he proposed, looking directly at Throst. "It is he that is to blame for the discord."

Momentarily meeting the nobleman's gaze, Throst sighed and clasped his hands upon the table. "Yes,

Lord Crawbrand. I must seek some path to peace, since my actions inadvertently caused such strife," he agreed. "Nay, I meant nothing but to ease the people of their yoke of suffering when I offered my cure."

Taken aback, Eyoés found the man's maturity remarkable.

He takes responsibility for his actions, and seems as concerned about the people as Vikar!

A light gleamed in Throst's eye as he leaned forward and met the eyes of the Lords each in turn. "Perhaps we should encourage the people to speak freely, and consider another man's opinion as his own certainty," he thought aloud. "As I have said before—the tyranny of silence is the death of a people."

Haral Rhys stifled a mocking laugh. "You propose to encourage two factions to speak their mind and expect the other to be *understanding*? Your view is simple-minded," he babbled.

Eyoés carefully eyed Throst, anticipating a biting reply to the blowhard's hasty words. To his surprise, Throst's expression remained calm and passive.

Looking to where the other man sat across from him, Throst inclined his head. "It might seem strange to some, but consider this, Lord Rhys—it's inevitable we would disagree with one another on some point. Even if you tried to sift your words to maintain harmony, how long would it be until your contrary belief escaped your watch and was exposed through your words?" he inquired, his tone pointed, yet respectful.

Haral hesitated, eyes darting to the faces of his fellows as he struggled to come up with a reply that would push forward his own view.

Throst continued without waiting for the man's reply. "To force a man to remain silent or else risk danger to himself is not honorable. Appealing to mankind's sense of liberty, rather than seeking a political alternative, might encourage peace," he maintained.

The Council of Lords sat in silence, reflecting upon the words spoken. Looking downward, Eyoés pondered the young Lord's reasoning.

What is the harm in Throst's way? He appears to speak sense—

He hesitated as he was once again reminded of the Guide's warning, and he struggled to understand its application.

So far, I have seen little danger of riches—but am I amid the company of evil?

Unsure, Eyoés sighed. Baron Vikar paused, waiting to see if any of the noblemen would venture to speak.

When no one spoke, he stood from his chair. "I propose this Council be adjourned in order to better consider Lord Ravenstrong's solution, or come up with a better one. We meet again tomorrow at this time," he declared. Following their Baron's example, the Lords pushed back their seats and hurried to the chamber door. Throst was one of the last to stand. Head lifted high with a confident conviction, he moved to follow.

Glancing to the wall, Throst noticed Gwair and Eyoés. As he locked eyes with Eyoés, he bowed in polite greeting and departed from the Council chamber.

<h1 style="text-align:center">15</h1>

Leaning against the uneven, rough pillar, Caywen Amberster cradled her bowed lyre in her arms. She gazed out the window, her mind lost in a maze of tales and ballads. As she drew the horsehair bow across the three strings, the reedy, ancient voice of the lyre spoke. Its song echoed in the halls of Hodholm, as the story it told wandered through dim forests and across empty moors. Notes grew and ebbed like the water's tide. Steadily, the song grew in intensity, rising to a crescendo like a warrior's battlecry. Then, all became still. A simple, haunting melody rose from the silence, mournful at the quest's end before fading away to nothing. Releasing her breath, Caywen smiled.

"Few times have I heard such beautiful notes. Your skill never ceases to amaze me," Throst declared, shaking his head in disbelief. "I only wish I had such remarkable talent, Caywen." With parchment in one hand, and a quill pen and inkwell in the other, Throst approached the place she sat, his footsteps muffled in the red carpet of the hallway.

Caywen sighed, and laid the bowed lyre flat on her lap. "There are others who play better. I spent a great deal of time learning, but more will be required if I am to play my best. What are you doing?" she said, indicating his parchment with a nod of her head.

Considering the writing utensils in his hands, Throst gave an exaggerated sigh. "I received a letter from my Steward in Herthere, full of his complaints over the many things needing attention in my absence," he explained with mild annoyance. "As Lord of Herthere, it is my duty to answer him and address all his concerns. May I sit with you while I write?"

Caywen's posture perked up, and she smiled. "You may," she said, eyes sparkling. Inclining his head in a polite bow, Throst seated himself on the stone bench across from her. He spread the parchment across the low windowsill and placed the inkwell beside it. Again, the haunting, captivating music of the bowed lyre flowed and ebbed though the castle hall. Dipping his quill pen in the ink, Throst began to write, the light scratching of the pointed tip on parchment adding a dimension of rhythm to the lyre's song. Every few words, Throst's eyes flitted up to glance at her.

As she drew the bow across the strings, Caywen noticed Throst's distracted glances toward her. A playful smile tugged at the corners of her mouth, and she tried in vain to put on a serious face. "Don't look at *me*! It would be intolerable if the people learned the Lord of Herthere was idle in his work," she chided.

Looking up again from his work, Throst saw her smile. He placed his quill pen in the inkwell. "You've been telling me that since we were children," he laughed. Caywen's face shone as she laughed in unison.

Her eyes wandered to the lands beyond the windowsill. The corners of her grin trembled, then fell as her face darkened like the coming of storm clouds. Propping the lyre against her left leg, she drew the bow across the strings. A mournful dirge rose from the instrument, its beauty and sadness complimenting each other in a slow dance.

Looking up from his writing, Throst noticed her grave expression. At the sudden disappearance of her jovial amusement, his face darkened in concern and he hastily set aside his writing tools. He leaned forward and set his hand on her knee. "Is something troubling you?" he questioned.

The music stopped. Caywen set aside her instrument and leaned against the stone wall. She glanced toward Throst. "It is the people, and the conflict dividing them into factions," she acknowledged. "I cannot help but fear what will come of it."

Moving to kneel at Caywen's feet, Throst lifted his other hand and gently stroked her cheek. His boyish amusement had vanished, replaced by an earnest sincerity. "I assure you I do not desire to undermine Vikar. I support and respect him as your father and my Baron," he promised, turning her head with his hand to look her in the eye. "The people are confused, Caywen. They seek to blame rather than understand the truth—hard times lead to greatness. You have a fine mind. Surely you understand."

With a weak smile, Caywen reached up, pulling his hand away from her cheek and clasping it tightly. Her forehead wrinkled as she searched within for an answer to her own confusion. "Yes, but I find it difficult to discern my part in all this. What am I destined to do? I seek the Guide's will in this," she replied.

Throst squeezed Caywen's hand and placed his forehead against hers. "You must discover that for *yourself*," he insisted. "*Decide* your place in this affair. I'm here for you, whatever your decision."

Caywen hesitated. Averting her gaze, she mulled over her friend's words of encouragement. During the years of close friendship, Throst had repeatedly sought solutions and philosophies that went against the Proverbs and the Guide's direction. Though she had learned to overlook his troubling advice, the incongruity continued to give her pause. Caywen returned his steady gaze. Deep within his eyes, she could see the earnest desire for her betterment.

Throst means no harm.

Throst's gaze lingered. With a smile of consolation, he kissed her hand and returned to his seat. He waved the matter aside. "Come now. Let us not dwell on such things," he declared. As he took his seat, his eyes fell on the ornament about her neck.

Nearly the size of a river stone, an amber pendant dangled from a golden chain, its polished, glossy finish reflecting the light from the window. The swirls within gave the illusion of movement, like stars in an orange sky. Encompassing the pendant, a golden festoon of twisted wire wrapped about it like a dragon's curling tail.

Enraptured by its beauty, Throst examined it closely, brows furrowing briefly. "This priceless pendant is quite fit for a such a lady of beauty. I've seen it before. Where did you come by it?" he inquired, looking up to Caywen.

Glad to leave her worries behind, she looked down at the pendant hanging from her neck and took it in hand. "When my family first visited Andieff, I took it upon myself to explore the small town while my father met with Lord Bardmond. I ventured outside the town and into the moors," she said, admiring the refracting light inside the amber. "A man in a white cloak met me there—calling me by name! He introduced himself as Ruach Shekhin of Taiseem, a priest of the Castle Sanctum. It was he that gave me this amber pendant, like the ones my ancestors used to create and trade. He claimed it was one of the few things blessed by the King, and told me I would know when to pass it on to another."

Throst cocked his head to the side, observing the pendant out of the corner of his eye. "A strange tale indeed, like one of the legends of old," he wondered aloud. "They say things blessed by the King's hand hold a hidden power. Could great strength reside in something so small?"

Taken aback by the question, Caywen searched for an answer. She smiled and clasped the pendant in her hand to hide it from view. "It is a symbol of something greater than any power in this world," she stammered, troubled by Throst's focus on power.

Clenching his jaw, Throst berated himself for his carelessness. "My apologies. I didn't mean to vex you," he said.

Caywen reluctantly released her tight grip on her pendant, and she smoothed out her dress. She picked up her lyre and gave a small smile. The scratching of Throst's quill pen filled in the silence as the lyre began its song once more.

16

Night strengthened its hold on Castle Hodholm as Eyoés and Gwair entered the stables. Asleep in their stalls, the Lords' steeds gave no warning as the stable door creaked open, allowing the dim light of a lantern into the dark space. Gibusil gave a chirp of greeting as he recognized the scent of his rider. The griffin had been placed in a large group stall to accommodate its size. Stepping into the aisle, Eyoés hung his lantern on the post next to the griffin's pen.

Gwair stood close behind, clutching a small bow in his hand as he remained alert. Although small in size, the weapon's composite construction of bone and sinew provided a power disproportionate to its size. During his travels around Alithell, Gwair had become fascinated with the distinct design and its use. "Are you sure we can draw Hranfist out?" he inquired, keeping his voice to a whisper.

Unlatching the gate to Gibusil's stable, Eyoés stepped inside. "If our suspicions about him are correct, we will," he assured his companion. He hoisted the custom saddle from the ground onto the griffin's back and secured it in place.

With a final tug at the cinches, Eyoés turned to face Gwair. "We deliver the message to Hranfist's room, fly to the keep, and wait for him to come to us," he whispered. "If we can *persuade* him to sign a written confession, the Phantom League will have lost one of their members and will be forced to act." Eyoés led Gibusil out of his stall and down the causeway.

Gwair followed beside him, hand fingering the bow at his side. "And what guarantee do we have it will work?" he inquired, his tone skeptical. As he reached the end of the stable, Eyoés unlatched the double doors from the inside and cracked one open. He released Gibusil's reins and peered out into the castle courtyard. Upon the ramparts, several sentries completed their rounds, the torches upon the battlements lighting their path.

If I time our exit right, we should be able to slip past unseen.

Turning to Gwair, Eyoés slipped a deep hood over his head and motioned for Gwair to do the same. "There is no assurance of our success. We will have to risk it," he replied. He slowly pushed the door open to avoid any sudden noise and looked to the top of the wall. As the last sentry disappeared from view, he hurried out the entrance with Gibusil and Gwair in tow. Quickly mounting the saddle, the two took to the night sky, unnoticed by the guards below.

The soft light of the waning moon illuminated Hranfist's personal quarters as midnight approached. Touched by a gentle breeze, curtains hanging to either side of the window flapped inward, occasionally blocking some of the moonlight. A small bed of simple construction lay opposite the window. A shoddy rug, worn from use and lack of cleaning covered the floor. A wardrobe was positioned against one of the walls. Nestled in a corner, a small table served as a meager work space. Despite these furnishings, and a single short sword hanging upon the wall, the room was surprisingly bare. Lying wrapped up in his blankets was the Baron's slumbering advisor.

Shooting through the open window, an arrow embedded into the frame of his bed, the shuddering shock of the blow startling Hranfist awake. Eyes wide and dazed with sleep, he threw the blankets aside and leapt from his bed, clumsily seizing the short sword hanging on the wall. The beating of wings sounded outside his window, then died away into the distance.

Drawing his sword, Hranfist leaned over the windowsill, searching for sign of the strange intruder, to no avail. As if expecting an enemy to leap through the window, Hranfist stepped back, the tip of his weapon pointed toward the opening.

"What could possibly—" he muttered, voice shaking. He glanced to where the arrow was embedded in his bedpost, the fletching dark in the dim light. Hranfist set aside his sword, bending to examine the arrow for any sign of its owner. Eyes narrowing, he noticed a thick parchment wrapped and fastened around the shaft. As he untied the cord, Hranfist unrolled the parchment in the stream of moonlight. The fear of attack faded as he read the scrawled words.

Meet at the top of the Western Tower by midnight. No exceptions.

Beneath the curt command was the L-shaped symbol of the Phantom League. Hranfist stood and cast the message onto his bed.

There must be an urgent change of plan, to forego our usual channel of communication.

Hurrying to the wardrobe, he slipped on a pair of boots and a simple robe. As he wrapped the robe around himself, Hranfist leaned over the windowsill again and looked up to the moon.

It's nearly midnight now, I must hurry.

The Baron's Advisor threw open the door of his chamber and raced down the stairs to the quickest pathway to the designated spot.

Gibusil gently set foot upon the top of the western tower. Dismounting, Gwair adjusted his mask and moved to the far side of the circular enclosure, leaning against one of the merlons. Eyoés slid off the griffin's back.

Making sure all he needed was in his possession, he laid a hand upon Gibusil's furry neck. "Return to the stables," he ordered. Although the creature did not understand his words, it knew what its master desired. Giving a warble of farewell, the griffin leapt off the tower battlements and glided across the sky, the moonlight reflecting on its golden feathers. Assured his steed was headed to its destination, Eyoés turned away. As he did so, his footstep made a hollow knock on the floor below. He glanced downward, locating the trap door in the dim light.

There it is.

Noting the placement of the hinges, Eyoés positioned himself behind it to avoid being seen prematurely.

Gwair nodded approvingly and followed his companion's example. "It was better to leave Vikar behind. This place is too crowded for more than three men," he whispered. Upon their return from the Council meeting, Eyoés had explained his plan in depth to both Gwair and the Baron. When Vikar had insisted on joining them, Eyoés refused.

Looking up, Eyoés regarded the moon's position. "We shouldn't have much longer to wait," he ascertained.

The silence of the night pervaded the place, save for the occasional cry of an animal carried on the wind. Clouds journeyed across the sky, passing in front of the moon and smothering its light.

Then, footsteps sounded from below the trap door. Gwair and Eyoés crouched in the shadows of the battlements, maintaining utter silence. The hatch swung upward on its hinges, and the robed figure of Hranfist emerged onto the top of the tower.

Shutting the trap door, the traitor turned as one of the hooded figures stood from the shadows. "What has changed, Amnedd? Has the League decided on another course of action?" he questioned. Eyoés drew his sword as Gwair stood, nocking an arrow to his bow and drawing back. Hranfist's confidence was replaced by an incredulous stare as the moonlight gleamed off Eyoés' blade. Eyes wide with shock and horror, the advisor took a step back, bracing himself against the merlons behind him. The two heroes stepped around the hatch, their weapons pointed toward the traitor's chest.

"Your traitorous ways have found you out, Hranfist," Eyoés said, stepping closer.

Hranfist stared at the man's blade and swallowed, his eyes wide with disbelief. "The message—how do you know the symbol?" he stuttered, rooted to the spot.

Eyoés' eyes flashed with anger, and he pressed the tip of his sword against the man's chest. "My sister was marked for death by your fellow Phantom Leaguers when she was young," he declared, envisioning the moment as he had when Gwyndel had first told her story.

Seeing the pain in the man's eyes, Hranfist gritted his teeth and pressed himself against the tip of Eyoés' blade. "Are you going to kill me?" he inquired, his tone daring. His eyes stared darkly at Eyoés with a morbid determination.

The young hero withdrew his sword. "No," he said.

Seeing his opportunity, Gwair released the tension on his bowstring and reached into the loose vest he wore. He set a piece of blank parchment, a pen, and an inkwell upon the stone floor.

"If you write your confession and leave the territory, you can live in peace," he announced, lowering his voice to avoid being recognized. Eyoés held his breath.

After a moment of silence, Hranfist crouched and took the items in hand. He regarded them as he stood. Then, with a spiteful laugh, he turned and threw them from the ramparts. "If I betrayed the Phantom League, my life would be forfeit," he spat.

Glancing at each other, Eyoés and Gwair moved to act. Hranfist guessed at their intentions and stepped into one of the crenels, his strong gaze fixed on them.

He closed his eyes, his expression twisted in wicked triumph. "Live in shadows, die in shadows!" he exclaimed, his voice seeming like thunder in the night stillness. As the two heroes hurried forward to restrain him, the traitor turned and leapt with a cry. Heart racing, Eyoés leaned over the battlements, vaguely seeing the dead form of Hranfist lying on the courtyard below.

It was now their unpleasant duty to report to Council—and hope the Phantom League did not become suspicious of them.

17

As the caravan of Loyalists journeyed westward to the abandoned fortress of Weomor, the forest thickened into a blanket of conifers. The boughs weaved so tightly together the daylight struggled to pierce through. Moss stained the bark a deep green, contrasting with the decaying brown hue of the fallen pine needles covering the forest floor. To gain knowledge of the enemy's fortifications, Beydan had ordered the platoon to make camp while he and several of his scouts surveyed the ruins of Weomor.

Sparsely stationed throughout the dark expanse, the Loyalist tents strove to maintain a defensible structure. The forest itself dictated their formation, as though seeking to weaken their united front. Torches fastened upon poles were thrust into the ground to light the encampment. Tied to low boughs and tree trunks, the horses chomped dully at what undergrowth there was, neighing and huffing in irritation.

Gwyndel clasped a short branch in her hand, whittling away the bark with her dagger. Eyes narrowed in impatient concentration, she forcibly pushed the blade away with each stroke, slicing off pieces of bark. Her face was bright with anticipation and an eagerness to reunite with Kiffyn. Recollections of the fond times they had spent together danced in her head, with hopeful thoughts for the well-being of her lost friend. Mind full of these imaginings, Gwyndel whittled with zeal.

Kiffyn is within our grasp! There must be some way I can aid the search while Beydan is out scouting with several of his men.

Sheathing her knife, Gwyndel threw the bare branch into the dark forest. Embarrassed to reveal her eagerness to the men, she feigned boredom and walked toward the center of the camp. While strolling among the arrangement of tents, she sought to sort through her thoughts and emotions.

What if something goes wrong, and the mission is abandoned?

Shaking her head in forceful denial, Gwyndel hurried her pace. As she strolled across the rolling, uneven surface of the forest floor, the recollection of Gwair's trust in Beydan surfaced.

Gwair would only believe in Beydan's capabilities if there was reason to. I must trust all will go well.

She paused, her trail of thought arriving at the beginnings of an intriguing idea. Gwyndel leaned against a nearby tree, the bump of a tied rope pressing like a fist into her shoulder.

Surely Beydan has a record of his findings in a journal, and possibly a strategy for action. Perhaps I can glean from it a more complete understanding of the situation at hand and how I can help.

She looked in the direction of Beydan's tent. Above the other tents, the blue and silver emblem of the Northern Guard flapped from a branch above the

Captain's quarters. She pushed away from the conifer she leaned against and started toward Beydan's quarters.

Glancing about to assure she was not watched, Gwyndel hurried her pace, weaving behind several vacant tents to hide her approach. The soft, wet ground muffled the elf's light footsteps. Trudging through a small patch of ferns, Gwyndel checked behind her.

No one must notice my approach, lest they interpret my actions as misconduct.

At the edge of the main camp, Gwyndel crouched behind a small tent, peering around the edge to examine the Captain's commanding tent from a reasonable distance. Standing beside the entry flap, a single guard stood watchful. Gwyndel pulled back slightly, rubbing her jaw in thought.

What am I going to do?

Tapping her fingers on her thigh, Gwyndel narrowed her eyes in focus.

I must find a way.

She watched as a second soldier approached the commanding tent. With a salute, he addressed the other and gestured behind him, though his exact words Gwyndel could not tell. Listening with patience, the guard spoke his agreement and followed his friend on their unknown task, leaving the Captain's quarters unguarded. Gwyndel smiled.

It must be the Guide's will that I do this.

She left cover and moved toward the tent entrance. Briefly looking behind to assure her actions were unobserved, Gwyndel brushed the tent flap aside and entered. Items were strewn upon the floor of Beydan's quarters in a careless manner, left at the mercy of dirty boots. Suppressing her nervousness, Gwyndel kneeled in the center of the floor. Gently sifting through the belongings, she briefly scanned crumpled pages of parchment before setting them aside with the other items of little interest. As she pushed aside a bundle of clothes, she caught sight of a small brown book in the corner of the tent. Her eyes widened in recognition.

This is the book Beydan was reading while I spoke with him about Brecc. Maybe it contains the information I need about Kiffyn.

Intrigued, Gwyndel took the volume in hand and undid the leather strap keeping it closed. She quickly glanced over her shoulder as she laid the book open on her lap. Taking a deep breath, she scanned the pages for a recent entry. Scrawled in an odd cursive was a compilation of journal entries, each marked with a date. As Gwyndel turned to the next page, she noticed an entry written in scarlet ink. The sight of faint water stains blotted several letters. Setting her finger upon the words, Gwyndel began to read.

The 17th day of Aevoran, in the year 2184 of the Second Era:

My brother is lost to me—and I am left alone. Upon the banks of the Wrolm River, I watched Caydell's life fade away, stolen by the blades of these cursed raiders of Norgalok. The rulers of that desolate wasteland of ice and snow claim the pirates are criminals in their own land, but I have none of it. Had the cursed swine left the remote river villages alone, my brother's life would still have been his own. I cried out to the King himself to save my brother—even swearing to give away all my possessions and leave myself cold and starving should Caydell be restored to health.

Despite my pleas, the King stayed his hand and did nothing. My brother believed Fohidras to be divine, capable and willing to restore those who sincerely invoked his royal mercies. Although Caydell and I disagreed upon this notion, it did not drive a wall between us. Now, I am convinced. The King is no more than a wolf feeding upon the earnest beliefs of the naive and foolish.

I wish to the end I was strong enough to protect the ones I care for. I must harden myself if I am to be.

Gwyndel looked up from the journal's pages, her mouth hanging open in an mixture of confusion and shame. Shutting the book in her hand, she realized she had read something not meant for her eyes.

I should not have harbored feelings of anger toward him.

Guilt over searching Beydan's private quarters seized her and she moved to set the book back in its place.

"Learned enough?" Beydan snapped. Spinning around to the tent's entrance, Gwyndel held out a hand in a gesture of peace.

Eyes watering, she stepped forward. "Beydan, I—"

Seizing her shirt and pulling her forward, Beydan gritted his teeth. His gaze bore a hot fury, yet tears began to form at the corners of his eyes. "You betrayed me and took the secret that was mine to hold!" he exclaimed, voice wavering. "That I will *never* forgive."

Gwyndel broke the Captain's hold on her shirt and stepped back. "I don't expect you to," she quavered, forcibly tightening her mouth to control herself. "This resentment toward the King and anger at your loss will only destroy you. I've seen it before."

Gripping the handle of his falchion, Beydan laughed in spite. "I'm not going to take advice from the likes of you," he spat. "This King you follow is a liar. He claims to care for you but will only leave you to die when your time comes, Forester. Fools like you fuel Fohidras' schemes. My brother deserves justice!"

Gwyndel stared at the ground, her brows furrowing as she struggled to rebuff the man's biting words. It was blatantly clear Beydan's beliefs were founded in his own emotions. Recollections of Eyoés' strong feelings seemed a mirror image to Beydan's struggles, and she sought a way to plant a seed of encouragement.

Looking up, she swallowed. "I lost my parents when I was young, and my brother was dead to me for years. I too know how loss cuts like a blade," she remarked. "I chose not to be bitter, and my life has been much sweeter."

Releasing the handle of his sword, Beydan said nothing. He jabbed an accusing finger at her. "I swear by my own blood I will leave you in the ruins of Weomor," he vowed through his teeth.

Outside the walls of the Captain's tent, a single Loyalist soldier held an armful of firewood in his grasp. As he heard the words of his commander, his eyebrows raised in thought. Leaning away from the canvas walls, the man hurried further into the camp, his footsteps muffled by the soft carpet of needles.

Beydan's secret wound could no longer be hidden.

18

Beydan shouted as he exited the cover of the trees. At their Captain's command, the Loyalist men formed ranks. The dim forest abruptly came to an end at the edge of a wide, open plain, providing a large area to assemble the men. Following at a distance, Gwyndel cleared her throat as she tried to appear normal before the men. Although Beydan's private words to her continued to stir up embarrassment, she kept a neutral demeanor to avoid revealing her true state of mind to the men. She had yet not fully processed the intensity of her confrontation with Beydan and her limited understanding of his struggle. She furtively watched the Captain as he approached his troops.

There must be some way to encourage him—to somehow change his mind.

Gwyndel recalled the hurt in Beydan's eyes and his written words. It was clear from the Captain's manner such a thing would not be simple. Standing before the still body of troops, Beydan let his gaze wander across the stoic faces of his men. He clenched his jaw, easing his worn nerves. As he gathered himself, he pushed away the thoughts of indignation, shock, and anger at Gwyndel's actions. Again the pain of his brother's loss welled up to grip him—only to be shoved back into the pit by Beydan's determined will.

He took several deep breaths.

Caydell will not be forgotten, and the knowledge of one brazen woman will be of no consequence.

Hearing Gwyndel move to stand slightly behind him, Beydan addressed his men. "I have scouted ahead with several of my trusted soldiers," he began, meeting the gazes of the men in the front lines. "No less than a few hours' travel by horse are signs of an isolated force —and from the tracks and evidence I saw, their numbers are nearly a quarter of ours." A murmur of triumph rippled through the ranks as the Loyalists spoke among themselves. Beydan held up a hand of silence. "Do not be so hasty! If it is true that members of the Phantom League have fortified themselves in the ruins of Weomor, the advantage is theirs," he explained. "There is still time to prepare ourselves, but until then, await further instructions. Any questions?"

Beydan stepped back to where Gwyndel stood. He searched the eyes of the men present, his demeanor expectant. Beside him, Gwyndel clenched her hands behind her back as she struggled to prepare her words of apology to the Captain. Hearing no immediate questions, Beydan opened his mouth to dismiss them.

Pushing through the front lines of his comrades, one of the Loyalists raised his hand to attract his Captain's attention. "I wish to speak," he declared, his tone more inquisitive than demanding. Raising an eyebrow, Beydan nodded for the man to continue.

The soldier leaned against his pike awkwardly, briefly glancing at the men behind him. Several of the Loyalists nodded in encouragement as they met his gaze. With a sigh, the single soldier relaxed his formal appearance. "Captain, word has gone around camp that your brother was gravely injured in some sort of skirmish, and you blame the King for letting him die of his wounds," he quavered. "We wish to know—is this true?" Gwyndel stifled a gasp and stepped back, her eyes wide with horror.

Mouth agape, Beydan stiffened as the fire of anger stirred to life. Regarding the man with a dazed stare, the Captain stepped forward, struggling to find the words to say. His silence was enough evidence. "Then it is true!" shouted one of the men deep in the ranks. "Yet another example of the King's tyrannical conduct!"

At this outburst, the ranks broke as each man roared in reply, whether for or against. "Such talk is treason!" a soldier cried above the others. Gripping his weapon, the man stepped back, the tip of his spear poised threateningly at the one who had instigated the chaos.

As he withdrew, nearly half of the other men rushed to his side. "Treason!" they chanted. Indignant, the others accused of sedition formed their own group, screaming insults to the King's divinity. Blades gleamed in preparation for battle. Standing apart from the two factions, a group of undecided Loyalists attempted to ease the conflict.

Watching the growing disorder in horror, Beydan drew his falchion, his expression harried with the possibility of violence among his own troops. He turned to Gwyndel. "*You* did this," he hissed, his voice quavering with rage and betrayal. Abruptly turning away from the speechless elf, he summoned the undecided and rushed into the ranks of rioters with a piercing shout for silence.

Clutching the Proverbs in her hand, Gwyndel raced into the moonlit night. The crunch of the underbrush underneath her boots spurred her on, promising the freedom of a moment unobserved. Guilt clung tight to her, and tears of regret rolled from her eyes.

What have I done? My reckless actions have now caused disunity. I have caused the failure of our mission to rescue Kiffyn.

Assured the Loyalist camp lie far enough behind her, Gwyndel fell to her knees, bruising them on the hard ground. The memories of the riot among the Loyalist ranks flashed through her memory. Although Beydan was able to calm the situation, division between those who agreed with their Captain's personal conclusions about the King and those who disagreed continued to fester. The striking similarities to the Loyalists' divisions and the Dwarf Draed only served to further Gwyndel's remorse.

I should not have rifled through Beydan's personal belongings. Why could I not have borne him with more patience?

Angered by her own imperfections, Gwyndel pounded the forest floor with her fist, scraping her knuckles on the bark of a fallen branch. Through her pain, thoughts of the Guide surfaced with mixed feeling.

What could I ever do to pay for my own recklessness? Surely there must be a way to make amends for what I've done.

She gripped the water-soaked book of Proverbs, as if by touching its pages wisdom would come to her mind. Assured by the silence of the forest and the knowledge of being alone, Gwyndel sobbed without fear of ridicule. She longed for comfort. As she grieved her lack of self-control in dealing with Beydan, the familiar voice of the Guide returned.

You can never pay for the wrong things you've done. You can only decide to act differently in the future, with my aid. Eyoés had to learn the same.

Recognizing the voice, Gwyndel wiped the tears from her eyes.

How can I be assured I will not choose poorly again?

Biting her lip, she hung her head in discouragement. A comforting warmth warded off the feeling of brokenness.

Doing what is right does not depend on perfection. It depends on the strength to keep fighting even when you fall.

The words of wisdom gave her comfort, despite her grief. Gwyndel took a deep, quavering breath inward, and looked up.

What must I change?

Thoughts of her past mistakes rose to shame her again, only to be repelled by her commitment to persevere. The tension of her guilt fell away like dragon scales, and relief took its place to back up the Guide's voice.

You felt proud for resisting Beydan's scathing attempts to provoke you. Pride began to grow, and you let it have its way. Rather, when others mistreat you and try to provoke you to wrong, act kindly, and out of compassion.

Considering the words of wisdom, Gwyndel recognized the truth in the Guide's correction. Her pride had gotten out of hand. As she knelt on the cold ground, she frowned in thought as a growing question stirred within.

What about Beydan?

The Guide's voice quickly put her thought to rest.

Let me convince Beydan of his wrong thoughts. It is only your duty to plant the seed and cultivate it when it has grown. In time, he will realize the error of his ways.

19

3rd of Iaulan, 2202 SE

The growing light of day glowed through the haze of overcast sky as Gwyndel journeyed to the Loyalist's camp. Unwilling to risk getting lost in the dark forest, she had slept under the cover of the pine boughs, waiting to return until dawn. The Guide's words of encouragement circled through her mind, acting as a constant anchor. Swallowing and adjusting her collar, Gwyndel ignored her growing unease.

Beydan will not be welcoming. I doubt he will accept my apology.

At the thought of the gruff Captain, a newfound compassion surprised her. Her thoughts were interrupted as she spotted the white canvas tents of the camp directly ahead. Gathering courage, Gwyndel hurried her pace. As she ventured further into the Loyalist encampment, her stomach clenched.

A large space now divided the tents into two distinct camps. In either division, a single flag flew above the innermost tent to identify it as the leader's quarters. One boasted the banner of the Northern Guard. The other, a simple green shirt tied to a pole. Gripping their weapons with white knuckles, sentries belonging to either party stood at watch. An air of anger and insubordination pervaded the place.

Gwyndel stopped in her tracks. Standing alongside the sentries posted at the Northern Guard's encampment, was Beydan, his dark gaze fixed on the forest she emerged from. Too late, Gwyndel moved to hide behind a nearby tree.

Spotting the lone Forester out of cover, Beydan nodded to his troops and marched toward her, his footsteps heavy as stray branches broke underneath. "Well, the prodigal has decided to rejoin us and make amends. Where have you been hiding? Gone to betray me to the Phantom League as well?" he spat, standing mere inches from Gwyndel. Involuntarily stepping back a pace, she said nothing. The Captain's accusations stoked a flare of indignant anger. For a moment, Gwyndel was tempted to speak her mind.

Have compassion. Forgive his faults as I have.

Mustering the strength to look directly into Beydan's aggressive stare, Gwyndel gripped the book of Proverbs for added courage. "I only ventured off to think," she replied, her steady gaze sincere. "I am sorry for my actions. I should not have torn open an old wound."

Beydan shoved her back and sent her reeling. Stooping and grabbing a fistful of dirt and dead needles, he thrust the mucky clump at her face. "Your apology is nothing but rotting refuse to me," he snapped, throwing the clump of soil against a nearby tree trunk. "I have already spoken to both camps. This rift can only be resolved with a duel." Wiping his hand on his shirt, he stepped back, chin held high in disdain. "You may choose any weapon, save a bow. We settle this at noon," he announced. Without any further word, Beydan abruptly turned away and strode into his encampment.

Gwyndel leaned against a nearby tree, shocked that his anger pushed him to such an extreme. As Beydan's challenge fully registered in her thoughts, she rubbed a hand through her hair.

Man's hubris knows no bounds.

Her head swam as she watched the Captain disappear into the dissenters' camp. Sharp remorse pierced through the haze of confusion and growing fear.

My rash actions have affected so many. This is my fault.

Turning toward the forest, Gwyndel rubbed her hand against her chest. The desire to retreat and think pulled her toward the solace of the trees. She glanced back and forth between the dim forest and the divided camp. One seemed to offer solace, while the other offered a chance for reconciliation. In truth, she knew neither could fulfill their promises. By avoiding the consequences of her actions, guilt would arise. If she moved to reconcile herself with Beydan, it could result in a nasty end. Still, it seemed the Guide would wish her to attempt some sort of resolution with her rival. Gwyndel kicked the trunk of a conifer with her boot.

I wish I could do something to remedy the situation. But I cannot fight him. To do so would only stoke his fiery temper.

A rustling from a nearby clump of bushes startled her from her thoughts. Sucking in a quick breath,

Gwyndel turned. "Who's there?" she said. Gwyndel realized the weakness of her fear and winced.

A moment of silence answered her. Emerging from the cover of brush, a young man stepped toward her. His white face was freckled, and wavy brown hair curled about his neck. A light vest covered the chainmail shirt hanging over his thin body. Taken aback, Gwyndel raised an eyebrow, glad to set aside her troubles for a moment.

He is younger than Eyoés was when we first met. He looks out of place in this military company.

Gathering his confidence, the youth cleared his throat. "Forgive me, miss. I overheard the Captain's challenge to you and wish to speak to you concerning it," he confessed.

Gwyndel examined the lean boy standing before her. "What is your name?" she asked.

The youth inclined his head and saluted. "Marc, son of Wilnor," he answered.

Gwyndel leaned against the conifer tree, her eyes narrowed. "Why have I never seen you before?" she questioned. Although impressed by the boy's boldness, she remained skeptical and unsure of his proposal.

Marc glanced at the two divided camps and sighed. "I'm part of the rear guard. Nobody ever minds us," he admitted.

At this, Gwyndel cocked her head and moved toward him. "How did you join the Northern Guard?" she asked, the thought of such a young man entering the ranks disconcerting.

Marc smiled briefly. "I didn't. My father read me stories, and I left my home of Gahidros in search of adventure no less than a year ago," he recalled. "Beydan allowed me to join the search for Kiffyn because he was in need of extra men."

Gwyndel's eyes brightened. "You come from Gahidros? The home of the Knights of the Lance?" she questioned, the mention of the famed castle and cavalry hearkening back to the stories of her childhood.

With a smile, Marc bowed. "The very same, Miss," he said. Regarding the youth with a new sense of respect, Gwyndel bowed in return. Memories returned to her of nights spent with Fychan, reading tales of honor and daring by firelight. The thought seemed to bring Fychan closer amid the dreary forests she found herself in.

Before Gwyndel could speak more, Marc raised a hand to ward off her questions. "As for the Captain's challenge," he remarked, his face growing stern. "He affronted you in a dishonorable way unfit for a man of his rank. He might have been hurt in the past, but he's blinded by his anger." Inclining his head, he exposed the heart of the matter. "I may not look like much, miss, but I'm skilled with a quarterstaff," he declared. "Those who support the King should honor his code. I will fight in your place."

A steady rainfall churned the grassy plain into mud as the two opposing factions gathered together. The men whispered among themselves and several shot distrustful glances to the enemy opposite. Encircling the large patch of ground serving as the dueling area, each party beckoned their champion forward. Standing at the front of the crowd, Gwyndel clenched and unclenched her fists as Marc stepped into the improvised arena.

This boy should not pay for my rashness.

Spotting Gwyndel among the small crowd, Marc gave her a quick wink. She flashed a false smile to hide her disquiet. Clustering about him, several men cheered him on, whispering encouragement into his ear. Gripping his quarterstaff, Marc prepared himself for the fight to come, deaf to the exhortations of his supporters.

Beydan stepped into the arena, concluding a conversation with one of his men. As he caught sight of his young opponent, his eyes widened in shock and anger. He spotted Gwyndel nearby and pointed an accusing finger. "You let a *boy* fight for you?" he exclaimed.

Before Beydan could speak more, Marc spoke up. "And *you* challenged a woman to a man's sport," he remarked, leaning against his quarterstaff. "You're letting your anger dull your senses!"

Beydan locked his fiery gaze on the young boy. "Say that again when you're bleeding," he dared. He yanked his falchion from its scabbard. The blade seemed eager to enter the fight, its tip like an eagle's talon. With one hand, Beydan untied his sword belt and cast it into the ranks of his men.

From where she stood, Gwyndel briefly closed her eyes.

May the Guide protect him.

Eager to witness the victory of their champion, the divided troops gave a shout to get the duel started. The men clustered about the two contenders fell back to their respective parties. Gripping the back end of his staff with both hands, Marc assumed a ready position.

Beydan circled as he examined his opponent. "We will see whose cause will triumph," he growled. With a shout, he lunged forward with a thrust. Marc stepped to the side and quickly struck his opponent's chest and ribs with two flicks of his staff. Gritting his teeth, Beydan stumbled forward and regained a stable stance. Marc swung at Beydan's head. The Captain barely deflected the blow and swung his falchion at Marc's exposed back. Slicing through the youth's dark tunic, the blade glanced harmlessly off his chainmail.

Clumsily, Marc struck Beydan's head with a glancing blow before retreating well out of reach. Beydan stepped back, feeling a shallow cut as he brought his hand to his forehead. Although the pain of his bruised ribs caused him to wince, the thought of being bested by a mere boy and his stick sent a flare of anger through him.

Gwyndel may have exposed my past and hired a scrawny boy to do her dirty work, but she will not claim victory.

With a renewed vigor, Beydan rushed his enemy with a cry. Unflinching, Marc forcefully thrust at his head. Gwyndel gasped as Beydan ducked under his blow. The Captain seized the staff with his free hand, and Marc nearly lost his footing in the mud. The falchion's blade raced toward his head. In desperation, Marc pivoted the back end of the staff and cracked Beydan across the forehead.

The Captain staggered back, instinctively releasing the staff. All faded to black, and he fell to the ground, unconscious. Marc stood over his fallen enemy, leaning on his staff.

All fell silent. Marc stepped back from his fallen superior, looking intently across the crowd. In the eyes of the dissenters, he could see a brooding indignation. For a brief moment, he caught sight of a dark mist weaving among them. He blinked, and saw no more of it. Gwyndel attracted his eye and nodded, her relief evident.

Returning his focus to the men, Marc plunged his quarterstaff into the muddy ground. "You've all had your duel. We are brothers at arms! The enemy is at hand, and will destroy us if we do not stand together. If we allow division to slip past our guard, we will *die* in Weomor," he announced with passion. "The Captain is still our leader, no matter our beliefs. Yet, he is still a man, as are we. As brothers, we support each other, regardless of rank. If one of us endangers his life, will we not try to save him?" He paused, letting his words sink in. Those who had cheered for Beydan's triumph with zeal now stood silent as the bond of combat tugged at their dissident hearts. Tears welled up in Gwyndel's eyes, which she quickly wiped away.

My mistakes have been amended—to some extent.

She glanced to where Beydan lay unconscious, his wet clothes smeared with mud. The likelihood of his attitude being friendly upon his waking was slim. From the weeks of traveling alongside him, Gwyndel knew it would take more than a knock to the head to change his mind.

Marc nodded as his fellows considered his exhortation to unity. "Brothers stand by each other, and that is what *we* will do," he concluded. "I must get the Captain back to his quarters." Rushing to where Beydan fell, Marc seized his ankles and heaved backward, clenching his jaw as he strained to drag him to camp.

The Loyalists closest to him dropped their weapons and came to his aid, lifting the Captain as one. As they started towards the tent, the remaining Loyalists—regardless of their former divisions—joined together as a single force and followed behind. Standing in the open field, Gwyndel fell to her knees, letting the relief sink in.

I cannot tarry for too long. I must aid in Beydan's recovery.

She looked up. Splattered with mud and rain, Marc's quarterstaff stood upright in the ground, the lone reminder of what transpired in the open clearing.

20

18th of Biarron, 2202 SE

"I regret to inform the Council that Hranfist, advisor to our Baron, was found dead in the courtyard this morning, apparently by suicide," Gwair announced, standing still as his gaze moved across the faces of the Council before him. For a moment, the seated Lords were silenced by shock as they came to understand what had transpired, then a wave of hushed conversation rose from those present. Slowly nodding as he mulled over Gwair's words, Vikar folded his hands upon the table.

Leaning against the far wall, Eyoés met Gwair's gaze. The unexpected events of the night played repeatedly through his thoughts. He abruptly broke eye contact with Gwair and lowered his head.

Gwair should have taken the lead. My actions and ideas only lead to disappointment and failure.

Noticing the young Baron of Taekohar's distraught bearing, Vikar met his gaze and raised an inquisitive eyebrow. Eyoés shook his head. Gwair saw the exchange and set a hand on Vikar's shoulder and whispered in his ear. The Baron frowned in thought, then patted Gwair's hand to dismiss him. With a nod, Gwair left Vikar's side and moved to where Eyoés stood.

Staring off into the distance, Eyoés pursed his lip.

I will follow Gwair's lead until this crisis is over. It is not my place to lead the way. I've already made one mistake.

Gwair stood beside his companion and leaned against the stone wall. He hesitated for a moment, then leaned toward Eyoés' ear. "I arranged for Vikar to meet us in the afternoon," he whispered. "Do you think the Phantom League could discover our trail from this incident?"

Eyoés quickly shook his head. "We left no evidence behind in the tower," he replied with false confidence. "Without some sort of proof, this incident could pass as a mere coincidence." Inwardly, his disappointment over his own actions caused doubt to grow beneath the appearance of confidence. His attention turned to the Council.

Reclining against the back of his chair, Gerall Bardmond stroked his chin and looked to Baron Vikar. "This entire affair is beyond me. Without more information, it is difficult to know how Hranfist's death came about," he stated, tapping his fingers on the tabletop.

Throst Ravenstrong leaned forward, his expression troubled. "According to Gwair, it seemed Hranfist's death was suicidal. Perhaps the stressing circumstances of the past months have weighed him down with depression," he reasoned.

Shaking his head, Vikar folded his arms across his chest. "He was my advisor, and little of him escaped my notice. I can assure you he was not suicidal from the beginning of this entire crisis," he objected. "It would be unlike him to take his own life for no reason."

Fidgeting in his seat, Haral Rhys nervously glanced at his fellow Lords, a look of fear pasted to his pompous face. "Do you think there could be treason involved?" he asked, voice wavering. The Lords present did not reply immediately. What once would have seemed an wild supposition now held them in uncertainty and mistrust.

Throst's eyes narrowed as he stabbed the table with his index finger. "It is not beyond reason," he cautioned. "As the Council, we know Hranfist did not always concur with the Baron's actions. Surely you all remember times when this has happened?" The Lords mumbled their agreement, looking to Vikar for confirmation. Taking a deep breath inward, the Baron met Throst's eye with a fixed look. "What are you implying?" he questioned.

Throst paused—then continued. "The people are both confused and passionate about their side of the debate. It might seem outlandish, but it is possible that radicals who are zealous in their devotion to Baron Vikar might have murdered Hranfist for his moments of opposition," he concluded.

Agnar Crawbrand shook his head and held his hand out in incredulity. "How would they get past the garrison?" he protested.

Throst stood from his chair, jaw set, and locked eyes with Lord Crawbrand. "They wouldn't need to if they were within these very halls," he replied in a cold tone. Eyoés and Gwair glanced at each other, the weight of their situation now openly exposed.

Hranfist's death was no longer mere coincidence.

Walking idly through the upper halls of Hodholm, Eyoés left the bustle of court life behind. To his left, open windows allowed the crisp air to blow against his face, heightening his awareness and clearing his mind. The suspicious words of Throst circled through his head. Scrubbing a hand over his face, Eyoés pushed the thought aside.

There may be only a short time until the League picks up our trail. What is the extent of this conspiracy?

Eyoés took a deep breath in, then forcefully exhaled through his mouth. If they were to stay ahead of the conspirators, more information had to be either gathered or reasoned. Focused with a stubborn determination, Eyoés increased his pace.

From what I have heard, the Phantom League is a group of assassins and mercenaries. Given their specialty, there would be no reason for their presence without a designated target.

He mentally filtered through the evidence gathered since their arrival in Rehillon. To his left, Eyoés spotted a single door, leading to one of the many castle towers. He moved toward it, then stopped as one man came to mind.

Could Vikar be their target?

Eyoés' eyes widened as he considered the possibility. Vikar had been at the center of the Everwheat crisis since the beginning. His growing anxiety was quickly checked by reason.

If the Phantom League's goal was to kill the Baron, he would have been poisoned by now. There must be more to their plans than assassination.

Eyoés continued to the tower door and pulled it open. The musty smell of an old, enclosed corridor met him at the doorway. The base of the staircase was illuminated by the light from the hall. Stepping inside, Eyoés shut the door behind him and began to climb the stairs.

Throst is perceived by the people as Vikar's rival—could he have something to do with this besides bringing the Everwheat remedy to the Council's attention?

Eyoés considered the matter. There was no evidence showing Throst had any connection with the Phantom League, yet something about him seemed odd.

At the top of the staircase, he stopped before another door. Now assured he would be away from any prying eyes, Eyoés' fears were eased. He pulled the door open and stepped through the doorway.

A waist-high wall enclosed the round tower pavilion. Several pillars replaced the customary walls to support a domed roof, giving a wide view of the castle grounds. Through the empty spaces between the pillars, a gust of wind tossed Eyoés' hair. Shutting the door behind him, he stepped further into the space, and abruptly stopped. Sitting with bent knees atop the pavilion wall directly in front of him—was Throst Ravenstrong.

21

At the sound of approaching steps, Throst looked up from his book. His eyes brightened as he recognized the newcomer. Shutting his book with a thump, he swung his legs down and casually sat on the wall's edge. "I've seen you at the Council meetings," he noted with a smile.

Eyoés hastily bowed in apology. "I didn't mean to disturb you," he muttered, abruptly turning to leave.

Holding out a hand to stay him, Throst leaned forward. "Please stay, I insist," he urged. "There are few outside visitors to this castle, and I could use some company." Eyoés hesitated, turning slowly to face the young Lord. His suspicions about the man warned him. Yet, he knew to leave after an invitation would be rude.

Eyoés stood face to face with him, and Throst nodded in satisfaction. "We haven't been properly introduced," he acknowledged with a customary bow. "Throst Ravenstrong."

Regarding the young Lord with curiosity, Eyoés bowed in return. "Eyoés Kingson," he replied, his gaze focused on his new acquaintance.

At the mention of the name, Throst tilted his head back with a smile. "Ah, you're the man who fought alongside the Dwarves in the North," he recalled, his fingertips skimming along the length of his jaw. "On behalf of my people, I honor you for your selfless actions to protect Alithell from destruction."

With a nervous laugh, Eyoés waved the matter aside. "It was the Guide's doing, not mine. I merely followed his counsel," he insisted, a visible flush creeping across his face.

Nodding, Throst looked off into the distance. "As you say," he remarked. Clouds heavy with rain crept along the sky, and the wind whispered across the stone walls of the castle.

Eyoés paused, then pointed to the closed book in Throst's lap. "What are you reading?" he inquired.

Pulled from his observation of the serene land beyond, Throst held the book and regarded its cover. "Mairwen of Ledale's 'The Art of Thought'. I recommend you read it. It is quite a masterful work," he sighed, opening the book to a certain page. "I was just reading her treatise on desire and prosperity. It says here 'Allow your desire to flower, and the wealth of a thousand kings will become its fruit. In time, you will find prosperity is a shield for those who find it'."

Eyoés stepped back involuntarily.

Beware the charm of gold and the company of evil.

Eyoés hastily suppressed his concern and clasped his hands together in an effort to compose himself.

Does he mean to convince me of this or are his intentions harmless?

Turning over the words in his mind, Throst closed the book. "Prosperity is a shield," he mused aloud. "Sometimes it seems such a distant hope, and we embark on a journey to claim it—only to realize it was hidden at home all along." He paused, then glanced to where Eyoés stood, silent. Flashing a brief smile, Throst cleared his throat. "I have also heard you are Baron of Taekohar," he said, tilting his head to the side. "How did that come to be?"

Eyoés sighed, and strode to the nearest pillar. Behind a mask of idle thought, he was glad the subject had changed.

The less I am faced with thoughts of prosperity, the better.

Leaning against one of the pillars, Eyoés watched the wind gently toss the pine boughs nearby. "I grew up without my father. When I was twelve years of age, I discovered he was the Protector of my homeland, and a hero—up until his death at the hands of the Phantom League. I idolized him, even embarking on a quest to become the man he was, and avenge the deaths of my people," he recalled. The strength of his conviction reminded Eyoés of his journey of transformation. "In time, I discovered the image of my Father did not define me, and my story was a different tale than his. At the end of my quest, King Fohidras granted me the Baronship of Taekohar."

Pushing himself off the short wall, Throst moved to Eyoés' side and set a light hand on his shoulder. "I too know the pain of fatherlessness," he admitted, closing his eyes and rubbing his forehead.

Caught off guard, Eyoés looked to the young Lord. The man's claim of sympathy bound them like kinsmen.

Could it be that he really understands?

Throst sighed. "My father, Fedrik, and my mother never married, and I was their illegitimate son. Because of that, my father treated me like a servant. I was given a pittance for my clothing and food. He might have lived in the same household, but was *not* my father in the truest sense of the word," he said, his voice hitching. "As evidenced by his behavior towards me. So the saying goes—fatherhood is an act, not just an office. From what you've told me, *your* father was more worthy of affection than mine."

Unsure of what to say, Eyoés paused as his wariness towards the man waned. The longing for his father's presence grew in strength. Eyoés blinked away several tears.

Does prosperity mean only treasure? Or can the people dearest to me become my wealth?

Nodding to himself, Eyoés stepped away from the pillar. "Yes, prosperity is a shield. The ones we care for become a place of safety," he mumbled under his breath.

Throst removed his hand. "That is a wise thought," he observed.

Eyoés smiled and bowed. "I am flattered," he said. "If you'll excuse me, it is about time I depart. I have business to attend to.

Throst returned the gesture of friendship. "Until we meet again," he declared. Silent, Eyoés opened the door and closed it behind him. As he traveled down the spiraling stairs, the suspicions about Throst faded like smoke.

22

Hurrying his pace, Eyoés neared his and Gwair's quarters. Banners adorned the walls to either side, richly decorated with interlacing designs of beasts and men, each telling a story of heroic deeds. As he passed by, Eyoés admired them, his thoughts revisiting his encounter with Throst.

Prosperity is a shield. Maybe I should find a copy of the 'Art of Thought' and read it.

He rounded a corner in the hall and spotted the door to his quarters. Catching his mind wandering, Eyoés mentally chided himself.

I must remain on guard. Whether I admire Throst or not, the Phantom League is still on the prowl.

Looking behind him, he searched for sign of a hidden pursuer. Nothing but the shadows lingered underneath the banners. Eyoés remained watchful as he stood before the door. He knocked on the door once, then scratched the door twice with his fingers. In reply, the door opened wide enough for him to slip inside.

Gwair shut the door behind him and locked it from the inside. He turned and crossed his arms. "Where were you?" he asked.

Eyoés raised a hand to ward off his companion's concerns. "I needed time to think," he replied, removing the courtier's cloak from his shoulders and tossing it on his bed. Although thankful Gwair had provided the fine raiment for daily wear during his stay, Eyoés disliked the heavy cloth weighing his shoulders down.

Across the room, standing in front of the window, Vikar turned with an understanding nod. "I have been thinking as well," he admitted, wandering toward the two heroes. "Something went awry with Hranfist's interrogation, didn't it?"

Eyoés clenched his fist in front of his chest. "We nearly had his confession!" he exclaimed bitterly. "I failed to anticipate his refusal and we lost any chance of physical evidence as a consequence."

Gwair set a comforting hand on Eyoés' shoulder. "He leapt from the battlements rather than betray the League," he explained. Disturbed by the violent image of this gruesome death, Vikar turned away.

Shaking his head in frustration, Eyoés paced about the room, pounding his fist into his open palm. "I am tired of living in uncertainty! We know without any doubt Hranfist was one of them, but if we reveal what we know, the Phantom League will find a way to destroy our alibi and frame us for sedition!" he growled through his teeth.

Avoiding direct eye contact with either Eyoés or the Baron, Gwair let out a pent up breath. "We are safe with the knowledge we have gathered. As long as the circumstances of Hranfist's demise remain hidden, the truth will only help us. But if the Phantom League uncovers the real cause for Hranfist's death, there *will* be retaliation."

Vikar leaned against the bookshelf and stroked his beard. "You may well keep the truth hidden, but how do you suggest we uncover more evidence?" he inquired.

Hesitating, Gwair looked out the window, watching the clouds roll by. Eyoés stopped his pacing and looked to his friend for guidance, his expression strained.

With a sigh, Gwair met the gazes of his confidants. "I don't yet know. Until the conspirators make their next move, their intentions remain hidden from us. We can only wait," he said.

Eyoés took a step forward."We might not have long until it is too late," he insisted. "I say we burn the forged letter and eliminate any chance of—" His voice faded to silence. Eyoés' face blanched, and a spike of panic surged through his chest.

He stared blankly at the wall. "The letter—it's still in Hranfist's room!" he exclaimed.

23

For a second time, Gwair and Eyoés ventured into the darkness of midnight. The night wind whistled through the arrow slits in the tower wall, accompanied by the calls of nocturnal birds. Holding a torch in one hand, Eyoés ascended the tower steps to Hranfist's quarters, with Gwair following immediately behind. The tamed glow of the torch illuminated just enough steps ahead of him to guide him onward. Eyoés cringed as one of the wooden steps creaked under his weight, but pushed on.

There is no one here to notice our approach save Gwair and I. Keep going—the sooner the letter is in our possession the less danger it poses.

Stopping for a moment, Eyoés turned to Gwair, bringing the torch to reveal his companion's face. "You are sure our entrance into this tower went unnoticed by the sentries?" he asked, unconsciously lowering his voice in secrecy.

Gwair nodded toward the steps ahead of them. "Yes, I am positive. Don't stop now to talk," he answered. Without a word, Eyoés turned away and hurried his pace, ignoring the creaking steps below his feet. His chest tightened as he fought to remain calm.

I trust Gwair has a plan for this undertaking. If our efforts are fruitless, the enemy might have us imprisoned in the near future.

The stairs leveled to a landing as a single door was lit by the torchlight. Slipping his left hand into his cloak pocket, Gwair stepped past his companion and grabbed the handle. With a creak, the door swung open with the slightest push.

Gwair's brow wrinkled with apprehension. "It should have been locked," he muttered, releasing the lock picking tools in his coat pocket.

Grasping at hope, Eyoés ignored the obvious conclusion. "Perhaps Hranfist forgot to lock the door that night. After all, he was planning on returning," he reasoned, inwardly grimacing at the reminder of their failure. Raising his eyebrows with a questioning look, Gwair stepped into the vacant room. Once Eyoés entered, Gwair shut the door and locked it from the inside. Blowing out the torch, Eyoés set it aside. For a moment, they stood still, allowing their eyes to adjust to the darkness.

After taking a quick survey of the room's arrangement, Gwair nodded. "Search everything," he said. The two of them scattered about the room, leaving no part of the room unturned. Eyoés pulled the covers off the single bed. Gwair opened the wardrobe and placed its contents onto the floor for further inspection. With each passing minute, the spike of dread pierced deeper into their hearts as the letter remained unfound. Gaze darting about the room, Eyoés rushed toward the solitary desk and rifled through its contents with increasing desperation. Before long, the room lay in shambles.

Eyoés looked to Gwair with a feverish gaze, the moonlight from the window glinting off the beads of sweat on his forehead. "It's not here! We're too late!" he gasped, seizing his hair. "What now?"

Searching the pockets of the clothes strewn about the floor, Gwair curled his hands into fists. "I don't know—do you have any suggestions?" he asked.

Eyoés shook his head, unwilling to accept Gwair's offer. "My plans are useless. You saw what happened to Hranfist!" he exclaimed, taking a step back.

Standing, Gwair seized the young Baron of Taekohar by his shoulders. Although filled with anxiety, his eyes softened. "You can't shy away from your own mistakes, Eyoés. I know you grew up without a father's guidance and wisdom concerning life, but you must take responsibility for your actions, learn from them, and *move on*," he said. "Don't let the fear of failure render you helpless and crippled."

The desperation in Eyoés' eyes waned as Gwair's wisdom penetrated his fear. Taking a deep breath, he hung his head. "Forgive me," he sighed. "I am uncertain about the next step to take." A moment of silence hung between them as they regained their composure.

Nodding, Gwair patted his friend's shoulder and stepped back, pushing several clothes out of his way with the heel of his boot. "It is clear someone has taken the evidence before we arrived. The only question is who," he said. He stopped, the beginnings of an idea dawning on his features. Turning away, he gathered his thoughts. "Tomorrow, on the twentieth of Biarron, the noblemen celebrate the Feast of Origins to commemorate the founding of Rehillon as a territory. During the proceedings, the servants and sentries will be stationed close to the Great Hall. The rest of the castle will be relatively empty," he mused, turning to face Eyoés. "We can search unnoticed for as long as we need—and I might have an idea where we can look first."

Holding his breath, Eyoés smiled in anticipation and curiosity. "Where?" he asked.

Stirred by his own conclusions, Gwair wasted no time in answering. "Throst's quarters," he revealed.

Eyoés' smile faded. The recollection of his private conversation with Throst only served to heighten his aversion. He opened his mouth to tell his companion of his encounter, then stopped.

If Gwair has his suspicions about Throst, what will he think when he learns I have associated with him? Will he think I am compromised?

Checking himself, Eyoés came up with a safer declaration. "From what I've seen, Throst is a hero. Do you not remember how he saved the people from the Everwheat addiction?" he asked incredulously. "I do not see any grounds for a search of his quarters."

Excitement curbed, Gwair mentally revisited his argument, then snapped his finger in recollection. "I shouldn't expect you to know about the turbulent past between the Ambersters and the Ravenstrongs. It is logical to first search where we know conflict already exists," he explained. "Besides, if Throst is innocent, I will find nothing compromising and we will move on."

Giving a wavering smile, Eyoés gathered himself. The thought of seeing Throst again after he had knowingly violated his privacy in searching his quarters reviled him.

He sympathized with me. How can I betray his trust? There must be a way to avoid this.

Letting his gaze wander about the room, Eyoés searched for a way to distance himself from Gwair's intentions. He swallowed. "You'd best go alone," he stammered. "There is a better chance for one to remain unnoticed than two. I will attend the feast and create a reason for your absence." He faltered, hoping Gwair would accept his reply.

As he considered his friend's claim, Gwair tilted his head. During his time with Eyoés over the past four years, he had become accustomed to his regular manner.

There's something about Throst that's bothering him. Something he's not willing to tell me.

Hiding his misgivings, Gwair nodded resolutely and bent down to pick up the clothes set on the floor. "Very well. Quickly—we must restore the room to its former state and return to our quarters before we are discovered."

24

The Feast of Origins, 20th of Biarron, 2202 SE

Cheerful voices filled the Great Hall as nobles celebrated around the table. Tapestries and heraldic flags adorned the stone walls, and fine furs covered the backs and armrests of the chairs. Hurrying about their duties, servants carried platters of food to the table and arranged the meal in an appealing display of bounty. The pungent scent of meat and heavy spices hung like an invisible, thick smoke over those present. At either end of the tabletop, two candelabras provided light for those seated. Thick bread trenchers lay in front of the partakers in preparation for the midday feast, along with mugs of mead and fine drink. Crowning the assembly of mince pies, rabbit, and spiced steak was a mock basilisk, created from the body of an eel and the head of a rooster.

Seated to the left of the Baron, Eyoés gazed off at the opposite wall, trying to smother the uneasiness in his gut. He furtively slipped his hands into his pockets underneath the tabletop.

Even if the people are distracted by the feast, Gwair is taking a risk by searching Throst's room.

Striving to calm himself, he slowed his breathing and took a draught of mead. He knew the purpose of his presence at the feast, and he intended to maintain a normal demeanor at all costs. Should someone question Gwair's lack of presence, Eyoés had a ready answer. In search of something to fiddle with, he reached for the napkin to his left. He clenched his jaw as Rodmer Estworth seated himself immediately beside him. Silent among the din of merry conversation, Rodmer pressed his fist against his mouth and sat still. Not wanting to catch the red-haired youth's eye, Eyoés shifted his seat slightly closer to where Vikar sat at the head of the table.

Eyoés looked up from his trencher to see Caywen sitting directly opposite him. She spoke idly with Vikar at his right hand, the velvet cloth of her emerald green dress glittering in the candlelight. Her smile lit her glowing face with happiness, and she clasped Vikar's hand lovingly. In return, Vikar smiled and pulled her into a close embrace. For a moment, Eyoés' unease subsided as his thoughts journeyed to other places.

What role does Caywen play in all this? Surely, as the Baron's daughter she must have some part in his affairs.

His musings were broken by her voice. "How has your stay in Hodholm been? I hope my family and fellow Rehils have been welcoming," she remarked, raising her eyebrows and leaning forward.

Returning a warm smile, Eyoés quickly filtered his words before speaking. It would do no good to mention the stress of the past few days. "It has been a pleasure to stay for a time in one of the oldest castles in Alithell," he replied, gaze wandering about the room. "There is a certain *magnificence* about the place I wish to bring to Castle Asdale. Perhaps there are some changes to be made to the building plans." Leaning back in her chair, Caywen beamed.

Dismissing an aide, Vikar clapped several times to get the attention of those present. The din waned to silence as the Lords awaited their Baron's words, until the only sounds came from the kitchen as the servants continued to work. Vikar briefly smiled to acknowledge the Lords' cooperation. "Food taster!" he shouted, turning partway in his seat toward the back of the Great Hall. Eyoés frowned, watching Vikar furtively as a tall, scrawny man approached with a towel in hand. The Baron shifted in his seat, attempting to hide his unrest. From the expressions of the others seated, it seemed no more than a typical routine. Eyoés observed as the tester dipped the corner of his towel on the meat and in the juices of the mock basilisk and brought it to his tongue. It seemed improbable the Phantom League would poison the Baron's food after such an extensive Everwheat plot, yet Eyoés found himself holding his breath.

Another reminder of the danger in these halls.

For a moment, the tester paused. Then with a nod, he moved on to the other dishes, until all had passed his inspection. With a final bow, he departed to the kitchen.

Closing his eyes briefly, Vikar released a low sigh. He smiled. "On this day, King Fohidras approved the acceptance of Rehillon as a territory of the kingdom. Let us celebrate the perseverance of our forefathers and the hope of a united Rehillon," he declared, lifting his mug of mead in toast.

Seated at the far end of the table, Throst Ravenstrong lifted his mug and met Vikar's gaze. His clothing was his finest, indicating his respect for the holiday. "To a united Rehillon—which *will* come to pass," he added, blinking away a tear. The other Lords followed their Baron's example with a loyal shout and took a draught of their mead.

The feast began. Rubbing his hands together in eagerness, Haral Rhys dove into the meal set before him, cutting a large chunk of stuffed meat from the mock basilisk and setting it on his trencher before greedily indulging himself. All present helped themselves to the bountiful collection of foods, downing a mouthful of fine drink when necessary. Eyoés took several bites of spiced rabbit, surprised at the hot bite of cinnamon combined with the savory flavor of meat. Conversation carried on where it had been set aside.

Wiping the corner of his mouth with a cloth napkin, Throst examined those present, then craned his neck to look at Eyoés. "Where's Gwair? Surely he planned to attend the meal," he said. The other Lords didn't seem to notice the inquiry.

Eyoés froze, sitting stock still in his seat. He tensed, mind racing to recall the excuse he had created. Making a show of swallowing a large mouthful, he hesitated, feeling the steady gaze of Throst upon him. Eyoés cleared his throat. "He is occupied with his records. He insisted I attend without him," he answered, his voice unsteady. Eyoés glanced to Vikar. The Baron gave a comforting nod and returned to his meal. Taking a deep breath, Eyoés looked to where Throst sat.

The chair was empty, and the door to the feast hall closed with a clang. Eyoés pressed himself against the back of his chair and gripped the armrests with white knuckles.

Glancing one last time down the hall, Gwair knelt at Throst's door. He removed a thin cloth bundle from his chest pocket, senses tuned for any danger of discovery. As he unrolled the wool pack, his fingers grasped a strangely shaped iron rod. While examining the lock on the door, Gwair pulled another instrument from the bundle.

Without Neifon's lock picking instruction, I would be in a sorry position. I'm glad he insisted, despite my opposition.

Putting his ear beside the lock, he inserted one of the thin iron devices into the keyhole and gently twisted. Two clicks sounded in succession, and he stopped, inserting the second iron instrument into the lock. Gwair bit his tongue to ease his tense nerves.

I cannot let my concentration be clouded by nervousness.

The sound of approaching footsteps upon the stone floor sent a spike of adrenaline through him. He froze and glanced down the hall.

The Feast is already underway—everyone should be occupied!

Talking in low voices, two servants headed his direction, oblivious to the secretive act going on ahead of them. Gwair turned back to the door and put his ear beside the lock as he fiddled with the second pick. They were nearly upon him. The lock clicked open, allowing the door to Throst's quarters to pop open. Shoving the two instruments into his pocket, Gwair hastily slipped inside, came to his feet, and closed the door behind him. He bowed his head as the servants' footsteps passed by and faded away.

Gathering himself, Gwair let his eyes adjust to the dark room. Among the dark shapes of furniture and personal items, a glow of natural light emanated at the edges of a thick curtain. Making sure his lock picking instruments were securely placed in his pocket, Gwair moved toward the obscured window. A movement caught his eye, and he froze.

In the dark recesses of the room, a black mist hovered above the floor like smoke, thick as the veil of night. Shaking his head to clear his vision, Gwair squinted into the darkness. Calming himself, he grasped the thick curtain, pulled it aside, and pinned it behind a nearby chair. Beams of light penetrated the dark recesses of the room. A shiver crept up his spine as he saw the cloud of mist retreat into the furthest corner. His hand wrapped around the handle of his concealed dagger. As daylight filled the room, the mist vanished from sight. Releasing the handle of his dagger, Gwair stared at the vacant corner.

I'm imagining things. The possibility of discovery is wearing at my senses.

He rubbed his forehead and focused on the task at hand. A single bed lay across from the window, draped in green sheets. An empty fireplace boasted intricate stonework, filled with the ashes of a dead fire. Laid atop the wood-covered floor was a thick rug. A dresser stood in the corner of the room, alongside a smaller cabinet.

Oriented, Gwair took a deep breath and moved toward the dresser.

I might not get a chance like this again—I must look for both the letter and anything that would provide insight about the remedy Throst discovered.

Although grateful for the young Lord of Herthere's remedy, Gwair could not help but feel a strange curiosity about it. Throst had only spoken of its healing capabilities, but not of its origin.

Gwair pulled open the drawers and rifled through their contents. Stacks of clothes and spare bedsheets were his only reward. Pursing his lips, he shut the dresser and moved to the cabinet. He pulled open the top drawer and was greeted by the musty scent of old paper. A thrill of excitement caused him to smile in triumph.

Inkwells, pens, paper, and other stationery lay in a meticulous fashion. Gwair grabbed the stack of paper within, pulled it out, and sifted through it. His eagerness sank as he regarded the blank pages. A single slip of paper fell from the diminishing stack in his hand, coming to rest on the floor at his feet. Gwair paused, regarded the fallen paper with narrowed eyes, and set the stack of blank pages atop the cabinet. Stooping, he grabbed the piece of paper and unfolded it. His eyes widened as he recognized the counterfeit symbol of the Phantom League.

Why does Throst have our forged message?

Folding the note in half, he put the blank pages back. Heavy footsteps sounded outside the door, and Gwair dropped the note into the open drawer. He spun around as the door swung open—and came face to face with Throst.

Standing in the open doorway, Throst regarded Gwair with a steady gaze. Gwair clenched his jaw, noticing the man's anger struggling to pierce a false facade of surprise. For several moments, the two did not venture to speak.

"I know why you're here," Throst said in a controlled tone.

Gwair resisted the urge to grab the forged note.

If the forged letter is found in my possession, it may provide the Phantom League with enough information to frame Eyoés and I for their dark deeds.

Flexing his fingers, Gwair feigned calm. "Do you, Lord Ravenstrong?" he asked, raising an eyebrow.

Throst took a step forward, his expression inquisitive. "Hranfist's death interests us both, it seems. Possibly even for the same reason," he proposed with a smile.

Steering clear of the obvious truth, Gwair glanced over Throst's shoulder with narrowed eyes, feigning suspicion. "You yourself suggested radicals siding with Vikar could have orchestrated Hranfist's demise. With the unrest among the people, and your controversial position, I fear you might be their next target," he suggested. "I overheard a strange conversation and learned there may be a threatening note in this room that may expose the situation."

Throst leaned against his bedpost. "Most interesting," he said, his tone noncommittal. "I have already reasoned the radicals would target me next. I seek to uncover their schemes and bring them to justice." An uneasy silence rested between the two of them again.

Then, clearing his throat, Gwair started toward the door, empty handed. "Take care," he mumbled. As he started past, Throst's hand shot out and seized his shoulder with a strong grip. Gwair stopped, forcing himself to meet Throst's gaze.

Looking downward, Throst sighed. "I heard about Kiffyn. It is truly a tragedy that a man lose his own brother. Although comforting, beware of nurturing false hope, my friend. Kiffyn may not return, if cruel fortune befalls him," he acknowledged.

Gwair's stomach rolled. Briskly, he pushed Throst's hand from his shoulder. "Don't speak to me of Kiffyn," he warned. Gritting his teeth, Gwair strode out of the room.

25

Stuffed full with delicacies and drink, the noblemen walked out the doors of the feast hall, followed by a crowd of servants. As the Lords departed to their quarters to rest, the clamor of conversation died to a trickle of quietly spoken words of parting. Emerging from the feasting hall behind the main body of folk, Eyoés stepped aside and looked about the main hall.

Gwair should have completed his search by now—unless something went awry.

He leaned against the stone wall. If Gwair had been found in Throst's quarters without permission, it could spell the end of their hard fought efforts. Eyoés frowned.

It would not be a pretty end, either.

He paused, pushing himself from the wall, straining to see through the crowd of servants. Gwair stood partially obscured by a pillar. His face was flushed red and he struggled to stay still, rubbing the back of his neck. Catching Eyoés' eye, Gwair gestured for him to follow as he started off down the hall.

Eyoés hesitated, then quickly weaved through the crowd of servants, following at a distance. It was clear from his manner that something was amiss. Searching for a possible explanation, Eyoés recalled Throst's early departure from the feast. His heart sank.

Did I give away Gwair's position?

Eyoés berated himself at the thought of yet another failed duty on his behalf. Drooping his head, he released a heavy sigh. In the midst of his frustration, he recalled Gwair's encouragement.

You must take responsibility for your actions, learn from them, and move on. Don't let the fear of failure render you helpless and crippled.

Briefly closing his eyes, he shut out the disappointment over his actions. Hurrying his pace to catch up with Gwair, Eyoés recalled Throst's return to the feast after his quick disappearance. His eyes widened as he came to a startling realization.

We told no one Throst's room was going to be searched, and I did not reveal that at the feast. If Throst was on edge and went to his room without clearly knowing beforehand, he must be hiding something.

Staring at the floor ahead of him with brows pulled inward, Eyoés struggled to accept his own conclusions. Recollections of his private discussion with Throst and their shared experiences rebuffed the accusation, and instead tugged at the bonds of sympathy. His thought wavered between suspicion and defense.

It is not certain Throst left the feast to go to check his quarters. For all I know, he might have had important business to attend to.

Ahead, Eyoés watched Gwair abruptly disappear around a corner. Wetting his lips, Eyoés slowed to a stop and glanced over his shoulder.

I refuse to see Throst as an enemy. Gwair will try to convince me of it.

Stepping out of cover for a brief moment, Gwair gestured urgently for him to follow. Eyoés leaned back slightly and took several hesitant steps forward.

The last time you refused to see the truth, you found yourself in the pit of despair. Do you really wish to repeat the same mistake?

The Guide's voice pierced through his reluctance, reminding Eyoés of his old faults. The pain of the recollection startled him. Closing his eyes, Eyoés sighed and pressed his lips together in a firm line.

The truth saved my life. It might do so again.

He hurried to where Gwair waited. Muttering to himself, Gwair looked up as Eyoés arrived.

He glanced about and grabbed Eyoés' shoulders. "This will be brief—this is not a safe place for lengthy discussion," he whispered, eyes darting. He shifted his position, accidentally hitting his heel against the wall. Gwair cringed. Eyoés recognized the same fear and uncertainty in Gwair's eyes that had greeted him at Merwic.

Gwair paused, making sure he would not be heard —then continued. "Throst has our letter in his possession. I don't know the reason for his special interest in Hranfist's death or why he would conceal his discovery of our note," he said.

Eyoés set a light hand on his companion's shoulder. "He might be trying to uncover the story behind Hranfist's death in order to protect the people of Hodholm. It's very much the thing he would do," he speculated, trying to comfort his friend's anguish.

Pushing Eyoés' hand from his shoulder, Gwair shook his head. "No! There's more to it than that," he insisted, his voice trailing off. He bit his tongue, reluctant to continue his thought. The questions provoking his anxiety surfaced in his mind once again.

What business does Throst have with my brother? How did he know Kiffyn was missing? I told only Vikar! I must seek the answers on my own. Eyoés does not seem to be open to the possibility of Throst's compromise.

Eyoés leaned forward and raised an eyebrow. "Such as?" he asked expectantly.

Gwair turned toward him and flashed a quick smile. "Never mind," he reassured dismissively.

Taking several hesitant steps back, Eyoés nodded toward the end of the hall. "I'm headed to the Great Library. It's about time I learn about the Ravenstrongs," he declared. "Andíamas radem."

Gwair's false smile faded as his courage was stirred by the motto of his order. Clasping arms with Eyoés, he nodded, his anguish replaced with a strong determination. "For Sword and Crown," he replied.

Shutting the door quietly behind him, Eyoés ventured into the Great Library of Hodholm. The musty scent of old pages mixed with the smoky odor of burning lamps. Only the fluttering whisper of candle flames heralded his arrival. Several large chandeliers hung from the roof to provide light to read by.

The room was circular in shape, supporting a domed roof atop several pillars equally spaced around the perimeter. Between each pillar, a wide, tall wooden shelf stretched to the top of the arched ceiling. Banners hung from several pillars, denoting the subject matter of each collection of books. A ladder was placed nearby each bookshelf to allow access to the uppermost volumes. Desks were arranged about the wide floor, and smaller shelves held books yet to be returned in their proper place. The quietness pervading the space reminded Eyoés of the stillness of twilight in the forest.

Admiring the Great Library with awe, Eyoés leaned against the nearest chair. From the meetings of the Five Heroes, he had come to know of this legendary collection—often called one of the crowning jewels of Rehillon. Few places boasted a library that could equal it, save Mithlon, the capital of Edeveros. Taekohar had much to envy in refinements of this extravagance. Eyoés made a mental note to add a grand library to Asdale's building plans for the betterment of his people. He felt a light tap on his arm from behind and turned.

To his astonishment, an elderly dwarf about half his height bowed in greeting. A finely combed grey beard tinged with streaks of white covered his chest.

His elegant maroon tunic and gilded belt outmatched the simple courtier's cloak Eyoés wore, and his white, wool head shawl gave him an aura of reverence. A pair of spectacles sat on his large nose, and his face was wrinkled with age. Eyoés' smile waned.

Even the dwarf assigned to arrange volumes and toil over these books through the night wears better finery than I.

"Welcome to the Great Library of Hodholm, sir," the dwarf declared with a warm smile. "I am Thruldin—the one in charge of the treasures here. Are you seeking something in particular?"

With a smile, Eyoés nodded and examined the shelves about him. "I wish to learn more about Rehillon's past, including the history of the noble families," he answered. The dwarf adjusted his spectacles and started toward one of the immense shelves, with Eyoés following behind.

Thruldin pointed upward to the pillars flanking either side of the shelf. Upon each was a blue banner, emblazoned with the symbol of a single tower. "This would be where the history books are kept," he explained, grasping the ladder in the middle of the shelf and beginning his ascent. "I haven't seen you before. Where do you come from?"

Eyoés steadied the ladder for the small dwarf. "Taekohar. I'm originally from Asdale," he answered. "It has been some time since I have seen a dwarf. The last I saw one of your folk was in the mountains of Iostan, near Nubaroz."

Lifting a glowing lamp from its hook on the shelf, Thruldin searched among the spines. "Ah, Nubaroz! I visited that place when all guests were welcomed—that is, before the Draed cut them off from the outside world," he remembered with a slight smile. "I was a youth in Qezul when the War of Adrógar ended. Seeking an escape from the chaos, I journeyed south to Rehillon as a book-keeper."

Squinting, the dwarf held the lamp close to the organized volumes and recited the names of each under his breath. He pulled one from its place and replaced the lamp upon its hook. "Ah, here. This is the best source I know of regarding Rehillon's history," he said, descending the ladder. Once his feet touched the floor, Thruldin handed the book to Eyoés.

Eyoés took it. "My thanks to you," he said. Clapping his fist to his opposite shoulder, he bowed in the tradition of the dwarves. Surprised, Thruldin smiled at the familiar gesture of his far-away homeland. Returning the gesture of gratitude, the dwarf adjusted his spectacles. "It is my pleasure. If you need anything more, I will be about the library," he announced. With a smile, the dwarf disappeared into the labyrinth of desks and smaller bookshelves.

Spotting a small reading desk and chair nearby, Eyoés strode toward it and seated himself. He made himself comfortable and laid the book on the table. Two leather straps held the volume closed. Upon the deep red leather cover was exquisite script inlaid with gold leaf.

The Lords of Rehillon: Founders, History, and Legacy.

Carefully undoing the leather bindings, Eyoés opened to the first page and scanned the table of contents with his finger. Finding the section he sought for, he pressed his lips together and hesitated.

Am I willing to let my own experience with Throst be challenged by another person's perspective?

Shoulders tense, he fought through his own hesitation and turned to the designated page.

The Tragedy of Eryndál Amberster and the Origins of the Ravenstrongs.

His desire for truth struggled to outweigh his common ground with Throst. Releasing a pent up breath, Eyoés started to read.

26

The Tragedy of Eryndál Amberster and the Origins of the Ravenstrongs

Baron Rhisiart Amberster's son, Eryndál, forged an early friendship with Aerard, son of Telor Lasandor, Lord of Herthere. Eryndál and Aerard stood together amid their every struggle, one supporting the other despite their differences. As noblemen, their fathers gathered together often to discuss the War of Adrógar, leaving the two sons to roam about in search of adventure. The time came when they might join their fathers' discussions and have their say as heirs. Elated and intrigued by the honor, Eryndál joined the matter wholeheartedly. However, when Aerard gained more favor in the eyes of both fathers, jealousy grew in Eryndál's heart, sowing seeds of bitterness. After nearly two years of hidden resentment, he sought out an enemy of the House of Lasandor and offered to betray his friend for a price. The man paid Eryndál handsomely, and gathered a band of villains together to accomplish the treacherous deed.

Accompanying Aerard on a forest run, Eryndál fell back, allowing his friend to charge ahead. When Aerard turned around, however, Eryndál was nowhere in sight. The enemy surrounded Aerard and took him captive. Eryndál departed the forest, with Aerard's *shouts for aid echoing behind him. Aerard was ransomed for the exact amount the embittered enemy had lost years earlier in the employ of Telor Lasandor. Shocked by the loss of his friend's son, Rhisiart Amberster cherished Eryndál all the more. Eryndál was pleased to be noticed once more by his father.*

Unfortunately for Aerard, one of the hired villains had other plans for him. Once an orphaned waif, Derwin dreamt of the prestige of nobility, and searched for opportunities to ascend to status through whatever means necessary.

Seeing his opportunity to ingratiate himself with a noble house, Derwin plotted to frame his employer as a murderer and deliver him to Aerard's family. He secretly slew Aerard under cover of night and placed his body in the Wrolm River.

When word came that Aerard, son of Telor Lasandor, had been found dead, Eryndál was plagued with guilt and hid his deed, mourning his friend's loss. He sought a way of life that would give him opportunities to do good.

Sneaking away from the band of villains, Derwin traveled to Hodholm and revealed the location of the enemy camp to Telor Lasandor in hopes of gaining his favor. Full of grief and rage, Telor assembled a large force with Rhisiart Amberster and followed Derwin's guidance into the mountains. They clashed with the band of brigands, and Telor was slain in the fight. So the Lasandor line came to an end.

In the years that passed, the War of Adrógar continued to ravage the land of Alithell. Now a grown man, Eryndál Amberster set out with the blessing of his father to join the war with an army of his own. Through times of fire and sword, Eryndál repeatedly made a name for himself by his honor and courage, and came to wed a woman and have a son of his own. Seeing his valor and skill, King Fohidras made him the Commander of the Armies of Men.

During his journeys, Eryndál received word from Hodholm bearing news of his father's death, and the passing of the Baronship to him. Torn between grief for his father and anticipation of his newfound status, Eryndál doubled his efforts in the military as the Baronship was in the temporary care of the Steward. In time, the cursing of Llumiel ended the centuries of conflict.

With an army of victors and the title of Baron, Eryndál Amberster returned to Castle Hodholm with his wife and son Arógym, who had fought alongside his father during the war. To his shock and dismay, however, the castle guard barred him from entry and threatened open battle.

Eryndál inquired as to the meaning of the uprising. As Steward of Hodholm, Derwin stood upon the ramparts and demanded Eryndál meet him privately and void of arms. In the halls of Hodholm, Derwin demanded Eryndál pledge an oath to bestow upon him noble status and a castle of his own. At first, Eryndál refused. Consumed with rage, Derwin threatened to expose the new Lord Amberster's treacherous role in Aerard's death. Anxious to rid himself of the danger of denunciation and take his rightful place as Baron,

Eryndál agreed to appoint Derwin as Lord of Castle Herthere after securing a promise of secrecy. Despite being Lady of Herthere, the dying wife of Telor Lasandor no longer remained fit to rule.

So it came to be that Derwin took upon the name Lord Ravenstrong, and became the founder of his family line. Before leaving for Herthere, Derwin sought out Arógym and revealed the details of his father Eryndál's treachery. Sickened and grieved, Arógym left his father and journeyed to Edeveros, and founded the Estworth family line. Father and son were never reunited.

Bound by his oath and the guilt of his previous betrayal, Eryndál did not challenge the Ravenstrong line, and let it continue as a noble house. The army settled back in their homes, and Eryndál did his best as Baron of Rehillon to prosper his people with the amber trade. Left without an heir, Eryndál had a second son, Nerthall, who continued the Amberster line.

After Derwin grew old and died, his hand in Aerard's death became known to history by his own entries in a private journal. Upon his deathbed, Eryndál wrote his own account to clear his conscience.

And so Eryndál Amberster fell from hero to villain in the eyes of his sons.

Slamming the book shut, Eyoés pushed it away, repulsed by the tale of treachery within. He clasped his hands together and rested his chin on his knuckles.

So this is Throst's heritage—murder, betrayal, and manipulation. Does the past serve as a warning?

A heaviness weighed upon his shoulders at the thought of Throst. The bond of kinship between them strained against his doubt. Even with firm convictions of the Ravenstrong's past, Eyoés hesitated to call Throst an enemy.

Vikar's ancestor Eryndál left a legacy of deceit and treachery, yet Vikar does not seem to commit such evil deeds. He seems to be one who highly values family and others above himself. Could it be Throst does not mirror his ancestors' faults?

Standing from his seat, Eyoés clasped his hands behind his back and started toward the library door, his face pensive. Such contradictions could only be solved with deep thought.

27

Adjusting the book underneath his arm, Throst turned a sharp left around a corner in the hallway. To his right, several pillars separated the hallway from a nearby balcony. A draft tossed his hair. Open to the outside, the balcony remained one of the few places in the castle exposed to the elements. The quiet ambience of the place provided the ideal place for contemplation and distance from the eyes of others. Looking down, he watched the stone floor pass beneath his feet.

Gwair knows about the note. What is he planning?

In the past few hours, reasons and theories had gathered as to the answer. Pursing his lips, Throst sorted through them all, and considered each on a rational level, yet found himself dissatisfied.

I will have to keep my eye on his actions. There is more going on than he would lead me to believe, and if I look close enough, there may be a chink in his armor.

Looking up, he stopped. Eyoés stood leaning against one of the balcony pillars. Throst put aside his troubling thoughts and moved toward him. Occupied with his own musings, Eyoés didn't notice the man's approach, instead fingering the beautiful amber inlays within the pillar's surface. Hesitantly, Throst cleared his throat as he came to stand alongside.

Startled, Eyoés recognized Throst. He stood straight up and moved back a step with a nod. Without a word, Eyoés looked out into the open sky.

Surprised by this cold greeting, Throst leaned against the balcony railing and set his book upon it. "Is something troubling you, Eyoés?" he inquired, the concern in his expression drawing his brows together.

Eyoés glanced at Throst out of the corner of his eye. In the light of the things he had read, the quiet, well groomed young Lord no longer seemed welcoming. The legacy of Derwin Ravenstrong stood fast between them. Drawing himself up, Eyoés hesitated as he continued to muse over the Guide's warning.

I cannot answer him. I must assume he means to lead me astray. It is better to be overly cautious in this time of uncertainty.

Seeing Eyoés' indecision, Throst moved closer and set a hand on his shoulder. "You can trust me," he insisted. "I only wish to help you."

Eyoés turned to Throst and met his gaze. A desire to share his thoughts with another man urged him to speak his mind. Hesitant to give in, Eyoés considered his options.

Might I go to Gwair and speak to him?

As he recalled the obvious anxiety of his fellow hero, Eyoés dismissed the idea.

He is not in his right mind. There are things he seeks to deal with on his own.

Uncomfortable with Throst's urging, Eyoés's eyes bounced about as he searched for a reason to refuse without upsetting him. The words left his mouth before he could stifle them. "After the feast today, I went to the Great Library, wanting to learn the history of Rehillon," he said. "I learned about your family's legacy." Realizing his lack of tact, Eyoés abruptly turned away and started to leave.

I have said too much already—I need to eliminate the chances of being tempted.

Watching the young Baron of Asdale depart, Throst nodded. "I understand. This is not the first time my ignoble heritage has caused unrest, Eyoés," he admitted, "but I have chosen to defy it."

Eyoés stopped. Turning to face the young Lord, he frowned. "What do you mean?" he asked, his tone uncertain. Pushing away from the railing, Throst took several steps forward. His face beamed with pride and confidence. Eyoés was reminded of the eagerness that had filled him to leave Asdale and see the world.

It was this eagerness to have my own will that led me on the path of revenge.

Throst smiled, his enthusiasm tugging at the walls of Eyoés' suspicion. "My forefather's reputation does not decide my destiny," he declared. "I forge my own legacy."

Eyoés held his breath, his mouth parting as Throst's statement struck him like a hammer. He closed his eyes. Even after nearly four years, the memory seemed new—the sharp bite of the wind, the cold touch of the rain, the musty odor of rotting wood, and the echoing calls of Zwaoi's terrors. For a brief moment, all seemed to disappear like a veil, billowing as an invisible hand pulled it into the sky above. Once again, Eyoés stood before the Guide, the muddy ground soft under his feet.

Leaning against his crooked staff, the Guide looked deep into his eyes, his kind gaze sending a wave of comfort to Eyoés amid his troubled mind. Through the thick fog of his own inner thoughts, the Guide spoke, his voice as clear as shimmering water.

Your father had a unique purpose. His legacy does not define you.

Then, as suddenly as it had come, the vision faded, leaving Eyoés standing on the balcony before a man he now hesitated to call friend. Standing silently before Throst, Eyoés struggled to find what to say.

Throst stepped closer and set his hands upon Eyoés' shoulders. "If it will assure you—I am more than willing to send a group of workers to aid in Asdale's construction, with your consent of course," he offered with a smile. "The glory of Hodholm could become the honor of Asdale!"

At these words, the vivid image of Asdale clad in the splendor of might and beauty, wreathed in clouds and sunlight filled Eyoés' thoughts. The tender whispers of great promises surrounded him like the sighing wind. His breath quickened, and a warmth flooded over him like the desert sun. Upon a chair of crafted stone and jewels he sat, with nearly ten chests full of gold resting at his feet. Eyoés sucked in a quick breath.

How it glimmers in the sun—and for it to be within my reach...

His fingers longed to reach out and touch the forbidden treasure.

Throst can give me this? What will he ask for in return?

A surge of anger welled up inside, stirring up the old vestiges of anger and fury that remained. Eyoés gritted his teeth.

He will never lay his hands on the gold. It is mine!

Eyoés stared at the vivid image, his mind enraptured by the manifestation of his struggle. A hand stretching from a white sleeve appeared from nothing, stretching out and sending a pillar of consuming fire at the chests of treasure. As the billowing flames of unearthly fire filled Eyoés' eyes, a voice reached through the darkness and seized him with incredible force.

What you see demands a heavy cost, and will only vanish in the flames. The purpose I have given you does not merely stand against the fire, but extinguishes it. Why exchange the everlasting for things which will pass away? There is something greater than mere wealth, and I have given it to you. Beware of fools who would tempt you with their fleeting promises.

The images faded from his mind. Looking into Throst's steady gaze, Eyoés stepped back. "I cannot accept your generosity, Throst," he said.

Giving a quick smile, Throst backed down and bowed. "As you wish," he conceded.

Eyoés paused, regarding Throst with a questioning eye. The vividness of what he had seen stoked a desire to fight. Tilting his head, he raised an eyebrow.

"Prosperity is a shield," he recalled. "Forgive my blatancy, but such a creed appears to be Derwin's greed in disguise. How do you reconcile this?" He drew himself up with a gleam in his eye.

Throst, impressed by the young Baron of Asdale's reasoning, wasted no time in answering. "Greed and desire are two different creatures—the former can never be satisfied, but the latter will be content once it finds what it seeks," he reasoned, gesturing with his hands to accentuate his point. "When you desire water, you quench your thirst, but if you drink the whole barrel, you will tear yourself apart from within. It all depends on your own discernment and self-control."

The confidence in Eyoés weakened. Despite the strength of his own judgement, the reasoning behind Throst's argument caught him off guard.

Are discernment and self-control really the only difference between greed and desire? Such an answer is hard to grasp.

With a wavering smile, Eyoés bowed. "I must be on my way," he said. "I have things to attend to." Throst bowed in return, and Eyoés pressed his lips into a firm line and turned away. As he disappeared from view, Throst smiled.

28

Gwair marched down the hall, face red as he mumbled to himself. His bewilderment at this unforeseen turn of events stirred up his agitation, filling his head with angry ramblings and wounded emotions.

Vikar must have spoken of Kiffyn, though I clearly asked him to keep it to himself.

Ahead, the closing of a door caused him to look up. Vikar started down the hall in Gwair's direction, rifling through papers. Scowling, Gwair clapped twice, palms stinging. At the sound, Vikar noticed him. Before he could speak, Gwair pointed to the closed door of the Baron's chamber. "You are not done here —I must speak with you in private," he demanded.

Taken aback by the straightforward challenge, Vikar halted, incredulous. He altered his course and opened the door to invite Gwair in. Interest surpassed the affront for the time being, and Vikar frowned.

Such gruffness is out of character for Gwair.

Shoving past the Baron, Gwair entered the room. Vikar shut the door and rubbed the back of his neck. "What is the matter, my friend?" he said.

Gwair swiftly spun on his heels to face the Baron. "You gave me your word," he scolded, the insult cutting deep. "Kiffyn's disappearance was to be our secret. No one was to know!"

Reflecting on his friend's words, Vikar wavered—then roughly scrubbed a hand over his face. "There was one time—I forgot Throst was in the room," he recalled. "During the delivery of my morning dispatches, I asked Hranfist if there was news of Kiffyn. At the time, I had thought the incident would be of little consequence, so I kept it to myself."

Gwair shook his head. "This castle is no longer a safe haven. Your slip of awareness may have put my brother in peril!" he exclaimed, leaning against Vikar's desk.

"Rigorous concealment and deception is not my way. With such a sudden shift to secrecy, I struggle to know what to reveal and what to keep unspoken," Vikar said.

Gwair closed his eyes and put his hand to his forehead. The turmoil kept him from thinking clearly. Anger at Vikar's actions urged him to retaliate with sharp words. Pity for the Baron's bad timing and ill fortune appealed to a higher sense of reconciliation.

How can I expect an honest man to navigate the world of deception with ease? I should have kept Kiffyn's disappearance to myself and revealed it to Vikar when he was ready.

Pressing his lips tightly together, Vikar stepped forward, unsure of himself as he set a hand on Gwair's shoulder. "I would never willingly put Kiffyn's life in danger—you know this," he maintained, sorrowful.

"My actions grieve me. I vow to guard my tongue in the future. I beg your forgiveness."

Lifting his head, Gwair regarded the hand on his shoulder, avoiding direct eye contact. "I forgive you," he said. He pushed away from the table and strode out of the room, conflicted.

Whether or not he meant it, he would have to decide.

Eyoés sauntered down the halls of Hodholm, the discussion with Throst tumbling through his head. Where once had been friendliness and trust in Throst, there was now uncertainty. The more Eyoés turned over Throst's viewpoints, the more he saw faults in them—as much as he hated to consider it.

Looking up, he spotted Gwair. Seated on a bench, he leaned forward, resting his forearms on his knees. His lips moved silently. From the man's gloomy expression, Eyoés could tell something wore away at him. He approached, reluctant to disturb him.

Gwair spotted him and sat up. "What have you found?" he asked, cutting straight to the point. The lack of cordiality in his tone warned Eyoés to speak carefully.

Deliberating on his words, Eyoés seated himself. "The dissension between the Ambersters and the Ravenstrongs is too far in the past. Whatever your suspicions about Throst, this would be an unlikely motive for ill," he said, keeping his voice down.

Gwair frowned and stroked his beard. "Are you certain? It is logical for a learned man such as Throst to find grounds for discord in the lore of his homeland," he reasoned.

Reluctantly, Eyoés considered the idea. "Possibly, but it is difficult to know for sure," he speculated. "We must be watchful." As much as he wished for Throst to remain a friend, Eyoés compelled himself to indulge Gwair's suspicions. He adjusted his seat, expression betraying his unease.

From the corner of his eye, Gwair noticed Eyoés' uncertainty, and sank back into the melancholy of contemplation.

29

Streams of colored light played upon Eyoés' face. Mesmerized by the stained glass window before him, he leaned in, his mouth parting in amazement. All else faded away in the splendor of the moment, giving him a much sought after respite.

Frozen in time was the scene of Eryndál Amberster's return to Hodholm. Stained a dark red in a testament to his wicked soul, Derwin Ravenstrong stood upon the ramparts of Castle Hodholm, glaring down at the army stationed before the gates. Seated on a mighty warhorse, Eryndál looked up at the traitor, a halo of light surrounding him like the sun. Above the heads of each man, was the coat of arms for his noble house.

Eyoés narrowed his eyes in thought as he regarded the tale immortalized in colorful glass.

How Eryndál would protest had he seen himself portrayed as a flawless man of honor! I pray to the King that, in my legacy, I would be depicted as I really am—a faulty man whose only claim to goodness is the mercy of his King.

The scuffing of light shoes came from the stone floor behind him, and Eyoés turned. To his surprise, Caywen stood before him, frozen to the spot. A flush grew across her face. "My deepest apologies—I did not mean to disturb you," she blurted, moving to leave.

Eyoés held out a hand to stay her. "No, please," he insisted with a welcoming smile. "I would be glad of the company." Relieved of her embarrassment, Caywen pursed her lips into a thin smile, entering the small nook surrounding the stained glass window. As she stood beside him, a rainbow of colored light flittered across her green dress. Her eyes gleamed as she admired the grandeur of the fine craftsmanship. Many times had she stopped in the middle of her rushed life to contemplate and seek solace from its beauty.

Caywen looked at Eyoés, the reds, greens, blues, and whites of the window gleaming in her eye. "I've heard stories about your journey to Zwaoi, and the battle you fought in the North alongside the Dwarves," she said.

The respect and admiration in her words caused Eyoés to shake his head with a smile of humorous disbelief. "People have praised me for my deeds many times since then—but the glory is the King's, not mine," he maintained. "I was blind to the truth in those days. I am glad they are over."

Looking back to the scene in glass, Caywen fixed her gaze on the forest portrayed in the background. Her eyes softened as she lost herself in the greens and browns, imagining herself walking beneath the shelter of the boughs. "For years, I have dreamed of packing my things, wishing my father goodbye, and embarking on an adventure of my own," she spoke, marveling at the escapades she imagined. "The lands I would see, the people I would meet, the excitement—"

Eyoés set a hand on her shoulder, and she turned to face him. Closing his eyes briefly, he collected his thoughts. He opened his eyes and looked steadily into hers. "I used to think the same, Caywen. I found, however, adventure is not always glorious. There's violence. Pain. Weariness," he said. "It is not for the faint of heart."

At this, Caywen's expression became pensive. "I might not always be strong, but in dark times, when strength is needed, I hope I will find the courage," she wondered aloud.

Eyoés leaned forward. "I do not doubt it," he declared with a smile. He released her shoulder and stepped back. Glancing toward the window, his smile faded. Behind his mighty father Eryndál, Arógym observed the tense standoff on a slightly smaller steed. His brows were pulled up, and lines of confusion and uncertainty creased his features. The very image interpreted in stained glass spoke of the tragic ending to the story.

Eyoés found himself unable to look away. "What is it like, growing up with a family?" he asked.

Unaware of her companion's longing, she smiled, chuckling to herself. "If there is any better example of devotion, I have yet to find it," she declared, her face upturned. "Family stands beside you, despite your struggles. They love you always, and guide you in your times of confusion and uncertainty." Her smile took a grim turn, and her voice became tearful. The sudden bleakness of her mood brought Eyoés down into the pit of melancholy. "It is a pity some are robbed of such a love. It's been only two years since mother died," Caywen muttered.

Eyoés began to reply when Rodmer's striding footsteps down the hall cut him off. His hands shot up in annoyance as he caught Caywen's eye. "There you are! Come, Caywen," he exclaimed, glancing toward Eyoés with a narrowed eye. "You have more *pressing* things to do." Taking hold of her by the shoulder, he pulled her away, leaving Eyoés alone under the unblinking eyes of Eryndál and Arógym.

30

3rd of Iaulan, 2202 SE

Laying on an improvised bed of folded blankets, Beydan let out a groan and opened his eyes. A throbbing headache pounded like several smithies in the middle of his forehead. He reached up to touch the spot, feeling the rough linen bandage wrapped around his skull. Blinking to clear his blurred vision, he moved to sit up. Beydan caught sight of a young man sitting at his bedside and stopped.

As the recollection of his lost duel, he wrinkled his nose in disgust and fell onto the bed with a laugh of spite. "You again," he growled. "What do you want now, whelp? You've already humiliated me once!" Leaning forward in his seat, Marc reached out to adjust Beydan's bandage. With a frown, the Captain batted his hand away.

Marc shifted his position on the hard floor of the tent and rubbed his sore knees. "I want nothing, Captain. I'm simply here to tend to your needs for the time being," he said. "You were unconscious for half an hour, but you'll be well enough by nightfall, except for a sore brow."

Propping himself on an elbow, Beydan looked toward the tent entrance and scowled. "I'll like to give *her* a sore brow! Where is she?" he asked.

Marc shook his head and regarded his Captain with a stern eye, even though Beydan avoided it. "Gwyndel bandaged your wounds! Even as we speak, she is encouraging the men to accept your orders," he exclaimed with indignant frustration. Taking a breath, Marc calmed himself and moved closer to Beydan's bedside. "Captain, I might not always agree with your character, but I can say this—you fought well. I respect you and forgive you for your actions," he said with finality. "I may not have been under your command for very long, but I can see the strength you instill in your men. They look up to you because of your confidence and courage, despite your faults. All men and women are marked by their own imperfections. You still have the makings of a great leader."

At this, Beydan met Marc's gaze with a blank look. After years of loneliness, he felt a connection to the boy's mannerisms and sense of principle.

Caydell spoke with the same peculiarity.

In a fleeting moment, he saw his brother standing before him, a smile on his face. A yearning to be reunited with Caydell caused Beydan to rise from the bed. The vision faded, a sullen hole tearing wider in Beydan's heart. Sitting back on the bed, he regarded Marc, recalling the fury that held him as he sought to end the boy's life. Narrowing his eyes, Beydan cleared his throat and sat up.

I fought to kill him, and he tells me I not only fight well, but inspire my own men? What does he mean by this?

Beydan absentmindedly rubbed at his ear. "What is your name? I can't remember the names of all my company," he inquired.

The young man saluted his superior. "Marcas, son of Wilnor—but those who make my acquaintance know me as Marc," he answered. "I'm part of the rear guard."

Eager for answers, Beydan nodded with a wave of his hand. "Very well, Marc," he said. "What do you mean by your compliments? I don't understand."

Marc smiled and removed a small book from the satchel laying beside him. "In my homeland of Edeveros, we live by a code of honor—to live by the King's Proverbs and treat others in a respectful, noble, and honorable way, even if they don't deserve it," he explained, extending the book to the Captain. "In the Proverbs, and in submission to the King, there is true honor that cannot be gained by a duel. Yes, we might win prestige and position, which is important in its own way. Yet it is *true* honor that separates us from the animals, who cannot honor their creator with their conduct and treatment of others."

Silently regarding the book, Beydan hesitantly took it in hand. Two leather straps held the book shut for safekeeping, and golden leather trim surrounded the edges. Painted in the middle of the cover was a golden wing and a crown meshed into one symbol, surrounded by a blue circle. Beydan regarded the small volume, tracing the edge of the book with his finger.

Such honor as Marc speaks of I have not considered since Caydell's death—yet it calls to me.

Marc noticed the Captain's interest. "I received this book of the King's Proverbs from my parents when I set out from my home of Gahidros. It has been a steady companion and place of solace to me," he added. "For the time being, it may be the same for you."

Beydan resolutely extended the book toward Marc. "I cannot take this from you," he said. The irritation and bitterness of his own defeat at the young man's hands seemed a trifle in light of his kindness.

Flashing a quick smile, Marc pushed the book back towards the Captain. "I would rather let you borrow it and learn of a better path, than keep it for myself and let you continue on," he maintained. Beydan looked at the book once again and laid it beside him without further refusal. Standing from the improvised bed, he walked to the tent entrance and pulled the flap aside with his hand to allow a view outside. Among the white canvas tents, he glimpsed the Forester elf speaking and associating with the men.

At the sight of her, Beydan stepped back from the tent entrance and let the flap fall back into place. "What motivated you to come to Gwyndel's aid? You knew I could kill you, yet you persisted," he asked, looking at his feet.

Marc stood, his small frame dwarfed by the Captain's. "You did the dishonorable by challenging her to a fight to the death. She would not be able to last long against your attack. Not only this, but you publicly treated her with contempt," he dared. "I could not have stood idly by while she died the death of an enemy. You lessened yourself in the eyes of the men."

Nodding, Beydan sat on the end of his bed. Caydell would have chastised him in the same way. Beydan realized the young man's input was valid. "It wasn't a wise thing for me to be carried away by my rage," he admitted. Swallowing hard, he hung his head as the pain of Gwyndel's actions surfaced. He cleared his throat.

She took advantage of my absence and delved into the most private memories from my past. The things I had sought to bury.

His shoulders drooped, and he turned to look at Marc. "Even if I had not challenged her, she betrayed my trust. The pain still grieves me. I cannot reconcile myself with her—not yet," he insisted with a quaver in his voice.

As he stood beside his wounded Captain, Marc sighed. "Not a wise choice, but I understand. In time you will forgive her," he assured, "but I advise caution —we are about to march into the jaws of the Phantom League. If you should fall in Weomor, Gwyndel will live the rest of her life in shame over her mistake—if she and the other men survive. Divisions do not just heal. It takes time and purposeful leadership to bind these wounds."

Abruptly standing, Beydan faced the young man and set his jaw. "I will not fall," he declared.

Marc smiled. "And the Loyalists will assure that," he answered with a salute. "We await your orders."

Beydan's countenance softened. Spotting his falchion sheathed at the head of his bed, he picked it up, fingering the leather scabbard. "I still cannot understand why the men would even consider me their leader. I allowed division in the camp, and was bested by a warrior half my age," he confessed. "Surely they will obey me with reluctance."

Stepping forward to challenge this notion, Marc clasped the falchion's scabbard alongside Beydan's hand in a gesture of friendship. "You are mistaken. We do not see ourselves as your men, but as your brothers. Brothers care for one another, and are loyal despite the other's faults. *That* is why we follow you," he said.

Beydan looked down at his hand, and the small hand of the soldier before him.

These men would die defending me, regardless of my faults. I will not continue to be one so undeserving of their loyalty.

"Tell the men to prepare to rise early tomorrow morning. We leave for Weomor at dawn," Beydan announced.

31

4th of Iaulan, 2202 SE

Gwyndel and Beydan ducked behind a stack of whitened boulders. Whistling through the boughs and across the exposed stone, the crisp morning wind chilled Gwyndel's face. Clouds gave way before the sun, allowing the land below to enjoy a brief moment of repose from the dreary weather.

Gwyndel took several deep breaths to calm herself. She envisioned breaking into Kiffyn's dark cell with the Loyalists and rescuing her old friend from the jaws of the Phantom League. Her heartbeat increased.

Kiffyn rescued me when I could do little to defend myself. It is my turn to return the favor.

Eyes glowing with eagerness, Gwyndel looked to where Beydan crouched beside her. His lips were pressed together in a slight grimace as he met her gaze and nodded. As one, they peered over the boulders hiding them from unwanted eyes.

The hill where they hid sloped downward into a large clearing, surrounded by forest. Rocks lay scattered in the tall grass, overgrown with moss and lichen. In the center of the open space stood a large ruin, a monument to a story of loss and woe. Like jagged mountain peaks, the remains of a large military fortification created an intimidating labyrinth. Rising above the maze of ruins was a towerhouse, nearly intact save for the occasional breach in its walls or the eroded surface of stone. To Gwyndel's eye, it seemed abandoned. Her excitement at the possibility of rescuing Kiffyn momentarily quelled the cautious nature of her Forester training.

Falling back into cover, Gwyndel smiled. "It seems deserted. The quicker we rescue Kiffyn the better," she whispered.

Her eagerness waned as Beydan gruffly shook his head and bit his lip to keep himself from speaking everything on his mind. He avoided her gaze and examined the castle ruins below with a probing eye. "My years in the Northern Guard have taught me otherwise. Never assume your own safety—we *are* dealing with the Phantom League," he remarked, his expression stern. "I can tell Kiffyn means much to you, but I know the Phantom League is hiding among those rocks. This time, we are the ones creeping through the shadows. But beware—men of secrecy know what to look for. They may pick us off if we are not watchful."

Gwyndel's eagerness turned to confusion. She was bewildered as to why his words were lacking their usual biting sarcasm. Her shoulders drooped as she glanced back to where the troops waited the command to enter Weomor.

Ever since the duel, he has been willing to work with me without complaint. Why does he no longer lash out in open anger or purposely provoke me?

She leaned closer to Beydan and studied his expression. Catching a glimpse of her movement,

Beydan glanced at Gwyndel and hastily looked away. His eyes bounced about as he furrowed his brow. Despite his attempts to keep his inner strife from her, Gwyndel could tell something was amiss.

Before the duel, Beydan did nothing about the disunity in his ranks, and it was Marc who spoke of unity to the men. Perhaps Beydan realizes that if we do not stand as one, we will fall to the enemy.

Beydan cleared his throat and interrupted the elf's thoughts. "Kiffyn is most likely locked away in the towerhouse, where intruders would have a more difficult time reaching him," he mused. "We have a better chance against the Phantom League if we break up into separate forces and approach the ruins from three sides. I will come from the south, you from the north, and Marc from the west. When we reach the towerhouse, we can join back together."

Gwyndel turned her thoughts toward the task at hand, evaluating the situation with the experience of her Forester training. She nodded in agreement and examined the deceptively tranquil castle further. "The Phantom League cannot ambush all three of the contingents, and it will be easier to maneuver in the confines of the ruins," she said.

Tightly grasping the handle of his falchion, Beydan gave a last, wary glance toward the ruins and started toward the place where the Loyalists were hidden. "I'll give the command," he said.

Gwyndel grasped Beydan's shoulder, causing him to turn. She steadily met his eye. "Thank you, Beydan —for helping me rescue my friend," she remarked.

Beydan gave a half-hearted smile, looked away, and descended down the hill to the Loyalists' location.

The crumbling walls of Weomor hemmed the Loyalists in on both sides, like the claws of a beast surrounding its prey. The smell of mildew hung in the air. Black streaks of ash told of a fiery end to the castle's past livelihood. The remains of arches crested over their heads, barely supported by the walls to either side. Crevices and empty corridors led to places of shadow. Above, a large cluster of clouds stifled the sunlight. The grass muffled the crunching of gravel and broken cobblestone under the men's boots.

Gripping Fóbehn, Gwyndel searched the crags and gaps in the ruins with wide eyes, tensed to fight. Yet, the desire to leave the danger ahead and return to safety slowed her steps.

A grim silence pervaded the shell of Castle Weomor, save the clink of chainmail as the Loyalists wove through the web of causeways. Whispering wind taunted the advancing force with its hushed voice. For a brief moment, a black mist wove in and out of the ruins. Like smoke, it enwreathed the broken stones and seeped through the cracks, curling and twisting. Gwyndel shivered and forced herself to look away, glancing over her shoulder to assure the men's formation remained steady.

Advancing further in, the Loyalist soldiers eyed the surrounding ruin with apprehension. Several men took the position of the rear guard, facing the opposite direction to assure there were no attacks from behind. Such precautions would rob the Phantom League of any easy opportunity. Of this they all knew. It was the fear of unexpected attack that preyed at their nerves, adding to the impression of unseen terrors.

A sudden cawing came from their left as a crow was startled from its perch. They halted and spun toward the noise, weapons poised. For minutes, they stood still. When no enemy appeared, the men lowered their weapons and resumed their march, shaken by the sudden rush of panic.

Glimpsing the towerhouse between the gaps in the surrounding ruins, Gwyndel aimed Fóbehn at the dark recesses.

Surely we should have stumbled upon the enemy by now. Something is amiss...

The images of what could be flashed through her mind and she rebuked them under her breath. The causeway broadened as the towerhouse came into full view before them. To their right, a patch of overgrown brush filled in a gap in the stone structures. Curving to the left, the causeway steered clear of the deep moat surrounding the towerhouse. Because of the dreary and wet weather of the region, the moat remained full of stagnant, stinking water. A weather-bleached bridge crossed over the moat's boggy mire and ended directly inside the entrance.

As Gwyndel and her contingent approached, the square towerhouse rose over them like a giant, topped with a sloping roof of weakened stone. A flock of sparrows took flight from the steeple. The keep walls were stained halfway up with streaks of ash.

On the other side of the bridge, Gwyndel saw Beydan and his group enter the open causeway. She raised a clenched fist, and the Loyalists behind her stopped, ready for orders. The rustling of brush from behind the towerhouse drew her attention. Emerging from the ruins with his glaive poised for combat, Marc circled around the moat to Gwyndel's position. He signaled for his assigned troops to follow.

Gwyndel hurried her pace, and urged her men on. The three groups of Loyalists converged at the bridge. Beydan stationed Marc's contingent to guard, then motioned for Gwyndel to come with him. With a nod, she stepped forward. He tightly gripped the handle of his falchion, his posture unflinching.

It was his eyes that alarmed her. His gaze held a morbid expectancy, strained with the uncertainty of escape. The usual gleam of sarcastic confidence was gone. His resignation sowed seeds of apprehension in Gwyndel's heart. Saying nothing, they hurriedly crossed the bridge to the towerhouse entrance, the stench of the putrid moat making Gwyndel gag.

There was no door. The event that destroyed the rest of the castle by fire had left the towerhouse unprotected. Only the hinges remained fast in the stone surrounding the entrance. Beydan leaned against the stonework and peered inside. The troops shifted uneasily, eyes alert for trouble. Gwyndel stood rigid as she observed the ruins around them for signs of danger. Her eyes scanned the destruction. Standing in a tall section of grass and weeds was an old mausoleum, its roof broken down. The vacant doorway of the sepulcher seemed to laugh in dark foreboding of things to come.

Beydan withdrew from the doorway. "Although we might not see it, the enemy is waiting for the right time to ensnare us. It is only a matter of when and where," he said in a low voice. "Tell Marc and the men to enter in single file and proceed up the stairs behind me. We must move quickly."

Gwyndel nodded and crossed the bridge to where the Loyalists waited. Standing at the front of the group, Marc clutched his glaive as Gwyndel relayed the Captain's order. The wide, single-edged blade of the pole weapon reminded her of a carving knife.

Assured the men understood, Beydan advanced. The Loyalists hastily followed, eager to escape the danger of exposure.

As they disappeared into the keep, Gwyndel followed, her lips stretched into a thin line. She forced herself to avoid dark thoughts.

May the Guide protect us.

Like a troop of ants, the line of soldiers disappeared through the keep's doorway, until the rear guard passed through. Returning the arrow to her quiver and shrugging Fóbehn onto her shoulder, Gwyndel started up the stairs with Marc and the others.

32

Breathless, Gwyndel pushed her way to the top of the stairs through the line of soldiers. Her heartbeat increased as she struggled to get to the front.

I'm coming Kiffyn!

Shoving past the last few Loyalists in her way, she passed through the wide entryway and stepped aside.

The chamber was capable of containing the entire unit of Loyalists, with room to spare. The stone tile ceiling soared above them, supported by old, rotting wood—tentatively keeping the roof from falling onto their heads. Chairs and other furniture were scattered across the room, along with the occasional weapon, old and unfit for use. Two large chandeliers hung from the wooden roof supports. A sizable window in the left wall allowed fresh air in. Cobwebs clung to the corners of the room, and an abandoned birds nest perched precariously upon one of the chandeliers.

Preoccupied with Kiffyn's rescue, Gwyndel barely noticed the surroundings. Seeing Beydan standing in the middle of the room, she strode toward him with a growing smile. The Captain raised a hand to ward off her approach—but she paid no heed. Grasping Beydan's shoulder, she pushed him aside. Her smile faded. She gasped, her hand flying to her mouth.

A vacant wood chair sat before them, stained with blood and sweat. Beside the chair were shackles and a pile of chains—lying next to that was a scrap of metal crudely fashioned into a lock pick.

Hot tears fell from Gwyndel's eyes, and she swallowed the lump in her throat.

Kiffyn escaped? Is he still alive? Where could he be?

Her expression contorted in confusion, and she slowly turned to face Beydan, chin trembling. The Captain's eyes grew ever wider, and his hands began to tremble. For a brief moment, they hesitated as the gravity of the situation came to rest fully in their minds.

Wild eyed, Beydan drew his falchion. "It's a ruse! Retreat! NOW!" he roared, voice breaking in panic.

Flaming arrows shot through the open doorway behind them, embedding into the already compromised roof supports. With an audible whoosh, the wood alighted in a burst of flames. Gwyndel and Beydan turned, weapons at the ready. Filling the entryway was a massive brute of a man, backed by shrouded Phantom Leaguers.

A wicked grin twisted his features. "Beware the wrath of the phoenix," Amnedd jeered. With a cry, the Loyalists rushed at the enemy. The double doors slammed shut, cutting off their escape. Throwing weapons aside, the frontmost soldiers rammed their shoulders into the door, to no avail. Their fear of sudden ambush had been realized.

The room filled with a smoky haze. Flames swept along the walls, licking up moss and other debris in its path. Desperate cries of confusion were choked off by the thick smoke. Several Loyalists hacked at the door with their weapons. With each breath, their strokes weakened as they struggled to breathe. In desperation, the others raced to the open window, wildly shoving each other out of the way for a precious gulp of cool air. One of the men leapt from the windowsill with a cry, falling to his death amid the ruins. A desperate few followed his example.

Using clothing to shield their faces, each man left strove to outlast the other in hopes of discovering a path to freedom. Smoke and flame smothered the daylight, enveloping them in growing darkness. The stone walls cracked in the heat. Beydan's shouted commands added to the turmoil as he struggled to gather his men. At the window, Marc gulped in a blast of cool air before being shoved aside. They lost track of each other in the enfolding smoke.

Trembling, Gwyndel stood amid the chaos, everything around her blurring. The old scars from dragon flame sent a wave of pain through her body. With a cry, she fell to the ground. Over the commotion, a screeching roar pierced her ears. Struggling to take a deep breath, Gwyndel lifted her head.

A dark, looming shape lingered behind the curtain of fire. Heavy footfalls pounded in a steady rhythm as the silhouette grew in size. Emerging from the flames with another piercing shriek, the pale Norzaid locked its crimson gaze on the fallen elf. Gwyndel screamed, clapping her hands over her ears. Contorted in a grim smile, its maw opened, revealing rows of jagged fangs. A deep orange glow flashed in its throat, and Gwyndel struggled to rise. The beast's wings spread wide above its head, sending smoke curling across the floor. Gwyndel gripped Fóbehn with resolve and nocked an arrow to the bowstring. Digging its claws into the stone floor, the Norzaid shot forward, flames coursing from its mouth. Gwyndel raised the weapon and drew back.

The dragon vanished, leaving Gwyndel standing with Fóbehn in hand. Sobbing, she fell to her knees. The cries of the Loyalists faded from her ears, as the pain of trauma and despair spread through her.

Then, through the dark voices of desperation, a quiet, recognizable voice caught her attention.

Your perseverance in the face of despair and darkness has pleased me.

The words seemed like fresh air amid the thick smoke about her. Lifting her head, Gwyndel watched the mayhem unfolding about her. Several Loyalists had succumbed to smoke and lay dead on the floor. Others, too exhausted to fight any longer, gave themselves up for lost. Smeared with ash, Beydan and Marc fought on, ripping off their outer shirts and batting the flames. The wooden supports above their heads creaked precariously, now struggling to bear the full weight of the stone roof.

Use the blessed bow. There is still hope—I am with you.

A surge of strength coursed through Gwyndel, despite her shock and fear. Gripping Fóbehn, she stood, searching for an opportunity. Across the room, she caught sight of a small door, barely wide enough to admit two men side by side. She looked upward to the chandeliers hanging in the flames above their heads.

Drawing the arrow back to her cheek, she isolated the single ring holding the main chain tethered to the ceiling and let fly. The arrow split the ring, and the chandelier smashed through the small door.

The Loyalists turned at the sudden crash. Seeing a path to freedom, they rushed the entry, each picking forsaken weapons and shields off the ground. The Loyalists charged through the opening.

Gwyndel's knees buckled, and she collapsed, overtaken by the tumultuous clash of terror, shock, and relief. Their throats dry and swollen, Beydan and Marc started for the door.

Marc's beaming expression faded. Through the haze of smoke to his right, he glimpsed a green Forester shirt. Marc raced back into the fiery chaos. In vain, Beydan reached out to stay him. His stomach clenched as the roof supports creaked and under the weight of the roof.

If this boy dies, I lose my greatest reminder of Caydell.

"Marc!" he roared, dashing after him, then skidding to an abrupt halt. Marc gritted his teeth and struggled to hoist Gwyndel onto his shoulder. Sheathing his falchion, Beydan fell to one knee at her side and heaved her from the floor with a grunt. The supports groaned. One broke away and fell to the floor with a shuddering crash. They raced for the open door.

Wielding his glaive, Marc sailed through the door first. As they left, the last of the supports gave way. Rubble rained down in a smoldering heap, shaking the entire towerhouse like an earthquake.

They bolted down the stairs, trailing the main force of Loyalists. From below, the Loyalists' roars of determination and bravery resounded against the old stone walls. Cries of panic accompanied the scurrying of feet.

With glaive poised for action, Marc led the way, scanning for signs of danger. Beydan urged him onward, struggling to hold Gwyndel steady in his arms. He glanced downward.

Her face was pale, and she stared upward, motionless—but not unconscious. As the irony of his predicament came to him, Beydan snorted under his breath.

I am now saving one who yesterday I would have left for dead. Quite an unexpected way of making amends.

Stumbling on the last stair, Beydan watched soldiers exit the towerhouse through the back door just feet in front of them. Hurrying their pace, Marc and Beydan fled out of the towerhouse and into the ruins. The courtyard was strewn with the bodies of assassins who had vainly attempted to push back the frenzied mob.

At the creaking of a bowstring, Marc spun on his heels. Beydan rushed by with Gwyndel and raced to the edge of the ruins. A single mercenary leapt to his feet from behind a pile of rubble and let fly. The arrow punched into Marc's right shoulder, shuddering as it pierced his chainmail shirt. Grunting in pain, he stumbled back. The assassin hurried to nock a second arrow.

Pushing past the pain, Marc hurled his glaive at the mercenary, piercing the man's light armor. The bow fell from the Phantom Leaguer's grasp as he collapsed. Retrieving his weapon, Marc turned and fled the towerhouse.

The ruins meshed into a mass of green and grey as he ran. He inhaled a deep draught of fresh air, seeing Beydan and the Loyalists vanishing into the forest ahead of him. Marc quickly covered the exposed ground and disappeared into the cover of the trees.

Having barely escaped the initial stampede of Loyalists, Amnedd stumbled from the ruins, his breath coming in ragged heaves. The smoke of his burning fury consumed him. His heartbeat resounded in his ears like the footsteps of his escaping foes. With a roar, Amnedd ripped the fur mantle from his shoulders and dashed it to the wet ground.

The wolf had lost its prey.

33

6th of Iaulan, 2202 SE

The familiar, fresh scent of new rain seemed an old companion of the garrison of Hodholm. The layered wool clothing of the guards shielded them from the cold, and steam rolled from their mouths with each breath. Raindrops tinkled on their steel vambraces and helmets. It was a quiet morning, when the civilians of the town indulged themselves with sleep in anticipation of the weekly holiday. Even in the garrison, minds were untroubled. In the courtyard of Hodholm, however, such was not the case.

Gwair completed his fifth lap around the castle courtyard. His shoulders were stiff, and his overall posture was rigid with tension. The wet, dreary weather mirrored his own troubled spirit.

The steady beat of pattering rain was stifled by the throbbing headache hammering away at his skull. Overwhelmed by his circling emotions and thoughts, Gwair stared at his moving feet. The grass occasionally growing through the cracks in the stone became a blur of green as Gwair's pace increased with the intensity of his mood. With a forceful sigh, he reluctantly faced the troubling thoughts one at a time.

How could Vikar tell others about Kiffyn? He knows the danger we face together, yet he spoke without thinking of the potential consequences! How could I trust him again?

The recollection sent a wave of heat over his face. His expression bore an obvious hurt that fought with the hard look of anger in his eyes. With each moment spent dwelling on the offense, Gwair's steps became more uneven, losing their speed and purpose. He put his hand to his forehead.

Vikar did not mean to hurt you. For his entire life, he never had to face an unseen enemy—and you expect him to know what to keep to himself and what to speak aloud?

With a sigh, Gwair slowed his steps and lifted his head. He had heard the voice before, and was familiar with it. Recognizing the one who spoke, he set aside his conflicted sentiments.

Gwair hesitated, unsure how to respond. Despite his own opinions, the Guide's words wore away as he considered truth.

In my years of knowing Vikar, he has faced clear and certain danger with boldness. It is not his way to be absentminded in such matters.

Pinching his lips together, Gwair abandoned his dying argument in favor of a new claim.

Why have you not given us a breakthrough in these matters? Why is our enemy still concealed in darkness with no evidence to expose his guilt?

Despite Gwair's persisting frustration, it was the reason for the trials of their mission he really longed for. Not knowing *why* played dark tricks in his heart. The tension in his muscles eased as his aggravation gave way to an eager desire for truth. From his time spent with the King, Gwair knew the Guide *would* answer.

Perhaps he will shine a new light on his situation, or reveal some secret only he could know.

The Guide addressed neither of these. His quiet voice was as gentle as the rain dampening Gwair's clothing.

Have patience, my son. Even in times of chaos, my hand is moving. In time, things will be revealed to you that will spur you onward. Remember the Proverb of Fydenir—The one who believes in the King's sovereign power will overcome. He will witness the coming of victory.

A sense of calm replaced his anxiety and frustration, assuring him of the truth. The strain in Gwair's countenance faded, and he looked upward. Drops of rain fell onto his face and rolled down his cheeks like tears of hope. Even though Gwair's faith did not manifest itself outwardly, he felt it spurring on his determination.

Gwair let his eyes wander about the courtyard. As he observed the high keep and towers of Hodholm, and the ramparts soaring above him, he paused.

What about the future of Rehillon? Even if the enemy is exposed, darkness will have its way if we are too late to deny its rule.

A crack of thunder rent the clouds above. Both Gwair and the garrison upon the ramparts jumped at the sudden sound. With a passionate fervor, the voice seemed clear and audible in Gwair's ears.

Truly, the skies will not weep over the triumph of darkness. The enemy will be knocked from his perch by the hands of those in whom his confidence has been placed.

It was then that the rain ceased.

Eyoés' eyes shot open as the shadow of midnight reached its strongest point. No light penetrated the darkness lingering about the room, save the small oil lamp glowing at the foot of his bed. Through bleary eyes, he sat up and cast aside his bedsheets. Although the reason for his sudden waking remained unclear to him, apprehension warned him of sinister things.

A desperate scratching came from the other side of the door. Drawing his sword, Eyoés stood from his bed and moved toward the sound. The hair on his arms lifted as it continued. As Eyoés passed by, Gwair woke, rubbing the sleep from his eyes.

Seeing the drawn blade, he leapt up and drew his own weapon. Again, the scratching came. This time, the low groan accompanying the frenzied sound sent chills down Gwair's spine. Covering the distance to the door in seconds, he gripped his dagger. As Gwair laid a hand on the door handle, Eyoés positioned himself for attack. Their eyes met, and Eyoés nodded. Gwair quickly pulled the doorhandle and stepped back.

With a groan, a man stumbled into the room and collapsed at their feet. His tattered cloak bore evidence of hard riding, and his bare feet were bruised and bleeding. Eyoés tossed his sword onto his bed and kneeled beside the stricken man, and Gwair did likewise. Grasping the man's shoulder, Eyoés rolled him onto his back. He cringed.

Blood was smeared over his face, and numerous wounds covered his exposed skin, barely clotted and some festering. His blonde hair was wet and disheveled, matted with mud. Staring blankly up at the ceiling, the man trembled, muttering incoherently under his breath.

Gwair gasped, and his face paled. "Kiffyn!"

34

14th of Iaulan, 2202 SE

Thruldin gently dipped a linen rag in the bowl beside Kiffyn. Drops of liquid rolled down his clenched hands as he wrung the cloth. The sharp smell of herbs and other medicinals tingled the inside of his nose.

Adjusting his spectacles with his left hand, he brought the rag to Kiffyn's exposed chest and lightly pressed it against a long, grisly cut. "Daily treatment is the quickest path to healing—and for this poor soul, the path to life," he sighed, treating each of Kiffyn's wounds with care.

Watching over Thruldin's shoulder with a blank, lifeless stare, Gwair wiped away the tears from his red eyes. Kiffyn slept soundly, recovering the sleep lost from terror and exhaustion. As Gwair watched his brother lie quiet under Thruldin's close ministrations, his heart ached over recollections of childhood adventures. He stood silent beside Thruldin, unwilling to leave his brother's side.

Across the room, Eyoés sat on his own bed, leaning forward and resting his chin on his clasped hands. Gwair had said little since Kiffyn's arrival. The mighty hero of Rehillon, who had carried himself with dignity and strength, now stood vulnerable at the mercy of his brother's fate. Gwair's shoulders drooped, and his head hung low. No food had touched his lips since Kiffyn's shocking appearance at their door. Eyoés clasped his hands tightly together as the gaunt face of his friend haunted him.

Gwair knew what he was sending his brother into when he sent him to summon us. Yet imagining such misery, and seeing it before your eyes in its grisly glory are two very different things.

Images of dead dwarves and Hobgoblins lying contorted on the battlefield of Nys-Felz sent a shiver through him. Eyoés looked to the still, resting form of Kiffyn.

He had a home, a family, and a purpose to his life —things any man could want. Now he is stripped of everything and transformed into a muttering madman. When trouble cuts us down, it becomes clear the things worth holding on to are the ones we love—and the King himself.

The door to the room opened and Eyoés jumped from his bed, clutching at his dagger. Startled from his brooding thoughts, Gwair spun on his heels. Suddenly, all the dark thoughts were chased to the corner of his mind.

Standing in the doorway was Gwyndel. Her appearance was ragged, and her Forester garb was stained and torn. Tears welled in her eyes. "Eyoés!" she exclaimed.

Eyoés embraced her tightly, the pent up worry and anxiety for her safety releasing in the form of tears. Holding her at arms length, he smiled. "I was afraid you had fallen to a cruel fate!" he said, "Thank the King you returned." Gwyndel smiled, chin trembling, then embraced him again. It was then that she saw Kiffyn over Eyoés' shoulder.

Her eyes widened in horror. Mouth agape, she dashed to his bedside, nearly knocking Thruldin over in her rush. "Kiffyn! Can you hear me?" she cried, her shaking hand reaching out to touch his arm.

Startled from sleep, Kiffyn quickly sat up, knocking the bowl of medicinal liquid onto the floor. His eyes were wild with terror. "Get away from me!" he screamed. The sudden recollection of torture triggered a wave of pain through his body. He shouted in agony and gasped for air, writhing and trembling as he tried to fight off the enemies in his mind.

Recovering his balance, Thruldin seized a damp cloth lying at the foot of the bed and passed it under Kiffyn's nose. The terrified Forester's eyes dimmed, and he slumped against the wall, fast asleep.

The dwarf turned to the shocked Gwyndel and brandished the cloth above his head. "Confound it, my Lady! I understand your shock, but he mustn't be startled to such an extreme!" he scolded. "I cannot give him many more doses of Naddamric to calm his nerves, or he'll suffer permanent damage." Shaking his head, Thruldin returned the cloth to its place and adjusted his white head shawl.

As the dwarf returned Kiffyn to a comfortable position, Gwyndel turned to Eyoés and Gwair, her hand pressed against her chest. Blinking to stop her tears, she struggled to put aside the image of Kiffyn's pain. "I remember that day so clearly—when he stood between me and the malicious Forester Initiates, defending me against their taunts," she stammered, blankly staring off at the wall. "When I set out with the Loyalists, I expected to be reunited with the same man —the same kind, loyal, and courageous Kiffyn I knew." She paused and turned to face Gwair and Eyoés. "We discovered he had escaped the League's clutches, and I had hoped that—"

Gwyndel's voice choked in her throat. Wiping her nose, she embraced Gwair. From the dark circles under his eyes, she knew her sadness was nothing compared to his own wretchedness. Gwair, used to being the strong pillar others leaned upon in their time of need, was averse to show his own weakness. Hesitantly, he returned her embrace. Gwyndel stepped back. "What happened while I was gone?"

Eyoés and Gwair explained the fruits of their efforts, pressed to share only the important discoveries. Gwair withheld a portion of his knowledge—Throst's awareness of Kiffyn's disappearance. Throst presented himself as man of integrity, but Gwair's apprehension toward the man had built over the course of their investigating. As Eyoés spoke of Throst's humility and loyalty to Vikar despite civil unrest, Gwair glanced at him out of the corner of his eye. Underneath his positive demeanor, he read conflict in Eyoés' eyes, revealing an uncertainty they shared.

Lord Ravenstrong's part in the situation at hand will come to light in time. Whether for good or ill, I do not know.

Gwair woke from his thoughts in time to heed Gwyndel's next question. "You haven't discovered any other evidence since finding the letter in Throst's room?" she inquired, unwilling to believe their bad fortune.

With a sigh, Gwair nodded. "It is true. Should we uncover the origins of Throst's Everwheat remedy, the enemy's identity could be unearthed—or at least, glimpsed," he answered.

As she considered Gwair's conclusion, Gwyndel's eyes gleamed with stoic inspiration. "I believe I have a solution," she revealed, "but I must first meet Baron Vikar."

"Captain Beydan!" Gwair shouted across the courtyard of Castle Hodholm, quickening his steps. A light rain pattered dully on his clothing, discoloring it with an army of small, dark spots. He hurried to receive Beydan's report on the expedition, while Eyoés showed Gwyndel her quarters.

Gathered in the middle of the courtyard like a herd of wild beasts, the clustered group of remaining Loyalists sat saddled on their steeds. Accustomed to both the desolate moors of the Northern Passage and the forests of Rehillon, they preferred the beauty of the untamed wild to the smooth stone under their feet. Their horses whinnied in displeasure at the tight quarters.

Beydan firmly cinched his saddle tight. He patted his horse on the neck and saluted Gwair with a courteous half-smile. "High Marshal!" he said, acknowledging the presence of his superior. Those within earshot stood at attention, but were dismissed by Gwair.

Scrutinizing his subordinate with a raised eyebrow, Gwair laughed to himself. "It appears as though you've been through quite a rough time," he noted. Wet mud was smeared over Beydan's leather jerkin, as well as ash, and several jagged holes were torn in his sleeves.

Briefly regarding his disheveled appearance, Beydan shrugged it aside, unconcerned over his looks. "Our undertaking was trying, to say the least," he said, his exhaustion telling in his manner. "It is a relief such struggles lie behind us."

Gwair's smile faded. With Kiffyn's unexpected arrival and the growing uncertainty over Throst, he doubted such optimism.

There is much more strain yet to come.

Clearing his throat, Gwair clasped his hands behind his back. "What have you to report?" he inquired. He spoke in a restrained manner, concealing his eagerness. The events of the expedition could provide new insight into the happenings in Hodholm.

Beydan adjusted the falchion on his belt. "From Merwic, my men and I traced the Phantom League's trail to Andieff, as you ordered. After some searching, our leads indicated the enemy had fled to the abandoned grounds of Castle Weomor," he declared.

Gwair frowned and inclined his head. "Weomor?" he repeated for confirmation. The history of the forsaken place remained immortalized in several books in the Great Library, and Gwair remembered the dark tale of its destruction. The tragedy had not lost its power on him over the years.

What ill fortune drove them there?

Perceiving his superior's unease, Beydan nodded his understanding. The tale of betrayal and death in the bleakness of Weomor struck him as similar to his own experience. "The very same. To our astonishment, the enemy ambushed us within the ruins. It was because of Gwyndel that we all draw breath today," he said, ducking his head to hide his expression for the sake of formality. "Give her my thanks, as well as the gratitude of my men. As it is, we lost several of our number."

Gwair nodded, patting Beydan's shoulder. "I shall. Have you more to report?" he asked. He knew there was more the Captain had not yet spoken of, and Gwair had a guess as to what he would say.

Should he speak of Kiffyn, I will disclose nothing. The fewer who know, the better.

Beydan collected himself and nodded. "Kiffyn eluded us—we have little knowledge as to where he is now," he sighed, muttering through his teeth at his inability to fulfill his assignment. "It is clear the Phantom League intends to claim this land for its own."

Gwair knew this as well—but speaking the bleak words aloud brought home their gravity anew.

35

Standing in the middle of Baron Vikar's personal quarters, Gwyndel bowed, her hastily-cleaned boots pressing into the exquisite Amiranooran rug lying on the stone. "I am Gwyndel, Daughter of Élorn and sister of Eyoés Kingson," she declared cordially. "It is an honor to stand in the renowned halls of Hodholm."

Vikar smiled and nodded in agreement. The wooden joints creaked as he put his weight on the backrest of his chair. "You are welcome here, and will be respected by myself and those who reside here," he replied, his gaze flitting between Eyoés, Gwair, and Gwyndel. "Allow me to introduce my family."

Turning to his two young relatives, Vikar grasped Rodmer's shoulder, pulling him forward. The young man eyed Gwyndel with narrowed eyes, and hesitantly stepped forward at his uncle's bidding. The Baron sensed his nephew's begrudging obedience and cleared his throat. Rodmer understood, and tried his best to appear genial. Vikar smiled at his new guest. "My nephew, Rodmer Estworth. He journeyed from Edeveros to reacquaint himself with family," he explained.

Flashing a beguiling smile, Rodmer bowed. "Welcome to Hodholm, my Lady," he said. Gwyndel, recalling his initial wariness, hesitated, then gave a weak smile and bowed in return.

Vikar turned to his beloved Caywen. Her hands were clasped in front of her as she waited until bidden to speak. Beaming with pride, the Baron gently took her hand and led her forward. "Caywen, my daughter," he said.

Caywen briefly bowed and embraced Gwyndel. "What a pleasure to meet another woman my age! Most of my old companions have left to attend to their own lives, while I remain here tediously attending to my duties," she exclaimed.

With the memory of Beydan's callous behavior still fresh on her mind, Gwyndel welcomed this gesture of friendship. She smiled, and clasped Caywen's hands in hers. "I understand the stress of leadership. Perhaps during my stay we will have time to speak together in peace," she replied with warmth.

Caywen nodded. A relief from her duties—the documenting, administration, and constant strain on the nerves—was something she longed for.

Stepping forward and setting his hand on Caywen's shoulder, Vikar nodded at the door. "I wish to speak with our guests in private," he indicated, glancing at his nephew. With a bow of respect for her father, Caywen started toward the door with Rodmer in tow.

As the door closed, Vikar stiffened, taking his seat behind his desk. Taking his quill pen in hand, he pulled the fine hawk feather through his fingers. His gaze wavered between the three standing before him. "I've spoken briefly with Gwair about Kiffyn after his arrival, but my duties and the ever watchful eye of the public have kept me from seeing about him personally," he spoke, shifting in his chair. "What is his current condition?"

Gwair's shoulders drooped. Shaking his head, he avoided Vikar's gaze as the poignant image of his brother rambling like a madman tore his heart in two. He leaned against the edge of the table.

If I could only escape for just one moment to make sense of all this.

Feeling the eyes of his companions upon him, Gwair collected himself.

I must stay strong. They have experienced enough uncertainty already. May the Guide strengthen me so I may encourage others.

He cleared his throat. "He's finally resting, but still delirious when woken. I doubt he will recover quickly." He forced the dark words from his lips. "He —endangers us all, and is in no condition to provide us *any* useful information." His dull voice cut off, and his chin trembled as he tightly pressed his lips together. No matter how hard Gwair tried to disguise the struggle with his emotions and his sense of duty, it bled through. Unsure what to say in reply, Gwyndel stood quietly by, increasingly strained with dismal thoughts.

Careful to respect Gwair's desire for strength, Eyoés kept his distance, only letting a hand lightly touch the man's shoulder in a sign of sympathy. It bound them together. The old pain of Asdale's destruction seized Eyoés, reminding him of death and the guilt of his own consuming vengeance. Weighed down by the grip of tragedy, he closed his eyes.

The King has forgiven me my past wrongs. I must focus on what lies ahead.

Understanding his friend's pain, Eyoés chose his words with caution. "I fear if we do not rush to conceal Kiffyn, the Phantom League will find him," he pointed out, "and finish him at the first opportunity. Having been in their midst, he is a dangerous liability."

Gwyndel shivered, and her anger bubbled over. Stepping forward, she pounded Vikar's table with her fist, shaking the inkwell and other loose items on its surface. "We owe it to Kiffyn!" she exclaimed with passion, her curly red hair bouncing about her ears. Turning to Gwair, she set a hand on his arm and leaned close to his face. "You know Hodholm well—you must know some place where your brother can be hidden. We must keep him from the Phantom League's clutches," she insisted.

Gwair looked up, tears building in the corners of his eyes.

I will not let my brother fall prey again. He will live!

Standing with determination, he nodded. "There are tunnels underneath the castle, prepared for escape in event of siege during the War of Adrógar. Kiffyn avoided the sentries by using these very passages to return. I am sure of it," he said. "Thruldin and I will conceal him there. I believe Thruldin can sustain Kiffyn underground with a small gathering of provisions."

Vikar set his quill pen in its inkwell with a quiet tink. Placing his hands on his desk, he pushed himself from his seat. His stern gaze locked on Gwair and Eyoés with such gravity that the two inadvertently stepped back. The commanding sense of authority in Vikar's bearing returned in strength, breaking the bonds of fear and tribulation. "Whether or not you hide Kiffyn will mean nothing if we do not act. If we continue in the blindness that has so far foiled our efforts at uncovering the enemy, the Phantom League will gain control of Hodholm. Kiffyn's life would not be out of the League's hands for long. We must discern more of their plot before it is too late!" Vikar exclaimed. "Gwair, I understand your concern for your brother. I have felt the pain of a loved one's loss, but you know I speak the truth."

Eyoés and Gwair said nothing. Since arriving in Hodholm, days had passed with little gain, save the dark suicide of Hranfist and the discovery of their letter in Throst Ravenstrong's quarters. Unsure of their enemies and fearful of revealing their true allegiances, they had searched unsuccessfully for signs. *Something* that would indicate the League was on the move.

As she watched her companions falter, a fire stirred in Gwyndel's heart.

Drastic action is needed. The enemy must be deceived into revealing a new lead.

She stepped forward. "It is time we *act*. You all rightly fear exposing yourselves to the Phantom League—but it has become clear mere searching will not save Rehillon," she announced.

Eyoés turned to his sister, expression doubtful. "What do you suggest?" he said.

Gwyndel jabbed a finger to her chest. "Whatever Everwheat remains in this castle will be mine to eat. We can procure another dose of Throst's remedy and analyze the substance to identify it," she declared with finality.

A sudden coldness chilled Eyoés to his core, and his face paled. Gwair's words concerning his own addiction warned him.

When the supply of Everwheat grain began to run out, the people of Rehillon began exhibiting strange symptoms—ranging from mood changes and insomnia to delirium, tremors, and in some cases, near madness.

Eyes wide, Eyoés leaned against a nearby chair for support. His head swam. "Surely not," he started, voice pained. Pushing himself to his feet, he stepped toward her. Images of Gwyndel writhing in the pain of withdrawal flashed through his mind.

I cannot bear to see her succumb to such torment!

"I forbid it! For you to sacrifice yourself because our lack of daring is too harrowing a fate," Eyoés exclaimed.

Gwyndel shook her head. "I must do this! If I don't, we will remain at the mercy of the enemy!" she retorted. Struggling to give voice to the overwhelming confusion and panic, Eyoés looked to Gwair and Vikar for aid.

Setting a hand on Gwyndel's shoulder, Gwair looked her steadfast in the eye. "You don't realize what you suggest," he reasoned, his manner grave. "The sudden seizure of the remedy without convincing symptoms would attract unwanted attention. You would have to eat Everwheat bread for several days in order to manifest such withdrawal symptoms." He paused. "There is a chance of death," he acknowledged, lowering his voice.

Gwyndel let the silence between them act as her witness. Returning his steady gaze, she made her case. "I am willing to risk it," she answered. "Time may be short."

Eyoés clenched his fists. "I FORBID YOU!" he shouted, moving to seize her.

Gwair stepped between them and restrained his friend. "Listen to me!" he commanded through clenched teeth. "I too struggle to allow this, but she is decided. The Guide holds her life in his hands. Whether or not I agree, I tell you this—I swear by my life I will do *all* in my power to keep her from death!"

Blinking to stay the tears, Eyoés hung his head in resignation. His troubled thoughts pored over Gwyndel's several close encounters with death. The Phantom League, the Kalakill, Skreon's Norzaid—all should have brought about her demise, yet something had foiled their attempts, and it was neither he or Gwyndel.

I have protected you and Gwyndel before. Do you trust me to do so again?

His brows furrowed. Eyoés felt the comforting presence of the Guide put his fears to rest. Proverbs from his childhood spurred on his courage.

Eyoés looked up at Gwair. It was through faith his hopes would come to pass. "So be it. Where must I find the bread?"

36

Ducking behind a pillar, Eyoés pulled his dark cloak tight about him. The clicking of boots on the stone floor of the castle passed by him. Pressing against the wall, Eyoés peered around the the pillar. Illuminated by a small torch, a guard's vague outline could be made out in the shadows of night. As the man's footsteps faded, Eyoés slipped out of cover.

Occasional stained glass windows allowed fractured light to pierce the darkness of the castle. Eyoés instinctively glanced over his shoulder. Darkness had a way of heightening a man's awareness, making him alert to the slightest sound in his ear, or touch of air on his skin. Whether for good or ill it mattered little.

He slowed his stride to a walk. Gwair and Thruldin carried Kiffyn into the shadows of the hallway leading to the tunnels beneath the castle. Eyoés pressed his lips tightly together and paused. It would be the last he saw of them until morning.

Should Kiffyn awake from his induced stupor and cry out, there will be little they can do—and I will be unable to come to their aid.

Clenching his fist, Eyoés continued on. It was out of his hands now. Now he must accomplish the task he had put himself up to.

To his right, a small passage broke off from the main hall. Through the darkness, Eyoés glimpsed a set of descending stairs. He diverted from his main course and entered the passage, removing a nearby torch from its place on the wall.

Eyoés proceeded with care, feeling the steps with his toes. Drafts of cool air wafted up from the depths below. His heart beat faster. The stone walls wound around him like a corkscrew as he descended the spiral stairs.

As his boot touched bottom, a solitary door came into view, lit by two torches. Dust covered the rough surface of the door in a film of grey. He recognized it from Gwair's description.

The castle cellar, without a doubt.

Straining his ear for any hint of danger, Eyoés cocked his head. He pulled back the hood concealing his face. The gravelly snoring of the sentry inside the storeroom could be heard through the door. Eyoés placed his torch into an empty sconce. Eyeing the iron handle and locking mechanism of the door, he reached into his pocket for several metal instruments. He knelt before the door and examined the lock. It was one of the easier locks Gwair had prepared him for. Apparently, much of the fortification had been concentrated on the outside of the castle, not the inside. Looking intently at the keyhole, he recited the steps in his head. Eyoés inserted the tools into the lock and began working the mechanism inside. All the while, he kept an ear tuned for sign of danger.

With a barely audible click, the lock gave way. Eyoés shoved the instruments in his pocket and pulled the door handle. A spike of adrenaline swept through his limbs as the door squeaked on its iron hinges. Eyoés set his hand on his concealed dagger. The droning of the sentry's snoring broke briefly—then resumed. Slowly, Eyoés peered around the doorframe and stepped into the cellar.

A coldness lingered like the chill air of a spring morning. Sputtering lanterns hung from the ceiling to provide light. Placed about the room in clear rows, shelves and barrels full of goods awaited use.

Closing the door behind him, Eyoés glimpsed the slouched form of the sentry seated in the corner. The pungent scent of mead emanated from several barrels next to him. The slumbering guard embraced a goblet against his chest. Eyoés smiled.

Appears that someone helped himself to the wares he was charged to keep secure.

He ventured among the stores, passing through each row with a critical eye and scanning the contents of each shelf. Squinting, he struggled to read the label tied to one of the barrels. He tilted it on its side and turned the label into the light of the nearest lantern. Confident the contents were not what he sought, Eyoés returned it to its place.

If the sentry wakes and finds something out of place, unnecessary suspicion will be aroused.

He moved to the next shelf. Skimming the basket labels, Eyoés paused. Seizing one with his sweaty hands, he pulled it from its place and set it on the cold floor. The large capital letters of the parchment label warned of dangerous contents. Eyoés peered closer.

Baked with Everwheat flour! Not for consumption!

Licking his dry lips, he slipped the small satchel off his shoulder. As he dumped the bread into the pack, he looked at the dozing sentry.

Thank the Guide Gwair decided to retain some as evidence. His suspicions of foul play have proven true.

Removing the parchment label, he returned the basket to the shelf. He darted to the furthest corner of the cellar and stuffed the label underneath a large sack of grain. In time, Gwyndel's consumption of Everwheat would be discovered. Adjusting the strap of the satchel on his shoulder, Eyoés slipped out of the cellar.

37

16th of Iaulan, 2202 SE

Tucking a book snugly under his arm, Eyoés exited the Great Library, shutting the large door behind him with a clang. Two days had passed since he had infiltrated the castle cellar. Though restless with lost sleep over Gwyndel's endangerment, he strove to forget it. His grip tightened on the book in his hand. Reading always soothed his anxiety. His footsteps evened into a steady trod as his mind churned.

How long until the Everwheat solidifies its grasp on Gwyndel? Will she be alright?

Slowing his breaths, Eyoés brought his musings to a conclusion. If there was to be any measure of peace in this time of risk, his mind would have to overcome its own uncertainties.

It is all in the Guide's hands. Today already has enough to worry about.

Grasping his book with both hands, Eyoés considered the deep navy blue cover. Worn from age, the edges were bent and scraped of their color, revealing a dark brown base. Upon the cover was a tender scene of a woman beneath an oak tree, chin resting on her hand in thought. In faded gold ink, the book's title hung above her head. Twisting patterns were embossed around the image, beautiful in their intentional simplicity.

"Ah, Eyoés—what a pleasant coincidence," spoke a familiar voice. Whisking the book under his arm, Eyoés hesitantly looked up. A smile of welcome grew on his features as Throst Ravenstrong approached.

Eyoés moved to meet him in the middle of the hall. "Indeed," he said, clasping arms with the young Lord of Herthere. "How might you be?"

Taking a deep breath inward, Throst gave a deep sigh of gratification. "I thought it would be a fine day for a new book," he declared, gesturing toward the thick doors of the Great Library. "May I walk with you?"

He paused, his forehead wrinkling for a brief moment. The objections over the forged letter discovered in Throst's room and the Ravenstrongs' troubled past surfaced and fought within him.

None of this evidence clearly proves Throst is an enemy. He said himself the reputation of his family's history did not define him.

Since his arrival in Hodholm, Throst had respected him as a guest and treated him as a close friend. Though his philosophy remained questionable at times, Eyoés found it strangely comforting. With no definitive evidence against Throst, Eyoés remained unsure of his allegiance. For all he could see, it appeared as though Throst knew nothing of the plot, and humbly submitted himself to Vikar's leadership despite the common folk's pleas. Eyoés came to a final conclusion.

I trust my own judgement.

With this in mind, he glanced back to the door behind him. "You may, but I do not wish to stand in the way of your scholarly pursuits," he inquired, nodding toward the library.

Throst shook his head and gestured down the hall with his open hand. "Another time. It is better to be in the company of good friends such as you," he remarked with a smile.

They started down the hall, the soles of their boots sinking into the red carpet. As they took a sharp left into a separate corridor, the Great Hall came into view. Occupied with the business of the noon hour, servants hurried about, arms full of dishes and other items needed for the midday meal.

Glancing at the book under Eyoés' arm, Throst raised an eyebrow. "What book have you borrowed?" he asked. He recognized the cover, though it bore marks his own edition did not have.

With one hand, Eyoés held the book out toward Throst. "'The Art of Thought', by Mairwen of Ledale," he replied, glancing up at his companion. "Your recommendation intrigued me."

Throst's expression brightened. Grinning, he threw an arm around Eyoés' shoulder. "It is a triumph whenever another man willingly increases his knowledge of the world through philosophy," he proclaimed. "You have proven yourself to be an intelligent man."

They laughed together. With his interest in the reasoning of Mairwen of Ledale, Eyoés had found common ground yet again.

Why is Gwair wary of Throst? It was unexpected to find our letter in his quarters, but surely there can be no harm behind it.

Eyoés let his eyes wander across the cover. "Though it interests me, I do not trust myself to fully comprehend it," he sighed, looking to Throst. "Help me to understand."

Throst Ravenstrong let his arm fall from his companion's shoulders. Ahead, he gestured towards a simple wooden bench at the end of the hall. He nodded. "With pleasure," he said.

38

19th of Iaulan, 2202 SE

"More water! Quickly!" Thruldin ordered, pressing the damp towel on Gwyndel's forehead. Tremors shook her as she gripped the blankets of Eyoés' bed. Eyes wide with the utter confusion of delirium, Gwyndel muttered incoherently to herself. Matted to her forehead, her hair was disheveled, and hung like loose rags about her head. Her voice rose and fell with a wretched despair that caused the hair on Gwair's neck to rise.

Ignoring the sweat stinging his eye, Gwair seized a nearby towel. He doused it in a large bowl, spilling water over the edge. He rushed to Thruldin's side and handed the dripping towel to him.

Writhing on the bed, Gwyndel cried out in pain. "Kiffyn! The sun rises in the night—leaves in the grass!" she yelled, eyes frantically bouncing about the room in search of something unseen. Her fist slammed into Thruldin's chest, sending him sprawling.

Clutching the sopping linen, the dwarf recovered his balance. "Confound it! Hold her still Gwair!" he shouted, rushing back to her bedside. Wiping his hands, Gwair gripped Gwyndel's shoulders and forcefully held her. He grit his teeth as she thrashed. His muscles cramped as he fought the suffering woman. Clenching his jaw, Gwair watched the dwarf retrieve another towel and cover her forehead.

Thruldin gently wiped Gwyndel's face. A weary sigh escaped him as her restlessness waned for a brief moment. With his free hand, he scrubbed the bags under his eyes. Much of the previous night he had spent at her bedside, comforting her through the beginnings of withdrawal—though the worst of the symptoms had now taken a firm hold. Thruldin glanced at his concealed alchemy kit in the corner of the room. Beneath the shroud was an assortment of tools. Thruldin averted his gaze from it, shaking his head.

It feels almost cruel to use some of the remedy for research—the remedy that would alleviate her pain. I can only hope both she and Kiffyn are safe and sound at the end of this.

Gwyndel's groans rose again. Tortured by the monsters of delirium, she sat up on her bed, fighting against Gwair's hold on her. "They're after me!" she screamed. "Claws, black mist!" Legs weak, Thruldin stumbled to retrieve a freshly dampened linen.

The door to the room burst open. Eyoés charged in, his face deathly pale. Spotting Thruldin, he seized the dwarf by his shoulders. "Throst is right behind me!" he whispered fiercely. Before the dwarf could respond, Eyoés raced to Gwyndel's bedside, tears streaming down his face. Kneeling beside her, he tightly clasped her hand and pulled her arm close to him. "Everything will be alright," he quavered, eyes dull with grief.

Towel in hand, Thruldin leaned close to Eyoés. "We must do everything we can to keep Throst's attention away from my alchemy kit!"

The sound of approaching footsteps arrested Eyoés' attention. As Throst strode into the room, Gwyndel screamed. Thruldin motioned for Eyoés to stand back. Looking to Throst, Eyoés reluctantly obeyed.

Throst Ravenstrong regarded Gwyndel with an expression of astonishment and anxiety, as expected. It was his posture that struck Eyoés. Throst's arms hung limply at his sides, and his concern over Gwyndel's well-being seemed halfhearted.

As Eyoés stared at the young Lord of Herthere's inaction, he pointed toward the struggling Gwyndel. "Well?" he asked in irritation, tone pointed like an arrow.

Looking up from his work in anger, Thruldin seconded the notion. "Don't just stand there like a fainthearted woman! Bring me the remedy!" he stormed, taking a threatening step in the man's direction. The natural dwarf brashness shook Throst from his stupor. To appease the fuming dwarf's wrath, the young Lord of Herthere held out a bottle in his right hand.

Clearing his throat, Throst hurried to Gwyndel's bedside. "Half of the bottle is enough to relieve the symptoms. Only use the other half if symptoms persist —too much, and she could become addicted to *it* as well," he explained, holding the bottle carefully away from Gwyndel's flailing limbs.

Thruldin took the bottle in hand. Muttering strange, harrowing things to herself, she finally broke away from Gwair's cramped grip, nearly throwing herself upon Thruldin. The dwarf leapt back as her clenched fist passed inches from the bottle he held. Shaking his cramped forearms, Gwair gritted his teeth and grabbed Gwyndel by the arms and pushed her onto the bed. Cautiously approaching his struggling patient, Thruldin cast an angry glance at Throst. "There has been enough delay! Gwair, hold her still! Eyoés, open her mouth and close it when I finish each small dose—we'll be lucky if she swallows a single drop!" he declared. Throst stepped back as Gwair positioned himself directly behind Gwyndel and pinned her arms. Eyoés rushed to the bed and seized her mouth in a vice-like grip. He pried her jaw open, wary of her teeth.

Thruldin gripped the bottle with both hands and poured a small amount of liquid into the side of Gwyndel's mouth. As soon as the dwarf pulled the bottle away, Eyoés shut her mouth. All present stood still in tense hopefulness as they watched the struggling Forester. Many in the room prayed to the Guide for mercy—save one, whose only guide was his strong mind.

Gwyndel swallowed. A cheer of victory went up from Eyoés and Gwair. The young Baron of Asdale shook with relief as he thanked the King for the small victory. Spurred on by their first triumph, Thruldin met Eyoés' eye and nodded. Pulling the stopper from the top of the bottle, he moved to administer another small dose.

Taking several steps back, Throst watched from a distance. He lowered his head and studied Gwyndel with a narrow gaze. "How did this happen?" he inquired. The lack of energy in his words made him seem apathetic.

Absorbed in Gwyndel's treatment, Eyoés hesitated, inattentive to Throst's question. Swallowing, he recalled the careful answer he had decided on. "It seems she visited the castle cellar and helped herself to some bread tainted by Everwheat," he hastily replied. "The loaves must not have been labeled." Several minutes passed as Throst looked on.

The muttered ramblings of Gwyndel slowly waned, as each dose of the Everwheat remedy lulled her closer to rest. Thankful for the sudden peace, Thruldin wiped the sweat from his face on a towel and cast it aside. Eyoés released his hold on Gwyndel's jaw and stood.

As the tumult came to its end, Throst pursed his lips together in thought, glancing toward Eyoés. "I will look into it," he said, speaking in a strangely flat voice. Adjusting the robe around his neck, he gave one last glance to where Gwyndel lay and turned to leave. "At least we are rid of the remaining Everwheat," he muttered under his breath. Without another word, Throst left the room.

Eyoés started as he mulled over Throst's final words. Putting his hand to his mouth, he shook his head. Images of Gwyndel writhing in the pain of withdrawal returned to haunt him as Throst's words turned over in his thoughts.

Does he think Gwyndel a mere tool for disposing of unwanted waste?

His eyes darkened with indignant anger. Tears welled in his eyes as he looked at the empty doorway. Eyoés grabbed a fistful of his shirt. Gritting his teeth, he slammed the door shut and locked it.

Thruldin held the bottle carefully in his hands as he poured the final portion of the dose into Gwyndel's mouth. As Gwair gently closed her mouth to prompt her to swallow, the dwarf held the bottle up to the window and examined its contents.

Good—exactly half empty. Plenty more to experiment with. We'll hope we don't need a second treatment.

Stopping the bottle, the dwarf stumbled to where his alchemy kit was hidden, legs weary from rushing about. "This will take a few moments," he said, voice hoarse from shouting orders. Eyoés stepped aside as Thruldin moved his kit to the middle of the floor and began his research.

Unaware of Eyoés' boiling anger, Gwair frowned at the dwarf. "The other half of the remedy—what if Gwyndel should need it later?" he asked.

Thruldin focused intently on his work. "She has only been exposed to the Ossinder in the Everwheat bread for a short period of time. The amount of medication she has taken will be more than adequate to heal her of this. She'll sleep for about three days," he concluded, adjusting his spectacles as he examined the setup of his equipment. Gwair had informed the dwarf of his journey to the Darmore Fells, and the discovery of Ossinder in the Everwheat flour. Though intrigued, it seemed Thruldin had saved his curiosity for his own experimenting.

As the dwarf went about his skilled labor, Gwair released Gwyndel's head. Cramping pain shot up his arms and through the muscles in his hand. He shook his hands to give vent to his own discomfort. Looking up, Gwair noticed Eyoés brooding to himself, his gaze sharp as flint. "What is it?" he asked, setting a kind hand on his friend's shoulder.

Eyoés glanced up. Heat flushed through his body as the flaring wildfire of anger strove to claim its place. An abundance of rash words rushed to take the reins of his tongue. Caught up in the hurt and fury of his own thoughts, Eyoés thought to indulge his own desires. A gleam of painful recollection woke him from his own daze.

Gwair knows my story, about the anger that used to torment me. I cannot give him reason to think I have traded the Guide's forgiveness for my old weakness.

The fire in his eyes retreated. Looking away, Eyoés halfheartedly waved the matter aside. "It's nothing," he stated.

Gwair paused, pulling his hand from his companion's shoulder. He could tell an unspoken matter was eating away at Eyoés. Despite his desire to console his friend in whatever ailed him, something urged him to respect his decision. Gwair took a seat and slumped against the side of the bed.

Minutes passed. Pouring varying amounts of the remaining solution into the twisted glass tubes and vials, Thruldin analyzed the results of his work, adding the heat of an oil lamp to certain areas as his experiment required. Though many considered him to be solely a man of letters and keeper of books, he appropriated many skills from the things he read. Whether for amusement or serious study, the wizened old dwarf delved deep into the books he studiously cared for.

He frowned. A foreboding seized his stomach. His face reddened, and he nearly upset his alchemy kit.

Could it be?

Adjusting his spectacles one final time, Thruldin examined the results of his own research. From where they waited, Eyoés and Gwair noticed the dwarf's agitation.

His own anger and pain momentarily forgotten, Eyoés stepped forward, his gaze riveted. "What have you found?" he asked, moistening his dry lips. Gwair stood up and advanced as well.

Removing his spectacles, Thruldin turned to face them, his expression grim. His gaze drifted between them. Shifting his position, he took a wary glance at the empty bottle. "This remedy is made of Terragyn. The Phantom League is known to sell it to addicts to alleviate their suffering—and in doing so, make a steady profit in both drug *and* remedy." He sighed. "It is rare to find it sold legally in Alithell—and definitely not in the quantities it would take to cure the people of South Rehillon of an Ossinder addiction. The only person who would have access to such a large amount is one allied with the Phantom League."

The two heroes of Alithell said nothing. Eyoés closed his eyes. From the depths of his memory, the Guide's warning returned.

Do not relax your guard. The mission to which you travel will endanger not only your life, but your purpose as well. Beware the charm of gold and the company of evil.

Eyoés took in a deep, pained breath. Blinded by the shows of sympathy and apparent wisdom, he had accepted Throst's words as truth. To his surprise, Eyoés found his bond to Throst easier to break than he had thought.

How did I not see this? Although inconclusive, the evidence for Throst's corruption should have been clear to me. I even bought into the lies of his own philosophy! I was not on my guard.

Repeatedly, Eyoés had come to suspect Throst's compromise, yet had been fooled into thinking his own discoveries were not what they seemed. Accustomed to these unsightly suspicions concerning Throst, Eyoés found the sudden affirmation of his conclusions strangely freeing. The enemy was now clearly in view.

Turning around, Eyoés brushed past Gwair and kneeled by Gwyndel's bedside, hearing her steady breaths in his ear as he groped about underneath the bed frame. His eyes darkened as his fingers clasped around the spine of a book.

Withdrawing *The Art of Thought* from under his bed, Eyoés stood and approached Thruldin. "We are grateful for your aid—it was sent from the Guide himself," he said, clapping his fist to his opposite shoulder in the dwarf salute. Thruldin inclined his head with a smile of appreciation and returned the gesture of friendship. Eyoés extended the book towards the dwarf. "Before you return to look after Kiffyn in the tunnels, could you return this to the Great Library?" he asked. "It is no longer of use to me." The last words he spat with contempt, his eyes gleaming with an inner anger.

39

23rd of Iaulan, 2202 SE

Letting her hand brush against the spines of the books, Gwyndel scanned the Great Library of Hodholm. She weaved through the labyrinth of bookshelves and tables. As she passed by, her eyes scanned the titles of the books, searching for anything of interest. The scent of old books and aged oak shelves rejuvenated her like the crisp smell of fresh air. Gwyndel scrubbed her hand over her face. Though three days of sleep had done her well, a lingering weariness remained from the intense struggle of her withdrawal. She blinked several times and returned to her searching, muttering the titles of the books under her breath.

Many of the book volumes lay awkwardly on the holding shelves. Some had fallen over into the empty space. The occasional cobweb traced a jagged line from one corner to the other. Gwyndel carefully shuffled through a small stack. The ragged and torn edges of the pages felt soft under her touch, yet firm like packed soil.

As Gwyndel rounded left in the maze of shelves, she came upon a group of tables. They provided a suitable place for study across a section of the Great

Library. A single, flickering candle was placed upon each tabletop.

The furious scratching of a quill pen attracted Gwyndel's attention. Turning to where the sound came from, she noticed Caywen seated at one of the far tables with a piece of parchment. Her face was twisted in concentration, and she gripped her pen, staring intently at the words she wrote. Taking several quiet steps toward her, Gwyndel cocked her head and leaned forward, unsure whether to disturb Caywen in her work.

The scratching of the quill abruptly ceased. Feeling the uncertain scrutiny of another person's gaze, Caywen paused, then looked up from her work. At the sight of Gwyndel, the tension in her body released. Eagerly, she set down her pen and moved to stand. "Gwyndel! I am so glad to see you!" she exclaimed.

Holding out a hand, Gwyndel gestured for her to sit as she came closer. "So am I," she replied with a welcoming smile.

Caywen's expression darkened with concern, and she reached out a hand to touch Gwyndel's arm. "I heard you were afflicted with the Everwheat addiction," she said, examining Gwyndel for any sign of her suffering. "Are you alright?"

Nodding, Gwyndel dragged one of the nearest chairs away from the nearest table. The wooden legs screeched along the stone floor. Placing the chair next to Caywen, Gwyndel seated herself. "I am. Thankfully, the amount of Everwheat I accidentally consumed was little compared to the others afflicted in South

Rehillon," she answered, clasping her hands together on the table. "What are you working on?"

With an exasperated sigh, Caywen rested her elbows on the tabletop and splayed her hands in the air with wide eyes. "Notes—I'm giving my weekly lesson on heraldry to some students later today," she growled. "I truly do enjoy my work educating others, but I have taken on more than I can handle *and* promised to delve into a subject I know little about."

Gwyndel slid closer to Caywen. During her Stewardship of Asdale, she had seen many of the laborers and servants struggle to read, or accomplish tasks that required more than strength and obedience. As one educated well by her mentor and adopted father Fychan, she felt pity for those who struggled to understand such things. She had felt inclined to teach on several occasions, only to be dragged back into the mire of Stewardship. Gwyndel leaned forward. "What is it like, teaching?" she asked, a certain wonder in her tone.

Pulling her gaze away from the shelves of books across the expanse of the Great Library, Caywen met Gwyndel's eye. "Such a thing cannot be completely explained. You pour your heart and soul into your students, hoping for the light to dawn. They become your children, in a sense, regardless of age. To show them the love of the King and the beauty of our world —that is the reason I teach," she declared, her gaze going distant. "Yet, I have been forced to bear the load of assisting my father for a time, and set aside teaching for once a week. With the Everwheat crisis and the people's unrest, Father has been unable to address many of his normal duties. Too much of his time is spent creating public proclamations of his innocence and searching for ways to remedy his situation."

She looked up to speak further, then noticed the odd scar on Gwyndel's cheekbone once again. Guessing at her curiosity, Gwyndel absentmindedly brought her hand up to touch it. "A result of an unfortunate situation of my childhood," she explained, purposefully excluding mention of the Phantom League.

Sensitive to Gwyndel's feelings, Caywen looked down at the parchment. Taking her quill pen in hand, Caywen dipped it into the inkwell and began sketching on the corner of the parchment. The image of distant mountains came to life, bearing craggy cliffs and the sharp spikes of conifer forests. "I wish I could travel our world, Gwyndel. Spending my days constantly caged in this castle with work seems a terrible way to live one's life," she protested, yearning for the beauty of the world outside the stone walls she called home.

A familiar sympathy was kindled by these words. Gwyndel leaned back in her chair. The nagging chatter of servants and courtiers fighting for her attention rang in her ears, coming alive in her memory. As she recalled the stress of having to juggle more than she could handle, a frown pulled at the corners of her mouth. Gwyndel absentmindedly fingered a faded red hair straying from the curls bound behind her head.

I too have felt the tension of leadership. One should not bear the weight alone and suffer on the wayside.

Reaching out to Caywen, Gwyndel squeezed her shoulder. "I understand the strain is pulling you down. While my brother learned the responsibilities of a Baron, I was put in the position to steward over his domain. For a time, it was a joy, being able to better the lives of others. Then, as the construction of the castle began, I found myself burdened with things I was unsure how to handle," she said gently. "It was because of the Guide's constant aid I managed to stay strong—and so shall you, with his help."

Caywen gave a weak smile. "It is as my friend Throst Ravenstrong says—one grows strong through reflection, and with calm mind, we can find the strength to save ourselves," she reasoned. "I disagree with the last statement, but the notion of finding strength through thought sounds true enough."

Gwyndel stiffened in her seat. Pursing her lips, she looked down into her lap. That morning, Eyoés and Gwair had told her of the implication of Throst's connection to the Phantom League. Though she had only seen him through the haze of her clouded mind, an enmity and spite for the man had taken a strong hold.

She respects him. Thinks him wise!

Furtively glancing at Caywen, Gwyndel pinched her bottom lip with her fingers.

Should I tell her the truth?

She watched Caywen continue her small sketch on the corner of her parchment. Mulling over the apparent wisdom of Throst, Gwyndel hesitated. Should she reveal the truth, the sympathy she had claimed to share could be disregarded as manipulative. In a time such as this, with unknown enemies plotting evil in the very halls of Hodholm, an ally who shared a common struggle was invaluable. Gwyndel made her decision.

Another time. To speak of Throst's treachery now might break her heart. Besides, it could reveal our secret investigation of the Phantom League's plot.

Clearing her throat, Gwyndel nodded toward the parchment. "May I help you with your notes?" she inquired. "I know enough about heraldry from my years as Steward of Asdale."

Caywen smiled and finished the final cloud on her sketch. Dipping the pen into the inkwell, she motioned for Gwyndel to move closer. "Your aid would be much appreciated, friend," she said. Shifting their positions, the two hunched over the manuscript. The scratching of the quill pen continued in the stillness of the Great Library.

40

A streak of light penetrated into the dim interior as Caywen pushed open the door to the castle stables and invited Gwyndel in. Politely inclining her head, Gwyndel entered, casually observing the interior. The pungent odor of old, mouldering hay and filthy animals stung her nose.

Pitchforks, shovels, and other equipment hung from the rafters above, securely held in place by thick straps. Bridles and reins dangled from several wooden support posts. Loose straw was scattered across the floor. A spider crawled on one of the rafters, then darted into the thatched roof. Sacks of oats were stacked in one corner, along with several small troughs. To the right, an aisle stretched the length of the castle stables, lined with individual stalls to either side. Nearly a hands-breadth wide, small vents allowed fresh air in from the top of the walls, as well as stray rays of light. The plain, unadorned fashion of the place reminded Gwyndel of days gone by, and the remote places she had visited as a Forester.

Shutting the door behind her, Caywen motioned down the aisle between the stalls. "Come, I will show you my horse," she insisted with eagerness, hurrying further down the stables. Gwyndel followed, stray pieces of straw crunching under her boots. Penned up in their stalls, the horses observed her curiously.

Caywen stopped before one of the pens, reaching inside and stroking the tawny horse inside. Its cropped, white mane stood upright, with a shock of black running through the middle down its neck. Intrigued by the strange appearance of the beast, Gwyndel approached, leaning slightly forward. "What an unusual breed. A beautiful creature," she remarked.

Patting the horse's neck, Caywen leaned against the stall gate. "This is Thyre," she said. "Father and I acquired her on my first trip to Andieff, when I was a child. She has been a fond companion of mine."

Gwyndel gave a smile of understanding. She knew firsthand the bond between a beast and its master, and the trust it forged. Looking down the rows of stalls, she envisioned herself once again in the mountains of Iostan, laughing alongside her brother as he tried in vain to mount Gibusil for the first time.

When Eyoés was consumed by his vengeance, Gibusil was a welcome companion during the lonely nights in the wilderness.

Stroking Thyre's coarse mane, Gwyndel motioned to Caywen. "Follow me," she said, starting down the aisle. Caywen patted her steed's neck and followed.

Her eyes widened as the bulky griffin came into closer view, its golden wings tucked neatly into the close quarters of the stables. Kept in a group stall to accommodate his size, Gibusil had curled up after a hearty morning meal of wild meats.

As Gwyndel approached, the griffin's ears perked up, and it came to its feet, the gate of the stall barely reaching up to its chest. With a chirrup of welcome, Gibusil nudged Gwyndel with his head. Tousling the creature's feathers, Gwyndel turned to Caywen, smiling at the awe on her face. "Meet Gibusil," she beamed.

Caywen's heart pounded in her chest. The glint of daylight streaming in from the vents glistened off the creature's feathers like sunlight. The beast appeared even more spectacular when compared to the drawings in the books. "I have never seen a griffin face to face, though I have heard their cries from afar. How did you tame such a magnificent beast?" she asked in wonder. Gibusil regarded her with an unblinking eye.

Letting her fingers rake through the griffin's furry chest, Gwyndel closed her eyes, revisiting the vivid memory. "My brother and I stumbled across the creature in the mountains of Iostan. He ate our bread and seemed willing to be our companion. I still wonder at Gibusil's readiness to let us ride him," she explained, looking up into the griffin's eyes. Gibusil let out a low rumble of contentment, appreciating the time spent with his rider.

As Caywen stared at the creature, she brought her hand to her chin. "I have heard stories. According to some accounts, the people of Iostan have trained these beasts in the past. It would be no surprise if Gibusil had come into contact with civilization before," she remarked.

Considering the possibility, Gwyndel paused, the griffin releasing a disappointed chirp. "Whatever the case, Eyoés and I are grateful for Gibusil's company," she said. Again, she tousled the griffin's feathered head.

Caywen's hand went up absentmindedly. Looking to Gwyndel, she pulled her hand back. "May I?" she asked. Understanding her friend's wish, Gwyndel motioned for her to continue. Tentatively, Caywen reached out, fingers curved.

With a glare, Gibusil pulled away, wary. Caywen hesitated. Gwyndel reassured the creature. As Caywen continued to reach out, Gibusil's determination wavered as his rider urged him to be friendly. Then, exchanging his wariness for the trust of his companion, the griffin let the woman's hand touch his beak.

41

Pacing his quarters, Eyoés clasped his hands tightly behind his back, his grip powered by the force of frustration. Gwair sat across the room on his bed, watching his friend stride from one end of the room to the next. As she stood next to Vikar, Gwyndel shifted her position, idly tapping her belt with her fingers. Though scattered about the room, one thing united them in both mind and presence—Throst.

Eyoés spun on his heels and faced Vikar. "We cannot stand idly by and let Throst have his way while we search for the ideal opportunity!" he insisted, extending a pleading hand to the Baron. "Throst must be exposed before the Council!"

Hunching over in his seat, Gwair held his head in his hands. The halting progress of their undertaking wore down his resolve. Weeks had passed, with little advancement or hope. His mind revisited the events of the past, and his heart sank.

I will not let Rehillon fall. It is time for action, whatever that may entail.

He slammed his fist into his open palm. "Action needs to be taken, whether that means standing before the Council with our accusations or something else!" he cried, leaping up from his seat. Surprised at Gwair's reaction, Eyoés turned, raising an eyebrow. His companion firmly met his gaze. Folding his arms across his chest, Eyoés smirked in triumph and nodded in approval. How he longed to draw his sword in defense of Rehillon and the King's virtues. He detested the restraint this constant secrecy demanded.

Standing rigid beside Gwyndel, Baron Vikar held his peace. His hands trembled, and he looked aside. A tear of anguish rolled out of the corner of his eye. Since the beginning of the turmoil in Rehillon, a lingering fear had festered inside him. As it often does during the test of time, fear becomes a brooding unease—until the tension of uncertainty and stress snaps in anger.

With a roar of despair, he kicked the bedstead with all the force he could muster. The corner of Eyoés' bed jumped off the floor several inches before slamming back down.

The room was silenced. All eyes turned to Vikar, taken aback by the show of hidden emotion. Leaning against the edge of the bedstead, Baron Vikar furtively glanced at those present. "Forgive me," he pleaded, his voice thick. His face burned with shame at his rash display. Gwyndel set a comforting hand on the Baron's shoulder. Emboldened by her compassion, Vikar cleared his throat. His eyes were red-rimmed. "There is no certainty the Council will even *consider* the accusation. Throst may have the people calling for his leadership, but the Council has known him long enough to believe he means the best for Rehillon," he declared, broken by his own words.

Gwyndel's silence unnerved those present. Her grave expression betrayed the thoughts she reflected on. Like a blank canvas, her face became as smooth as still water. Walking with slow, heavy steps, she approached the window. "Our hand is forced—if we act now, we compromise our own mission. If we wait, we might be too late to save the Rehils," she pondered aloud. She flinched, struck by the despair in her own statement. Neither option provided a conceivable solution. The chasm of uncertain answers brought forth a recollection—the time when a similar uncertainty had gripped her while flying through the misty skies of Zwaoi, lost without hope. Gwyndel frowned. When compared to the despair of *that* moment, their current situation did not seem as desperate—yet.

There must be a way. The King has delivered us from times of uncertainty before, and he will do so again. I am sure of it.

Turning to face her companions, Gwyndel fingered the handle of her dagger. "Overcoming Throst in one move will not defeat the Phantom League. When you fight the dragon, don't only cut off the claw unless you wish to be bitten. One must go to the source to destroy such a wily foe," she said.

With a hard smile, Eyoés glanced to Gwyndel, eyes narrowed. Provoked by frustration, the fires of indignant anger slyly shone through. "What do *you* suppose we do?" he snapped. Once the words left his mouth, Eyoés realized his error.

To entertain thoughts of anger would be to lose my sensitivity for the Guide's voice.

Grimacing, he looked away, unable to meet Gwyndel's eye. "I'm sorry," he apologized, admonishing himself for his outburst. Gwyndel flashed a weak smile of mercy. Her smile faded. Seeking an answer to her brother's question, she paused, pushing a stray lock of hair behind her ear.

She took several steps toward him. Steeling herself, Gwyndel gently grasped his chin and lifted his head. "I do not know what we should do," she answered, meeting his eye. "Whatever may happen, I can only say this—we must trust the Guide. He will lead us."

No one sought to rebuff her. Those present were aware of the grave situation at hand. They knew the truth. Without a clear plan of action, they could only know and wait, watching the enemy's moves carefully for an opportunity to see justice served. All had paid a price to know their enemy, whether in health, family, or trust. Whether they would see the fruit of their sacrifice remained uncertain.

Gathering himself, Vikar wiped away the traces of tears from his face. He held his chin high in an attempt to remain strong. As his eyes drifted between the others, he nodded in agreement. "Then we shall wait on the Guide's timing," he said, lifting a finger in warning. "But promise me this—do *not* speak of this to Caywen. She and Throst have been close friends since childhood. I fear uprooting something so deep would destroy her."

42

24th of Iaulan, 2202 SE

Eyes glowing with bright eagerness, Caywen hastily walked toward Throst's personal chamber. A grin was pasted on her face. Turning a corner in the hall, she glanced down at the journal in her hand.

Throst is always fond of writing down his own musings. This will be a fitting gift.

She fingered the spine of the leather-bound journal. A flutter of excitement spurred her to hurry. Seven years had passed since Throst had saved her from a harsh punishment she didn't deserve. Time had only increased her gratitude for his actions. Caywen's gaze drifted across the trimmings and banners gracing the walls.

These halls have changed little since that day.

With a shallow sigh, she clasped the journal tightly. Directly ahead, she could see the doorway to Throst's quarters. Fixing her eye on her destination, Caywen recalled the words she wished to say. She held this day dearly with every passing year, and she looked forward to time alone with Throst. Stepping up to the door, she repressed her grin of eagerness into a friendly smile. Though it was slightly ajar, she raised a loose fist to knock out of courtesy—then stopped.

The low murmur of voices reached her ears from the opposite side of the door. Caywen's smile faded, and she let her hand fall to her side. She moved to leave.

He must be occupied. I will speak to him later.

"*Now* you speak to me of this?" a voice from within snapped. The brooding anger and scorn in the words sent a chill down Caywen's arms. Though she recognized the voice, it was not what she'd come to expect.

Throst?

Hands shaking, she leaned close to the opening and peered through. Her mouth slackened.

Throst faced the open window overlooking the courtyard, legs planted wide in a stance of defiance. Though impossible to see his face from this angle, his demeanor exuded a brooding hatred. Caywen stared in disbelief, dreading what she would see next, yet unable to pull away.

Crouching before Throst, on the stone windowsill he'd entered, a hardened man with a grey beard looked on. His appearance reminded Caywen of a seasoned soldier, whose eyes had seen so much death they no longer shone.

The man watched Throst carefully. "I came as soon as I was able, Lord Ravenstrong," he said with smooth arrogance. "My men had to establish themselves in the town before I could act."

Steadily regarding his guest with a cold, ominous eye, Throst took several threatening steps forward. "Amnedd, are you certain this escaped prisoner of yours is inside Castle Hodholm?" he inquired, cocking his head.

The man gave a firm nod. "As a Knight of the Phantom League, I swear it. Where else would he go? His brother is here. My men and I will search every corridor of this castle in order to find him," he declared.

Throst cursed under his breath. Waving aside the matter, he gave a snort of disgust. "I would have expected the Phantom League to be skilled enough to retain their own captives," he scoffed, "but no matter. We must act quickly. Begin final preparations." Having accomplished what he had set out to do, Amnedd gave a nod and grasped the top of the protruding lintel, moving to hoist himself out of the window. Throst quickly seized the man's shirt and pulled him back down. "Find this runaway of yours and do away with him. I have no use for babbling fools," he commanded, voice brought dangerously low.

Amnedd's expression hardened like stone. Shoving Throst's hand away, he grasped the hilt of his dagger in warning. "It is against our Code to do so without contract. He is not our target," he said with finality.

Throst slipped his hand into his pocket. Amnedd started and drew his dagger. The young Lord of Herthere raised a hand of assurance and pulled out a small sack, tossing it at Amnedd. The assassin caught the jingling packet and sheathed his dagger. Quickly, he undid the string.

As the Phantom Leaguer rifled through its contents, Throst smirked in cunning triumph. "How much is your *Code* worth to you?" he asked. Caywen held her breath as tears clouded her vision. A moment of silence passed.

Amnedd looked up with a growing smile. Tying the sack of coins tight, he attached it securely to his belt. "It will be done," he said. "I must take my leave. I already have overstayed my welcome." The Phantom Leaguer heaved himself out of the window and disappeared.

Stepping back from the door, Caywen covered her mouth. Her head swam with lightheadedness. The shocking exposure of Throst's villainy continued to sink in, yet she struggled to believe what she had seen. Caywen's stomach hardened, and she shook her head.

All those years—a lie. He pretended to care for me, yet plotted wickedness behind my back. Surely someone knows of this.

Her hand slowly fell to her side.

When I reminded Father about the anniversary of my friendship with Throst, he seemed on edge, as if there was something he wished to speak to me about, but thought better of.

Clenching her fist, Caywen punched the book clutched in her other hand, her face reddening in indignant outrage.

He knows.

Face dark with rage, she stormed down the hall from which she had come, casting aside her gift for Throst with disgust.

Lost in concentration, Vikar hunched over his desk, his pen scratching the parchment with furious strokes. Disturbed by his conversation with Eyoés, Gwyndel, and Gwair, he had set his mind on discovering a reasonable political strategy. Surely there had to be a way to put the people's fears to rest. His eyes brightened as a new thought came to him, and he jotted it down below his other notes.

The door to his chamber burst open. A splat of ink marred the parchment as his pen flew from his fingers. Leaping from his chair, he looked toward the entryway of his chamber. Caywen glared at her father and slammed the door shut behind her. The doorframe shuddered.

Stomping toward her father, she shoved aside a nearby chair. It wavered unsteadily, then fell with a bang onto the stone floor. "Why did you withhold the truth from me?" she accused, stabbing her index finger at him. "You *knew* Throst was working with the Phantom League?"

Taken aback, Vikar leaned against his desk for support. He struggled to find the words to explain himself. Pressed by his daughter's stormy questioning, he met Caywen's eye. "I feared I would hurt you," he stammered, leaving his desk to stand trial before her passionate scrutiny.

Caywen cocked her head, disbelieving. "You know I desire honesty, and that it is a mark of one loyal to the King—yet you held your peace?" she stormed, unwilling to believe her own father had shrouded her in a lie. Wiping away her hot tears with an angry growl, she swallowed hard.

Stricken, Vikar said nothing. For years, he had sought to do his best to teach his daughter the Guide's tenets. He had remained patient despite the tears, sleepless nights, and torment, all for the joy of raising his daughter. Faced with the truth that he had both angered her *and* disobeyed the King's own wisdom, Vikar pulled his hair with both hands in remorse. "I admit it!" he shouted. "I was wrong to keep you in the dark. I knew how close you and Throst had become, and I feared to end such a bond. Forgive me."

Caywen stepped back, collecting herself. Her father's honesty partially quenched her own fury. Not yet willing to completely leave her anger behind, she frowned. "For the King's sake, and not yours, I forgive you. But do not only seek my forgiveness. You strayed from the King's Proverbs with your actions. Seek his absolution," she answered in a controlled manner.

Reaching out to place a hand on her shoulder, Vikar hesitated, then pulled back. "You know I will," he said, chin trembling. "Tell no one of this. The present circumstances are too *dangerous* to reveal such matters."

Caywen briskly turned away and started toward the door. "Very well," she growled. Gripping the door handle, she opened the door and hastily left the room, slamming it behind her.

Had she seen her father's tears, her anger would have been roused to pity.

43

Gwyndel pushed open the door to the Great Hall and slipped inside. Adjusting her shirt, she searched for her quarry with reluctance. Her lip curled in disgust as she recalled her given assignment.

Me? To speak with Throst and attempt to deduce the Phantom League's ambitions? I cannot even bear to think of looking him in the eye.

Her throat burned in disgust at the very notion. Discussions with Eyoés and Gwair had painted Throst as a spiteful foe with a forked tongue. Pausing at the doorway, she fidgeted uncomfortably with the pleated shoulders of her dress and looked about.

To her right, the feasting table was prepared for the evening meal. Goblets and mugs were neatly placed at each seat, along with a set of cutlery. Across the room, the door to the kitchen stood partially ajar. Gwyndel could hear the low murmur of hushed gossip and conversation from within. High above her head, two large windows looked down upon the Great Hall. Pennants bearing the coat of arms of each Baron of Rehillon hung from the central beam of the roof, swaying gently. The room was kept clean and neat, and two smaller tables with benches provided enough seating for a sizable feast.

Seated at one of these tables, a lone man wrote in polite silence. As she caught sight of him, Gwyndel instinctively shrank back. From the description her brother had given, it was clear she had found her target.

Compelling herself to appear calm, Gwyndel started toward Throst. She steeled herself in preparation.

Whatever he says, be wary, and believe none of it.

Gwyndel strove to exude a positive attitude, dismissing the emptiness in her stomach as a lingering effect of her recovery. She detested pretending. As she approached, Throst looked up from his work.

For a moment, he paused, eyes narrowing in uncertainty as to her identity. Then with a smile, he stood, giving a polite bow as was custom in the presence of a lady. "I remember you—you're Eyoés sister, are you not?" he asked, inquisitive. She appeared infinitely better than the last time he saw her—in the throes of the Addiction.

Gwyndel slowed to a stop, her contempt for the man held in check. Through the haze of her withdrawal, she had seen little of Throst. With the discovery of his wicked deeds, she had construed the image of a villainous, repugnant man in her mind. However, the young, neatly dressed man standing before her, however, did not seem to be the type responsible for the crimes he was accused of.

It is in the most alluring guises the enemy conceals himself.

Faking a smile of friendship, Gwyndel nodded and bowed in return. "I am," she replied. Gwyndel recoiled inwardly. The fact that this man recognized her in the first place made her skin crawl.

May the Guide keep me from his influence!

She hoped she could hold up against deception. It was a tricky business. In times of suspicion and aversion, the intentions of others became unclear. Hasty, negative conclusions were often based on little more than a single, provocative occurrence, the byproduct of a biased perspective. Sometimes, they exposed bias and showed the concern was unfounded. Other times, they rang true. Gwyndel had seen it during her years as a Forester, and had been victim to it herself. Covering her true emotions, she stepped closer, placing a hand on her chest. "I've come to give you my deepest thanks. Had you not provided the remedy for my addiction, there's no telling what my fate could have been," she said, grateful. To her surprise, an appreciation for his intervention fought against her contempt.

Throst inclined his head and smiled. "The honor is mine. I could never stand aside while a lovely damsel suffers as you did," he observed.

It took little effort for Gwyndel to feign embarrassment. She froze in place, dipping her chin down and avoiding Throst's gaze. As she furtively glanced toward the door to the Great Hall, she considered making a hasty retreat.

We may have little time until the Phantom League makes its final move. If I learn nothing from this, we may be too late to act.

The conversation had begun, and Gwyndel hesitated to leave without gaining some kind of information Eyoés and Gwair needed. Looking past Throst, she saw the parchment spread out on the table behind, corners held in place by several stones. Smooth, elegant script was neatly fit into a rectangle.

Noticing Gwyndel's interest, Throst seated himself and eagerly removed the weights holding his work to the table. "I am transcribing my reflections for the betterment of others," he explained, words rushed with the excitement of sharing one's hard work. Lifting the parchment from the table, he turned to face Gwyndel. "At the moment, I am addressing the subject of leadership—a topic of apparent concern to the people of Rehillon," he declared.

Gwyndel's smile went rigid.

Why mention the people's unrest? Could it be simply his concern for them, or is Throst pressing something unspoken?

Holding the parchment up to his scrutiny, Throst examined his writing carefully with rapt attention. "I shall read you an excerpt," he said, clearing his throat. "The greatest leader is one who assumes the role of public servant, not tyrant. In times of crisis, the leader becomes one with the people, and when all has reached its end, they shout 'We did it together'."

Throst peered up over the edge of his parchment at Gwyndel. The young elf shifted uncomfortably. Her desire to flee the scene was impeded by a fear of discovery. Pulled in opposite directions by her nerves, Gwyndel searched for a way out. As she looked at

Throst, she could have sworn she had seen the creases of a smirk pulling at his face. "You speak wisdom," she stated, speaking her words with care in order to keep from stumbling over them. "It will inspire others, as it should."

Smiling, Throst set his written work onto the table, adjusting his inkwell. Gwyndel played with her dress as she glanced back at the door. She had been in the presence of this devious villain for too long, and the reading of Throst's philosophy gave her an eerie sense she had found what she had sought for.

She partly wished she hadn't. "I must be on my way. I do not wish to keep you from your important work," she said. She was fearful to say more lest Throst manipulated her into a compromising position. Giving a quick bow, she turned to the door and made her retreat.

As Throst watched Gwyndel depart, his expression darkened. He reached for the dagger hanging unseen under the folds of his mantle.

Something is amiss.

44

25th of Iaulan, 2202 SE

Encompassed in a thick darkness, Lord Haral Rhys' room seemed more like a hole in the ground than a place of rest and comfort. Curtains kept out the light of the stars, leaving the room in shadows. Silhouettes of simple chairs and other furniture were barely visible. The bed nestled against the curved wall could easily have been mistaken for a table. Darkness made everything equal, eliminating forms and shapes into a simple presence, not seen, but felt with sense of physical position.

Out of the depths of inky shadow, the deep, rattling snore of Haral Rhys rang like a wrong note on a bowed lyre. On the nightstand beside his bed, a plate of leftover food waited till the Lord of Enfalls was next stricken by hunger.

The steep, conical roof came to a point above him. On one side of the roof a large hatch was sealed shut. When open, it acted as a miniature skylight accessible by a nearby ladder. At the top of one of Hodholm's towers, it seemed unlikely to receive unwanted visitors at the midnight hour.

The roof hatch creaked open, allowing a beam of starlight to penetrate the thick gloom below. Exposed in the light, a rat darted away, scrambling into a hole in the stone. Again, the snore of Lord Rhys roared up from the depths like a monster's growl. Slipping through the open hatch, a figure grasped the wooden beams supporting the conical roof. His plain clothing flapped in the night breeze issuing into the room. Adjusting the mask covering his face, the figure climbed down from the rafters as far as he could, then dropped to the floor in his soft shoes. The gentle impact was veiled by the snoring of the room's occupant.

Pulling his hood tighter over his head, Amnedd strode toward the closed window and whipped the curtains away. He leaned as far out from the windowsill as he could and spoke, craning his neck upward. His words merged with the whispering of the breeze, yet his comrades understood. Two more figures slipped through the roof hatch and descended in a similar fashion. Their clothing bore no distinguishing marks. Nothing extravagant, just what would mark them as everyday members of society—even if that meant of the lowest status.

Their only unique mark was the black tattoo of the Phantom League symbol on their necks, hidden beneath the collars of their shirts.

Once assured his men had entered without incident, Amnedd approached the bed at the far end of the room. Sprawled under the covers, Haral Rhys continued to snore. Beneath his mask, Amnedd gave a sneer of contempt for the fat noble.

What a pity he is to join our undertaking.

Ripping the covers off the bed, Amnedd shook Lord Rhys so violently, he nearly tore the man's nightshirt from his shoulders. With a cry, Haral abruptly sat up, shaking. Seeing the three looming figures at his bedside, his face paled. "Who are you?" he sputtered, staring. One of the Phantom Leaguers behind Amnedd took a step forward. Haral pressed himself against the wall, lips trembling. "Keep away from me, or I'll have you hanged!" he threatened, his voice shrill.

Angered by the worthless threat, a Phantom Leaguer drew his dagger with a growl. "Hold your tongue, braggart, or I'll silence you myself!" he snarled.

With the speed of a dragon, Amnedd whipped his rondel dagger from its sheath and knocked his subordinate backward, causing the man's knife to fall to the floor. Slamming the assassin against the wall, Amnedd pressed the spike blade of the dagger against the man's throat. "You know the penalty for speaking rashly," Amnedd hissed, his fearsome demeanor demanding obedience. Raising his hands in submission, the mercenary eyed his commander, the light of his violent rebellion extinguished. Amnedd let the moment of terror rest between them, then stepped back.

He turned to face Haral Rhys, sheathing his rondel dagger. "You're going to do us a favor," he said.

45

As the main gate to Hodholm swung out, the sentries stepped aside, standing at attention with their pikes upright. Leading the others, Lord Haral Rhys strode into the courtyard. Along with Lord Crawbrand, Lord Bardmond, and Lord Ravenstrong, Baron Vikar followed closely behind. Woven among the leaders of Rehillon, Eyoés, Gwyndel, and Gwair followed down the descending stairs, pushed and shoved by this small crowd. The Baron's family flanked either side of him, with Caywen's position on the right as befitted her direct relation to her father.

Vikar rubbed his brow as if to ward off the upcoming headache resulting from Haral's blathering. "What is the meaning of this urgent assembly of the Council, Lord Rhys?" he sighed. The Lords of Rehillon had learned over the years to take Lord Rhys' word lightly. Often the man spoke with little thought, or became concerned over matters that meant little—or nothing—to the welfare of their homeland. In truth, it was quite remarkable the man served his people well at all. Whispering mocking quips amongst themselves, the other Lords followed Lord Rhys in anticipation of a good laugh.

Slowing to a more moderate pace, Haral looked over his shoulder, his lips moving rapidly as he searched for the right words. "There is a pressing matter that must be addressed," he answered, not meeting the Baron's eye.

A mutter of disgruntled disbelief rose from Gerall Bardmond and Agnar Crawbrand. Looking on with a raised eyebrow, Throst alone considered Haral's words seriously. Vikar growled under his breath and hurried his pace. "Of what kind?" he asked again, leaning forward as he attempted in vain to glean some kind of information.

Lord Rhys didn't break his stride. "The kind that brings into question things that are. Disorder could erupt because of it," he said, curtly.

Eyoés furtively glanced at Gwair. In light of their most recent discoveries, the prospect of a public airing loomed like a hangman's noose before them. Such an ominous foreshadowing could only lead into dark places.

If this truly warrants urgency, Hodholm will not be the same by nightfall.

Meeting Eyoés' eye, Gwair grimaced in dark expectation and peered at Throst. From the rear, there was little danger of being seen, but Eyoés was reluctant to even glimpse the Lord of Herthere. The fear of his own suspicions being read in his demeanor kept his eyes fixed on Haral Rhys.

Gwyndel noticed her brother's hand touch his dagger. She frowned, tapping his shoulder to attract his attention. They exchanged a look of uneasy understanding.

The group came to a halt in front of the castle stables. Stretching nearly half the length of the eastern wall of Hodholm, the stables consisted of thick stone walls and a thatched roof, heavily insulated to keep the animals within comfortable. The simple wooden entry door hung open, allowing a glimpse of several stalls within. Two massive sentries stood at either side of the doorway, cradling large axes in their burly hands. The emblem of the Amberster line—three drops of amber surrounding a single conifer on a blue shield—was stitched on their tunics.

Attracting the sentries' attention, Haral Rhys nodded. With a salute, the two guards set aside their weapons on the wet stone of the courtyard and entered the stable. Lord Rhys turned to the skeptical group. Pulling a handkerchief from his pocket, he patted away the beads of sweat forming on his forehead and neck. He fought to maintain his righteous facade, knowing his part in what he was about to reveal. Then, stuffing the handkerchief back in its place, he cleared his throat. "While tending my horse yesterday, I had the ill luck to step through some weak floorboards—perhaps too many mince pies—and stumbled upon this object," he said as the two guards reappeared at the stable entrance.

Clenching their teeth, they hauled a large, iron-covered chest out into the open by the sturdy rope handles on either side. On either side of the broken lock, the words "Var Hynlest" could be roughly made out, inscribed in the metal. Other than the inscription, the box seemed simple, and of little interest. Except to Vikar.

At the sight of the chest, he frowned, closely inspecting it. A hint of familiarity seemed to register in the Baron's mind. A dread as to its significance nearly overpowered Eyoés.

The fate of Rehillon may lie within that chest.

It didn't take long to find out. Casting aside the broken lock, the guards heaved the lid open. The assembly gasped aloud.

A mound of gold coins glittered with the allure of forbidden wealth. Astonished, Eyoés stared as everything else faded from his awareness. The massive pile of wealth beckoned him like the whispering voice of a forbidden friendship. His stupor cleared, and he felt disgust at his weakness. Recoiling with a curled lip, Eyoés tore his gaze from the chest.

I will not give in. It is not mine to take.

Lord Haral Rhys stepped up and blocked the chest from view. "The exact amount of the *missing* payment for the Everwheat. We Rehils were thrown into addiction when the Everwheat supplier didn't receive *this payment*," he reminded, turning to face Vikar with a hard stare. "Here it sits—undelivered. There is only one responsible for such an atrocity."

Eyoés placed a hand on his dagger.

The Phantom League has made their move.

Gwair stepped back, stoic as he struggled to suppress his emotions. Gwyndel covered her mouth with her hand. She looked to where Caywen stood. Horrified, Caywen moved closer to her father. Looks of confusion, shock, and utter mistrust passed between the Lords of Rehillon. They turned to Vikar for an immediate explanation.

Frozen in place, Vikar stared at the strongbox in dismay. His legs trembled as he strained to remain standing. Bringing a shaking hand to his forehead, he stepped back, nearly falling into the arms of Gwair. He could produce no explanation for the discovery.

Lord Rhys forcefully adjusted his thick mantle. "I resign from my seat on this Council and depart for Enfalls at once. My rejection of you, Vikar, will speak *for* me," he spat. Lifting his chin in haughty defiance, he spun on his heels and started for the gates. His horse fearfully awaited the long, painful task of carrying such a large burden.

As the group watched Lord Haral's departure, Throst shook his head in disbelief, pressing a clenched fist against his lips. Slowly, he backed away. "For years have we followed our Baron faithfully—only to uncover *this* treachery?" he accused, taking a shaky breath inward. "Perhaps the people are correct in their presumptions." Spinning on his heels, he stormed back to the castle, with the Lords of Rehillon in his wake.

46

29th of Iaulan, 2202 SE

Word spread like wildfire. At first, only the sentries on guard spoke of it, and only among themselves. Then, compelled by the weight and meaning of the incident, they spread the word under cover of idle conversation. The waves of news that had broken violently against the inner walls of Hodholm broke through to the masses, and the people of the town whispered words of shock. Few took heed of the power of their remarks.

Words scattered and sowed into the very fabric of society. They appeared soft, but cut like a knife, and kindled fires—flames of the dragon within the fickle heart of man. With the news of Baron Vikar's apparent misconduct, the divisive factions running rampant among the Rehils flamed into outright war. Within four days, news of riots and brutality streamed into Hodholm. The wrath of a dragon had poured out on the masses—and moved ever nearer to the gates of Hodholm itself. The truth soon became clear—even the Baron's strong heart could be melted by the searing flames of anarchy.

Inside Eyoés and Gwair's personal quarters, Vikar sat on the side of the bed, head held in his hands. His back slumped under the weight of his betrayal. Tangled in the disarray of sleepless nights, his hair lay disheveled. A hollowness filled his chest, reminding him of his own broken heart. Still, despite the onslaught of ill fortune, the last vestiges of his former strength motivated him to continue on.

Gripping the edge of the bed with the fierceness of determination, he looked purposefully at Gwair and Eyoés. "Never have I felt such betrayal," he quavered, striking the side of the bed with his fist. "Surely it is not too late to strike a final blow against the enemy!"

Eyoés glanced at Gwair. His head spun with shocking news of riots and unrest. Swallowing, he leaned against one of the supporting pillars and avoided Vikar's gaze.

What can we do against an enemy who has the people's support? All we claim and do will appear to be more trickery in their eyes.

Eyoés closed his eyes, recalling the fury and hatred in Skreon's eyes as his blade swung in a downward arc, thirsty for blood. At the time, it had seemed such a foe of physical strength remained the most fearsome a man could face. Yet, it was the cunning of Throst and his superior, devious mind, that pinned them to the wall. It had become clear the scheming words of Throst Ravenstrong cut deeper than the sword of Skreon. Every scheme they devised to escape his grip only served to strengthen Throst's hold.

How could such a crafty foe be brought to his knees by a simple boy?

Blinking to stay the tears, Eyoés rebuked the spiteful thought.

The King himself appointed me as Baron. Perhaps it is because of my forwardness and willingness to follow the Guide's instruction that he promoted me to such high standing. A man of cunning cannot be trusted with power—he will abuse it.

He looked up. A newfound courage surged within, and he pushed himself off the pillar to face his companions. "Perhaps there is something," he wondered, a revelation dawning on his features.

Gwair shook his head and moved to confront his friend. "How is that possible? It is clear from the evidence Throst has some hand in this attempt to soil Vikar's reputation," he declared, despairing. "I believe the Baronship of Rehillon is at stake, and the people swallow his lies."

To Gwair's surprise, Eyoés nodded enthusiastically with a growing smile of triumph. "And if those lies are exposed for what they are, Throst's true intentions are revealed!" he pointed out. "If we snatch our forged letter from his chamber, is it possible we can implicate Throst despite the lack of hard evidence?"

Throwing his hands up in a gesture of despair, Vikar stood and ran his hands through his hair. "You should have learned by now that nothing is as straightforward as it appears," he argued in irritation. "It will take a confession from Throst before the people to undo what has already been set in motion. I think we all agree upon the impossibility of this. We cannot restore Rehillon in such a hasty manner. It is a task that will take years to accomplish—should all be put right in the end." The Baron muttered the last words under his breath, to hide his own doubt from the others.

Eyoés clenched his fists in tenacious determination. A dark gleam of malicious anger glimmered in his eye. "We could force Throst into a confession," he said with contempt, keenly feeling the betrayal himself.

Having seated herself beside Vikar in an attempt to console him, Gwyndel rose. "You might as well be asking if we can tell a dragon to change its nature—it is impossible," she said.

Eyoés began to pace about the room. "There must be something!" he insisted, grimacing as he stubbed his toe against a nearby chair.

Gwair stroked his beard. "What if Lord Rhys retracted his accusations?" he thought aloud.

Clenching his jaw, Vikar pondered his old companion's suggestion. He shook his head in dejected resignation. "The damage is done—slander often becomes truth in the eyes of the misguided. I am afraid there is nothing we can do to remedy it," he sighed. "I will speak to Rodmer. He is an Estworth, not an Amberster. Perhaps he could travel to Merwic, Herthere, and Enfalls to try and at least calm the people down," He moved to the door.

Despite the Baron's confidence, Gwair wasn't so sure. "Do you trust him?" he inquired. Though Rodmer was a kinsman of the Baron, Gwair had noticed his cold, hostile demeanor. With the betrayal of Throst fresh in his memory, Gwair could not help but regard the Baron's nephew as an enemy of sorts. Erring on the side of caution appeared to be the prudent choice.

Weary of secrecy, the Baron's nerves were worn thin. "He may be a distant relation, but Rodmer is no villain," Vikar asserted. "Do you doubt my word?"

Words of strife, assurance of good intentions, and eagerness for action crashed together like the waves of the sea. Assured of complete secrecy, the friends spoke their minds openly, only serving to fuel the disagreement. There was one who witnessed it all.

Caywen pulled her head away from the other side of the door. Considering the words she overheard, she frowned, glancing up and down the hall to assure she was unobserved.

It is time I learned the full truth.

As she carefully muted her steps on the red carpet lining the halls, Caywen hurried to her quarters. There was much to prepare for her journey.

47

29th of Iaulan, 2202 SE

Pulling the hood further over her face, Caywen pressed herself against the nearest wall. The rush of night wind brushed through the castle halls. Caywen suppressed a shiver. She focused on the soothing patter of rain upon the stone outside. Moonlight shimmered through the windows lining the hallway, revealing specks of dust floating in the air.

A surge of adrenaline caused her to tremble in excitement. Caywen bit down a smile. Until now, she had responsibly deferred her dreams of heroic exploits.

Finally, an adventure to call my own!

She paused, excitement checked as Eyoés' words of warning returned to confront her.

I found adventure is not always glorious. There's violence. Pain. Weariness. It is not for the faint of heart.

As she considered his words, her zeal was reined in. It would be foolish to jump headlong into danger without heeding the wisdom of one who had gone before. Selfish fervor would only plunge her into a tight situation. She shook her head, reprimanding herself.

It is for my father that I dare to leave Hodholm, not my own eagerness.

The mystery of Lord Rhys' accusations against her father had kept her awake for hours. She had tossed and turned, mind filled with questions. Though known as a braggart, such a sudden act of sedition was too much even for Lord Rhys. The man had been content to follow Vikar's leading since his appointment as Lord of Enfalls. To suddenly adopt an attitude of contempt for one he had willingly followed through troubling times was contradictory. Her stomach was uneasy.

I must know the truth. Father needs me.

Peering around the corner, Caywen spotted a sentry on duty. His face was partially exposed by the orange glow of his lantern. Caywen pulled back as the man glanced her direction, nearly losing her footing on the smooth floor. Her heart raced. She pulled a coin from the folds of her cloak. Stepping around the corner, she threw it as far as she could. The coin knocked against a far wall, catching the attention of the guard. He swung his lamp in the direction of the sound and moved to investigate.

Caywen breezed past and dove into a separate corridor to her left. A stairway led down to the wide vestibule, then to the main gate itself. The dark space stretched in unseen directions like the depths of the sea. Partly lit by the dim light coming in through the windows, the bulking outline of the door stood fast, guarding the ancient halls of Hodholm with a stern resolve.

Holding her hands out to steady herself, Caywen descended the stairs into the vestibule, her dark cloak becoming one with the shadows. She stared intently at the main entrance, occasionally glancing about to discern any potential chance of discovery. The hem of her cloak dragged on the stone floor behind her. A few lanterns barely lit the vestibule, and ornamental pennants and banners hung from the decorative pillars pressed up against the wall, dimly illuminated.

As she stopped before the looming door, Caywen paused. She had become acquainted with the rounds and positions of many of the sentries over the years. On the other side of the main entry, she knew, two guards held their post long into the night. To attempt an exit out the main door would be folly, and a sure way to be caught.

Pursing her lips, she looked further down the wall to the right. The small servant's door allowed access to the courtyard, but barred entry from outside, being locked from within. Oftentimes, servants within the castle were assigned temporary duties in the courtyard, whether it be caring for the animals in the stables or gathering water for the kitchen. The door proved a convenience on a regular basis, and it did so now.

Hastening toward it, Caywen undid the draw bar and pulled the door open. Her cloak billowed wildly as the night wind picked up. A light creak squealed a warning to the sentries outside. Caywen released the handle, holding it still with her foot.

I should be able to fit through.

Gathering the wild folds of her cloak about her, she gradually eased her way through the half-opened doorway. Her face brushed against the door as she passed out into the courtyard. She pulled it shut.

She paused against the wall, glancing at the guards standing at the main entrance. The moonlight glinted off their vambraces. Beneath the visor of their helmets, the sentries' faces were barely visible. Holding themselves upright, they observed the empty courtyard with dignity, taking their task as soldiers of Hodholm seriously.

Looking to the right, Caywen could make out the large shape of the castle stables. The occasional whinny of horses drifted out into the night. Caywen glanced at the guards, muscles tense. Adjusting the cloth tied around the soles of her shoes, she moved smoothly out into the shadows cast by the looming towers of the castle.

Concentrating on her safe passage, she nearly crashed into the wall of the stable. Resisting the urge to glance back to where she had come from, Caywen pulled the stable door open just wide enough to squeeze inside.

The pungent odors assaulted her senses. At her entry, the horses lifted their heads, some stamping on the packed floor at the unexpected visitor. Leaning back against the closed door, Caywen coughed and shook her head. The dust in the air nearly made her sneeze. She felt her way along the wall to avoid stumbling.

Pushing off the wall in a step of faith, Caywen moved into the narrow aisle. She felt the drowsy gazes of the animals as they observed in silence, locked into their stalls by simple gates. She paid them no heed, instead searching each stall intently.

I know you're here…

From the recesses of the stable, a flash of feathers appeared above a gate not far away. Rubbing her hands together, Caywen hurried in that direction. Untying the cloth bound to her feet, she tossed it into the corner of a stall. She stood before the large group pen, looking on in wonder.

Nestled comfortably in the large pen, Gibusil looked up, tail curled behind him. His golden feathers brushed against the wood of the stall. At the sight of the cloaked figure, the griffin pulled back with a growl, raising the crowning feathers on the back of his head. His eyes were luminous in the dark.

Caywen threw back her hood. "It's me," she whispered, extending her hands to soothe the creature. Recognizing her from her previous visits with Gwyndel, Gibusil relaxed, stepping forward to nudge her hand. Caywen smiled as her fingers stroked the smooth surface of the griffin's black, curved beak. The creature gave a chirp of welcome, rearing up to place its front claws on the edge of the pen. Caywen's eyes widened at the size of the beast.

He's bigger than I realized.

Setting her hand on Gibusil's scaled forearm, she unlatched the gate to the stall. Gibusil stepped back as it swung open, then moved forward, sniffing curiously at Caywen. Stepping back, Caywen laughed to herself. She noticed a worn leather saddle set over the wall of the griffin's pen. Awkwardly moving past the creature, Caywen ducked under the edge of the saddle and grasped it with both hands. Gibusil followed her, observing closely.

Caywen clenched her jaw and stood up under the saddle. Balancing it on her head, she hastened to Gibusil's side and slid it over the griffin's back. Gibusil, knowing the familiar process of saddling, stood still.

Caywen paused to rub her aching neck. Exhaling, she cinched the saddle straps tight around the griffin's midsection as she would have for her own horse. Lifting a set of reins off a nearby nail, she gently put the bit in the griffin's mouth. Gibusil growled in discomfort, trying to work the bit to a more comfortable position with his tongue. Caywen tugged the reins in her hand, stepping back into the aisle and looking to the back of the stable. A pair of double doors at the far end of the building allowed access for larger animals to the courtyard. She coaxed Gibusil to follow. "Come along, boy," she urged, walking backwards to the doors. Stepping into the narrow aisle as best he could, Gibusil obeyed.

As they passed by the other stalls, several horses hung their heads over the tops of their gates, peering curiously at them. Gibusil gave a low growl of annoyance, and the other animals retreated into the safety of their pens.

Releasing the reins, Caywen undid the latch keeping the doors shut. She grasped both handles and pushed the double doors open with little effort. The western side of the castle courtyard spread out ahead.

Caywen took Gibusil's reins in hand. Quickly glancing about to assure no one observed, she hastened out of the stable and into the courtyard with the griffin in tow. She loosely wrapped the reins around the saddlehorn and heaved herself up into the saddle.

Gibusil needed little prodding. With a single flap of his wings, he soared upward into the night sky. The cold wind rushed into Caywen's face, making her eyes water. She clung desperately to the saddlehorn, stomach clenching as the griffin rapidly ascended. Staring into the nothingness of night, she held back a scream.

The griffin evened its flight to a horizontal path, wings spread out wide to catch the air. Caywen felt the surging strength of the wind propel them forward, as the waves of the sea thrust a boat forward into uncharted waters. As her panic faded, a thrill of excitement took its place. A wide grin spread across her face as the wind coursed through her hair, and caused her cloak to billow behind. The raw cold of the air sent an invigorating shiver through her body.

Untying the reins from the saddlehorn, Caywen looked to where Hodholm lay below. The place she had called home seemed a set of child's toys, with its magnificent towers, mighty walls, and humble town. Moon and stars lit the place, fighting against the glowing orange light of taverns and other establishments.

Caywen shifted her seat and tucked the reins underneath her leg. Reaching into her pocket, she pulled out a small compass and held it in front of her, reading the inscribed compass rose inside by moonlight. With her other hand, she clumsily righted their course with the reins. Though her skills at handling the griffin left much to be desired, Gibusil sensed where she wished to go and corrected accordingly.

Replacing the compass in her pocket, Caywen looked out into the vast land ahead, and the stars above that led to Enfalls.

It was time she learned the truth.

48

30th of Iaulan, 2202 SE

With the savory flavor of breakfast still upon his tongue, Vikar stood before the door to Caywen's bedchamber. His daughter had been absent at the morning meal, leaving her seat vacant at her father's right hand. Unsettled, Vikar had spent the morning in silence, trying to reason out an explanation.

It was unlike her to miss such a regular occasion. The more he considered it, Vikar believed he knew the answer. Staring at the floor in front of her door, he leaned against the doorframe.

She is still hurt by my reluctance to tell her about Throst.

Lifting his head, he sighed and reached for the door handle.

I will ask for her forgiveness again.

He knocked with his other hand. "Caywen," he said, leaning close to the door to make his voice heard. A minute passed, with no response. Pulling at the collar of his shirt, Vikar pushed against the door. It swung inward. Hesitantly stepping into the room, he looked about. "Caywen?" he called.

The room spanned nearly half the size of Vikar's personal chamber. Once his daughter had reached the age to have her own quarters, the Baron had tried to convince her to claim one of the larger rooms for herself. Despite his insistence, her mind was set on a smaller vision. A finely crafted bed sat unused, sheets neatly tucked into the frame. Hanging on the wall was a tapestry crafted by his daughter's own careful hand, portraying scene of a woman gazing longingly into the distance. Every time he set foot in her quarters, Vikar paused to treasure its artistry, and the yearning conveyed through it. The red curtain hanging above the window was drawn back. The room was prepared for the day—before the servants had even been there to ready it.

Vikar stepped further into the room. Caywen was nowhere in sight. Shaking his head, the Baron refused to believe the dread rising inside him. He glimpsed a white parchment lying on top of the neatly made bed he had not noticed earlier. Vikar rushed to take the note in his cold fingers. His stomach rolled as he read the hastily written words.

Father, or whoever finds this note -
Since I must leave soon, I will make this short. After much thought, I still cannot make sense of Lord Haral Rhys' sudden accusations against you. For years he has been content in your service, with no reason to betray you. To suddenly adopt an attitude of contempt for you is unlike him. I also overheard you discussing the matter with Eyoés, Gwair, and Gwyndel. I plan to learn the truth for myself. I assure you I will return by tomorrow.
Caywen

The note crumpled under Vikar's anxious grip. Letting his hand fall to his side, he stepped back from the bed, harried by the news.

She could very well be walking into the Phantom League's hands!

The room around him began to spin. Baron Vikar turned and fled from the room, breath coming in strained heaves.

"She departed without speaking to me! Jumped into the dragon's maw! There's no telling if the Phantom League has her in their clutches!" Vikar shouted, pounding the wall with his fist. Eyoés and Gwair looked on, their expressions grave. They were unwilling to look the stricken Baron in the eye. A moment of silence passed in mourning Caywen's loss.

Gwyndel stood in front of the far window, the overcast light painting her face with grey shadows. Heaviness weighed on her heart. She closed her eyes, remembering Caywen's caring sense of commitment to her students, and her sacrifice to aid her father in his duties. She recalled the vastness of the Great Library as she and Caywen prepared her notes for teaching. Their companionship had brought her much joy. The thought of Caywen being lost to the enemy made her cry.

"We have to ride to Enfalls before its too late!" Vikar pleaded, eyes wild. Choked with emotion, he reached out in an imploring gesture. Gwair grasped the Baron's shoulders. He understood Vikar's pain.

Gwair's eyes were kind. "To do such a thing would only provoke the League to violence," he reasoned, his quiet tone soothing to Vikar's nerves. "Even if we were able to intercept them with Caywen in their hands, do you believe they will simply hand her over to us? They would *kill* her." Baron Vikar looked aside with a pained stare. Fumbling for words, Gwair stopped, allowing Vikar space to breathe and think. He released the Baron's shoulders. "It hurts me to say this, but by staying behind, we may be keeping her alive," he said.

While Gwair whispered words of comfort to his old friend and leader, Eyoés held his peace. He recalled his short time with Caywen.

She wanted an adventure—and got one. Whether she returns alive has yet to be seen.

It was time this strained conversation came to an end. "The situation is getting out of hand. There will soon come a time to use force. I *know* it," Eyoés said. "We can only prepare ourselves and pray the King delivers Caywen from the enemy."

Mutters of quiet agreement rose about the room. Eyoés found himself strangely calm.

The King will protect Caywen. As long as we put our faith in him, all will be put right.

Though he found it difficult to believe, he knew it to be true in the depths of his inner being.

49

30th of Iaulan, 2202 SE

A day passed before Caywen and Gibusil reached Enfalls. The horizon glowed a deep orange-red as dusk settled. Peeking above the trees, the moon began its ascent into the starry sky, proclaiming its reign over the land below. Calls of nocturnal animals issued from the forests as the daytime creatures settled down to sleep.

Drifting on the calm air, Gibusil soared over the forested hills and valleys below. A flock of birds scattered as he passed close by. The griffin ignored them, already full from an earlier meal. Seated in the saddle, Caywen squinted, looking ahead. She referenced her bearings with her compass yet again. She noticed a dark silhouette cast on a nearby hill and steered Gibusil in its direction. The castle came into view, partially illuminated from the side.

Castle Enfalls paled in comparison to the size and grandeur of Hodholm. Built upon a rock outcropping, a single tower overlooked the valley, topped with a hexagonal, gabled roof. In the upper keep, only two windows allowed in light and fresh air. A rampart surrounded the castle in an odd, scraggly formation, as if part of the mountain itself. The stone wall blended seamlessly into the foundation below. Crowding the already small courtyard, several smaller houses provided quarters for the few servants who lived there. The design of the structures was plain, akin to the simplicity of a common merchant's home. From the sky, the castle was very unimpressive. Caywen sighed.

I had expected something grander.

She dismissed her trivial disappointment. The griffin soared toward the small fortification, its gold feather coat reflecting the deep hue of the dusk horizon. Gibusil slowed to a gentle glide before pulling up short of the keep. Caywen indicated one of the windows, from where a glow of light hinted at habitation. Silently gliding below the window, Gibusil latched his claws into the stone. Caywen precariously scrambled up the griffin's back, heaved herself onto the windowsill, and slipped into the room. Gibusil glided back into the night, landing on the flat roof of the servant's quarters nearby. Caywen ducked behind a long, draping curtain.

The rectangular room was nearly the same size as Caywen's personal chamber, large enough to provide a suitable living space, but too small for much else. A bed was pressed up in the furthest corner of the room. Cracks traced the length of the bed frame, hinting at a struggle to keep its occupant off the ground. The sheets were sloppily wadded and unkempt. A tapestry hung beside the window, bearing the respectful image of an ancestor. At the far end of the room, furthest from Caywen's hiding place, was an angled desk, along with an empty chair. An elegant rug was placed in the middle of the floor.

Lord Haral Rhys rocked on the balls of his feet in the middle of the room. Turned away from the window, he fanned himself with his hand. He muttered to himself, voice quivering with dread and guilt. Although Caywen could not quite make out what he spoke of, bits and pieces of his rambling words she understood.

"Oh, how could I have done this?" he moaned. "It wasn't him—*it wasn't Vikar!* Curse those brigands!" His hands flapped about in wild gesticulations. Tugging at the collar of his shirt, Lord Rhys glanced at the desk and the piece of parchment lying there. He wrung his hands, taking a pained breath. "I can't live with such guilt!" he exclaimed, stomping his foot. Shuffling to the desk, he seated himself precariously on the chair.

As the Lord of Enfalls furiously wrote, Caywen fingered the curtain veiling her from view.

Now is the time to act. I have to know the truth in full.

She began to move from behind cover. A quick knock on the door sent her back into hiding. Woken from his burst of guilty inspiration, Lord Rhys ceased his writing and hurriedly flipped the page over to expose its blank side. He cleared his throat to gain his composure and looked toward the door to his chamber. "Come in," he called.

A spike of fear ran through Caywen as the door opened. Amnedd strode into the room, flanked by three others clothed as servants. Caywen's eyes widened as she recognized him.

Retreating further into cover, she observed from a crack between two chairs. As his men barred the door from within, Amnedd sauntered further into the room. Malice gleamed in Amnedd's eyes as his gaze settled on Haral. "Good evening, Lord Rhys," he sneered, his manner cooly malevolent. "I must congratulate you on your fine work."

Face pale with terror, Lord Rhys stuttered, unable to speak. Placing a hand on the back of the chair, Amnedd leaned down to Haral's level, noticing the parchment lying upon the desk. Hastily written words bled through to the other side of the page. A smirk of spiteful glee pulled at Amnedd's mouth. He flipped the parchment over and took it in hand, briefly scanning its contents. "What's this? A confession?" he inquired in mock surprise. "I expected such double-dealing from you, if I were to be honest."

Caywen's expression became somber as a contemptuous determination broke through Lord Rhys' fear. He gave a scoffing laugh and spat on Amnedd's boot. "Filth such as you don't care for honesty," he snapped, standing from his chair and taking a step back.

Amnedd raised a questioning eyebrow. Forcefully shoving the chair underneath the desk, he moved a threatening step forward. "And do you assign that judgement to yourself as well?" he sneered.

Haral Rhys cringed, looking away as he clenched his fists. "I have done wrong, but I must make it right," he declared in defiance. Planting himself in a solid stance, he watched as Amnedd circled around behind him like a predator sizing up its prey. Lord Rhys faced him, turning his back to the three other assassins.

Amnedd meandered forward, each step pushing Haral Rhys back toward his subordinates. "I think not," he said with a harsh squint. Looking over to the other Phantom Leaguers, Amnedd gave a firm nod. "Get the rope and throw it over the uppermost rafter," he ordered with a smile.

With a salute, one of the men pulled an object from his satchel—a rope with an iron weight at one end and a noose at the other. The Phantom Leaguer tossed it up and over the main rafter bracing the base of the roof. One of the others caught the weighed end and held it tightly. Dangling menacingly, the noose waited patiently for the inevitable.

Eying it with sudden terror, Haral stepped back, bumping into Amnedd. His heart raced. Trembling, Lord Rhys looked over his shoulder, beads of sweat forming on his forehead and upper lip. "What are you doing, Amnedd?" he asked, his whimpering voice barely audible. "I did what you asked of me!"

Pushing his terrified captive forward, Amnedd laughed. It was a laugh Caywen would never forget. A restless evil lay unspoken in it, joyous at the thought of death. From behind cover, Caywen shivered.

The head Phantom Leaguer took the noose in hand. "Why, assisting you in your suicide," he answered. "I understand how *deep* the pain of Vikar's betrayal must be to you—the hurt has to end, somehow." Widening the noose to fit around Haral's wide neck, Amnedd looped it around his victim. "There's nothing to look forward to now—and your confession will never be brought to light," he declared in wicked victory.

Lord Rhys' hands slowly went up to touch the rope around his neck. Taking a moment to comprehend the depth of his misfortune, he stared blankly at the floor. Caywen bit her trembling lip as tears raced down her cheeks. A moment passed. Lord Rhys felt tears welling in his eyes. The smirk on Amnedd's face faded. Behind the man's fear and sadness was a determined resolve.

The man about to die now bore himself with confidence. Haral Rhys swallowed and clenched his jaw, face drawn in unwavering courage. "For Rehillon," he said.

With a sneer, Amnedd snatched a hood from one of his subordinates and pulled it over Haral's head. He stepped back, folding his arms across his chest. "Kill the fop," he commanded. The three henchmen pulled the rope down to the floor, heaving Lord Rhys upwards. Caywen looked away, hearing the rafter creak under the weight of the dying Lord of Enfalls. Minutes passed under a tense silence, as Lord Haral Rhys embarked on his journey to the Kingdom under the stars.

One tied the loose end of the rope to the bedpost, leaving the shrouded body to hang limp. Taking the desk chair in hand, they set it on its side beneath the body of the Lord of Enfalls. The suggestion of suicide would cover their tracks.

Quenching her sobs, Caywen glanced at the window.

I'm trapped in this room!

Stricken with both the fear of the enemy and the horror at the sights she had seen, she darted from behind the curtain. She whistled loudly, preparing to leap out of the window and onto Gibusil's back.

The Phantom Leaguers seized Caywen by the shoulders and pulled her back into the room as Gibusil flew past, anticipating her jump. As Caywen struggled against her captors, the griffin turned with a screech, diving for the window with outstretched claws. "No Gibusil!" Caywen cried. The impact, she knew, would likely send the griffin hurtling to its death with a broken wing. Reluctantly, Gibusil changed his course and rocketed into the sky above.

Pulling Caywen's arms behind her back, the men forced her to her knees. A smile grew on Amnedd's face. "What have we here? A witness?" he thought aloud in hopes to intimidate his freshly caught captive.

Enraged, Caywen lunged forward, baring her teeth. "Get away from me, mongrel," she snarled. A flush of heat wafted over her like fire, stoking her anger. Twisting, she attempted to break their grip on her.

Amnedd leaned forward, his piercing stare causing Caywen to flinch. "Such a sharp tongue for a child," he hissed in warning. His hand wrapped around the handle of his dagger in consideration.

Noticing their commander's action, one of them glanced at the hanging form of Haral Rhys. "Should we let her swing?" he inquired.

Amnedd paused, pursing his lip as he mulled over the proposal. Releasing his dagger, he shook his head. "No—we only have one rope, you dullard. Her body would only raise questions. We keep this one alive. She's the Baron's daughter," he explained. His tall frame loomed over her like a giant. With a grin of mock friendship, he clasped his hands behind his back. "Allow me to introduce myself—I am Amnedd, Knight of the Phantom League," he announced, bowing with mock flourish.

Eyes flinty with hatred, Caywen glared at him. "I know who you are," she growled. Had she been in possession of her senses, she would have known resistance was useless. Reason clouded by raw emotion, she strained forward, muscles quivering.

Considering Caywen's words, Amnedd raised an eyebrow. "Do you?" he asked. This time, Caywen noticed a sincere surprise in his tone, partially masked by scorn. The desire to fight waned, and she pulled back, unsure of the right words. Seeing her hesitation, Amnedd looked to his subordinates. "She knows something. Gag her and prepare to depart for Hodholm," he instructed. "I believe Lord Ravenstrong would like to speak with her."

The wolf had caught its prey.

50

3rd of Merchen, 2202 SE

Caywen knew from the toll of the evening bell she and her captors had entered the town of Hodholm. Hands tied behind her back, she lay on her side within the horse cart's secret compartment. Bales of hay were stacked above her upon the cart's false bottom. The ropes bit into her wrists, the rough dried hemp leaving red rashes. The earthy smell of hay choked Caywen. Inside the hidden compartment, the hot air caused her to sweat, drying her throat with every inhale. Wafts of fresh air drifted through the gaps in the boards beneath. Though she had been hidden in the hay cart for only a short time, Caywen felt ill.

The cart bumped over a stone in the path. Caywen was jolted onto her back, twisting her bound hands. Grimacing, she rolled back onto her side. A linen sack lay under her head, bound into a roll. Her head throbbed from the constant jolting of the ride. The comfort of a pillow, no matter how crude, was most welcome.

The bustle of the townsfolk talking among themselves was an incomprehensible murmur from within the cart. Clanging in a steady rhythm, the evening bell informed the people of the coming night hours. One of the horses pulling the cart neighed as the driver pulled hard on the reins. Caywen felt the cart lurch to the right, then stabilize. She shifted her position, blowing away the hair blocking her face. The cart came to a stop.

Where in Hodholm are we? Where are they taking me?

Caywen flinched as the bales of hay above her were removed, and the false bottom detached from its place. She sat up, disoriented. Amnedd set aside the reins and seized the rolled up linen sack from the back of the cart. Quickly untying its leather strap, he unraveled a thick shroud and pulled it over Caywen's head. Darkness blinded her once again as she was pulled from the cart by her captors.

Her feet dangled in nothingness, then touched the familiar firmness of the street. Caywen staggered into a barrel. The Phantom Leaguers grabbed her and ushered her along, eager to leave the scene of the crime.

All was darkness as Caywen stumbled, blindly guided through the alleys. The crisp, fresh scent of new rain cleansed her nostrils from the cloying smell of hay. Off in the more distant part of the town, she heard the repetition of the blacksmith's hammer. Turning corners here and there, Caywen struggled to keep up the pace, straining to see through the fabric hood. Several times, the setting sun illuminated one of the henchmen from the side, allowing Caywen to glimpse the man's shadow.

They came to a sudden halt, jarring Caywen as she stumbled forward. Her shoulders wrenched as her captors jerked on her arms to pull her back. From under the sack, her breaths quickened, adding to the trapped hot air. A drop of sweat rolled into her eye.

The door opened. A quick exchange of words passed between Amnedd and some stranger. Shuffling feet could be heard, then Caywen was pushed forward. Her toe caught the rim of the threshold. She fell onto her face with a grunt. Two of the men hoisted her up before shoving her forward again. A second door opened, the squeak from the hinges sounding directly in front of her.

Suddenly, she was shoved into a hard wooden seat. Caywen's tailbone ached from the blow. This time, when the door shut, the creak came from behind her.

The hood was yanked off, pulling some of her hair with it. Clenching her jaw, Caywen bore the pain in silence.

I will not show weakness to these brutes.

The space was completely barren, except for a table before her. Cracks traced jagged paths across the wall. Covered in old, broken tiles, the floor seemed untouched by man, coated with a layer of dust and grime. The ceiling sagged above her. Caywen glanced toward one of the two doors allowing access to the crumbling room. Her eyes darted from one to the next, unsure which she had entered from. The uncertainty disoriented her.

Amnedd addressed his subordinates. "I will bring him in," he said. Leaving the three Phantom Leaguers to keep a close watch, he walked to one of the doors and passed through, slamming it behind him.

In the furthest corner of the next room, Throst sat on the edge of a barrel, hunched over. His fingers fidgeted anxiously as he stared at the floor. Expression tight, he glanced up at the door across the room. As he thought of what lay on the other side, his stomach fluttered.

She's here—and I can't bring myself to speak to her.

Closing his eyes, Throst envisioned the kindness in Caywen's eyes and the soft glow of her face. A smile spread across his features, though he didn't know it. The restless desire to be with her drew him in.

I cannot be without her.

His heart hammered in his chest—until his tender smile faded. Covering his face with his hands, Throst hung his head, despondent. With the revelation of his true nature, his relationship with Caywen would come to an abrupt end. Wiping his eyes, Throst envisioned Caywen on the other side of the door. The dreaded end coming ever nearer was hard to accept.

I had hoped to sweep Vikar from power and still keep Caywen by my side. Innocence is often confused for virtue, even when that innocence is false. Had Caywen still believed in my innocence, I may have lived in peace. Now, there is no turning back.

Throst felt an emptiness inside he could not fill by himself. He understood fully the consequences of his actions. There would be no reconciliation. No final goodbye. Only glares of anger and hurt.

Is such sacrifice worth the gain?

He was torn between transcending the wounds of his childhood by ascension to wealth and power—and keeping his love for her intact. Throst could not bring himself to a final decision. The door opened as Amnedd entered the dark room. Only a small window near the ceiling allowed light in. Standing before the young Lord of Herthere, the head Phantom Leaguer folded his arms across his chest. "She knows something," he stated flatly, wasting no time in speech.

Throst looked up at Amnedd. A sinking sensation pulled him toward the door. Hanging slightly ajar, it allowed a view into the next room. Throst leaned against the doorframe and peered through the crack. Strangely, the same exhilaration that filled him at the sight of her transformed into a conflicted reluctance.

He looked fixedly at her. "I'm torn, Amnedd," he muttered, afraid of being overheard by Caywen. "I wish her to be my wife, but she cannot know what I've done." Pulling away from the door, he turned to face the mercenary. "I cannot bring myself to show her what I've become," he said, casting a longing glance at the door.

Amnedd cocked his head. "Do you not remember the reason behind your scheming?" he questioned. "Your father, Fedrik, beat you—treated you as a slave. You told me yourself the pain continues to haunt you."

Throst nodded. "Indeed," he replied. "I promised myself in time I would ascend to such a status that such pain would never touch me again." The pain of his old wounds seared his back and arms anew. Wincing, Throst put his hand to his forehead, hearing his father's shouts of rage echoing in his ear. His heart ached.

Am I so quick to dismiss the wrongs done to me for the hand of a lady? Do I so easily forget?

A tear of anger dropped from his eye. Throst hastily wiped it away.

I must have the power to shield myself.

Seeing the incensed anger in Throst's face, Amnedd smiled. "As you have said—'Prosperity is a shield'," he declared.

Throst faced the Phantom Leaguer head on. "It is the truth," he said. Gripping the door handle, he pulled it open and strode through the entryway, with Amnedd following. At the sound of footsteps, Caywen looked to the door.

Seeing Throst, she tensed, eyes gleaming with hatred. "Treacherous swine! Traitor to House Amberster and the people of Rehillon! How could you trade the truth for heinous lies?" she yelled, restrained by the Phantom Leaguers guarding her. The tendons of her neck strained against her skin as she panted.

Throst Ravenstrong regarded her calmly, his expression smooth as polished stone. His fingers gently traced the edge of the table as he moved around to where she sat. As her glare traced his every move, Throst met it with a casual stare of his own. "You speak such travesty. Why do you claim these things?"

Grinding her teeth in rage, Caywen raised her eyebrows incredulously. "You purposely painted my father as the villain before the Council of Lords and the people themselves! Your scheming with the Phantom League only reveals the evil within you," she spat.

Throst leaned against the edge of the table, standing directly beside her. Taking several breaths, he examined the room around him. The contemplative silence held Caywen in tense expectancy as she awaited his reply. Throst let the moment linger, then moved around to the other side of the table. "Such a conclusion depends on the definition of 'evil'. Tell me, is it a crime to heed the concerns of the public? To investigate the rumors as a responsible leader?" he questioned. "The people are discontented with Vikar's leadership. You know this."

Caywen's anger waned. "Not everyone in Rehillon wishes you were Baron. There are others—"

"Others who have been under the old rule for so long they cannot accept a change even if it is for the better!" Throst interrupted cooly. "The tyranny of silence is the death of a people. Should we not listen and at least *consider* their concerns?"

Mouth agape, Caywen leaned forward, disbelieving. "You sound as though you're giving a *speech*—what happened to the old Throst Ravenstrong? The one who spoke to me as I played the bowed lyre? The one I confided in during times of trouble? The one who—"

Throst pounded the table with his fist with such force that Amnedd flinched. "Enough!" he shouted, the pain hidden deep inside him rearing its ugly face. "That man was weak, beaten by his monster of a father for *years*!" He leaned across the table, tense with wrath. "Do you not see it? I'm going to reclaim what he *stole* from me—the chance to become a man no one can wound! With the power of the Baronship behind me, my word will be final," he said. His low, menacing tone drove his words deeper into Caywen.

She pressed herself against the back of the chair with a quiet gasp. Fond memories of her childhood days spent alongside Throst surfaced, only to be torn in two by the open revelation of treachery. The young, laughing boy she once knew was dead. In his place, a vengeful serpent had reared its head, posing as a sheep. A pity for Throst's personal pain checked her anger.

I knew Throst's father was mean-spirited, but I never realized the extent of his father's tyranny.

An old vestige of friendship implored her to comfort her close companion. Yet, when she looked into Throst's eyes, she knew he would never accept her consolation. "Prosperity is a shield—so you told me once, when I thought your word was honest," she confessed. "Now, I realize I have been deceived by your smooth words, Throst Ravenstrong."

Stepping back from the table, Throst briefly closed his eyes, regaining his composure. He smoothed out his clothing. "Your father will be worried to death for you. I would be surprised if he has not sent a search party already," he said. "I will let you go free, should you pay me heed one more time."

Caywen's expression hardened. "You want information," she guessed, holding herself with pride. "I will never betray Rehillon—or Father."

Clenching his jaw, Throst turned to where Amnedd stood. "Feed her the White Flower," he insisted. "You will get the information you seek soon enough."

51

3rd of Merchen, 2202 SE

Standing before Eyoés, Gwair, and Gwyndel, Thruldin folded his hands, shoulders drooping under the weight of an unspoken confession. The heroes regarded the dwarf. The dark and heavy way he bore himself spoke for him.

Leery of yet more bad news, Gwair stalled for time, taking a minute to respond. "Why have you come, Thruldin?" he asked. The words left his mouth like the sputtering burst of a new well.

Thruldin chose his words carefully. "Kiffyn," he said, voice tearful. "This morning, in the tunnels—I woke to find him dead, stabbed in his sleep. I can only explain it as the Phantom League's doing."

Gwair fell to his knees, putting his head in his hands. Sobs shook his frame as he grieved. He wept openly, forgetting his former determination to remain strong in the presence of his friends. Gwyndel moaned in anguish, pulling at her curly red locks. As her whimpering cries of grief paid tribute to her childhood friend, Eyoés was also compelled to tears. His sister's heartache became his own, and for the first time, he truly felt Kiffyn to be a close friend. Though their meeting had been distant, Eyoés had appreciated the man's personable character. He embraced his sister in consolation, their tears staining the shoulder of the other.

The time for strategy had passed. The time for mourning had come.

That day, the sun hid its face, and the quiet funeral procession walked to the rhythm of a dismal dirge. The deceased—a man of wood and stream. A gentle rain pattered on the cobblestone as the clouds wept along with those below.

All were dressed in the appropriate fashion. Baron Vikar wore his finest, the thick mantle hanging on his shoulders damp from the rain. At his side, Rodmer followed in somber quietness. Bearing their coat of arms on their surcoats, the Lords of Rehillon honored the death of the exemplary youth, following directly behind the Baron.

A group of three Foresters carried a simple linen stretcher, signifying the simplicity and rigor of camp life. Upon it, lay Kiffyn, his face smooth and at peace as one whose pain has finally ended. His arms were crossed over his chest. Under one hand, rested a short pine bough, and under the other, a bow of yew, with a quiver of arrows lying at his feet.

The flag of the House of Amberster—and Rehillon itself—hung dully on its post as the youth bearing the standard paved the path for the departed. Rising and falling like the wailing of mourners, the reediness of the bowed lyre accompanied the gentle song of the traveler's harp. The harp player plucked a dirge, the melody accentuated by the lyre's emotion. There were few that day who did not shed a tear.

Gwair walked alongside his fallen brother. His bloodshot eyes were fixed on Kiffyn's still body. Determined to carry himself with honor for his brother's courage, he stifled his sobs, chest aching with the effort.

Trailing behind the group of Lords, Eyoés, Gwyndel, and Thruldin hung their heads. Eyoés fought for composure as his sister's sobs tugged at his heart. The loss of both Caywen and Kiffyn was too much of a burden to bear.

How could the King allow this? He knows how hard we strive to follow his direction.

Eyoés saw Throst standing in the procession. His hair hung loose and unbound in a show of respect, rather than being bound behind his head in the jaunty fashion of young nobles. His expression was pensive, contemplating the meaning of death, perhaps. To Eyoés' disgust, he even glimpsed a tear on Throst's face. He detested the treacherous man had the gall to be in attendance.

The procession approached the gatehouse. Standing upon the ramparts, the soldiers there removed their helmets and placed them at their feet in a show of respect and sympathy. With a metallic clatter, the portcullis lifted, revealing its iron teeth. The exterior gate swung open, allowing a direct path to the outside of the castle. As they passed under the gatehouse and out of the castle of Hodholm, the procession turned to the left, following alongside the wall. Eyoés reached out, letting his cold fingers brush against the uneven, moist surface of the stone.

At the corner of the wall, the land sloped down into a small ravine, guarded by a large copse of conifers. Though the boughs partially guarded them from the rain, drops continued to fall from the needles above. The forest ahead of them opened up into a small clearing. An ethereal glow seemed to linger about the forest with a enchanting peace. Ferns, shrubs, and small trees grew on the outskirts of the glade, gleaming with wet rain. Nailed to a nearby tree was a simple wood sign—"Final Resting Place". Freshly dug near the edge of the clearing was an empty grave, with a pile of fresh dirt beside it.

Eyoés let his eyes wander as he took in the alluring beauty of the forest. Despite his sadness, he admired the canopy of trees above him.

The forest was where Kiffyn belonged, and this is where he will rest.

He looked to Gwyndel. "Kiffyn would have been at peace here," he said. Meeting his gaze with tear filled eyes, Gwyndel nodded, lips trembling. The burden of her emotions could not be done justice by words.

Coming to stand in the middle of the grove, the Foresters carrying Kiffyn's body lay the stretcher at the side of the grave. One of them stepped forward, eyes lingering on the still form of Kiffyn. "In honor of our brother's passing, the oath he swore to follow shall be read aloud. By this oath, Kiffyn became a Forester. With this oath, he will be remembered," he declared, raising his voice. Reaching underneath his cloak, the man pulled out a parchment and unfolded it. The Forester drew himself up with honor, as generations had upon reciting this pledge. "I vow, from this day forward, to remain steadfast, and to stand for what is right, no matter the price. With bow, sword, and diplomacy, I will always be there for those in need. I will fight for virtue, and if need be, die in the service of others. I am a Forester—and my word is my pledge," he read. With a sense of finality, he folded the parchment and slipped it under his cloak. He exchanged a somber look with the other two Foresters. With a salute, the two took the stretcher in hand and lowered it into the grave along with Kiffyn's body. They draped a linen shroud over him reverently.

With each spadeful of dirt, Gwyndel wept.

52

Caywen remembered little after Amnedd poured the juice of the White Flower down her throat—only a haze of jumbled words and the pain of blows as the enemy beat her after confession. Leaning against the wall with hands tied, Caywen attempted to fall asleep to the tolling of the town bell. Through the fog of exhaustion, melancholy thoughts stirred.

Will I wither away in this room alone?

Unanswered questions hounded her. Shifting her position, Caywen opened her eyes and flinched as her bruised ribs bumped against a barrel. A hollowness permeated her body as if her fighting spirit had been torn out by her exultant enemies.

Will I ever see Father again? Or will I die by the assassin's knife?

Strangely, the isolation of the empty room comforted her. Here, she could think in peace, without fear of imminent danger. Still, the apprehension of her approaching demise disturbed her like the marks on her back and ribs. She now knew peace was just an illusion inside this room. Slumping against the wall, Caywen felt a despondency welling inside her.

They're keeping me here for ransom. If Father cannot pay, I am doomed to a gruesome fate. Torture before death. This is the end.

The lock clicked open. Caywen's head snapped up as the door opened, hinges creaking in protest after several hours of rest. Stepping into the room, a tall man held a lantern ahead of him.

She scrambled into the corner. "Stay back!" she hissed, voice quiet for fear of attracting more of the enemy.

Holding his hand out in a gesture of peace, the man approached. Exposed by the lantern light, his eyes exuded a genuine concern that confused Caywen. "I'm not going to hurt you," he promised, setting the lantern on top of the nearby barrel.

Caywen's tense posture loosened. Frowning, she glanced around, looking for answers. Her mind raced for an explanation. "Do not lie to me! I know you are murderers," she said, tone uncertain. For some reason, she wasn't so sure.

Kneeling before her, the man drew his dagger and gently set it aside. "It is not as you assume—I'm here to rescue you. Call me Lanyon," he said.

She drew back behind the barrel, shielding herself from the stranger. "I don't believe your lies," she retorted.

Though the room was dark, Caywen could detect his intent gaze through the lantern's light. "What would it take to earn your trust, even just for the moment?" he asked, sincere.

Caywen thought for a moment. "Your mask," she demanded. Without question, Lanyon reached up to his face, untied the cloth mask, and pulled it away. In the dim light, Caywen noticed his thin, chiseled features. His wide forehead and tapering jaw gave him the slightest appearance of a proud stag.

Lanyon waited, letting Caywen get a good look at his face. He had come to learn trust was best established over time. Unhurried moments of vulnerability had also personally brought him to trust —on occasion. "I will assure you further," he said, moving into the lamp's light. Pulling the collar of his shirt down, he exposed his shoulder, revealing the dark Phantom League tattoo on his skin. His fingers enclosed around the wrapped handle of his knife, and he slid the tip of his blade into the burning lantern. The flame licked the steel with hungry expectation. Overcome by the fire, a black stain of ash started at the tip of the knife, spreading until nearly half the blade was covered. Withdrawing the blade, Lanyon pulled the collar of his shirt further down with his free hand. He closed his eyes and braced himself. Looking away, he pressed the blade onto his shoulder. The acrid stench of burning skin caused Caywen to gag. Lanyon clenched his teeth as a tear slipped past his guard, giving voice to his pain. Determined to break the evil covenant, he let the blade smolder on his skin. Pulling the blade away, he set it aside, grimacing. An angry red mark defaced the symbol scarred into his shoulder with rebellious contempt.

As Caywen watched in disbelief, Lanyon pulled his collar up, wincing as the cloth touched the raw skin. "There once was a time I was proud of that mark—now, I despise it," he muttered in contempt.

Caywen regarded Lanyon curiously, indecisive as to her feelings about him.

What does he mean by this? Why does he speak to me?

"How do I know this is not a trap?" she questioned. Caywen listened intently for his reply. The mistrust in her manner was evident. From what she had heard and experienced about the Phantom League, she was *not* going to take chances.

He gestured for her to turn around, to which Caywen reluctantly complied. Lanyon drew a second dagger. "I have made myself an enemy of the League," he explained, severing the rope binding her hands with his knife. "I no longer belong here. Tonight will be *my* escape too."

Caywen rubbed at the raw skin around her wrists. The peculiar nature of this situation bewildered her. Though she did not understand it, she was glad for the aid.

Perhaps the Guide is using me to set him free.

She turned back around to face him. "Lanyon. Is that your real name?" she asked. Lanyon stood, grasping Caywen's wrist and pulling her up.

He blew out the lantern. "No. My real identity I keep to myself. Perhaps you could remember me as the Crimson Mark," he said. Holding Caywen's hand in a gentle grasp, he hurried to the open doorway, pulling her along. Caywen came to an abrupt halt as the man leaned against the doorframe, thoughtfully examining the surroundings.

She tried to push past him. "Quickly!" she insisted. She saw her escape within reach, and a zeal for freedom clouded her judgement.

Lanyon shook his head and restrained her. "The room may be empty, but be assured—there are ears listening," he whispered, pointing to the door exiting the room. "There are sentries posted outside the door and the one leading to the street. That is not the way."

Glancing about, he glided across the room to the furthest corner and crouched, feeling along the floorboards. Intrigued, Caywen hurried to his side. Lanyon closed his eyes. His fingertips glided across the edge of one slightly upraised board, then stopped. With a jerk, he pulled the wood up to reveal a hidden tunnel.

Lanyon quickly jumped down into the passage. "This will lead us out. Follow me," he whispered urgently. As she slipped past him and into the tunnel, Lanyon carefully replaced the floorboards above his head.

Peeking out from the second secret hatch, Lanyon and Caywen searched the alley wreathed in shadows. Sounds of merriment and friendly conversation carried to them from the nearest tavern. Lights from several establishments lit the streets, with patches of darkness in between.

Holding up the hatch, Lanyon searched the alley for movement. He understood even the most secretive made mistakes. It was only a matter of time. Caywen shuffled restlessly next to him. He glanced at her. "We're not safe yet. The League knows to expect all methods of escape—this one included. They will be hidden in the gloom, waiting for an over-confident escapee they can take captive again," he explained. He frowned.

Or they kill the prisoner.

"We'll be seen if we linger. If we steal away to the edge of town, there is a chance we can slip through their fingers," he whispered. Lanyon emerged from the secret tunnel and pulled Caywen behind him. Lanyon closed the hatch in silence, eyes bouncing about.

Moving to the mouth of the alley, they peered up and down the empty street. Save the occasional tavern patron stumbling into the shadows or small animal scurrying away, the path remained clear. Lanyon set his hand on Caywen's shoulder and urged her forward. "Make for the edge of town, where the trees grow outside of the castle gate," he whispered, pointing to the end of the street. "Don't look behind—I will be right beside you." With these words of instruction, he pushed her into the street.

Caywen stumbled at first as the weariness of her travels slowed her steps more than she wished. Then, gaining control of her tired legs, she hastened down the street to where Lanyon had indicated. She fixed her eyes on the towering shape of Castle Hodholm.

The light of several street lamps flickered. Keeping to the shadows, Lanyon accompanied Caywen as they neared an establishment. Raucous laughter erupted from within. Wrinkling his nose, the Crimson Mark quickened his pace. Caywen rushed ahead of him for a time, goaded by fear. Lanyon kept a moderate pace, taking time to check his surroundings.

Emerging from the tavern, a man in a dark cloak locked eyes with Lanyon. The Crimson Mark froze, regarding his fellow mercenary blankly. Raising an inquisitive eyebrow, the man glanced down the street.

The assassin recognized Caywen. Before he could raise the alarm, the Crimson Mark slammed a fist into the man's abdomen, driving the air from his lungs. Lanyon knocked the man out cold and ran to catch up with Caywen.

She felt Lanyon's breath as he leaned close to her ear. "We've been seen—hurry!" he whispered. Her breath caught in her throat at the echo of additional footsteps. Glancing over her shoulder, Caywen saw several dark shapes glide into the shadows like wraiths. The enemy's steps quickened.

Lanyon swallowed. He knew what they were capable of. He had seen captives tortured and murdered with callous cruelty. To fall into the clutches of the mercenaries would prove a bloody fate.

They turned into a separate causeway, out of sight from their pursuers. Caywen's lungs ached with the weight of fear and exhaustion as they dashed down the street. The footsteps pursued them with relentless hatred. Her panicked mind raced, searching for a way of escape. A shadowy figure leapt out, hands grasping wildly at her. The man grabbed Caywen's arm to pull her into the shadows, but Lanyon knocked him to the ground. The two fugitives fled.

Air rushed past Caywen's head as a throwing knife thudded into a nearby wall. Weaving through the maze of streets, Lanyon sprinted like a cat, with Caywen in his firm grasp. Barely able to keep up, she stumbled.

A large shape above them cast a darkening shadow over the alley with a whoosh. Caywen looked up as the winged form darted behind a nearby rooftop and out of sight. Caught up in the thrill of pursuit, they dove into another alley.

The two skidded to a stop. At the end of the causeway, the back wall of a house blocked their escape. Lanyon and Caywen turned to run. Standing at the mouth of the alley, four Phantom Leaguers closed in. Caywen backed away. Lanyon stood his ground. The killers hesitated, wary of seeing one of their own turn on his accomplices.

One of the assassins rushed Lanyon head on, knocking them both to the ground. Lanyon leapt up first and kicked the rising man to the ground. Knocking his head on the stone, he fell limp. Another assassin yanked a knife from its sheath. Caywen furtively reached for a nearby piece of wood. She swung as he lunged, knocking dully against the man's skull. He fell to the ground as Caywen and Lanyon faced the remaining two.

A blur careened down from the sky. Diving into the causeway, Gibusil snatched up the two remaining mercenaries in his talons. They cried out as the griffin flew above the town and dropped them onto the unforgiving streets. As Gibusil circled back, Caywen rushed to Lanyon's side. Tucking in his wings, Gibusil landed inside the alley and thundered forward with a snarl. Lanyon backed away, hands extended in peace.

Caywen stepped between them. "Thank the King!" she said, shaking as she wrapped her arms around the griffin's neck. "It's alright Gibusil." With a chirp of friendship, Gibusil nudged Caywen with his ebony beak.

Hands still raised in defense, Lanyon kept his distance, leery of the large creature. "*Easy,*" he urged in a appeasing tone. He had seen the beast dispatch two of his former accomplices with ease. The few griffins in his memory paled in comparison to the magnificence and might of the beast before him.

The griffin seemed to cast a dark look of spite at the former Phantom Leaguer. Caywen turned to Lanyon. "He trusts *me,*" she explained. "If he sees *I* trust you, he will not treat you like a threat."

53

As the night rain pattered dully on the stone outside, Eyoés woke from his slumber to the feeling of an unseen presence. His heart raced in anticipation of danger. The fear of a sudden attack from the Phantom League flooded his already sleep-hazed mind. Throwing aside his blanket, he reached over the side of his bed and grasped the handle of his sword. He sat up and jerked the weapon from its sheath.

Perched on a chair at the end of his bed, a dark figure soundlessly observed him, his narrow features faintly revealed by the dim light of nighttime. A glistening sheen of rain covered the stranger's clothing, nearly making him shimmer. Eyoés threatened the intruder with the tip of his blade and glanced to where Gwair slept soundly, exhausted from grief.

Seeing him begin to cry out, the dark figure stretched out a hand. "Be still! I mean you no ill will," he whispered. His voice carried the boldness of sincerity. Eyoés shut his mouth, adjusted his awkward position, and kneeled on his bed. The blade remained poised at the stranger's throat. Slowly, Eyoés glanced behind him. He sought for sign of a second enemy, but noticed nothing, save his own dusty bundle of supplies.

"Identify yourself," Eyoés commanded, keeping his voice low to avoid waking Gwair. Though he wished to rouse his friend and outnumber the man before him, there was no telling what would transpire.

The shadowy figure pulled down the collar of his shirt to reveal a smooth, scarlet wound. It looked fresh. "I am the Crimson Mark—but you may call me Lanyon for the time being," he answered.

His calm manner and ease of speech heightened Eyoés' wariness.

Sly, dangerous men always profess good intentions at first. There's no telling what lies beneath the shroud, waiting to be uncovered.

Sliding off the edge of the bed, Eyoés circled behind the Crimson Mark, causing the man to stand from the chair and turn with his back facing the door. "Very well, Lanyon," he urged, prodding the man to speak the truth, "what is your purpose here?" He soon discovered the man's tongue needed no persuasion.

Lanyon wasted no time. "I have returned Caywen Amberster to her home. We both fled from the Phantom League this very night," he said. Sincerity had a way of revealing itself in the form of confidence, and from the upright stance of this "Crimson Mark", Eyoés found himself believing the man's claims.

The point of his sword lowered. "Why have *you* fled?" he asked, studying Lanyon's reaction. He listened carefully, half expecting to catch the man in a lie—his story seemed too bewildering to believe.

Repulsed by his ties to the brotherhood of blood, Lanyon shook his head vehemently, angling his body away from Eyoés. "That is behind me," he affirmed. "I have severed my ties to the League."

Still not fully convinced of the Crimson Mark's claim, Eyoés kept his distance. "Where is Caywen now?" he questioned. The notion that a Phantom Leaguer had broken ties with his order and rescued his own captive was too bizarre to believe.

Sensing Eyoés' disbelief, Lanyon turned and gestured to the door. "Resting in her bedchamber. There will be a happy reunion at dawn—test my word," he stated.

Eyoés wavered. Though the strange tale seemed too outlandish to take seriously, the Guide's gentle voice contradicted Eyoés' misgivings.

His word stands true. Though he may not know it, he has been my vessel for Caywen's deliverance.

Lowering his sword, Eyoés sighed. Though the Crimson Mark had not fully gained his trust, he determined to follow the Guide's counsel despite his doubts. As he weighed the evidence, Eyoés considered a disturbing conclusion.

Are there dark motives behind this show of benevolence?

"What price does your 'rescue' demand?" he questioned. "You may not be one of the Leaguers, but surely—"

Lanyon raised a hand. "There is no price. No longer will I be slave to the coin," he declared with resolution. Abruptly turning to the door on the smooth soles of his boots, he paused. "I must take my leave. There are things I must make right, things I must know, and things yet to come," he said.

Eyoés advanced a step. "Where will you go? Your allegiance to avarice has cut you off from every other bond. You have no home, or people to call your own," he said. While he may have had reservations about the Crimson Mark, the thought of one wandering homeless reminded him of his lonely wandering after Asdale's destruction.

The Crimson Mark turned halfway to face him, waiting as he considered his answer. "I will go wherever the path may lead," he concluded. "Perhaps we will meet again." With these brief words of parting, Lanyon drifted like a passing mist through the open door and out into the hall. An unusual void followed his departure, as it often does with the passing of one horizon. As Eyoés stood still, Gwair's steady breathing grew and faded like a gentle bellows. Tiptoeing past Gwair's bed, Eyoés hurried to the doorway. He took the handle in one hand and searched the hallway.

The Crimson Mark was nowhere to be seen.

5th of Merchen, 2202 SE

Gwyndel strode into Eyoés and Gwair's quarters, waving a folded parchment above her head. It crinkled in her fingers as it flopped back and forth. The simple red wax seal holding it shut had been broken. Polishing their weapons, Eyoés and Gwair looked up.

Gwyndel brandished the parchment again, and it wilted like a dying flower in her grasp. "We received a letter from Beydan, brought by a messenger moments ago," she declared. "It carries grave news." Eyoés set down his polishing cloth and stood, noticing how Gwyndel's grip wrinkled the missive.

Kneeling to retrieve another component of his cleaning kit, Gwair shook his head. His expression was grave, and gave Eyoés the impression he already knew of its contents.

After the numerous failures and unforeseen dangers, has Gwair come to expect the worst?

Gwair nodded at the letter in her hand. "Read it aloud," he said. Attitude bleak, Gwyndel cleared her throat as she unfolded the letter.

To Gwair, former High Marshal of the Northern Guard —

I would rather write to you bearing good tidings than be the bearer of dreary news. Therefore, I will venture to make this brief to spare you the pain. As you know already, riots have continued to rise in number among our people, continually threatening the safety of both sides.

Not long after our brief return to Hodholm, my men and I traveled to Herthere to attain supplies from a certain connection I knew from my younger years. During a riot in the town, my connection with you and the Baron were uncovered. Two of my men were slain and the rest of us routed by the pursuing mob.

As I write this to you, my men and I are establishing camp on the rocky shores of the Jagged

Falls. We hope the treacherous terrain will protect us. I believe it will—for now.

A storm is coming, and it will not be long before it claims you also. There may soon be a time when those loyal to Baron Vikar will be forced to take refuge in the wilderness. I hope to the King that does not come to pass.

Also, tell Gwyndel I have come to miss her presence here in camp. There is much to speak of when we see each other again.

Beydan

Staring at the floor, Gwyndel folded the letter thoughtfully, the fine dirt coating the rough surface of the parchment rubbing off on her fingers. For the time being, Beydan's final words fell on deaf ears. With somber gravity, Gwyndel pondered the hopeless times brewing on the horizon.

Leaning against the side of his bed, Gwair sat quietly with his sword lying at his feet, hands folded in his lap. "A storm is coming," he mumbled. The image fit the circumstances—a tempest, brooding with tyranny as it bore down on the fleeing dissidents. When such ruthlessness rose up in society, men became like beasts, doing whatever they desired while treading on the heads of others.

Gwyndel slapped the letter onto Eyoés' bed. "Do you really think it will come to that? Fleeing Hodholm?" she asked, twisting her finger in her hair to hide her worry. The suggestion of hasty escape seemed a rational one, but the meaning behind the action was abhorrent. Escape could be construed as guilt, stirring up the people's fickle emotions. Their anger meant violence. Violence meant death, or the loss of a close companion. With Kiffyn's recent passing, none wished to suffer yet another loss.

Arms hanging at his sides, Eyoés faced her, the passion and determination to triumph dwindling like the last embers of a dying campfire. "Consider, Gwyndel—if the territory of Rehillon falls for Throst's lies, what could we do to stem the tide?" he reasoned. "When evil exerts its dominance, fleeing Hodholm would be the only way out." Even as he spoke, Eyoés looked to where his father's sword lay. He longed to wield it now, and end Throst's conniving. There had been a time when the sword had seemed the best way to confront an enemy. Now, even his father's blade could do little.

There are few heroes in a place like this. The sword means nothing to those who live by the dagger. Aványn spoke the truth when she warned me of the evil in this world.

Gwair rose and regarded the two of them. "It is not in open combat that the corrupt will be defeated. Only through the power of words and cunning can that be achieved. However, if it comes to violence, we must make a stand," he declared, shaking his clenched fist. "Remember this—as vassals bound to the King, we stand as an example of good to this world. To back down would be to exchange our hope for deceit."

Eyoés swallowed. Although the vestiges of Gwair's strength encouraged him to press on, it struck him as forced, though meant to be an insult to the face of defeat. Eyoés remembered a similar frustration.

Despite my failures and the darkness in my heart, the Guide did not give up on me. Why should I not follow his example of steadfast patience and support?

As he returned Gwair's gaze, Eyoés exuded a determination born from the trials of uncertainty. "Then we hold fast and prepare ourselves for the coming darkness. With the Guide's aid, we will triumph," he said.

Several knocks rang from the other side of the door. All conversation immediately arrested. Tense with panic, Eyoés looked to Gwair. Bringing his alarm under control, Gwair walked to the door and opened it, expression smooth and without disquiet. "Lord Ravenstrong!" he exclaimed, feigning glad surprise.

Standing outside the doorway with hands politely clasped, Throst inclined his head and smiled. "I wish to speak with Vikar. He was not in his quarters, and Rodmer told me the Baron often visits you," he said. Hidden by Gwair's bulking frame and the partially closed door, Eyoés sent a wary glance at his sister.

Slowing his breathing, Gwair gave no hint to the uneasy caution, flashing a quick smile. "Unfortunately, he is absent from here also," he sighed. Gwair knew this for certain. For much of the day, Vikar had remained hidden away in the bowels of Hodholm. He suppressed a smirk of sarcasm.

I do not blame him for seeking solace from the chaos you created, Throst.

Throst waved aside the matter with a friendly grin. "Ah, it is no trouble. I'm sure he is simply occupied with his duties," he assumed. "I wish to make amends with Vikar. My outburst at the revelation of the hidden gold was most childish. Tonight, I will be holding a small gathering in memory of your brother, and also to toast Rehillon's future unity."

At this unexpected proposal, Gwair gave a slight nod. It was strange enough for Lord Ravenstrong to attend Kiffyn's funeral—he was no friend and definitely not related by blood. For him to declare a feast in Kiffyn's honor was too outlandish to take seriously.

He intends villainy—there is no other explanation.

Gwair held his breath, resisting the urge to grab Throst by the throat and release his pent-up agitation. Unsure what to make of the strange silence, Throst tarried. "You will deliver my invitation to the Baron, will you not?" he inquired.

With a firm nod, Gwair backed away from the door. "Of course," he said. Although a man of his word, he despised carrying out Throst's will. Behind the veil of friendship, Gwair seethed.

Now you bend me to your desire, and not just the others. Shrewd devil.

Satisfied with Gwair's reply, Throst backed away from the door. "Excellent. I shall look forward to seeing you all," he announced with a customary bow. He sauntered down the hall, his confident steps spurring on Gwair's nerves.

Gwair firmly closed the door, wishing he could slam it in Throst's face.

54

Bursts of intermittent laughter harmonized with lively conversation in the Great Hall. The Lords of Rehillon feasted on fine meats and pies laid out on thick bread trenchers. Candelabras ushered in the coming of night with a warm light. Again Eyoés felt the sharp scent of expensive spices fill his senses, a symbol of wealth and social standing. Compared with Fychan's homey, simple stew and the traditional dishes of his own homeland, Eyoés found the extravagant foods overpowering.

Sitting comfortably at a distance from the table, a musician entertained the guests with her traveler's harp. A smile formed on her lips. The troubles of life were gone, carried away in the solace of music.

The venturesome mood of the music reminded Eyoés of Caywen's adventurous spirit. Vikar had found her in the early morning, and they both had wept with joy. With the sensitive nature of her return, Eyoés and Gwair had decided to keep Rodmer in the dark until a more fitting time. Vikar had feverishly asked for details of what occurred, but she would reveal nothing, knowing it would stress him further. Eyoés, Vikar, Gwair, and Gwyndel *all* wished for answers surrounding her disappearance and return. However, when faced with the formidable task of besting

Caywen's stubbornness, they all realized the information would not be forthcoming. For now, she remained hidden. Vikar would have to put on a convincing air of distress and anxiety as to Caywen's supposed disappearance.

Eyoés looked across the table to where Gwair sat, idly picking at his meal. Underneath the table, the tapping of his heel on the floor caught Eyoés' ear. Swallowing a small bite of his roasted ham, he set aside his utensils, losing his appetite to his anxiety. He caught Gwair's eye.

Throst does not want to make amends with Vikar. After the public revelation of the lost payment, Throst would likely alienate himself from the Baron—not be cordial to him.

There was an unspoken motive beneath the appearance of cordiality, and both he and Gwair knew it. Gwyndel suspected it also. She had insisted she stay behind to guard Caywen. Eyoés and Gwair had consented. Now, seated among the celebrants, Eyoés and Gwair kept a close watch on the proceedings, tense with the anticipation of sudden conflict.

Pushing his chair back and standing tall above the heads of his guests, Throst Ravenstrong clapped several times to get their attention. "Honored guests and friends," he said, spreading his hands wide, "tonight's gathering is in remembrance of Kiffyn, our dear friend Gwair's brother." At the mention of Gwair, those present rose from their seats and bowed to him as a token of friendship and support. Gwair awkwardly cleared his throat and nodded his thanks. With a motion from Throst, everyone was seated. "As we partake, let us recall with fondness his time in this world," Throst declared.

The servants entered the Great Hall from the kitchen with the main course, carrying platters of savory foods, along with a hearty serving of potatoes. Loading their trenchers with food, the guests eagerly began digging in. The rich, juicy meats nearly enticed Eyoés despite his unease. He sat rigid, hands fidgeting under the table. Watchful, Eyoés examined the faces of those present for a glimmer of malice, or any hint as to the real purpose of the night.

The meal passed without incident, leaving Gwair and Eyoés on edge, suspicions eating away at their composure. There was no sudden burst of violence. No betrayal. No trickery—as far as they could tell. Fingering the corner of his napkin, Eyoés took a small portion of stuffing and set it on his trencher, attempting to appear at ease. He took several small bites. Three servers stood at various points about the room, patiently waiting to be beckoned. They appeared earnestly involved in their work, filling up goblets of mead when asked and awaiting any orders.

Yet, despite the work transpiring in the kitchens, none of these three left the room. Thoughtfully chewing a bite of stuffing, Eyoés studied them closely.

Surely one of them would have returned to the kitchens by now. Why stay together?

The music stopped. As Throst stood, the three servers nonchalantly moved closer to him. Taking his goblet of mead in hand, Throst lifted it high. "Honored guests and Lords, let us toast to the future Rehillon, a place of unity and—"

Drawing their daggers from the folds of their clothing, the three servers lunged at Throst. The Lord of Herthere threw his goblet at the nearest assassin and drew his own dagger. Leaping from their seats, Eyoés and Gwair moved to defend their own enemy in the eyes of the shocked and angry guests.

Stepping back, Throst dodged the nearest blow, thrusting his knife into his opponent's body, letting the man fall to the floor with a groan. Deflecting the other assassin's blade, Throst kicked the man away, sending him crashing into the feast table. Pushing away from the table, the assassin scrambled to his feet, barging through the door and fleeing into the hall. The third killer, wary of Throst's strength, fell back, examining his opponent. Eyoés and Gwair ran to surround him. Shrugging his mantle from his back, Throst grasped it with his free hand and held it in front of him like a shield. He rushed his foe before anyone could react, plunging his dagger into the enemy while shielding himself with the mantle.

The few guards watching in shock had barely enough time to draw their swords. Throst cast aside his mantle and pointed to the open doorway. "Seize the filthy rogue! Let justice be served!" he shouted. The guards sprinted out the door in pursuit.

Shaken, Throst turned to his guests, regarding each one with a dazed stare. "Who has done this?" he questioned, demanding an answer. No one delivered the answer he sought. Stunned by the sudden upheaval,

Eyoés did not meet Throst's probing gaze. The tension in the room robbed them of their speech, holding them all in stunned silence. Throst kneeled by one of the fallen assassins, rifling through his pockets.

As Throst searched for evidence, Eyoés looked to where Vikar stood bracing himself against his chair. Eyoés already knew where the current circumstances were leading.

Pulling a folded parchment from the fallen assassin's pocket, Throst stood and unfolded it, eyes flitting between the missive and the people standing trial before him. As he scanned the parchment, his brows furrowed further the longer he read. He crinkled the message in his grip. His eyes locked on the Baron. "Vikar—*you* are responsible?" he asked, disbelieving. The brokenness in his voice would have fooled Eyoés —had he not known the truth.

All eyes turned to Vikar. A sinking sensation held fast to Eyoés, and he drew back.

This is the final thrust of the knife. The Baronship is slipping from Vikar's grasp.

Eyes wide with incredulity, Vikar had arrived at the same conclusion. Mustering strength through his fear, he confronted Throst publicly. "That is an outright lie! I would never even *consider* such a thing!" he retorted.

Stepping dangerously toward the Baron, Throst pushed himself at Vikar. "Then explain to me how *your* signature came to be on this order of assassination!" he commanded, shoving the parchment into the Baron's chest. Snatching it from Throst's hand, Vikar quickly scrutinized its contents.

His face blanched. Turning to the guests behind him, Vikar struggled to speak. In the eyes of those present, his delay in responding proved his guilt. Having inadvertently witnessed the shocking events, the servants in the kitchen cried out in rage. Lord Gerall Bardmond and Lord Agnar Crawbrand slowly shook their heads in disbelief. In the melting pot of betrayal, their once cordial friendship with their Baron wavered.

Breaths coming in quick succession, Vikar tore the parchment in half with panic in his eyes. Clenching each fistful, he fought to clear his name, though he knew their minds were set. "I did no such thing! This is a forgery!" he shouted.

Throst pounded the table with his fist, adding to the outcry. "You despicable wretch of a man! When the people desire change, you smother their wishes and use treachery to achieve your purpose," he spat. "The people were right to think you a tyrant."

Pointing at Vikar, Throst met the gazes of all those present, his deception disguised as righteous anger. "A deceiver has no place in leadership! He must be held to await just punishment!" he shouted. Shaken by the violence, the Lords of Rehillon submitted to the authority in his voice. They escorted Vikar from the room—conflicted. Snatching the two pieces of torn parchment, Throst gruffly stuffed them in his pocket.

Triumphant, he marched out of the Great Hall along with the deceived. Only two loyal to the Baron remained—speechless.

Throst thundered into the town of Hodholm on horseback. Save the drumming of hooves echoing in the streets, all was quiet. Even the tavern patrons, tired from their carousing, lay unconscious in their beds. Breathless with anticipation, Throst grinned, envisioning Baron Vikar as a victim of the people's violent passion.

When stirred up, the fervor over a mistaken belief becomes all they see. Blinded by their outrage, they do not stop to consider their beliefs. They choose mindless conviction over discernment.

The towering frame of the town bell came into view. Bringing his steed to an abrupt stop, Throst dismounted, running to the base of the bell tower. His boots knocked dully against the packed ground. Above him, the bell hung securely from the sturdy framework of the tower, unmoved by the gentle breeze. A rope hung to the bottom of the structure. Throst seized it and yanked downward.

Across town, the citizens were roused by the thundering clang of the bell. Doors swung open, and the growing cacophony of confused voices sounded like the singing of Gahrim to Throst's ears. A crowd swarmed around the tower. Whispering among themselves, several pointed at the tall figure standing before them.

Throst smiled, eyes drifting over the crowd. Assured of their attention, he shouted, "People of

Hodholm! I am Throst Ravenstrong, Lord of Herthere and advocate for the common man in the Council of Lords! I come with grave news. Alas, your Baron, Vikar Amberster, attempted to *murder* me tonight, with his signature on the order of assassination!"

A gasp went up from a group of women assembled together. The others cried out in indignation and shock. Several men folded their arms across their chests, unable to consider Throst's wild accusations. One even laughed mockingly. "What proof do you have of this?" he yelled, extending an criticizing finger.

Pulling a torn parchment from his pocket, Throst drew his dagger. Recalling the turmoil at the feast, he praised himself for his cunning. The section of missive carrying Vikar's signature was a condemning tool for his purposes—in the confusion and emotion of the moment, no one had noticed his retrieval of the false evidence. Throst staked the parchment into the wooden frame of the bell tower. "See for yourselves!" he cried.

The few men standing at the head of the crowd moved forward. One yanked the missive away and examined its contents. At the sight of Vikar's signature, the man held it aloft with a confirming exclamation of outrage, and shouts of bitter betrayal rose from the crowd.

Throst threw down the gauntlet. "Ever since the Everwheat addiction ravaged your homes and loved ones, you yourselves have called for a *new* Baron—one who will lead you into times of peace and prosperity, not death and pain," he declared, waving his hand across the span of the throng.

A fist was raised, with a farm knife in its grip. "Down with his house!" a man cried. More of the townsfolk took up the cry, the tension of their disunity igniting with little effort.

Holding his shoulders back, Throst shook his fists. "If that is your conviction, then why not seize this moment, and take your future in your own hands?" he remarked, voice trembling with fervency.

Though Throst had heard of the riots occurring across Rehillon, he soon found himself taken aback by their power. A group of younger men broke from the crowd, shattering barrels and crates in violent zeal. Taking broken boards in hand, they lit the tips with a burning lantern and distributed them throughout the shouting horde. Emboldened by memories of their loved ones dying in the throes of the Addiction, the men raised up cries for justice.

Eyes wide, Throst cried out in conquest. "Tonight, Vikar Amberster will fall!" he shouted, raising his fist in victory. The rioters gave a rumbling roar of vigorous agreement. Throst smirked. "And those allied with him," he muttered.

55

Eyoés flinched, casting aside his blankets. The smell of smoke wafted through the open window, and a commotion of shouts sounded from the perimeter of the castle outside. The recollection of the night's feast pierced through the haze of sleep. As he paused to listen to the turmoil outside, Eyoés came to realize its meaning. His eyes widened.

The reckoning has come—Hodholm is in Throst's hands!

Rushing to Gwair's bedside, Eyoés roughly shook his companion, startling him from sleep. "Gather your weapons. If we do not flee, Vikar will die," he said, suppressing a shudder. A mob ruled by its own standard of justice, based off raw emotion rather than valid reasoning. The coming act of false justice would prove a grim ending for the innocent Baron.

Gwair leapt up, slipped on his boots, and buckled his sword to his side, along with a trio of matching daggers. Drawing his sword, he readied himself for battle. "I will *not* leave Hodholm! We must stand!" he declared.

More cries of chaos rose from the castle courtyard. Suppressing his growing panic, Eyoés held out his hands to stay the gleaming fire of Gwair's fervor. "In time, we will return—but a swift retreat to the Jagged

Falls is our only chance of survival. We can assemble a larger force with Beydan and the Loyalists supporting us," he said.

Gwair halted, struggling to tear himself away from his home. An explosion of voices outside decided the matter for him. Though haunted by his choice, Gwair sheathed his sword. Eyoés buckled his father's sword at his side, comforted by its familiar weight. He strapped a buckler over his shoulder, glancing at the pile of supply bags in the corner of the room. They would only hinder a quick exit. Armed and focused, the two raced down the hall.

Eyoés and Gwair nearly collided with Rodmer, Caywen, and Gwyndel as they rounded a corner. Eyoés embraced his sister, nearly causing her to drop Fóbehn. "Thank the King you're alright!" he exclaimed. He envisioned his sister in the hands of the rioters. Danger still lurked at their door.

Caywen hesitantly stepped forward, anxious over the shadows. "What's happening?" she asked.

"The division among the people has reached its breaking point," Eyoés explained, looking to Gwair. "Where is Vikar being held?"

Gwair looked down the hall, forehead creased. The imminent peril gave them little time. "The dungeon," he said. "Gwyndel, take Rodmer and Caywen to the Great Hall. The kitchen windows will allow you access to the back of the courtyard, where a small passage— just large enough to squeeze through—will give you access to the forest. Sneak in behind the back of the crowd, secure four horses, and quietly release Gibusil.

Head for the Jagged Falls and I will catch up with you. Eyoés, follow me!"

Tightening her grip on Fóbehn, Gwyndel dashed out of sight down the dark corridors of the castle, with Caywen and Rodmer following. Gwair and Eyoés ran in the direction of the dungeon.

The commotion outside dimmed to a muted rumble in Eyoés' pounding ears. Slipping on the smooth floor, he fell to a knee and quickly recovered. His vision blurred, senses overwhelmed. Following Gwair blindly, he felt the jolting impact of every footstep. The path abruptly led down a spiraling staircase into the depths of the castle. He recalled infiltrating the cellars, but realized this passageway was unfamiliar to him.

He stumbled down the last stair into a small antechamber alongside Gwair. The tumult outside was barely audible, stifled by the thick stone walls. Several lanterns lit the walls, revealing rusted cell gates, covered by cobwebs. Dashing forward, Eyoés and Gwair knocked the two guards unconscious before they could draw their weapons. Baron Vikar leaned against the bars of one cell, sagging under the weight of despondency.

Vikar leapt back, startled by the sudden commotion. Incredulous, he stared as Eyoés snatched the keys from one of the fallen sentries. Eyoés unlocked and heaved open the gate as Gwair pulled Vikar from captivity. Sensing the urgency, the Baron raced up the stairs, followed by the two younger men.

They ran toward the hallway leading to the tunnels underneath the castle. Through murder, betrayal, and uncertainty, they had stood together, united—and as they descended into the tunnel, the alliance still remained.

Pulling an unlit torch from its sconce, Gwair kneeled, removing a flint and steel from his pocket. After several attempts, the torch lit, causing rats to scamper away into the darkness. Wielding the torch, Gwair led his companions through the intersecting pathways, navigating the musty, confined spaces by memory. Eyoés and Gwair both struggled to shut out the horror of Kiffyn's death in these very tunnels.

Their steps splashed in puddles of gathered rainwater near the end of the tunnel. A large bush concealed the exit from any prying eyes, providing just enough room to squeeze out. Dousing the torch in the water, Gwair cast it aside. Eyoés rushed ahead, bursting from cover with Vikar and Gwair behind him. The forest appeared calm with the serenity of night. Assured of safety, Gwair disappeared into the brush. According to the plan they had devised, Eyoés lifted his fingers to whistle.

The throng of rioters emerged from the forest with a loud crash, startling Eyoés. With shouts of victory, the mob surrounded its quarry like a pack of wolves, torchlight dancing in the dark. Eyoés knew the odds of their escape would be better in the open than the confined space of the tunnels.

The rioters rushed forward, seizing Vikar and forcing him to his knees. "Kill the tyrant!" they cried in a storm of anarchy. A man clad in a hooded farmer's cloak moved to the forefront. He clenched an axe with both hands. Eyoés looked at Vikar. Despite the appearance of defeat, calm confidence gave testimony to his innocence. Tears clouded Eyoés' vision.

Where is the Guide? Is there no hope to be found?

Peering at the hooded figure, Eyoés choked down the urge to vomit. The masked face of Throst Ravenstrong regarded Vikar in smug triumph. Throst had out-maneuvered them—again. Eyoés gnashed his teeth.

As Throst raised the axe, Vikar averted his eyes, expecting the end.

Eyoés gave a shrill whistle. The answering screech arrested everyone's attention. A hulking shape dove from the sky, giving Eyoés a surge of hope. Spreading his wings, Gibusil slammed into the ground in front of Vikar, forcing Throst and the rioters back.

At the griffin's roars of defiance, the mob covered their ears in fear. Fanning his vast wings in a display of dominance, Gibusil crouched low, preparing to pounce. Eyoés leapt atop the griffin and helped Vikar up. Throst rushed the creature with a shout of rage, only to be swatted aside with violence. Supporting his cracked rib, he struggled to regain his feet.

"Andíamas Radem—for Sword and Crown!" Eyoés yelled, raising his father's sword. Gibusil took to the sky with the Baron safe on his back.

Throst cursed under his breath.

56

8th of Merchen, 2202 SE

As the low roar of rushing water joined the ambience of the deep green wood, four horses trod upon the forest path, hooves sinking into the saturated layer of needles and soil. Sitting upon Thyre's back, Caywen slumped in the saddle. Gwyndel rode by her side, with Rodmer and Gwair riding their own steeds close by. Their hearts ached for the home they left behind, and the memories there. Everyone carried a burden of their own, foisted upon them by Throst's sudden coup. Three days of silent travel had stretched for what seemed an age, with little conversation.

Twisting through the moss-covered pines, the trail guided them into the depths of the timberlands. The forest appeared to pity them, offering its fine beauty as a consolation to the defeated. Two squirrels scampered up the side of a conifer, chatting as they raced to the top. Songbirds watched the proceeding group from the branches. A raven burst into the air as they passed by, croaking wildly as it flew into the dark recesses of the forest.

The trail widened as the forest fell away, ushering them into open ground. Booming directly ahead, the waters of the Jagged Falls rushed in torrents over hidden stones. The ground turned to hard stone, and the dark grey waters came into view, bubbling and spraying like a wild beast. Sloping down in a jagged pattern, pillars of basalt formed a forbidding precipice. At the edge of the falls, a camp was stationed. Two sentries saw the dejected group emerge from the timber, and sent up a cry of warning.

Restless, Eyoés ran to greet the four riders. Gibusil's ears perked up at their arrival, and he gave a chirp of affection. Beydan strode out of the camp, glad to welcome his friends. "Gwair! Gwyndel!" he exclaimed, arms outstretched.

A genuine smile broke through Gwair's despondency. He saluted and embraced his friend. "I cannot tell you how relieved I am to see you again," he said, eased by the presence of an old companion.

Beydan released Gwair and stepped back. "As am I, High Marshal," he declared, firmly clasping Gwair's hand. As Gwyndel released the reins of her horse, the Captain turned to her and extended a hand of pleasant greeting. "Gwyndel! I have missed your company," he said, clasping her forearm.

Holding his forearm in her loose grip, Gwyndel regarded Beydan strangely, taken aback by his uncharacteristic kindness toward her. She recalled the hatred in his eyes as he challenged her to duel, and the bitter words he had spoken.

Where is his scorn? His anger? What has changed?

Awkwardly, she saluted with her other hand. "Thank you," she replied, hesitantly. She had become accustomed to Beydan's old manner, and struggled to respond adequately. As Gwair saw the astonishment in her expression, his welcoming smile faded.

Realizing the awkwardness of the situation, Beydan coughed and looked to Gwair, Rodmer, and Caywen. "I wish to speak with Gwyndel privately. Excuse us," he requested. He took her arm and gently led her away from the group. Looking intently at Beydan, Gwyndel followed.

Beydan leaned close to her. "I can see my cordiality puzzles you," he noted in a lowered voice. He recalled the old scorn he had embraced, when an attitude of superiority had overcome his sense of justice.

Gwyndel rubbed her forehead in doubt. "Last time we saw each other, you wished to kill me—now you welcome me with open arms, with no sign of hostility?" she asked. She recalled the strange note on the message they had received from Beydan three days ago.

Also, tell Gwyndel I have come to miss her presence here in camp. There is much to speak of when we see each other again.

Beydan nodded in understanding, eyes wandering to the forest as he collected his thoughts. "When we left you in Hodholm, I began to ponder. Despite my constant prodding and outbursts of anger, you remained patient. You tried to apologize for causing me hurt, but I cast you away," he said, pained with the knowledge that such an act could not be undone. "That was wrong of me. While I recovered from our duel, Marc spoke to me. Both his words and the King's

Proverbs convicted me of my wrongdoing. I learned honor and mercy was of more importance than my pride. I determined to do the honorable thing and forgive you, and I now ask of you the same."

Gwyndel's doubts fell away as she came to realize the reason for Beydan's transformation.

I beseeched the King to change his heart, and he kept his word.

She clasped his forearm in a firm grip, encouraged by his willingness to sacrifice his old habits for what was right. "You have my forgiveness," she said. "Where's Marc?" Peering over his shoulder, she searched for sign of the freckled youth.

Turning to the camp, Beydan pointed to the commanders tent, stationed in the midst of a forest of canvas. "He is holding counsel with several of the higher ranking men and briefing them on our escape strategy, should things go awry," he explained. "Upon your departure, I promoted him to Lieutenant. With his courage and noble heart, he deserved it. Come, I will show you."

Sheltered from the fine spray of rain, Eyoés ducked further under the lean-to, hearing the drops pattering against the canvas roof. The wind rushed through the camp with a mighty breath, adding to the roar of the falls. The late afternoon sky was a dull grey, the clouds heavily laden with water. Shivering in the cold, Eyoés lay down on the thick wool blanket, wrapping himself in it. Exhausted from near constant travel, he yawned, rolling onto his side.

"You and Gwyndel must depart Rehillon. There is nothing for you here," Vikar sighed, sitting beside Eyoés. An exhaustion of a different kind weighed Vikar down. Fingering his dagger, he placed it upon a flat rock and spun it.

Eyoés stared out into the camp, pondering Vikar's plea. The warmth of the laborers' campfires and the comfort of his own home called him back to Asdale. He yearned for the people he left behind, and the heritage that awaited him there. Yet, when faced with the choice of abandoning Vikar and Caywen to Throst's merciless cruelty or fighting alongside, he knew the choice he would make.

Sitting up in his blanket, Eyoés watched Vikar rub his eyes to hide his woe. "Until this is put right, we will be by your side," he assured his friend.

Baron Vikar flashed a false smile and patted the young Baron of Asdale's arm. "I appreciate your willingness to come to my aid, but I will not watch as you and your sister are murdered on my account," he decided. "Return to your home—Rehillon is no longer a safe place. In time, the House of Amberster will fall."

As Vikar urged him to take his leave, the warmth in Eyoés' chest rose in resistance. Eyoés punched the hard ground. "I will *not* abandon one who is in need, and neither will Gwyndel. We do not fight simply for a united Rehillon, but for the principles of honesty and virtue," he maintained. In a peculiar way, he felt the fervor of the King's Proverbs backing his words.

Mulling over Eyoés' words, Vikar lay down on the hard ground, the unforgiving stone forcing his back into an uncomfortable position. "How could the King allow such deception and treachery? Does he not take pity?" he asked, voicing the thoughts circulating in his head.

Occupied with his own emotions, Eyoés did not expect the question. His mind already whirled with the regret and guilt of the mistakes he'd made on this mission. He was tempted to ignore Vikar's question in favor of wrestling with and answering his own, before a realization struck him. Looking across the camp, he spotted the Commander's Tent, where Gwyndel spoke with her new companions.

When I struggled to understand, Gwyndel bore herself with patience and never let her emotions and struggles get in the way of encouraging me.

Hiding his troubles from his friend, Eyoés leaned closer to Vikar. "The King does not pity—he feels a higher empathy we could never understand. He allows struggle so we may become stronger because of it. There is not a time when he is not with us," he said. "I know this from experience."

A splash of water wetted Eyoés' blanket. He turned, facing Rodmer as he stood outside the lean-to, his boot in a large puddle. Damp firewood lay cradled in his arms. Roughly, he threw the pile into the corner of the shelter and seated himself beside the other two. "So you cover up their despair with a message of false hope?" he questioned. "Eyoés, this whole mission was a search for truth, and now you hide it!"

As Eyoés started to retort, Rodmer held up a hand and regarded them through dark, narrowed eyes. "There is no hope—there will come a time when Throst kills us all. We may delay the inevitable for as long as we can, but in the end, we will all face the same fate," he declared, convinced of his own opinion.

Flashing a dark look at Rodmer, Eyoés turned to comfort Vikar, only to find him lying wrapped up in a blanket, fast asleep.

57

A bright glow woke Eyoés from a troubled sleep, sparing him from the claws of his nightmare. Squinting, he sat up. The rain had ceased, encouraging the crickets to chirp from the depths of the forest. As Eyoés slipped from his blanket and stepped out from under the lean-to, the bright glow faded like a dying moonlit night, revealing the crook of a staff. All tension left Eyoés as a surge of hope coursed through him. Sitting on the ground with staff in hand was the Guide, his face radiant with a gleaming smile.

Falling to his knees before him, Eyoés bowed low. "My Lord!" he exclaimed, keeping his voice low to keep the others from waking. "Tell me this is no dream."

The Guide's laugh sent waves of warm strength through the young Baron's bones. "Feel my hand," he said, stretching out a hand, which Eyoés eagerly took. "Have you any doubt now?"

Shaking, Eyoés released the Guide's hand. He averted his gaze, as the guilt of his failures upset his stomach. "I am unworthy to be in your presence, my King," he objected. Keeping a respectful distance, he kept his eyes turned away.

The Guide regarded him patiently, with a sympathy Eyoés felt keenly. As he tapped the end of his staff on the stone, the crook of his staff glowed, illuminating Eyoés with a wholesome, pure light. "None are worthy, but the Light of Gald-Behn cleanses," he spoke, setting a light hand on the youth's back. "Tell me your cares, my son."

Eyoés looked up with tears in his eyes. "I let my vices cloud my vision. My desire for wealth blinded me to the enemy before me," he mourned. "Trusting my deficient discernment, I let myself be ensnared."

Expression thoughtful, the Guide moved closer to Eyoés. "And because of your guilt, you partly blame yourself for Throst's coup," he reasoned.

Shaking his head, Eyoés pounded his leg with his hand. "There must have been something I could have done, something that would have set us on a different course," he said, scolding himself fiercely. It was natural to assign blame to himself.

The Guide looked at Eyoés, his stern, yet doting gaze piercing through the lies he told himself. "The past is dead to you. Learn from your failures and continue on. Walk in the truth. I will not keep my strength from those who need it most," he promised.

Still, Eyoés struggled to accept this simple answer, inadvertently clinging to his self-deprecation. "Why did I have to be afflicted with these faults—greed, and an arrogant trust in my own ability to judge?" he said, asking himself more than the comforter beside him.

Working out his care for Eyoés with steady patience, the Guide leaned on his staff. "Wealth tempts a man new to power. It promises unending reward, but cannot fulfill what it assures. *All* in power have heard its call—what you do with it determines the hold it has on you. Ponder wealth's summoning, and it ensnares you. Take it captive and slay it," he said.

Eyoés took a deep breath and abruptly stood. "Then by considering avarice, I have failed," he murmured. Seeing only his past failures, he became convinced of this conclusion, to the exclusion of his victories.

How can I do what is right if all I do is fall?

The Guide stood as well, laying his arm across Eyoés' shoulders and facing the Jagged Falls. Watching the rolling water twist, turn and spray, he admired its crystal beauty. "Quite the opposite. I have seen you from afar, fighting against the pull of greed. I have made you strong," he contended.

Rubbing the back of his neck, Eyoés faced the Guide. Though he struggled to believe this inspiring statement, he knew deep within he *had* resisted the allure of greed and prosperity. "Even so, I fear to trust my judgement again," he replied.

I have stumbled too many times to be innocent!

The Guide sensed the struggle. "To discern is to examine—it is not something instinctual. Discernment is a learned skill on a path with many stumbling blocks," he said. "Eyoés, each stumbling block provides an opportunity to learn and discern. As you continue to follow my Proverbs and heed my voice, you learn to avoid the pitfalls."

With the thundering roll of the falls in his ears, Eyoés was reluctant to dismiss his guilt. However, he trusted the Guide, and knew he spoke the truth always.

Forcibly setting aside his preconceived ideas, he reexamined his guilty conscience with a critical eye.

Just as I blamed myself for Asdale's destruction, I blame myself for Hodholm's fall. Why am I so quick to hold myself responsible?

The similarity of the two instances troubled him. Since his quest for revenge, Eyoés had seen a change for the better in his manner and thoughts. He knew the Guide alone was to thank for such a transformation, but the notion of not applying his deliverance to even the smallest parts of his life startled him.

When things go wrong, I am quick to accuse myself because I know I am guilty of other transgressions.

Irritated for letting a remnant of his old self remain, he curled his toes in his boots.

Did I not leave such self-condemnation in Zwaoi? Does the King not have the power to pardon all of my misdeeds?

As he scrutinized the prodding of his conscience, Eyoés came to realize the weight of guilt was in truth a mindset of self pity. Though he had done wrong, the stubbornness with which he held onto his feeling of guilt, mourning his vices with woeful tears, was clearly a degradation of the Guide's absolution. Dwelling on past wrongs mocked forgiveness as forgery, denying the King's promises were of any more worth than a sluggard's vow. Eyoés felt the Guide's arm wrap tighter around his shoulders, and as he looked up, a glint of kindness gave voice to unspoken mercy. Expression pensive, Eyoés walked back to the lean-to. "Even when I was your enemy, you knew I could change—that you could stir me to life again," he recalled, bringing his hand up to his chin. "Could Throst turn from his ways?"

The end of the Guide's staff tapped on the stone as he walked. "I have seen him, listened to his frustrations, and waited for him to regain his senses and come to me for aid," he sighed, surprising Eyoés with the regret in his tone. "It is the wound from his father which causes him to seek the Baronship and the security it brings."

Briskly facing the Guide, Eyoés formed an idea. "Could he be plucked from the gloom and brought back into the light?" he inquired. Though angered by Throst's treachery, with this open revelation of past hurt, Eyoés felt a pity for the man.

Throst has wounds of his own, as I once did. If the Guide can restore me, can he not heal Throst as well? Perhaps the deceit of the recent past can be put behind us.

Hearing Eyoés' thoughts, the Guide looked across the camp to the forest, in the direction Hodholm lay. "You will see Throst again soon. Speak with him about his father," he suggested. "Whether he admits his wrong or continues on a treacherous path is his choice."

The night wind picked up, coursing through the Guide's smooth hair and billowing his white cloak. Pulling his hood over his head, he embraced Eyoés. "Do not give up hope, Eyoés," he encouraged. "All will be put right." Stepping back, he leaned against his staff. A glow of white light grew from the crook of the staff, expanding in size until its magnificence forced Eyoés to avert his eyes. The light suddenly dimmed. Eyoés looked back to the empty place where the Guide had stood.

Unable to sleep with the Guide's words swirling in his head, Eyoés cast aside his blankets and sat up. Vikar and Rodmer breathed gently beside him, lost in the vastness of sleep. Eyoés took his cloak from where it lay at the head of his simple bed and fastened it around his neck. The cool of the night pulled him out from under the shelter of the lean-to. Slipping on his boots, Eyoés squinted into the night. Night birds sang in the trees.

A sudden, low roar vibrated in Eyoés' chest. He froze, feeling rooted to the spot. The strange sound repeated. Inclining his head, he carefully sought the source of the noise.

It sounds like it's coming from further down the Wrolm River.

He caught sight of two figures standing at the edge of the falls several feet away. Keeping a wary eye on the river, he started toward them. Their faces were hard to distinguish in the dim light.

Beydan and Gwair keened their ears toward the sound, brows furrowed. As Eyoés neared, Gwair raised a hand to demand silence. Carefully stepping over patches of gravelly stone, the young Baron of Asdale came to stand beside them. They strained to hear any unusual sound above the rushing water over the Jagged Falls.

Bursting with renewed ferocity, the hoarse roar grew in intensity until it became a strained bellow. From further down the river, a wail of pain accompanied several massive splashes. All went silent.

Eyoés peered into the darkness. "What beasts lurk in these lands?" he questioned. The ferocity and haunting timbre of the howls brought imaginings of horrid devils lurking in the deep waters.

Grasping his sword to bolster his confidence, Gwair steeled himself to mask his unease. "Dragons of a different kind," he replied. He knew what creatures lurked in his homeland, and the knowledge did not ease him.

Beydan nodded in confirmation. "Seems a Wavelasher, to my ears," he guessed. "The creatures thrive in the waters, snatching unsuspecting prey upon the shore. From my experience, I have seen many larger than Gibusil." He gestured to where the griffin slept soundly nearby, exhausted.

Gwair grabbed the Captain's shoulders and turned him about. "Is it safe to pitch camp here?" he said. Eyoés stepped toward Beydan, demanding an answer.

The Captain met their gazes in turn, unflinching. "We are at a sufficient height above the river. It is unlikely the brute will trouble itself when the opposite shore lies closer to the water," he stated blankly. "We are safe." Again, the low, rumbling roar sounded from a distance, growing fainter. Eyoés swallowed. Grasping

Beydan's arm, Gwair started back into the camp. Eyoés remained at the edge, watching his two companions.

Turning back to the falls, Eyoés scanned the surface of the dark water. His heart raced as a large ripple quaked the reflection of the moon on the surface.

58

9th of Merchen, 2202 SE

In celebration of morning, the birds sang from the treetops, gliding with ease over the Loyalist encampment. Gwyndel could see her breath roll in the crisp, cold air. The morning campfires crackled nearby, just loud enough to be heard over the Jagged Falls. Gwyndel inhaled the pleasant smells of camp cooking wafting on the air.

Though she enjoyed the peace and calm, a heavy load hurried her steps. During the early moments of sleep, when one hovers between the void and wakefulness, she had pondered over Caywen. She had learned of Caywen's argument with Vikar over concealing Throst's true character in Hodholm. Her nagging desire to live up to her own expectations guilted her into a confession.

I knew Throst was the enemy, yet I was too weak to bring myself to tell her.

With this consideration in mind, she spotted Caywen kneeling by one of the campfires, warding off the morning chill. Slowing her steps, Gwyndel reconsidered her choice, embarrassed to expose her wrongdoing. Before she could turn away, Caywen caught sight of her.

Smiling, Caywen motioned for her friend to sit. Trying to keep an open expression, Gwyndel took her seat, keeping a relative distance from Caywen. Gwyndel rubbed her nose, thinking of how to express her thoughts. "Caywen, I must confess I have not been truthful with you," she began, preparing to elaborate.

Caywen looked up from the flames of the campfire. "You knew about Throst's true nature as well, didn't you?" she said, more of a statement than a question. Taken aback, Gwyndel pursed her lips and nodded. Caywen picked up a dead pine needle and threw it into the hungry fire. "Since you are involved in this whole affair, I expected such. I am not at odds with you, my friend," she declared, reasoning as to Gwyndel's hesitation. "My father is the one who should have told me. It was his mistake to keep the truth hidden from me."

Collecting herself, Gwyndel moved closer to Caywen. "Whether it was Vikar's responsibility or not, I apologize for not telling you myself," she insisted. "I do not want to mar our friendship, no matter how new it might be."

Caywen picked a section of moss off a rock with her fingernail and idly fiddled with it. "Gwyndel, for years I have had few other women to call my companion," she said. "From what I have seen, I can say this—I will have no better friend than you. Your honesty now only convinces me further."

Free from her contrition, Gwyndel put her arm around Caywen's shoulders like an older sister. "Then my fears have been put to rest," she concluded.

Shouts of alarm rose from the border of the encampment, startling them both. Leaping up, Gwyndel dashed to her nearby tent, snatching Fóbehn and its quiver. The Loyalists left their breakfast behind as they seized their weapons and rushed to the aid of the sentries in a mass stampede. Gibusil vaulted over a group of men with a cry as he readied for battle. As Gwyndel ran along with them, Caywen close behind, she saw Eyoés and Gwair just ahead. They emerged into the open space between camp and the forest.

Confronted by a number of guards, Throst and several others raised their hands in a gesture of peace. The charging Loyalists skidded to a stop. As Gibusil started toward Throst, Eyoés raised a hand to ward him off. The griffin obeyed.

Throst regarded the soldiers surrounding him. Several spearpoints were poised in anticipation. "I must say, Gwair, your troops are quick to rush to violence," he taunted with a grin of amusement.

Beydan stepped forward, falchion drawn. "They're *my* men, and they do what I command them to," he stormed. The morning sun shone brightly, glinting off the Captain's bare blade.

Gwair glared at Throst, flexing the muscles in his hand. "What do you want, you scamp?" he demanded curtly. He was not in the mood to listen to the traitor's scoffing talk.

Throst put his arms down. "I wish to speak with Vikar Amberster," he said. His narrowed eyes scanned the Loyalist ranks.

Pushing through the crowd, Vikar stepped out from the throng. Though cautious of the turncoat's cunning speech, he was curious as to what the man would say. "Speak your piece, Throst. I am listening," he said.

Throst pointed threateningly at Vikar. "I propose a fair compromise to settle our—disagreement, if you will," he stated. "As a nobleman and *Baron* of Rehillon, I challenge you to trial by combat, in the traditional fashion of our forefathers." Hushed words were exchanged within the Loyalist force.

Incredulous, Eyoés cocked his head and gestured at Vikar. "You first rob the man of his home, and nearly his family," he started, chortling in utter astonishment, "and then move to take his *life*?"

Throst ignored the youth's comment. "My challenge stands—unless Vikar would instead choose to prove himself a *milksop*," he smirked, taking joy in his insult. Gwyndel nocked an arrow to Fóbehn and drew back. The blades of Eyoés and Gwair poised dangerously, wavering in midair as if considering an attack.

Vikar spread his arms wide. "Stand down! I accept your challenge, Throst Ravenstrong. After the noon meal, we shall meet here," he decided. Lowering his weapon, Eyoés shot an uneasy glance at Gwair. Putting Vikar in open opposition of the young and cunning Throst seemed an ill choice.

Expression tightening in anticipation of combat, Throst stared at his opponent. "So be it. I will bring a number of my supporters to observe," he declared. "We will see who is the better man." With a nod, he turned back to the cover of trees as the Loyalist sentries fell back. Everyone returned to camp, unsure of the future.

Gwair paced about, stroking his beard. "Do you realize what you've gotten yourself into, Vikar?" he asked, doubting if his old friend really understood. He pinched his lip.

Seated inside the lean-to, Vikar steadily watched Gwair walk back and forth. He was decided on his course of action. "I know full well, Gwair," he replied emphatically. "For too long have I stood passively by while Throst brings Rehillon to its knees."

Exasperated, Gwair stopped in front of his true Baron and leaned closer to him. "You are not as young as you once were," he maintained, rubbing an eyebrow. "Throst would not challenge you if he did not detect weakness—it is not his way."

Vikar emerged from the lean-to and stood, his bulky frame matching that of his friend. "I care not! Until now, the sword has been forsaken in favor of shrewd tactics. I welcome direct combat against this devious enemy. Though I may be old, I have seen Throst train on occasion. There are several weaknesses of his own he does not realize," he said, gathering hope from the very notion.

Gwyndel broke in. "Pardon my ignorance," she interrupted before the two could continue their dispute.

"I heard Throst mention this combat would be done in a *traditional* manner. What does that entail?"

Glad for a change of conversation, Gwair turned to Gwyndel. "In these lands, a duel is not simply about settling differences—it is designed to demonstrate to the onlookers who is the better warrior," he explained, "The first match is fought with sword and shield. It is forbidden for one to kill the other. They are instructed to simply best the other in combat. The second match has no such rule. Armed with longswords, the combatants duel to the death. Whoever remains alive is declared the victor." The significance of such an occasion registered through Gwair's words.

Analyzing the process itself, Eyoés calculated the risk. "Such a prolonged clash will require an immense amount of stamina, strength, and tactics," he deduced. A duel in the traditional style of Rehillon was clearly a daunting feat.

Hasty to rebuff his verdict, Vikar adjusted his sword belt. "I will triumph!" he insisted, unwilling to admit any chance of defeat. "With the King's strength I will do it!"

Eyoés approached the matter from a calm, rational perspective. "Even should you possess the skills required, they will be no match against a hidden dagger," he asserted. They all knew the meaning of such a challenge.

Still, Gwair stated the obvious. "You suggest treachery?" he inquired.

Eyoés folded his arms. He believed he had seen enough of Throst's behavior to understand the man's capabilities. "It is not out of the question," he said.

Setting a hand on Eyoés and Gwair's shoulders, Vikar regarded them with confidence. "I trust you both to watch my back," he spoke, his faith evident. "But whatever may come, I tell you this—virtue must be defended, and if my accepting Throst's challenge accomplishes this, so be it."

Whether it would be accomplished through death or life, none knew.

59

Gathered around the designated arena, the crowd muttered to themselves as they debated the identity of the winner. Several weaved through the masses, accepting bets on the contenders. On the side nearest the encampment, the Loyalists gathered together, making up nearly half of the crowd gathered. The other half was composed of commoners, summoned from Throst's mob for the purpose of witnessing their new leader's triumph.

Eyoés twisted the button of his cloak, avoiding conversation with the surrounding multitude. A tingling restlessness took hold of his limbs. Though his body quivered with suspense over the duel's outcome, his mind had a vastly deeper outlook.

The future of Rehillon hangs in the balance—and the life of a friend.

Though he had only known Vikar for a short time, he felt a connection with him. Eyoés had reasoned it to be pity for Vikar's situation that bonded their friendship. An uneasiness swirled through his head at the possibility of Vikar's death.

He felt Gwyndel lock arms with him. Eyoés knew the same anxiety he felt was shared. In an effort to ease her nerves, he caught her attention and flashed a brief smile. She simply pressed her lips together even tighter, making an effort to keep her emotions hidden. Eyoés' mood darkened as Gwyndel's tension transferred to him.

At either end of the oval, the crowd parted, allowing the two contenders to enter the arena. On the right, Throst bore himself with smug confidence as the crowd applauded his entry. To the left, Vikar entered in silence, his appearance rousing no applause. The Loyalists caught his gaze and gave their support, whether it be a nod of encouragement or a word of inspiration. Eyoés looked down the ranks of Loyalists and bit his tongue.

I'm not the only one anxious over the outcome.

Beydan, standing in the middle of the arena, regarded the two rivals. "Let the combatants claim their weapons!" he demanded, his lackluster tone revealing his heavy heart. Gwair stepped out from the group of Loyalists with shield and blunted sword in hand. Expression grave, he handed the weapons to Vikar, forcing himself to meet his gaze with solidarity. Vikar set his shield at his feet and partly embraced his friend, lips quivering as he whispered words of comfort. Gwyndel winced and regarded the other side of the arena. Throst practiced his deft skills, shifting his stance and position of his weapons in anticipation.

Observing the preparations, Caywen shivered as she recognized Amnedd. Both distress and fury fought for preeminence in her mind. Standing beside Throst, Amnedd whispered in his ear. Letting Vikar say his parting words to Gwair, Beydan waited until both men were ready. He raised his falchion. "Begin!" he shouted, falling back into the Loyalist ranks and leaving the arena open.

The two contenders stepped into the arena warily. As they circled each other, the soles of their boots slid across the smooth stone. While the crowd cheered him on, Throst grinned. "So it has begun, Vikar," he taunted. "There is still time to surrender—I am merciful to those who are humble." Vikar said nothing, scrutinizing his opponent with the trained eye of a seasoned fighter. This was no time for talk.

Disappointed by his foe's refusal to reply, Throst glared at Vikar, glancing briefly at his own blade to admire its craftsmanship and beauty. "So—you continue in your villainy and insist on your despotism! Then feel the bite of my blade!" he cried.

They clashed, swords knocking dully on shields as they exchanged blows in sequence, blocking and taking advantage of small errors. Caywen forced herself to watch, eyes wide in horror. The crowd cheered for their champion, and the Loyalists joined their chaotic cries with shouts of encouragement. Throst whirled his blade overhead as Vikar raised his shield to protect his head from the blow. Eyoés held his breath. Knocking the enemy's sword aside with his shield, Vikar ducked low and sliced at Throst's legs, only to be quickly blocked. They drew back, holding their weapons at the ready.

Eyoés instinctively raised his hands, chest hitching. Vikar approached his opponent from an angle with shield outstretched, baiting Throst to strike. Throst bashed the shield with his own, sending Vikar stumbling back. Gwyndel flinched as their swords struck, ringing sharply. Blocking another blow, Vikar kicked Throst backwards and lunged. Vikar countered Throst's wild swing just in time.

They withdrew, considering the weaknesses and strengths they had seen in the other as they plotted their next move. As one, they collided, exchanging blows and struggling for domination. Throst lashed out with a kick, upsetting his balance as Vikar stepped back. The Baron rushed forward and slammed into him, knocking the usurper onto his back.

Throst came to his feet as Beydan stepped between the two with arms outstretched. "Vikar Amberster claims the victory for this round!" he proclaimed, with a wide smile of triumph. "Should Throst defeat him in the second match, he will redeem himself."

Cheers went up from Marc and the other Loyalists at their Baron's first victory. Disappointed by the defeat, the commoners expressed their disapproval with jeers and disgusted looks, trying to stir up the anger and determination of their champion. The two contenders returned to their designated end of the arena. Gwair eagerly accepted Vikar's blunt sword and shield, hurriedly setting them aside and clasping forearms with his superior. A surge of hope ran through Eyoés, and he embraced Gwyndel.

Perhaps there is a chance—Throst is not unbeatable!

The joy was short lived as Beydan stepped into the arena again. Gwair and Amnedd each handed their respective warrior longswords for the next match. Vikar swung his weapon experimentally. His familiarity with the sword bolstered his confidence. Throst gripped his sword with white knuckles. His pride was injured by the jeers of his supporters and the ease of his defeat. He regarded Vikar darkly. "Just a stroke of good fortune," he muttered under his breath.

Once assured the two contenders were ready, Beydan whistled to catch the people's attention. "Let the final match begin!" he commanded. Knowing such a proclamation meant blood, Throst's crowd applauded with even greater intensity as the two stepped closer and circled each other.

Throst spat at Vikar's feet. "Tell me—how many people died from the Addiction while you did nothing?" he questioned. Gripping the handle of his sword with both hands, he assumed a ready stance.

Expression hard, Vikar felt regret over the misery resulting from his allowance of the Everwheat trade. He sought a way to wound his opponent in return. "You poisoned the people's grain and then *withheld* the remedy!" he shouted. The crowd was visibly stirred as they pondered the allegation. The Baron had always been a benevolent leader.

Warily eying the throng of his supporters, Throst quickly shot back a reply. "You have no proof of this," he countered, sword poised for battle. "The time has come for you to pay for your lies."

The two contenders met in a flurry of blows. Vikar blew aside Throst's blade and nicked his opponent's shoulder. A shout went up from the crowd. With the pain fueling his attack, Throst pummeled his enemy, redirecting his cuts with every block Vikar could manage. Vikar maneuvered to repel a blow to the head, spinning around and striking Throst's cheekbone with the pommel of his sword. A sickening crack caused Eyoés to wince as Throst cried out in pain, his handsome appearance marred. Throst renewed his attack with a unearthly scream of rage. Swatting Vikar's stroke aside, Throst kicked him to the ground. Vikar's sword spun out of reach as Throst paused to catch his breath. Vikar rushed Throst in a bear hug and received a knee to the stomach. He fell onto his side and scrambled to get up. Vision blurred by his swelling face, Throst misjudged the distance and swung wildly, accidentally cutting the back of Vikar's thigh rather than severing his leg.

Caywen screamed, struggling against Gwair's restraining arms. Eyoés watched in horror, heart thumping in a steady beat as time slowed. Beside him, Gwyndel covered her mouth, tears in her eyes. As Vikar lay gritting his teeth in pain, Throst loomed with sword poised to deliver a killing blow. A section of the crowd of Throst's supporters chanted his name in unison, while others averted their eyes. Some felt guilt.

Throst met Vikar's terrified gaze. "Such a wretched way to die—feeling the hatred of those who once regarded you as their leader. A man's trouble dictates the people's memory of him. When ill-fortune strikes, the people ignore his pleas for mercy and instead blame him for his poor luck," he smirked. "That is your fate." Throst pulled back for a final blow.

Eyoés leapt into the fray, knocking Throst back and assuming a ready stance, his father's sword gleaming.

Gwyndel cried out, but Eyoés shot her a warning glance. Stepping back, Throst turned to Beydan with a look of disgust. On the ground, Vikar closed his eyes in relief as Caywen and Beydan grabbed his arm and pulled him to the edge of the arena. "Objection! Such interference goes against tradition!" Throst protested.

Eyoés maintained a steady guard, narrowed eyes trained on his enemy. "Maybe so, but what have you to lose from such a trespass? To best me would be to rise in the people's eyes—surely you cannot ignore such an opportunity," he claimed, gesturing to the crowd.

Faced with the chance of seeing their champion best *two* opponents, the throng urged him on, the din of their voices drowning out any more of Throst's objections. Holding up his hand to command silence, Throst wiped away the blood on his face. "Very well, Eyoés," he said, holding his sword steady.

Eyoés lashed out, his initial flurry of furious blows startling Throst as he found himself on the defensive. Recollections of his training returned to Eyoés, flowing from his mind to his limbs. The Loyalists cheered. Gwyndel held her breath, eyes wide with fear at her brother's risk. Throst tactfully evaded a blow and struck out with his own. The skill of one rivaled the next as the advantage changed hands repeatedly. Ducking low to avoid a cut to the head, Eyoés circled around Throst and pressed him back into the crowd of Loyalists. The throng hastily scrambled out of the way as Throst stumbled back into one of the canvas tents.

Throst rose just in time to avoid Eyoés' strike and tried in vain to repel his opponent. Eyoés pressed his advantage, pushing Throst further into the camp. The crowds followed. Throst heard the roaring waters of the Jagged Falls behind him and realized his plight. For one fleeting moment, his attention lay elsewhere. Swatting his blade aside, Eyoés knocked Throst flat on his back at the edge of the precipice. Before he could rise, Throst felt Eyoés' boot on his chest. The gleaming blade was poised at his throat.

A collective gasp went up from Throst's supporters. Breathing hard, Eyoés leaned forward, pressing harder on the enemy's chest. Staring in disbelief, Throst gaped at Eyoés. "You—bested me," he stuttered, struggling to breathe under the dominating foot.

Swallowing, Eyoés pulled his sword away. "But I will not kill you," he whispered. "Throst, your father mistreated you—"

A rush of anger crossed Throst's face. "What of it?" he demanded. Eyoés paused, bolstering his courage to continue extending grace in the face of such animosity.

The man will make his own choice. I cannot force him to admit his wrongdoing.

He stepped off Throst's chest, expression compassionate as he strove to be an example of the King's kindness. "He mistreated you, and such enslavement was *not* the King's will," he maintained, lowering his voice for private conversation. "If you are seeking protection from further hurt, you will not find it in prosperity. You can choose a different way. It is not too late."

Throst paled. "You know nothing of my life," he snapped—yet now, he wasn't so sure.

Recognizing his stubbornness, Eyoés felt drawn to Throst by sympathy. "Set aside your pain, as I once did," he said, reaching out to help Throst up. "You can still lead the people in your given position as Lord of Herthere—any man of sincere benevolence can do good, no matter his status!"

Consumed with indignant anger, Throst swatted his hand aside. "You think I care for these people?" he yelled. "They are *simpletons*—merely a means to achieve my own ends!" He realized his exposure too late. A heavy silence hung in the air, and Throst's face blanched as he looked at the crowd. For the first time, Eyoés saw terror on Throst's face.

As the Proverbs say—one who uses his tongue rashly and for foul ends will be betrayed by his own tongue.

The looks of the crowd darkened as they realized the truth. One of the older men seized a nearby spear. It trembled in his grip. "We have been *deceived*!" he shouted, face turning a crimson red. Grasping the fact, several more took up the cry—until the entire crowd roared in unison. Eyoés hastily pulled away from Throst. He dared not stand in the way.

Wielding his spear wildly, the commoner charged Throst, veins straining in his neck. Throst leapt up, dodging the blow and forcefully shoving the man from behind. With a scream, the man stumbled over the precipice, spear flying from his grip.

Bursting from the turbulent waters, a Wavelasher leapt high into the air, its long, narrow jaws clamping around the falling man. Its claws latched onto the basalt rock face, and two lifeless green eyes glared at the terrified crowd. Mottled grey-blue scales covered the dragon's body. Waves surged onto the cliff, soaking the Loyalist camp as the dragon heaved itself partly onto the top of the precipice, jaw snapping.

Everyone seized what weapons they could find. Throst scrambled across the slippery stone, hastily retreating further downstream and out of his captors' clutches.

Charging the Wavelasher, Beydan and Gwair brandished their weapons and shouted to attract the water dragon's attention. In the sky above, Gibusil circled, anxious to help. Panicked, Eyoés waved the griffin away. Amnedd and his fellows thrashed about in vain to free the crowd's hold on them. Pushing the mercenaries to the edge of the falls, the crowd heaved their quarry at the roaring Wavelasher. The dragon dove after the screaming mercenaries with a ravenous roar, snatching several in its jaws while swatting others into the river. Water splashed violently upward, then fell like a fresh rain.

Eyoés and Gwyndel witnessed the carnage with wide eyes, faces ashen at the power of the beast. Victorious, the crowds celebrated with cheers in a spirit of kinship. Eyoés peered over the edge. The black shadow of the Wavelasher faded as it descended deeper into the water, along with the crushed bodies of its prey. Shuddering, Eyoés backed away.

Several of the mob spotted Throst quietly creeping upstream in hopes of escape. "The fox is slipping away!" the men shouted, rallying the others to their cause. Consumed with hatred for the one who deceived them, the mob followed in haste, with whatever weapon they could find clutched in their hands.

Finally free from the crushing mass of the crowd, Gwyndel took a deep breath. Though her body ached, her spirit soared.

All has been made right. Throst's treachery will continue no longer.

Looking up, she spotted Caywen cradling Vikar's head in her lap. His leg was bound tightly to stop the bleeding. Caywen wept with relief, comforted by her father's whispers of encouragement. Behind, Rodmer sat quietly, regarding the two ominously. With blinding speed, he drew his dagger and lunged at the wounded Baron.

Gwyndel raised Fóbehn with the agility of her elven race. "Caywen!" she screamed, loosing an arrow. Caywen stared, horrified as the arrow shot through the heart of Rodmer Estworth, knocking him to the ground. The dagger rolled from his hand. Caywen gasped, moving away from Vikar to examine the body of her cousin. She pulled away the shirt from the wound.

Tattooed on his shoulder was the black symbol of the Phantom League.

60

12th of Merchen, 2202 SE

Crowding the Council chamber of Castle Hodholm, the servants and guards stood in rows along the aisle spanning the length of the room. Eyoés, Gwyndel, and Gwair watched as a new Rehillon was forged before their eyes. For the first time since his arrival in Hodholm, Eyoés smiled in earnest, unburdened of the stress and anxiety of danger. A warmth spread through his chest. Contented, he glanced to where Gwair stood beside him. Upon Gwair's broad shoulders lay his crimson robe, emblazoned with the white emblem of a clenched fist. The sight of the familiar attire brought back fond memories. Gwyndel stood to his left, her curly red hair tucked behind her pointed ears and cascading past the shoulders of her fine emerald gown. The sense of calm and order was soothing.

Leaning on a crutch, Baron Vikar beamed with pride. It had been a relief when Thruldin had declared Vikar's leg would not require amputation. Though the old Baron was destined to depend on a crutch for the rest of his days, he found it a mere trifle compared to the peace now resting in his house. After negotiating with the people of Hodholm, they had reached a suitable compromise.

Eyoés took a deep, satisfied breath.

Thank the Guide for delivering us from the wiles of our enemy. Rehillon is at peace. May the King preserve the order.

Caywen was ushered into the room by a small group of guards. She came to stand at the opposite end of the walkway from her father. A red cape flowed down to her feet, and ceremonial armor ornamented with amber inlays covered her shoulders. Her long, dark tresses were parted by a finely woven tiara. Even from a distance, her face shone with excitement. She adjusted the amber pendant hanging around her neck.

Vikar gazed lovingly at her from across the room, a tear rolling down his cheek. "Fellow Rehils," he began, clearing his throat and looking at the crowd gathered for the occasion. "For years, it has been an honor to serve you in a manner honoring our King—but now, it is time I pass down the honor to my daughter."

Caywen furtively wiped away a tear. Gwyndel smiled.

Caywen claimed the burden without care for herself. She longed for adventure, and it has come to her—not in the way she expected, but it has come.

Nodding, Vikar beckoned Caywen forward onto the dais. Led by the guards, she followed, surreptitiously clasping her hands in nervous expectancy. As she approached her father, Gwair leaned close to Eyoés' ear. "Such a blessing I have not seen in many years. Yet, I find myself wishing it could have come to pass without turmoil. The loss of Kiffyn and so many of our people was tragic," he whispered.

Gwair continued to grieve for his brother's death in private. The raw wound still bit, though he tried to tame it. Eyoés saw the tears building in Gwair's eyes at the mention of Kiffyn, and set a consoling hand on his friend's shoulder.

"Your brother rests in the Kingdom above the stars now. In peace, he awaits your arrival," Eyoés replied. "I too wish such evil had not befallen Rehillon." He looked at the opposite wall. Shields bearing emblems of the Lords of Rehillon hung on the wall—save one. The shield bearing the Ravenstrong coat of arms had been torn away, leaving a vacant hole. As Eyoés regarded the empty space, his expression turned pensive. "Through all of this, I have learned much. Greed is never content. Peace is knowing the wisdom of enough," he mused. "We must be ever watchful for pitfalls. Discernment is our compass on the journey of life."

Gwair nodded his agreement as Caywen came to stand before her father. The guards escorting her fell away, mixing with the observing crowd. Standing with their former Baron, Lord Agnar and Lord Gerall suppressed smiles of delight as they recalled a similar ceremony from their youth. Vikar said nothing, his gaze locked on his daughter. After a moment of silence, he collected himself the best he could. "Caywen Amberster, daughter and heir of House Amberster, do you swear to lead the people of Rehillon by example with honor, use wisdom, discernment, and uphold virtue in every decision?" he asked.

"I swear it," she declared, voice strong. The dedication and binding commitment of her words was not lost to her in the emotion of the moment, and she spoke them in truth.

Vikar repositioned his crutch. "And do promise to follow the King's Proverbs, and remain sensitive to the Guide's voice when he speaks?" he questioned.

Caywen held herself tall, unconsciously reaching for her amber pendant. "I swear it," she stated with increasing conviction. Smiling, Vikar awkwardly leaned on his crutch. Disregarding ceremony, Caywen reached out and steadied her father as he pulled a beautifully engraved signet ring from his finger.

Nodding, Vikar signaled for Caywen to release him. He slid the ring onto her finger. "Then by the authority vested in me by King Fohidras of Alithell, I proclaim you Baroness of Rehillon, and my successor," he announced. As cheers rose from the crowd, Vikar leaned close to Caywen's ear. "As Baroness, it is your responsibility to appoint a new Lord of Herthere as soon as possible," he whispered. Vikar traded places with his daughter, and made his way back down the aisle. As he passed by, Eyoés and Gwair saluted him, wishing their friend the best. Returning the smile, Vikar joined the crowd in the back of the room.

Caywen raised her hands, and the applause and cheers died down. "I wish to call forward two friends of mine. Though our friendship is yet young, I am proud and honored to be known by them. Welcome Eyoés Kingson and Gwyndel, daughter of Élorn," she announced. Caught off guard, Eyoés glanced at

Gwyndel. Linking her arm into his, Gwyndel gave him a little tug and stepped out into the aisle. Eyoés followed her down the walkway and up onto the dais where Caywen stood.

They bowed. With a laugh, Caywen motioned for them to rise, and beckoned a nearby servant forward. Eyoés raised an eyebrow at her ready authority as the servant brought a soft pillow with a bound scroll upon it.

Caywen took the scroll in hand and whispered her thanks to the attendant. Extending it to Eyoés, she looked at him intently, the warmth in her eyes captivating him. "I give to you a complete reproduction of the plans from Hodholm's design. I hope the beauty and grandeur of Hodholm can be brought to Asdale," she said.

Taking the scroll eagerly, Eyoés embraced Caywen. "You must visit when it is complete. I hope it will please you," He glanced over his shoulder to where Gwair stood with a sly grin. Eyoés cocked his head in question.

Gwair had a hand in this.

Caywen turned to Gwyndel, pulling the amber pendant up and over her head. "To you, Gwyndel—my dearest friend—I give this," she declared, extending the pendant. Accepting it with wonder, Gwyndel admired the refracting light inside the amber, and the golden festoon of twisted wire wrapped about it.

A smile lit up her face like the dawn. "I cannot thank you enough," she said, struggling to voice her gratitude.

Caywen put a hand on her shoulder and leaned closer. "It is more than a beautiful thing. I learned this pendant was one of the few things blessed by the King himself," she whispered. "When one submits to the King and his will, magnificence and clarity come because of it."

As Caywen stood upright, Gwyndel examined the amber pendant closely, her nose wrinkling as she probed the minute details with a close eye.

What could such a strange thing mean?

Such a question was to be answered another time. Setting her hands on their shoulders, Caywen turned Eyoés and Gwyndel around to face the crowd. "Without these faithful friends, the future of Rehillon would still be uncertain, or worse. Fellow Rehils, let us give honor to whom it is due!" she decreed.

Applause rang throughout the council chamber as the crowd stood to their feet, cheering for two of the true heroes of Rehillon.

61

Having cinched the saddle onto Gibusil's back, Eyoés checked their supplies, testing the straps with a firm yank to assure himself of their security. Gwyndel stroked the griffin's neck, her fingers raking through the soft fur coat. As they prepared for their departure, their thoughts turned to home. Though their hearts broke at leaving Hodholm behind, a longing for the peace and familiarity of Asdale pulled them away.

Eyoés stepped back from Gibusil, satisfied with his handiwork. Over the griffin's neck, he glimpsed Caywen, Gwair, and Marc, son of Wilnor approaching. Eyoés ducked under the creature's massive wings. Gwyndel noticed his movement and turned.

Coming to stand before them, the three visitors regarded Gibusil with wonder, though Eyoés clearly saw their sadness at the coming departure. Still clad in her ceremonial attire, Caywen gave a quivering smile. "If I could, I would ask you both to stay," she said, tearful, "but you have a world of your own, and it is not my right to deny your people your leadership. I hear Taekohar is quite beautiful."

Gwyndel embraced Caywen with a tight lipped smile. "It is *most* beautiful," she affirmed, her sadness at odds with the longing for home. "One day, you may see it for yourself."

"You are always welcome here, Gwyndel," she declared. Restraining their emotions, they bowed to each other. Fingering the amber pendant around her neck, Gwyndel turned to where Marc stood, waiting patiently. Beydan had bid a somber farewell the previous day, summoned away to the Northern Passage to continue his service. Gwyndel's brow furrowed. "Where will you go now?" she questioned. With the passing of the Phantom League threat, there was no need for the ragtag Loyalist forces. Many had returned to their homes, while others returned to serve under the Northern Guard. As a volunteer soldier, Marc now found himself without station or occupation.

Marc clasped Gwyndel's arm, gazing off into the distance. "I do not know where the path will take me— but one day, I will ride among the Knights of the Lance in my homeland. Once again, I will see the green, rolling highlands of Gahidros," he said.

As Marc and Gwyndel spoke together, Eyoés embraced Gwair, blinking away tears. As fellow members of the Five Heroes, their friendship had begun. The bond between them now had been fashioned in the of forge of struggle and vulnerability. It was with heavy heart Eyoés bid him goodbye. "It has been a pleasure to serve at your side, my friend," Eyoés declared, meaning every word in earnest.

Gwair smiled. "I can say the same," he said, eyes bright with expectation. "We will meet again at the next assembly of the Five Heroes." They released each other and stepped back with a bow.

Eyoés set a hand on Gwyndel's shoulder. "It is time," he sighed. With a knot in her throat, Gwyndel followed her brother, her steps hesitant. They mounted onto Gibusil's back, tying themselves onto the saddle with sturdy leather straps. Grasping the reins, Eyoés exhaled as he focused on the journey ahead.

One day, we will return. This farewell is not forever.

With a snap of the reins, Gibusil leapt into the sky. The cool wind of Rehillon caressed Gwyndel's face as she watched Castle Hodholm recede into the distance. The might of the castle and the town surrounding it shrank into nothingness.

Eyoés and Gwyndel looked ahead with hearts set for home.

18th of Merchen, 2202 SE

Eyoés' boots swept through the tall, wet grass. Birds alighted on Asdale's keep, singing songs of rejoicing. A light breeze tousled Gwyndel's hair as she walked beside her brother. The din of construction continued. Once only a partially built wall, the outer ramparts stood tall, guarding Asdale. Eyoés admired the beauty of his home.

Upon their arrival at Asdale two days previous, Eyoés had hastily held council with his advisor Ayleril. To the pleasure of the young Baron, he had graciously approved the last minute addition of borrowed elements from Hodholm. Craftsmen milled about, entrusted with the finer tasks of adding embellishments. The interwoven emerald inlays gracing the door to the inner courtyard brought Asdale to a new level of magnificence. Eyoés inhaled deeply, mouth partly agape.

It is beyond understanding that one so unworthy as I have been gifted with the responsibility of caring for such splendor.

He sighed, taking in a deep breath of the clean air. "If only Gwair were here," he said aloud, momentarily forgetting Gwyndel's presence.

His sister nodded, taking in the magnificence of Asdale with a somber eye. "He would appreciate the beauty and care you have brought to this place," she agreed. The temperature of the land wavered as small clouds passed briefly in front of the sun.

Lost in thought, Eyoés spotted the window to his quarters, and glimpsed the tapestry within. "There was a time when such beauty enticed me with a hunger for riches, promising things avarice could never fulfill," he recalled. "I thank the King he has given me strength to resist it. I desperately need the Guide's direction and discernment as I lead my people."

Turning around, Gwyndel faced the main gate of Asdale. Above the newly finished ramparts, the peaks of the nearby mountains could be seen, covered in a thick carpet of conifers. Gwyndel licked her lips, bracing herself to deliver her long considered decision. "The time has come, Eyoés. No longer can I share the

Stewardship of Asdale," she said, waiting for her brother's response.

Eyoés nodded in understanding. "I know. The burdens of authority are mine to bear, as they have been given to me by my King," he concurred, moving to stand by her side. He followed her gaze. The mountains reminded him of the days he had spent trekking through the wilderness of Alithell with her.

Heart beating ever faster, Gwyndel took in a calm breath in preparation to reveal her resolve. "Since I am free of the Stewardship, I have decided to rejoin the Foresters," she declared. "For too long I have been locked away in Asdale's keep."

Eyoés paused, his face turning somber as he considered the ramifications of her decision. "You desire to return to your home among the trees. I will not stop you," he conceded, looking her in the eye. "I will miss you, Gwyndel." This parting brought him pain, though only a short distance would separate them.

Gwyndel embraced him. Straightening his green cloak, she smoothed it over his shoulders. The golden flame symbol on his robe reminded her of all they had shared the last four years. "Our time together has been a gift, brother," she said.

EPILOGUE

The cries of wildlife were muffled inside Gwyndel's treehouse. The darkness of the forest allowed little light to enter the small cabin. Shadows played on the walls, lingering in the corners of the room, hiding to the side of the bookshelf and under the bed. Two candles fought against the dark of night.

Gwyndel sat at her desk, oblivious to the coming of night. Laid upon the smooth wood surface was Caywen's amber pendant. Gwyndel watched the wavering candle flames cause the small fissures to dance deep within. She traced the wire festoon with her finger tip, the metal cold to the touch. Caywen's words continued to intrigue her.

It is more than a beautiful thing. I learned this pendant was one of the few things blessed by the King himself. When one submits to the King and his will, magnificence and clarity come because of it.

As she pondered her friend's words, Gwyndel leaned against the back of her chair and took the pendant in hand.

What could her explanation mean? How can I uncover this secret?

The smooth surface of the amber felt glossy under her fingertips. Gwyndel pursed her lips.

The Guide will know.

Setting the pendant on her desk, she closed her eyes, face pulled tight in concentration.

You never let anything happen without reason. I know I have been given this for a purpose—make it clear to me, so I may understand.

As her thoughts progressed, a growing devotion intensified her words. Gwyndel pressed on, determined to know.

Show me. What is it I must seek?

With the abruptness of a reflex action, her eyes shot open as a wave of dizziness caused her to fall from her chair. As soon as it had come, the moment passed and her head cleared. Briefly closing her eyes to clear her head, Gwyndel looked about the room.

She gasped.

Everything about her seemed vibrant with color, the edges and outlines of each shape standing out starkly. Differing shades and colors abounded in the room with a clarity that took her breath away. It seemed nothing escaped her eye, from the cobwebs in the corners of the ceiling to the smallest thread in her bedsheets. A pure sense of weightlessness peeled away anything burdening her mind. Freedom had never seemed so tangible.

Euphoric, Gwyndel felt her gaze pulled toward the bookshelf. Among the spines, the Proverbs glowed like the morning dawn. Hurrying to the bookshelf, she pulled the Proverbs off the shelf and opened to a random page. As her eyes scanned the words, each proverb unfolded before her with the sharpness and realism of a witnessed event. Before her eyes, she watched as good deeds were played out in front of her, and others were encouraged in their loyalty to their King. Consumed with a love for others and a desire to do good, Gwyndel sat on the desk and pored over the Proverbs, taking in every word.

Her emerald green irises were half blue, shining like the ocean.

To access exciting Sword and Scion freebies,
please visit the Exclusive Content page on my
website:

www.jacksonegraham.wix.com/jackson-e-graham

Password: AndiamasRademSS

PROLOGUE

12th of Biarron, 2204 SE

The hard-hearted winds of Norgalok seized the breath from Baron Ednor's lungs. The cold tore at his sore ears. Pain raced across his exposed face as the blinding snow obscured his vision. Shielding his eyes with his gloved hand, he pressed on, stumbling through the thick mountain snow impeding his progress. The chill wind nipped his nostrils as he inhaled. Although grateful for the protection his thick fur cloak offered against the ruthless climate of his homeland, he longed for the comforting warmth of a fire.

Ednor pulled the wrapped bundle tighter under his arm, the contours of the hidden item pressing uncomfortably against his side. Reminded of his repulsive burden, the baron curled his lip and spat into the snow. Nausea compelled him to retch. Clearing his mind of fear and disgust, Ednor furrowed his brow.

I must sever the bonds of this abomination. It will be safe under the mountain's watch. I have nothing to lose since that sorcerer murdered my wife.

Even as he assured himself, Baron Ednor glanced around, an unnerving blanket of white impeding his sight. His chest tightened. Shaking, he fled. The blizzard tossed his greying hair, exposing his forehead to the snow's onslaught.

As he strained with all his might, the snow pulled at him. The many years he had spent in the frozen South told him he was in a dangerous predicament. The weather fought against his advance as much as the silent hunter pursuing him. It was only a matter of which enemy he would succumb to first. Ednor shook his head with violence and repeated his commitment under his breath.

I must press further on! The Kòakran must never be found!

He stopped. An unseen presence arrested him, holding him to the spot, muscles seizing. Tremors shook him. Gasping for air, Baron Ednor felt eyes scrutinizing him, concealed behind the blizzard's blanket. He clenched his jaw, eyes wide and stinging from the sleet. Forcing himself to face the terror, Ednor turned.

A sudden coldness crept into his heart like the tendrils of the blizzard itself, wrapping around his heart and freezing him from within. His heartbeat slowed as spikes of ice spread through his chest, the intensity of the pain robbing him of breath. The cold gripped him. He raked his chest with clawed fingers. Dropping to his knees, he writhed in agony.

Footsteps crunched beside him as a looming figure circled to watch his quarry die. "I know what you carry," the figure shouted. As his voice fused with the blizzard's roar, the storm itself stood before Baron Ednor embodied as a fearsome guardian.

Gritting his teeth, Ednor looked up. He knew who challenged him. His heart slowed further under the cold, invisible hand that clutched it.

Two hollow black eyes were set in a gaunt face. Wiry black hair hung loosely from the figure's head, dyed with streaks of red and gold. His long, pointed ears were coated in snow. An elaborate tunic covered his body, at odds with the rest of his plain adornment. The elf needed no shelter from the blizzard's torment. His deep, calm breaths relished the frigid air. He squinted harshly at the dying baron, apathetic to his suffering.

Trembling with each small breath, Baron Ednor made a valiant attempt to rise. He knew his fate, yet embraced his conviction. "This effigy you worship is a deception! It must meet its end—I regret nothing I have sworn to do," he stated boldly, his terror subsiding.

Ednor fell to his knees again as the grip around his heart intensified. The wrapped bundle slipped from underneath his arm. Shaklun clenched his extended fist, his glare slowly sapping the baron's courage. "The gods have entrusted it to *me* alone!" he exclaimed.

Grabbing at his chest, the baron stared at the elf.

The ferocity of his wrath is like an avalanche. How can I stand?

Spots of black flashed before Baron Ednor's eyes, pulling him further into the abyss of death. Fighting it, he shook his head, impulsively reaching out to Shaklun to beg for mercy. Disgusted at his weakness, Ednor yanked his hand back, huddling under the comforting warmth of his fur cloak. "I may have failed to destroy the Kòakran, but another will rise up to challenge you," he gasped.

Baring his teeth, Shaklun tightened his fist. The baron's heart twitched in a vain attempt to spark itself back to life. Darkness obscured Ednor's vision, and the overwhelming deluge of suffocation sent panic into his eyes.

The howling winds screamed.